GW01005728

YOU ARE HERE

Steve Horsfall

ATHENA PRESS
LONDON

ISBN 1 84401 305 7

First Published 2004 by
ATHENA PRESS
Queen's House, 2 Holly Road
Twickenham TW1 4EG
United Kingdom

Printed for Athena Press

YOU ARE HERE

Contents

Men will be Boys

The traffic moved along without a hint of haste or bustle. Dave was part of this motion, sitting behind the wheel of his silver Golf GTi convertible, top down of course.

It was a warm Friday in August, work was over, and it was time to make the most of a long, summer evening. The options for the night were many, but the choice was simple and had already been made: just a quick change and a few cool bottles of lagers with the lads. The beer garden at the Riverside Inn was to be the venue.

The warmth of the evening felt good as it brushed Dave's face. He was heading home at a slow pace. The radio was emitting bad tunes, crap music; it was not in tune with his buoyant mood. All this manufactured boy-band shite, thought Dave. Whatever happened to the *real* bands?

Dave grew up with the sounds of The Jam, The Clash and The Stranglers. He felt reborn when Britpop came along in the nineties. Oasis, Cast, Ocean Colour Scene. Even Weller was back in vogue.

His hand fumbled under the dashboard for a tape as the other hand firmly gripped the steering wheel. Dave pulled out a cassette without a cover; it was one he had recorded himself. He jammed the tape into the stereo, instantly killing the gargled warble of some easily forgettable ballad, which was now replaced by the rousing sound of 'My World' by Secret Affair; a sound from the mod revival of the late seventies. They only made two decent records, and this was one of them.

'Sorted!' shouted Dave.

He proceeded to sing along with the tape at the top of his voice and his mood was raised to an even greater height. The tape spooled on, playing track after track from the days of Dave's youth.

'*This is the Modern World…*' spouted Weller with an arrogant virulence.

Dave echoed the line and mimicked the sentiment of the song, just as he had done all those years ago. He felt really good now.

Young people were marching along the pavement in never-ending groups. These youngsters were all in their early twenties, but to Dave they were just out of nappies. They were all heading for the same 'popular' pub in their ridiculous oversized jeans and garish T-shirts. Some of the girls looked hot though, thought Dave.

The heads of the youngsters turn as a gleaming silver GTi convertible glides towards the crossroads; propelled by music, and cool music at that.

A screech of brakes suddenly eclipses Weller's forceful vocals. The group of youngsters pivot as one and see the Silver GTi, motionless at the crossroads, as a battered green Vauxhall ambles down the road to the front of it. The young group laugh and Dave turns a bright red – with embarrassment not anger – as the two occupants of the green Vauxhall, blissfully unaware of the scene they have created, crawl away. Two immaculate straw hats are perched by the rear window. Neither of them will see seventy again.

Dave shook his head but remained silent as he shifted the gear stick into first and moved away. A round of applause, mingled with Jerry Springer style whooping, came from the group of youngsters.

'Fucking kids,' mumbled Dave, as he picked up speed.

Five minutes later Dave pulled up outside his pad; a two-bedroomed flat, converted from one floor of a four-storey Edwardian town house. It's a cool abode and his fellow flat owners give him no jip.

Dave grabbed a Bud Ice from the fridge and downed half the bottle by the time he reached the stereo. He selected a CD to instil some tempo and stimulate the senses of his weekend mood. 'Staying Out For The Summer', by Dodgy was soon resounding around the flat and out the open lounge window to the street below.

A hard jet of warm water hit Dave's body. He'd grabbed another Bud Ice and the stereo was completely audible from the locale of the shower. Life was good!

Brown chinos, white lambretta sleeveless shirt, blue deck shoes. Dave looked cool but casual as he stood in front of the full-length mirror in the spare room. He nodded his approval to his reflection and then walked into the lounge.

'Phil!' Dave half shouted into the mouthpiece of the phone, as he sprawled himself across the settee. The TV had now replaced the stereo. Baldwin and Barlow were squaring up on *Coronation Street* again; *Top Of The Pops* was on the other side, but it wasn't worth watching.

'What time are you going out?' Dave enquired of Phil. 'Yeah. Sorted… I thought we could just hit the Riverside for a few and see how we feel from there,' he continued.

Dave chuckled as he listened to Phil's retort. 'Nice one, all right mate, I'm just going to grab a bite and then I'm ready to rumble. See ya about eight-thirty then… looking forward to it man. Cheers.'

At Eight-fifteen, Dave was strutting down the road on course for the Riverside Inn. The air was still warm and dusk had not yet settled.

The Riverside would be kicking tonight. Everyone would be in the garden in harmony with the calmness of summer; sitting in groups around wooden picnic tables, lying on the grass, standing in groups on the patio. Inside a few couples would be sharing a romantic moment, interrupted by the frequent human traffic through the garden doors. Hard-earned pay packets would pass across the bar to stack endless rounds of drinks on small round tin trays.

Dave knew the scene well. It had been part of his way of life for the last seventeen years. As he strolled along the pavement he began to think deeply; his thoughts were reflective as he whiled away the time.

Dave Holliman was in his thirty-fifth year and still living the single life. His childhood had been carefree and he'd been bright enough to attend polytechnic. Dave opted for American Studies – an easy option, he felt, to lead the student life. These days he worked in the unit trust department of a large life assurance company, Mutual Life. Apart from a few interim temp jobs, Dave had slowly moved up the corporate ladder since his heady student days. Progress was slow, but each year did bring a respectable pay rise. Dave always got pissed at the Christmas party and went on a lads' summer holiday every August.

Some things in life are a constant, and that included Dave's mates. The other mainstay in his life was the effortless pursuit of women. If there was an Olympic sport for notching up conquest after conquest, without ever forging a long-lasting relationship, then Dave would be a gold-medal contender.

Dave grimaced. He remembered that rebel spirit he'd had as a student; a cocky lad who had no time for authority. Ready to take on the world, and the world had better be ready. And how did he take on the world? He travelled, worked in bars, slept on golden beaches, surfed the waves, and was constantly pissed. No! Did he fuck? He got a job with Mutual Life. Now he had a female boss, six years younger than himself, and, although he would never openly admit it, he was actually quite intimidated by her. It was the authority you see, to which Dave offered respect and not rebellion. At least he still got pissed every weekend, when the rebel was reborn once more.

Dave chuckled to himself and thought of the sitcom *The Young Ones*. Where would Rik and the boys be now? All working in insurance probably. The revolutionists are dead; long live the conformists. Just look at today's young generation – the kiddies. Totally content with their computer games, mobile phones and hair gel. There is now no shame is sharing your musical tastes with your parents, because everyone loves Robbie Williams! Have those kiddies never seen *Quadrophenia*?

Dave was approaching the Riverside. The pub sat proudly on its own, just to the right of the bridge that led into town, and crossed the very river that prompted the name of the notorious local boozer. Swarms of revellers spanned the length of the bridge, traversing in and out of town. The mood of the swarm was relaxed, stimulated by the warmth of the evening. There were no herd-like advances reminiscent of the rank and file who work in the city of London, and who crowded the platforms of Waterloo Station, like sheep that have lost the will to live. Dave hates going to visit the head office of Mutual Life in London, as he has to witness and share the sad existence of these people. He doesn't hate them, just pities them. Some of them, maybe all, wanted to be rebels too, at one time.

A beer garden was situated at the rear of the pub, sandwiched by a wide free-flowing river. The water was pretty clear, and looked almost inviting in the haze of the evening. One thing was certain; someone would take the plunge before the night was over.

The garden was full. Three men in their mid-thirties sat at a wooden table; there was enough room for one more: Dave.

'Okay, boys?' beamed Dave as he stood before the table.

'About bloody time! You've been poncing with your hair again?' Tony grinned as he acknowledged his own wit.

Opposite Tony sat Gavin, and the trio was completed by Phil.

'At least I have some, mate. This one mine?' Dave picked up a cold bottle of Becks, took a swig, and sat next to Gavin. Tony and Phil took a gulp from their own bottles of lager in almost harmonious accord, whilst Gavin sat clutching a pint of bitter.

Gavin looked serious for a moment. 'Are we going to the Taj later?'

'The night is young, Gav. Let's take it as it comes. Be spontaneous,' declared Dave.

'Yeah, Gav, I hope you're not going to be Mr Itinerary on the Campaign. You know what happened last year.' Phil spoke with some irritation.

Gavin shook his head at Phil's remark, and cast his mind back to last year's Campaign.

Campaign is the title the quartet thought up for their annual holiday. It was their name, their holiday; the Campaign was greeted like a much loved relative who came to visit only once a year. But each Campaign was never the same, as the destination was always different, never repeated. The series started when Dave and Phil were both twenty-two. Dave had attained his degree at a polytechnic and had begun working at Mutual Life. Phil had been working as a credit controller for a builder's merchant, a job he had taken straight from school. They had known each other since the age of eleven, remaining the best of mates through the punk-fuelled aggression of the late seventies into the bland new romantic vision of the eighties. The first

Campaign (unofficially as the name was not yet born) was a camping holiday in the South of France. Gavin joined in for Campaign two on the Costa Brava. He got to know the others after becoming Phil's flatmate. Tony completed the foursome a year later on a Campaign to mainland Greece. His connection was through Gavin, with whom he worked at the local branch of an electrical store called Carters. It was on that trip that Phil came up with the name, apt timing, as the team was now complete.

Last year's Campaign took the foursome to Southern Turkey. Aside from the standard drinking and debauchery, there was an opportunity to take in some culture: a chance to get up early and join couples and families on a day out in a cranky old coach. Gavin had been on day trips on previous Campaigns, but by himself. The other three just wanted to sleep off the night before, either in their beds or by the pool, and not on a decrepit boneshaker of an old bus. They did show some interest once, on a Campaign to Northern Italy when Gavin got pissed and managed to tap off on a trip to a vineyard. The only other exception was the obligatory boat trip, but that was different; it was a party!

In Turkey, Gavin managed to persuade the other three to go on a day trip to Ephesus.

'It's one of the Seven Wonders of the World, you cretins!'

So the lads went with Gavin. They nearly missed the bus, and Gavin sulked for half an hour. The journey was lousy. Every comfort stop was highlighted by a mad stampede for the toilets. It has always been stated that ninety-eight percent of Brits who visit Turkey end up with Turkish tummy. That statistic was borne out by the peaky disposition of the majority of the bus passengers.

'It's because they cook everything in olive oil you know,' beamed an old man. He was one of two on the bus unaffected by the lurgi.

'Yeah. You're right,' acknowledged Gavin, the other member of the unaffected pair.

Ephesus itself was a success; the lads loved it. They photographed each other sitting on ancient communal toilets and sang raucous rugby songs from the stage of the massive amphitheatre.

The trip was a triumph for Gavin. He had a chance to organise something, to put some structure into the day, and the lads enjoyed it. He should have quit whilst he was ahead, but he didn't.

Early the same evening: 'I think we should just stay in the Bulldog tonight and give the bar crawl a miss. Let's just have some beers, and they do serve real ale in the Bulldog. It's easily the best pub in town.'

The others looked at Gavin in horror as they sat out on the balcony of their apartment.

'Oh! And also why don't we stay in one night this week. Thursday would be good, 'cos we could then get up early and go on that trip to the leather factory.'

That was it. Gavin had gone too far, a fucking leather factory. The lads looked at each other.

Dave spoke for them all. 'Gav, you tosser. We just go with the flow. Find a bar with some life in it and move on with the buzz. If that means going to a bar with a pseudo British name, then fine. Why do you always want to find a favourite pub and then not want to go anywhere else? It's the same every year. And what are we going to do if we stay in... play cards?'

Gavin looked pleased with the cards suggestion.

'Don't go there, mate,' snapped Dave. He hated card games. 'And why do I want to buy a leather jacket in the middle of summer?'

Gavin knew he had lost. He mumbled something about monotony and every Campaign being the same, before heading off to the bathroom to brush his hair. The other three smiled at each other. A lesson needed to be learned.

To Gavin the rest of the night was a blur, induced by the vodka-spiked beers that came in quick succession. Soon it was morning, and Dave was shaking him from his hangover slumber.

'You all right, Gav? Here, drink some of this.' Dave handed Gavin a bottle of still mineral water. Gavin took a large swig as his eyes begin to unstick.

'What hit me?'

'I dunno, but you were knocking them back for England last night, mate,' Dave said with insincere concern.

'I can't remember a thing. We were all in the Beach Bar and

then wham!' Gavin held out his hands looking for an explanation.

'So you don't remember dancing naked in Barry's?' Dave managed to keep a straight face.

Gavin looked startled. 'Fuck off!'

Dave grinned. 'Only joking, it's good for morale. But I tell you something that you did do last night. You tried to tap off with a local.'

'What?' Gavin had gone even whiter.

'She was a good-looker and she certainly liked you. Plus, you both disappeared for about half an hour. You came back with a big smile on your face, saying you'll never guess what I've done?' Dave struggled to keep a straight face.

'What? I shagged her?' Gavin's head was clearing quickly.

'Dunno, you wouldn't tell us.' Dave now had to look away.

Gavin stood up shaking his head and swigging endlessly from the bottle of water. He was wearing a pair of faded grey boxer shorts, a small paunch of a beer belly hung over this. Gavin never worked out and had a love of beer and junk food. His mousy brown hair was tousled beyond control and his body showed very little signs of tanning.

Tony and Phil were both sitting out on the balcony, reading and taking in some early morning rays. Gavin staggered out and mumbled at them. Dave followed just behind and winked.

For ten minutes Gavin sat with his head between his hands, taking deep breaths and moving only to take gulps of cool water. Suddenly, there was a loud banging on the apartment door.

'I'll go,' said Phil, already halfway to the door. He soon returned, followed by two Turkish lads.

'Um, Gav. I think you might be in a spot of bother.' Phil also wore a perfect deadpan face.

Gavin looked up and saw two Turks through blood-red eyes. 'Uh!'

One of the Turks stared daggers at Gavin. 'Have you forgotten your promise?'

'What promise?' Gavin looked like he had just drunk a pint of vinegar.

'Today, my friend, you are to marry my sister,' was the stern reply.

'You what?' Gavin shouted.

'Last night you planned the wedding to a very fine detail, and you told my sister how your future would be, as a couple.' Only one Turk spoke. The other just stared.

'Gav, it must be that local girl that you tap...er met last night,' interjected Dave.

'Shit!' The reality had hit Gavin.

'We will wait for you. Please go and dress,' the vocal Turk held out a hand and pointed Gavin towards the bathroom to get ready.

Gavin got up and headed towards the bathroom. He smiled at the Turks and closed the door behind him. Once the door was shut, Gavin headed straight for the window. He opened it and started to squeeze his frame outside. Soon he was on a ledge and preparing to clamber to the balcony below. The move was easy, even with a hangover. He then jumped from the balcony to the ground. A camera flash greeted him.

'Gotcha!' Dave, Tony and Phil were standing in front of him, grinning inanely. The two Turks were in raptures behind them.

'Meet Siad and Hitesh,' said Dave. 'They're good lads. They both work in the Hell Bar, and were well up for taking part in a little joke played on an English lad who had made one boring plan too many.'

Gavin stood and scowled at the scene in front of him.

A year later, Gavin scowled again in the beer garden of the Riverside. The memory of the lads' little jape was still painful.

'Wankers!' exclaimed Gavin, further mimicking his reaction from a year ago.

Dave and Phil chuckled, but Tony was lost, deep in thought, as he stared towards a group of girls over near the river's edge.

'Who're you letching at, Tone?' Dave enquired as he scanned the vicinity for signs of top totty.

Tony's face cracked into a large grin. 'Not letching, mate. Just a bit of déjà vu. I could have sworn I'd seen those three girls before.' Tony gestured towards a group of girls with his half empty bottle of Becks.

The others looked around without a hint of disguise.

'Bloody hell, Tone, you haven't?' Phil's face screwed up. 'They certainly are not lookers.'

'No, you tosser. Look, you've got one tall, one with no chin and a big nose; you've got a large, chunky one who's sprayed her hair so much it's almost an afro... and the third is small, stocky and squat.'

The others all looked puzzled.

Tony starts to sing a well-known cartoon theme tune from his youth. 'In the Wonderland Zoo, where the certain bears who stay at home every night, never quarrel, or fight. Hey we don't even bite...'

One by one the penny dropped with the rest of the lads. They all joined in the chorus at the top of their voices.

'So don't yell. Help! Help! Here come the bears. Help! Help! Here come the bears. It's the Hair Bear Bunch.'

The three girls in question looked around, along with half the occupants of the beer garden, as the lads reached the end of their crescendo. Quite a few other thirtysomethings sniggered as they got the joke. The girls themselves were much too young to realise, but shifted awkwardly in their none too flattering mini skirts, as they realised that maybe the crack was on them.

'Top Ace. The fucking Hair Bear Bunch.' Dave at once reminisced with a smile.

'Ooh, ooh, Mr Peevly, Mr Peevly.' Tony drew more laughter with an excellent impression of one of the main characters.

Dave drained the dregs of his Becks. 'Same again, boys?'

Fervent nods from the lads as each in turn gulped the remains of their beer.

Soon Dave was standing at the bar throwing a cheeky grin at a nicely shaped barmaid, although the face was nothing to write home about. His grin widened as he mumbled under his breath, 'Nice legs, shame about the boat race.' A line from a novelty punk song by the Monks, that was said at the time to be inspired by Angela Rippon's appearance on the Morcambe and Wise show.

The barmaid smiled back at Dave with a "you're not too bad" glance. Dave looked good for thirty-five, he looked more like thirty and acted like he was twenty-five. He measured six foot, and was athletic build with cropped, spiked black hair and a brown complexion verging on the Latin.

'Three Becks, a pint of Directors and some chilli nuts, love.'

'I'll get the beers, but what can I do about your cold bollocks?' A real hyena pitched laugh followed, and continued as the beers were plonked on the bar.

Any thoughts of passion disappeared from Dave's mind. Now, if she'd delivered a sassy retort like, 'Well I'd better make sure my hands get nice and cold handling your beers,' followed by a subtle humming giggle. Well, some sensual action could have been on the cards. But, this was not Hollywood and he was not that desperate for a shag anyway. Dave paid for the beers, turned on his heels, and headed back to the garden, clutching three cold bottles by their necks and an overfilled, dripping pint. The barmaid swiftly moved on to the next customer, and her guffaw soon rung through the air, following Dave into the garden.

'*Pixie and Dixie*,' shouted Phil, as Dave returned.

'What's the crack?' Dave wanted to join in.

Tony updated him. 'We're talking cool cartoons, which obviously does not include any Japanese shite. No, real classics, like *Top Cat*.'

'I hate meeces to pieces!' Dave does his best Mr Jinx.

'I always liked the Arabian Knights. Do you remember... size of an elephant?' Gavin boomed the catchphrase.

'Banana Splits, nice one!' shouted Dave.

Phil thought hard. 'Fleegle, Snorky and... shit! Who were the other two?'

'Drooper.' Gavin added a third.

'I used to have the theme tune version, by The Dickies on yellow vinyl. God knows what I did with it, probably worth a fortune now.' Dave moaned as he remembered his old singles collection.

'But who was the fourth?' Phil was getting pissed off trying to remember and it was obvious none of the lads could help.

The conversation soon moved on to children's programmes from a bygone age; the group's childhood.

'The ones I remember best were during the school holidays. *Daktari*, Herge's Adventures of *Tin Tin*, The Black and White *Flash Gordon*, and of course the *Double Deckers*.' Tony paused and then quietly sang a couple of lines from the *Double Deckers*' theme tune. 'Get on board, get on board...'

'Cool.' Dave found himself humming along, mainly because he and Tony couldn't remember the rest of the words. 'My faves were the *Tomorrow People* and *Murphy's Mob*, plus of course *Grange Hill*.'

'Flippin' heck, Tucker. The best programmes were always on just before the early evening news. Before *Neighbours* came on the scene.' Phil was in full swing again, the nightmare of the forgotten fourth Banana Split pushed to the back of his mind. 'You remember? *Captain Pugwash, Hector's House, The Magic Roundabout, Wilo the Wisp* and of course… *Roobarb and Custard*.'

All the lads suddenly start bouncing vigorously from their seated position, loudly mumbling the *Roobarb and Custard* theme tune. 'Na na na na… na na na na… na… na na… na na.'

All eyes were on Gavin.

'What about you, Gav?' Phil forcefully asked.

'Well, I was more of yer *Blue Peter, Vision-on, Swap Shop* sort of guy.'

'Figures.' Phil smacked his lips. 'I bet you were the sort of kid who would never have been seen dead watching *Tiswas*.'

'Too right… anyway, I used to fancy Maggie Philbin.'

'No way! Sally James pissed on Maggie Philbin.'

'Now there's a thought.' Dave raised his eyebrows. The group were all in hysterics, amplified by their semi-drunken stupor.

Phil giggled. 'Yeah, instead of Dragsters or Tanks as themes for trump cards, they should have had kids' programmes top totty. It would have been a sure-fire winner. Sarah Greene's legs trump Floella Benjamin's.' More raucous laughter ensued and echoed around the beer garden.

The lads continued to drink round after round of ice-cold lager and pints of bitter, maintaining a mood of reminiscence amid roars of approving cheers. Dusk saw the garden almost empty as the summer revellers either headed for home or on to a club. As last orders were called, only the lads were left and they were pissed.

'I'm too bloody knackered to go on any where, it's been a hard week.' The others didn't challenge Dave's half mumbled statement. They all look heavy-eyed, weary and inebriated. A few years back they would have all moved on to a club at this stage of the evening; but not now. The following Friday they were due to head off on another two-week 'Campaign'. Another lads' holiday in a series that had run nearly as long as *Eastenders*. Phil, like Dave, was thirty-five, Gavin thirty-six and Tony thirty-eight.

Gavin was thinking about the forthcoming holiday. 'We are going to have to pace ourselves on the Campaign, lads, or we'll be hiring Zimmer frames instead of scooters.'

Phil gave Gavin a hard stare. Of all the lads, he was the last to accept he was no longer in the 'youth' bracket. He'd even suggested a Club 18–30 holiday for this year's Campaign, to derision and ribbing from the others.

'Gav,' Phil waved an unsteady finger at him to make a point, 'on this Campaign we are all going to rediscover the elixir of youth, and show the kiddies what it's like to live it up. Regeneration, my friend. Regeneration. Talking 'bout my regeneration...'

Gavin tutted at Phil's drunken Roger Daltry impression. 'Shit, Phil, you make us sound like the cast of *Cocoon*.'

''Zactly!' Phil could hardly talk.

Dave had had enough. 'Come on, let's go and get a Phil Babb. I'm dying to eat some shit, and nobody does it better than Zak.'

Dave stumbled awkwardly to his feet and led a tottering trek towards Zak's kebab shop on the high street. It was only ten minutes walk but it took the lads nearly twenty due to their slow stagger, and the inevitable piss stops on the way. Phil even managed to fall over and land in the only puddle for miles around. It hadn't rained for about six weeks, but for some unexplained reason there was a big puddle at the entrance to a small alleyway down which Phil had gone for a piss. Tony reckoned he'd done it on purpose on account that he had probably just peed down his white chinos, and wanted to mask the mishap. Phil was not amused by this suggestion.

'Chicken legs open, my good man,' Phil shouted loudly as he entered Zak's kebab shop. A young couple looked at Phil with disdain. They were the only other customers in the shop, and by now were keen to collect their char grilled burgers and leave. They feared trouble.

'Phillip, you are so funny man!' Zak shouted with a jovial happy lilt. 'Not!'

Phil staggered to the counter and was soon joined by the other three. The young couple collected their food and hastily departed.

'Four Zak Zeniths, please, Zak, and make 'em deadly,' Dave spluttered.

'Four ZZs. You guys, always living life on the edge, never yer basic doner. No matter what, gotta have the taste of an inferno. And Zak, he happy to burn yer bloody mouths off!'

Zak is a kebab shop owner in the best tradition of Harry Enfield's creation, Stavros. Tousled black hair, dark olive skin, unshaven and wearing a whitish, badly stained apron, covering an equally unclean uniform of grey T-shirt, blue jeans and trainers. His partner in crime, behind the counter, is Baz, with an identical uniform, but his bum fluff of a beard does not quite cut it. Unlike Zak, Baz has yet to adopt the rapport and banter. Instead, he chooses to smile inanely at every one of Zak's jibes. Baz aspires to making the grade and entertaining as a Turk of great wit.

'Hey, Zak, make the ZZs lethal. They'll be the last for a few weeks.' Tony is hungry and in need of some spice to enhance his senses.

'Where you going?'

'Campaign 2001!' Phil screamed.

Zak roared a gargled laugh. Baz sort of imitated him. Zak mocked the lads. 'You guys, you're all Peter Pans; never get old. When're Mrs Zak and me gonna get a wedding invite? Why you boys never marry? You all Julian Clarey or what?'

'Fuck off!' Phil is hurt. 'We're just out for a good time. Just wanna experience as many women as possible before settling down. Sow those wild oats, man!'

'Yeah, right, because we all tap off like crazy these days.' Gavin seemed almost sober.

'Yeah,' Phil pondered. 'But this Campaign will be different. We're all gonna score. Promise yer.'

Gavin is unconvinced. 'Right. Either some nubile young twenty-year-old will be desperate for a father figure or there'll be a group of thirtysomethings just like us desperate not to be left on the shelf. We'll be fighting them off.'

''Zactly!' Phil had not spotted the sarcasm.

Dave grimaced in semi bewilderment.

Zak was already preparing the ZZs. Baz passed him four spicy pitta breads and Zak dropped two chillies in each, followed by a stuffing of peppers and onions, and then cubes of curried chicken. With a gleeful smile Zak squirted a layer of chilli sauce on top. He placed all four finished masterpieces on the counter. 'There you go, boys. Make your tongues hot for the ladies. They love it, don't they.'

The lads all grabbed their ZZs. Phil didn't hesitate and plunged his mouth towards the mound of spice. His face was soon splattered with chilli sauce. The others were more hesitant, preferring to take small bites.

Gavin grimaced. 'Fuck! That's hot!'

'Nah, well tame, man.' Phil's drunkenness had numbed his senses; he'd almost finished his.

'Give him another Zak, and make it really hot.' Gavin had had enough of Phil for the evening. This would teach him.

'Gav!' Dave protested.

Zak winked at Gavin. 'Phil, my man, if you eat all this ZZ, it's on the house. My gift to you.'

'You're on!' Phil is now looking a little queasy.

Zak created another ZZ with four chillies and a hotter chilli sauce. He went to hand it to Phil but then pulled it back towards his chest. 'Hey, man, you realise you eat this, you may never taste all that beach pussy waiting for you abroad.'

'Bollocks, hand it over.'

Zak passed the ZZ to Phil. He grabbed it and devoured it just like the first. Just as the last mouthful was swallowed, Phil's complexion turned incredibly pale and his lips puckered. Seconds later the door to Zak's shop was flung open and Phil disappeared. A roar of laughter followed him.

Dave was a little concerned. 'Do you think I should go and check on him?'

'Nah. Phil likes his own personal space when puking. Give him a few minutes,' Gavin said, still chuckling.

'You guys, where you going on this year's Campaign? asked Zak. Eastbourne, me reckon. Find some old bird your own age.' Zak grinned from ear to ear. Baz guessed Zak was joking and tittered nervously to prove it.

'You guys, you very old.' Baz laughed loudly as he delivered his own line. He had contributed to the conversation and now his night was complete.

'Bastards.' Dave smirked at Baz. 'If you must know, we're off to Crete, to a place called Hersonissos. It's full of top continental totty aimed at your more discerning British lads abroad. None of yer Magaluf slappers, know what I mean?'

'Sounds great, guys. Hey, if Mrs Zak would let me I'd come too. Get you some totty for sure, but no, she's a jealous lady. Baz could go, though.'

Baz looks excited. Tony suddenly found the power of speech again. 'Yeah that would be great… trouble is, it's fully booked.'

Tony smiled ruefully at Zak as he prised himself away from the fruit machine on which he had been leaning since entering the shop. The last half-hour had almost passed him by, but Zak's suggestion brought Tony from his semi-comatose state.

'Nah, you okay, Tone. See I already booked for Baz to go there. Didn't know that you were going too, man; just thought the lad needed a break. Find himself a lady, thought he couldn't do any worse than you guys. What you call a fluck, eh?'

Tony looked worried and puzzled. 'A fluck?'

'Yeah, a fluck, like when you do something and it turns out to be something else that you like but did not mean.'

'A fluke.' Gavin answered like he has just won a game of charades.

'Yeah, man, a fluck.'

'Except that this fluck is also known as bollocks.' Dave is not taken in.

Zak looked serious before beaming a smile. 'Got Tony though, eh?'

Tony was annoyed and tired. He wanted his bed. He often had a habit of going into his shell after a few beers, not in a morbid way, though. Tony was a thinker, and a bit of a dreamer. Always deliberating on how things might have been or how they still could be. His friends knew him too well, and knew when to leave him be. He would soon snap out of the trance and re-join the real world. Tonight, Tony has been thinking on the lines of why he was still going on holiday with the lads and not a girl, a fiancée, or even a wife and family. To be truthful he did get a little down for a while, but managed to quickly cheer himself up with the notion that this could be the year; the year when he finally meets the girl of his dreams. True, he did take the notion into pure fantasy at one stage. He imagined he would meet some single top totty celebrity on the hunt for an ordinary guy. A short guy with receding mousy brown hair, a complexion so pale he could have been hired out for hauntings and whose wardrobe was full of khaki trousers and white long-sleeved shirts. One of the girls from S-Club 7 maybe, or Cat Deeley, would be nice. Tony started daydreaming his very own *Notting Hill* script. His favourite film incidentally, and now he wanted to get home to bed and turn the daydream into a long, lingering night dream.

'I'm off home, lads,' Tony confirmed.

'Thought you went ages ago, Tone,' Dave chuckled. 'But I think you're right. I'm ready to crash myself. Better go and find Phil though.'

'Look no further,' Gavin pointed to the door just as Phil entered. He looks rejuvenated.

'Zak, those ZZs were the best. Now I'm ready for a club,' Phil now seemed wired.

'Nah, Phil, we want to call it a night. Save all the energy for the Campaign. Sleep now, party next week.' Dave had definitely had enough.

Tony and Gavin nodded heartily at Dave's rebuke. Phil grumbled and went into a sulk. 'And I can't even remember the fourth Banana Split. Fleegle, Snorky, Drooper … and who was the other fucker?'

'Bingo, innit?' said Zak.

Phil walked across and kissed Zak on the head.

Zak recoiled and wiped his forehead. 'There, told you all, Julian Clarey.'

Long Live the Weekend

The weekend passed quickly through a summer swelter. All the lads did their own thing.

Phil spent most of Saturday in bed, nursing a serious hangover. He even missed *SMTV*, and managed only a few bites from a slice of toast for a breakfast-cum-lunch. The day was filled with endless glasses of mineral water as Phil sat motionless in his garden, save for the times he changed the CDs booming from his stereo. He felt better by the evening, ordered a takeaway pizza and even managed a few glasses of wine. Beer was off the menu for once as he wasn't feeling that great. Phil watched some crap film with Richard Gere and went to bed early. Dull and boring, but he'd had fun the night before and the Campaign was getting closer. Sunday was hardly any better than Saturday, but the weather was good and he could enjoy the Sunday papers with a couple of cool beers as the neighbours worked tirelessly to get their gardens in order. The afternoon was spent at his mum's, for some good old home cooking. Phil liked his food. Phil liked his beer. Phil was lazy. No wonder his belly was growing.

Home for Phil was a little two-bedroomed terrace. He had bought the place over five years ago and made it into a real bachelor pad. Couples occupied all the other houses in the close, young cohabiters recreating the pristine abodes of their parents. Phil's house had its own style, its own stamp.

Phil had moved out of a flat he'd shared with Gavin five year ago to start life on the property ladder; Gavin had remained the eternal lodger. Like a gypsy he moved from place to place, after expertly scanning the 'To Rent' section of the local paper. Since Phil had left, Gavin endured numerous flatmates with varying characteristics. There was the quiet, introvert genre – tidy, considerate and of no harm to anyone, but dull. Then there was the slob - usually young with no respect for cleanliness, their surrounding or the personal space of others. Surely someone would clean or wash-up if things were left long enough. So what if they brought friends back at four in the morning for a party – he punched one once for doing just that on a Wednesday morning. What was their flatmate doing in bed anyway? Gavin hated the slob. Finally, there was the mysterious stranger – friendly and sociable enough, but with a past: an ex-con, a divorcee, a refugee; the list was long.

Gavin's current flatmate fell into the final category. Patrick was from Ireland. A nice guy who liked a drink and an intelligent conversation. Just like Gavin in fact, right down to their common love for real ale. Patrick was about forty-five and worked for a telecommunications company. He had very few belongings, and possessed no photographs of loved ones. Patrick was born in Dublin, and that was about as much as Gavin knew about his past. Phil's theory placed him in the IRA.

Gavin liked Patrick, or Parrick as he called him. He had only moved in two months ago following the swift departure of Gavin's last flatmate, Derek. He had been of the quiet, introvert genre, and one warm, barmy Saturday evening, he had been happily writing some letters in his bedroom. The bedroom window was open wide, and Gavin and Phil were just returning from a drinking session down the local; both were pissed. They staggered up the path propping each other up as they went. Phil suddenly looked up and grinned inanely at the open window above him. He proceeded to pick up a lump of soil from the garden and, before Gavin had a chance to intervene, a mud missile was hurtling upwards. Unfortunately it missed and smashed through the pane of glass next to the open window. The large stone entombed in the soil hit Derek on the head and he was out for about five minutes, until Gavin brought him round with some brandy. Phil even managed to persuade Derek that the missile had been thrown by some passing yobs... that was until two days later, when the lady next door gave her eyewitness account to Derek. He was out of there fast.

On the penultimate Saturday before the Campaign, Gavin and Patrick went to a mini beer festival at a country pub. Both had their fill of real ale, and both felt like shit the next day.

Dave had a great weekend; he spent it shopping for Campaign essentials. New snazzy shorts, sun tan lotion, batteries for the CD Walkman and T-shirts by the dozen. He even started some packing. That Saturday evening he had a date.

Her name was Sally and she was a trainee midwife. Dave had met her in Tesco, when he was shopping and she was stacking shelves to supplement her student income. Each week Dave would strike up a conversation with the petite brunette as she stacked boxes of cornflakes. Each week she would respond with a cheeky twinkle in her eye. Dave told his mates about this pretty young thing, but always ended by dismissing her as being too young for him. She was at most twenty-two. In the end Phil goaded Dave into going for it, basically by threatening to have a go himself. So Dave went for the kill, but not with the usual Holliman calm and cool approach, as witnessed in so many bars and clubs across Europe. If fact it was slow. Just how do you ask out a supermarket girl busy with her chores and surrounded by customers? He paced the shop many times before heading for the cereal aisle, determined not to come across as a sad old cradle-snatcher. Maybe he would test her medical skills by faking a heart attack and ask her out as she gave him the kiss off life.

Sally smiled as Dave approached. 'Here he is, the man who loves his cereal.'

Sally was loud and confident. Dave smiled and just knew he had to have her.

'Oh yes, breakfast, lunch and dinner, I can't eat anything else,' said Dave.

'So you mean to say that if I ever get invited to dinner, I can look forward to Weetabix followed by Special K with Alpen to finish.'

Dave now had an opportunity that was too good to miss.

'Well I could maybe change the menu just this once. I'm a mean cook you know... pukka, as that Oliver bloke on the advert says.' Dave hesitated and then coolly added, 'Would you like me to prove it?'

Sally said yes without hesitation and now Dave was spending Saturday afternoon preparing a culinary delight. He had not shared his triumph with the lads. When Phil brought up the subject of Sally the previous night, Dave quickly changed the subject. He almost felt guilty because of the age gap and knew it would lead to more piss taking than he could be bothered with. And this was despite the initial encouragement to go for it.

The meal went well. Melon to start, followed by a chicken pasta dish, and cheesecake for desert. Nothing too taxing to prepare and it was all washed down with two bottles of Rioja, and supplemented with conversation, lots of conversation.

They talked about family, music, film, work and their aspirations for life in general. There was a rapport from the start and no nervous silences. No incongruent body language. No disagreements. Dave admitting a liking for Steps, Ricky Martin and Leonardo Di Caprio helped the latter. Up until that evening he had detested them all.

In return, Sally had heard of the Jam, but not any of their music. Mention of The Alarm or The Undertones, however, brought a blank expression. Dave resisted taking the Robbie Williams CD (well you can't go wrong can you) off the stereo and replacing it with 'Where Were You Hiding When The Storm Broke?' or 'Teenage Kicks'. This was not the time to start the music education. Just as it was not the right time to stick *The Godfather* in the video for Sally's premier viewing. No, instead they continued to lazily talk over a soundtrack of easy going tunes. Sally left at 1 o'clock in the morning. Dave called her a cab and he was rewarded with a simple and innocent peck on the cheek.

The newly fledged couple met again on Sunday. Sally turned up at Dave's flat at exactly eleven o'clock in the morning. She arrived on a bright red scooter. Her shapely pert figure sat alluringly astride the compact machine. Dave marvelled at the sight before him as he observed Sally's arrival from the lounge window. As she removed her helmet and gave her brown bob a gentle shake, Dave's eyes moved down her body, which was tightly wrapped in a white T-shirt and faded blue jeans. You could almost hear the guitar-laden tune filling the air like a scene from some trendy advert. Dave was filled with lust.

The thirtysomething guy smiled with serenity at the young brunette stood before him. She was in full voice, and as bubbly as ever. The day was going so quickly and everything was so effortless. They had walked through the park, fed the ducks, lay in the grass, and acted in total harmony with a scene from every romantic B movie. They enjoyed a pub lunch and Sally even admitted that she was quite partial to the odd pint of beer. Dave jokingly stated that she would therefore have to marry him.

Dave was about to bid Sally goodnight when he wondered how far this would really go. Was it just lust between both of them? One day she would find out that he hated Steps. What then?

Sally pecked Dave on the cheek again, and with a little wink she almost skipped towards her scooter. Dave really wasn't sure what the future held, but he was going to have some fun finding out. He had arranged to see Sally, once more before the Campaign, on Thursday night. She was working at the hospital the rest of the time, including antenatal classes in the evenings. Dave pursed his lips together and then smiled.

'Roll on Thursday.'

Tony felt sad when he woke up on Saturday morning. He had a nice flat that was decorated and furnished to a minimalist style. Art deco adorned the spotless white walls. There was no clutter and no washing up to be done. No magazines strewn on the lounge floor. Quite the opposite to Phil's house, where the walls were plastered with movie posters and the magnolia backdrop covered in pin-ups, untouched since its original occupation. Phil had large deep comfy sofas; Tony had a prim leather couch.

Tony made himself a cup of tea with filtered water and sat on his sturdy leather chair. He sat thinking for over an hour as Springsteen's album, 'Nebraska', mellow and calming, played in the background.

All the lads needed something new in their lives, something to change their directions before they hit forty. Dave had Sally, Gavin had a new buddy in Patrick, and Phil had opted to obliterate everything with drink. Tony still needed to find something new. Sure he could drink like Phil, but when the high wore off he was back to reality and contemplation. The difference with Phil was that he seemed to simply contemplate the next drink up, or the next Campaign. Tony wanted, and was ready, for far more.

Tony was still pondering his lot as he strolled around Waterstones, trying to select various paperbacks to read on the Campaign. He was the most avid reader of all the lads, and would normally take five or six books to last the two weeks. Gavin usually got through a couple and Dave only ever took one, normally the biography of a sporting hero, which he never finished. Phil made do with some lads' magazines like *Maxim* and *FHM* for his reading matter, with a copy of *Viz* thrown in for good measure. He had progressed; on earlier Campaigns he'd been know to take *Mayfair* or *Escort*, and very little reading. Tony took a good hour to select six books for his holiday readathon. They ranged in style from the comic observation tale to the fast-paced thriller mystery. Something to heighten his senses of imagination; something to make him laugh; something to help him escape, and all were in the three for the price of two bins.

After buying a few more Campaign essentials, including the hopeful pack of condoms, Tony treated himself to a Cappuccino and quietly read *The Mirror* in a quaint little coffee shop. The young waitress smiled as she delivered the frothing cup to his table. Tony half smiled back and thanked her. He was a small, unassuming and lonely guy, who was rapidly losing his hair. The coffee shop was a Saturday routine, and all the staff recognised his face. Tony chuckled to himself, if only there was something in the waitress's smile other than the politeness of customer service. He dismissed any further sentiment as pity – 'Mr Saddo's in the building and sitting where he always sits' was what she must be really thinking. If only she could view him differently. The girl was quite pretty and seemed to have a friendly sweet nature, but no, she was probably off to share a joke at his expense with the rest of the staff in the kitchen. No doubt the older waitresses, and we are talking a couple that won't see sixty again, would jokingly offer to mother him. Tony could picture the scene, but he didn't care. He enjoyed the caffeine and the chance to deliberate in peace.

The reality was that Kim, the young waitress (a very young looking twenty-eight actually), had a crush on Tony. Each week she would try and grab his attention to start a conversation. And each week Tony would totally misread her advances as attributes of a friendly waitress trying to do her job. Kim was too shy to throw herself at him and Tony was too thick-skinned to ever read or believe the signs. Were the two hearts ever destined to meet?

Tony and Kim spent Saturday night watching a video. Both watched the new Charlie's Angels movie: Kim at home with her parents, Tony on his own with a bottle of wine.

You Have to Work to Play

Monday morning. Nothing manic about it as the bangles would have you believe. This one was only slightly dreary compared to the norm, as for the lads it was the last working Monday for a few weeks. They just needed to get it out of the way and notch it off on the calendar, like a jailbird etching the days to freedom on his cell wall. Freedom was the Campaign and Thursday night was the time of release.

Tony parked his red Astra outside the office and moved swiftly for cover through a summer shower. Work for Tony no longer involved selling electrical goods in high street stores, that all changed about five years ago when Tony decided to try his hand at selling something bigger – houses. He was now an employee of Elson & Smythe, a small family run estate agent.

Until about six months ago, Tony was doing all right. His sales were consistently good but then apathy set in. He was bored with life in general and his job in particular.

Tony was the last to arrive at the office. It was 8.45 a.m., and the other three estate agents had already been at their cramped, tiny wooden desks for over an hour, preparing their action plans for the day.

'Morning,' Tony mumbled to the others as he trudged to his desk, head bowed.

Some incoherent grunts of acknowledgement came back at him. Karen grinned inanely and shook her head ever so slightly, showing her professional disapproval for Tony's tardiness at work. Tony sat down at the small desk in front of Karen. A small radio was perched on her in-tray and the local station was playing the infamous Bangles tunes, so originally selected by the DJ.

'What a lovely bright tune,' Karen was filled with glee.

Tony pondered and responded dryly. 'You see, what I don't understand is why does she wish it was Sunday? I mean it's only a quick hop to another bloody Monday. Surely she should wish for

Friday night, although obviously it wouldn't make any sense to call it a fun day.'

Karen smiled with pity at Tony, and quickly turned her attention to her PC. Frantically she hit the keys on the keyboard and ignored Tony. She had always viewed him with disdain, like a teacher tolerating a slow learning, and infuriating, pupil. The other two, Jeff and Rob, were loading their briefcases and would soon exit at pace. Sales were there to be made.

Tony opened his briefcase and pulled out *The Mirror*. He placed his feet on the desk and lazily read the day's news. It might as well be Sunday.

An hour later Karen had also long departed the office, only Tony remained. He supped his fifth coffee of the morning and scoffed his ninth digestive biscuit. Suddenly Tony sprung to his feet.

'Right, let's go and move that property. Today I am irrepressible… yeah, right Jeff, you tosser. Mmm, I smell money to be made… loadsamoney… fuck off, Rob, and update your jokes. Oh, I'm selling a quaint little thing for a sweet little man to a divine older gentleman… Oh, I'm so hoity-toity, I could never marry a man who didn't vote Conservative. I mean he would have to be an oik fwar fwar.'

Tony's impression of Karen mirrored her yuppie laugh to a tee. In fact he had honed the impressions of all his workmates. He could even do their partners at a push, from memories of an awful Christmas do, when he was a pitiful singleton amongst smirking lovers.

Reluctantly, Tony opened his appointment book. He was down to cover the office until eleven-thirty and then had to marshal three viewings of a little two-bedroomed starter home.

Eleven-thirty came slowly. The rain had kept any browsers from the street, although a large number of shoppers had huddled in the doorway to take shelter. A few had even ventured in to while away some time, as a shower became a downpour.

Tony was actually pleased to get out of the office, although he had become so blasé to the art of selling. He arrived at the small terraced property in a nonchalant mood. A young couple with a baby was selling it; with another one on the way they now had to think bigger.

After letting himself in (The young couple were both at work, and the baby was with the girl's mum), Tony sat down in the lounge and waited for the first of his trio of viewers.

Fifteen minutes later there was a timid knock at the door. Tony opened the door to be greeted by a youngish hippy-looking girl. She was soaked from head to foot.

'I'm here for the viewing,' she announced and then continued to squelch her way into the hallway.

'Are you? Okay.' Tony looked her up and down.

'Oh yea, just a spot of rain and I had a three-mile hike to get here.'

'You walked?'

'Don't believe in cars and I keep getting knocked off my bike.'

Tony shook his head and continued to shake it as the hippy squelched around the house, even after she had removed her shoes.

Hippy Girl opened every cupboard door for a good pry, and even had a look under the couple's bed and the baby's cot. She said very little and instead just twitched her nose, a la Samantha in *Bewitched*, at every opportunity. When the tour was over she seemed unimpressed.

'A little too modern for my taste, I'm afraid.' Hippy Girl was slipping on her old brown boots.

'I can see that.' Tony wondered why the girl wasn't living in a wigwam on the common.

'Oh well, time to hike off home.' Hippy Girl actually smiled at Tony. 'Don't suppose you'd be heading towards the Ashbury estate would you?'

'I'm afraid not. I'm stuck here and besides I wouldn't want you to forsake your boycott of cars.' Tony was smug in the extreme.

Hippy girl huffed and walked out into the torrential rain.

It wasn't long before the second viewing was in full swing. This time it was a young couple who seemed ideally suited to the property. She was very short and very polite and pleasant. He was a hulk of a man, several feet taller and wider than his beau. Tony wondered how they had sex without a near-death experience for the girl. The missionary position was surely out of the question.

'Excuse me, Tony, are you okay?' enquired Sweet Girl.

'Uh… sorry,' Tony had lingered on the thought of the couple having sex a little too long.

'We were just wondering where the main heating control is?'

'I'll show you.' Tony quickly recovered his composure.

'Tone, any chance I could pop and use the lav?' the Hulk was actually looking green.

'Er… sure, it's directly at the top of the stairs.'

'Smart,' and the Hulk was gone.

Tony demonstrated the heating control to Sweet Girl. 'It's very simple, as you can see…' He paused as a number of large grunting noises emanated from upstairs. Sweet Girl smiled. The noises became louder and louder. Sweet Girl smiled more and more. Relief came with the sound of the toilet flushing, and the Hulk was soon plodding back down the stairs.

'Sorry, Tone, bit of a heavy sesh last night and one hell of a ruby.' The Hulk looked less green. Instead the colour transferred to Tony and Sweet Girl, as a stench from the depths of hell wafted down the stairs after its master.

Tony gulped loudly. He was totally thrown and felt ill. He was saved by Sweet Girl, who, with a look of immense embarrassment, announced that the house was not quite what she wanted and pulled the Hulk towards the door.

Tony was soon opening every window whilst trying not to be sick. He dared not check the toilet for fear of anything that had not flushed away.

The foul smell had nearly disappeared by the time viewer number three stood at the front door. Tony recognised her instantly. It was Cheryl the serial snoop.

Cheryl was a spinster in her fifties who had a strange hobby – nosing around other people's houses. She was harmless but a complete time-waster. Tony had not seen her for a while as Elson & Smyth had all but banned her, just like every other estate agent in town. Karen had slotted the appointment in at the last minute. The spiteful bitch, no wonder she had smiled when she told Tony she had done him a favour and found 'the perfect buyer for his little house.'

Running her finger along the top of the fridge, Cheryl tutted at the fair amount of dust it had picked up.

'Young people don't care to clean, do they? I bet you 10p that your house is the same, young man.' Cheryl moved swiftly into the lounge, stopping briefly to sniff the air. A puzzled look crossed her face as she sampled the remnants of the Hulk's stench.

'Oh look at those curtains, so plain. A nice floral, that's what this room needs. And why do they have all those videos? Whatever happened to proper family entertainment? A game of cards, draughts, even plain old conversation. Oh young people today.'

And so it went on, and on, and on. Tony followed Cheryl around in a silent daze. He was soon gazing out of the back bedroom window, lost in thought as Cheryl checked under the bed. A sudden screech interrupted Tony's pondering. He ran out of the room to be greeted by Cheryl emerging from the bathroom. She was pale, shaking and sobbing.

'It was horrible, so horrible. I couldn't breathe. Why oh why? I feel terrible, I must lie down.'

Cheryl was pretty incoherent. Tony led her into the bedroom and got her to lie down. She continued to mumble for another ten minutes, and then asked to leave as the colour came back to her cheeks.

'I am certainly not interested in buying this house, young man.' Tony smiled, she never was. 'And I am quite sure that I will never be able to lift a toilet seat again.'

With that Cheryl was off towards her small green Ford Fiesta. The reason for hysteria was now apparent – a gratuity from the bowels of the Hulk. Tony flushed the toilet ten times before checking for the all clear, allowing himself a wry smile as he did so.

By Tuesday, Gavin's head had just about cleared the after effects of the real ale festival from Saturday. A few hairs of the dog – in other words, a few pints of Old Grumbler on the Sunday had not really helped.

Gavin was still selling electrical goods, using the same sales technique practiced over the last fifteen years. But recently Gavin had made a life-changing decision; he had moved his employment from one high street chain to another. The prompt for this momentous change had been the arrival of an abhorrent new manager at Carters, Gavin's now former employer. He was a cross between the TV character Gordon Brittass and the Dickens character Uriah Heep.

On the day that was to be the beginning of the end, Gavin was completing the sale of a state of the art washing machine, already spending the commission money in his mind. And then suddenly up popped the pompous creep, real name Ian Small.

'Good day, dear people, Ian Small, store manager, at your humble service. Just checking that you are getting the very best service that Scarts can offer.' This was all delivered with an insincere toothy smile, gleaming from a slightly tilted head. The young couple preparing to pay for their purchase were slightly taken aback.

'We're fine, mate, your man here has been very helpful.' The stocky young man had placed his credit card on the counter.

'Oh yes, young Gavin is coming on nicely, but has he adorned you with the wonderful guarantee package currently on offer?' Gavin cringed. He was at least twelve years older than the snide creep.

'Yeah, he has, but unfortunately we can only just stretch to buying the machine itself.'

That was it. With sneering pomposity, the Creep explored every avenue on how the young couple could cough up the extra money. He nearly went as far as to suggest that the girl pawn her engagement ring. At that stage the boyfriend grabbed his girl's hand and stormed towards the door, and with that the sale was lost. The Creep followed with cupped hands, declaring his humbleness and sincerity as he shuffled beside them. Soon they were gone and the creep was marching towards Gavin.

'Rogers. How have you lasted in sales for so long when you continue to blow every deal that comes your way? I suggest you pull your socks up, young man, as my eye is now firmly upon you.' The Creep was now sounding unerringly like Brian Clough.

That was it. Gavin's structured life had to change and he knew it. Six sales had been blown in one week and all down to this creep. He managed to pull in a favour from an old friend at the high street rival, Moxies, and he was out of there. He made the Creep pay on his last day though.

The night before, Gavin recorded some special soundtrack CDs. One simply repeated the hissed word of 'creep' over and over again, whilst the second recurrently whispered the word 'snide', and a third delivered various slurping noises.

The next day, with the assistance of the head of sales from the entertainment department (who was also leaving), each CD was placed in various top-of-the-range music systems. Then, whenever the creep was in range, the CDs were activated by remote control, alternating from one to the other in short blasts and at full volume. The Creep shuffled around nervously, shouting for assistance to search for the source of the distressing sounds. The shop floor was devoid of staff as they strategically hid from view. Only a few bewildered customers looked on. Within ten minutes the Creep was on the verge of a fit, as his head twitched incessantly, scanning for the offending machines. He just could not work it out, such was the dexterity in which Gavin and his conspirator operated the various remote controls.

The Creep went home with a migraine; his suspicions of Gavin correct, but unproven – it had been a lesson taught.

Gavin smiled to himself as he paced the floor of the large Moxies superstore. There were only a few customers perusing the goods, mostly hovering around the vacuum cleaner section. Gavin looked on with contentment as he had quickly settled into a nice mundane niche, the shock of change overridden, it was like he had worked for Moxies all his life. He felt a buzz as he wondered if he would sell more cookers or dishwashers today. Of course it would have to be the latter if current shopping trends were anything to go by. Gavin was so proud of his job, encompassed by a smart demeanour and an informed methodical, and always polite and understated, sales technique. He always arrived for work dead on time, and left for home dead on time. In between, he had exactly an hour for lunch, during which he would read a newspaper whilst munching on a homemade sandwich, made with precision the night before. Gavin was a man of routine in everything that he did and woe betide anyone who blocked his chosen path. The Creep had tried and received his just deserts.

Gavin huffed. It was nearly eleven and there had not been a sale in sight. Everyone was buying vacuum cleaners today, and all Dysons at that. Its aerodynamic look had even attracted single blokes to part with their cash. Even Phil had bought one recently to replace a knackered old vacuum cleaner that spit out more than it sucked up.

'Gav, the bloody thing is great. You can see all the dirt whizzing around as you go. It's totally wicked.' To Phil, cleaning was no longer a chore but a game on a par with Tomb Raider, although he would have preferred to watch Lara Croft in action with the machine in his front room.

Gavin's attention was suddenly drawn to a middle-aged couple looking around the cookers. Well, at least the lady was, whilst her husband kept glancing and edging towards Moxies' impressive selection of mammoth state-of-the-art televisions. Gavin could read his mind – 'sod the bloody cooker, I want one of those'. The husband would never say it though; it was more than his life was worth. At work he was ruthless and feared, but the boss at home wore a skirt and she was beyond defiance. The wife shook her head several times and was soon heading for the exit, with her husband firmly in tow.

Gavin wandered over towards the television section and gave a hello smile to Barry, the young sales assistant.

'How're things, Baz?'

'Not bad, old boy, selling some nifty hardware. The way they keep updating these babies, I'll be upgrading my own system every week.'

Barry talked about televisions in the same way that Jeremy Clarkson talked about cars. He continued, 'See that little tease over there? Now *that* is a beauty.'

Gavin turned around, half expecting to see some gorgeous female, instead he was looking at a large, slim silver television.

Barry was in full flow, building literally towards a verbal orgasm.

'She's got Nicam digital, virtual Dolby, built in DVD, ninety-nine channel capacity, twin scart, front games connection, and all wrapped in a thirty-two inch wide, sublime slim body,' Barry was licking his lips almost seductively.

'Do you remember your first colour TV? I do.' Barry looked slightly startled as Gavin continued. 'It was about nineteen seventy-four, I think. The old black and white had packed up for good, and Dad had decided to go for a colour set after speaking to Radio Rentals. I can remember it like it was yesterday. Coming home from school and sitting in amazement before this big black magical box. First thing I ever watched was *Top Cat*, Brilliant! And look how TVs have evolved now, as well as the advent of Video and DVD. Amazing! If you wanted to see a good film when I was little you had to stick with the TV schedules.'

'Yeah, right, Gav. Looks like I might have a sale old boy, so catch yer later.' Barry sidled off towards a very young couple gazing in awe at a 48" monster set. They almost mirrored the young Gavin as he sat on the rug in his parents' living room, watching the family's colour TV set for the very first time.

By Wednesday Phil was feeling good. It was getting closer to Friday and therefore closer to the Campaign. Two weeks of debauchery and lads behaving badly, where he could really let go, really let off some steam. Time to move out of the mundane and find an alter ego. Somebody with no conception of work, time or rules.

For now, Phil followed the normal weekly script. He arrived at work for eight-thirty in the morning, made himself a coffee, logged on to his computer and pulled some files from the 'in' tray. It was Wednesday, but it could really have been any day, save the date shown on Phil's Ally McBeal desk calendar. Phil ripped off Tuesday's sheet and stored it for use as notepaper. Wednesday's read as 15 August 2001, and showed a captioned picture of Ally and Elaine. Phil wished he could offer Ally a good, wholesome meal, to put some more meat on her bony figure. Ditto every time he saw her picture. Phil's working life was more than a routine; it was a scene from *Groundhog Day*. Gavin loved the security of a much-practiced schedule. Phil despised it.

Phil was a senior credit controller at Shipp and Hall's Building Merchants. He had been working in the same department for over fifteen years and knew the job inside out. Outside of work Phil was a real lad, a man's man with a likeable roguish cheek. At work he was respected by the customers, revered by his bosses and admired by the staff. Mild mannered Clark Kent transformed into Superman in the nearest telephone box; likeable, stocky Phil Mockley transformed into mad-for-it lad in the nearest pub.

Apart from the bespectacled Alan, who had worked for Phil for eight years, staff came and went. Today Phil was to interview a candidate for a current vacancy in the team, and then begin the handover of responsibility to Alan before jetting off to the sun.

By ten Phil had cleared four outstanding invoices and had drunk as many cups of coffee. Bang on time, reception called to announce the arrival of the interviewee. Phil grabbed some papers, smiled at Alan, and headed for the conference room.

Jenny, a young college leaver, looked up from her work. 'Where's Phil gone, Al?'

'Interviewing.' Alan didn't look up from his paperwork.

Jenny stood up, straightened her micro miniskirt an inch lower towards her knees, and walked over to Alan's desk. 'Sharon in accounts reckons that Phil's an alky, brought on by the fact that he's still a virgin who lives with his mum. However, Sarah over there reckons he's had loads of girls. Although, Jane in sales says that's rubbish and that he is actually gay, and living with a guy called Dave. She saw them having a beer together one night. Tracey King says that could be true as she gave him the right come on once and he wasn't the slightest bit interested. Is he gay, Al?'

'Long live office gossip. Jen, as far as I know Phil is totally hetro, and always has been. He has his own house, which is just slightly bigger than Tracey King, and really enjoys a few beers with his mates.' Alan allowed himself a wry smile.

'Hetro? Does that mean he likes men and women?' Jenny looked excited and ready to dash back to her desk and call her mates with some news hot off the press.

Alan was stunned. 'Get back to work girl.'

Phil sat silently in the conference room, staring at the interviewee whilst flicking a biro up and down against his teeth. Phil's stocky build was quite intimidating, but it was sadly based around a growing portly thirtysomething tummy rather than a six-pack developed in the gym. Phil was very conscious of his weight, and very touchy when it was mentioned. His hair was thinning badly; the once proud blond mane was no more. He often wished he had married young, just so the wedding pictures would capture him at his best. Around the age of twenty-six, that was when he was in his prime, at that time he'd spent his evenings in the gym, and little time in the pub. The time he was truly in love, but it was the cruellest love of all. Unrequited love.

Aged twenty-six, Phil tried to become someone he was not. He went for a change of image and became an actor. Not someone who literally trod the boards, but a thespian in a real life drama. Phil's life.

Cary Grant once said that the hardest role he had ever played was himself. Phil's mum always told him to be himself. Phil tried to be someone else to win the heart of Kerry.

Phil first spotted Kerry one Friday evening after work. He was in the Grasmere, a pub across the road from Shipp and Hall's. Several other offices congregated around the Grasmere, and on Friday nights it was like a company bar for all of them. Kerry worked for Paul Harte, a small stock brokerage firm that was part of the congregation.

Every Friday, Phil would religiously drink in the Grasmere and admire Kerry from afar. She was just over five foot with gypsy black hair and a pale complexion. Her face was pretty, although a little plain.

Phil finally got to speak to Kerry through a mutual friend who had done some contract work at Paul Harte's. The friend told Phil to give her a wide berth, but did not explain any further. Phil could not understand, and soon forgot about his friend's caution as he chatted the night away with the sweet demure girl in front of him. She seemed so innocent in the ways of the world, and so vulnerable. Phil wanted to protect her from the harsh reality of her apparent virginal naivety. He thought it was love at first sight and he was desperate to claim Kerry as his own. To the onlooker love really was blind.

The couple did everything together: lunch; walks; a casual drink, and went to the cinema. To the outsider's eye, the couple looked good together. But that was as far as it went. During a pleasant lunchtime stroll, Phil was confident enough to reach out a hand to pull Kerry close. He was ready, and so wanted to show some real affection. Until now Phil had been unsure. He so loved being with Kerry, it would have been foolish to rush in with ungainly passion as he had done in the past. This time he was being subtle and romantic, and he longed for reciprocity.

Kerry's reaction was an explosion that blew Phil's world to pieces. His hand was coldly cast aside. 'Phil, I really like you as a friend but that's as far as it must go.'

Kerry might as well have knifed Phil in the heart there and then. From that moment he was numb, and for several days that followed. The pub was once again his solace. He should have just let it go and moved on, but his heart was in charge and still held out some hope. This was a challenge. He called Kerry and said he would like to continue their 'friendship' and that he accepted that they would only ever just be friends. Of course he did not mean it. Part of him did want to continue to enjoy the companionship, but part of him truly believed that there was a chance to change Kerry's mind. So Phil transformed himself to win his fair maiden's heart. He lay off the booze, worked out, bought a new wardrobe and changed his outlook. Phil tried really hard, but the harder he tried, the weirder Kerry would get. She began to play mind games, flirting with Phil's friends and work colleagues, whilst manipulating all around her with lies and gossip. One by one people began to see through her, and they would all take their turn to warn Phil. The word 'psycho' was repeated many times. Dave thought that she was a lesbian out for revenge on all men. Phil was deaf to all the warnings and still blinded by love. He defended Kerry at all times and isolated himself from those who truly cared about him.

This unrequited love took Phil to the depths of despair. He gave everything to find the key to Kerry's heart, only to find it cold and protected by barbed wire. None of the lads could get through to their once fun-loving mate. Phil was even talking about giving the Campaign a miss. The remedy came from Kerry herself. Phil accompanied her to a house party, and during the evening Kerry was casually chatting to a lad who had not long seen twenty. The scene was so reminiscent of when Phil first met Kerry. Phil smiled and walked over to hand Kerry a drink, and then came the blow. The glass was struck from Phil's grasp with one viscous slap of Kerry's hand.

'You creep,' Kerry shouted at Phil with an ugly sneer. 'Why won't you let me talk to any other men? You are a pest, a worm, and a perverted stalker. I hate you! Why do you follow me? Why? Why?' She looked evil and her words were spat out with real venom.

Phil looked directly at Kerry like he had just woken up from a coma.

'You are one weird bitch. Goodbye.'

And with those words, Phil turned on his heels and left the party, Kerry and unrequited love behind. Kerry's new young beau also made a hasty retreat. He was on life's learning curve for all things female, but this was a lesson he was going to skip. Phil was free at last and did he feel good.

Back in the present, Phil smiled at the young interviewee. A young guy, in an old man's suit, with an extremely polite nature.

Phil chortled loudly. 'It's funny isn't it, the jobs we end up doing.'

'Sorry, sir?' the lad looked puzzled.

'Well, I mean, I've worked in credit control all my life. But when I was a kid I had a romantic notion that my future career would be heroic or exciting. My mates wanted to be astronauts, firemen or sport stars, but they grew up to be bank clerks, estate agents and store managers. I wanted to be an archaeologist. Not a boring old fart with a beard holding a toothbrush for meticulously dusting down old artefacts. No, I wanted to be Indiana Jones, finding treasures with a supernatural origin. How about you? What did you always want to be when you were small?'

'A credit controller, sir,' came the confident reply, as if the young lad had not been fooled by the trick question.

Phil sighed.

Thursday was a long time coming for Dave, and his date with Sally was still a day's work away. The aroma of the ground beans smelled as good as ever that morning, as Dave queued for his espresso, in the company coffee shop. To be fair, those around him also maintained a buoyant, cheerful disposition. Only two days to the weekend and the weather forecast looked good. But for Dave it was going to be hot and sunny for two weeks, guaranteed. He was going to be away from here and to quote Phil it was party on.

Dave drained the last drop of his espresso, getting a real kick from the molten black beans. He was already logged on to his computer, and had amended five unit trust certificates by the time Mel arrived. Mel sat opposite Dave and had worked with him for two years now. She had a really athletic figure, and today was wearing a light mid-length skirt and sleeveless blouse that highlighted every curve. Her legs, arms and face were beautifully tanned, and her face was cherubic with hazel eyes and framed with a slightly wild brown bob. Dave's eyes filled with lust, as ever.

'Hey, D, still intent on leaving me?' Mel spoke softly and very seductively.

'Sorry, M. It's just meant to be, but you have sole custody of my millionaire desk calendar.'

Dave and Mel had only recently started to address each other in initials, and all courtesy of *Big Brother 2*. They had both been addicted throughout the summer and spent the mornings discussing the goings on in the house of the voyeuristic real life soap.

'Well, it's just not good enough. I'm just going to have to tie you to that chair and keep you for my pleasure,' Mel is pouting outrageously.

Dave's trousers are starting to bulge under the desk. All this innuendo never failed to hit the spot, and Dave was now feeling very warm in the cool air-conditioned office. It was not as though he could get up and walk to the water dispenser to cool down. The bulge had now grown out of all proportion.

'Just release me on a Friday night and I promise to return,' Dave played along with the fun.

'Done. I'll have it written in to your objectives immediately.' Mel was also Dave's supervisor.

The banter was typical of most mornings over the last two years, but Mel has been engaged for twice that length of time to a quiet unassuming aerobics instructor. To be honest the double entendres had driven Dave to distraction. He had even been out for some casual drinks with Mel and they had always got on so well. So well that Mel would talk openly about her relationship with Richard, her fiancé, right down to his penchant for Mel to wear stocking and suspenders for their lovemaking. Dave did some serious masturbating that night. But, and it was a big but, it was clear that Mel wanted to marry Richard, and that is why Dave never ever tried to take things further. He feared a lost friendship and possible humiliation, too much. Their sexual games remained forever in his head. This was one girl who Dave would not score with.

Dave and Mel were also united in a dislike for their immediate manager, Susan.

'Where's Jabba's sister?' scoffed Dave, as he used his very non-affectionate pet name for Susan. She was a large lady, although not unattractive, so the comparison to the *Star Wars* character was a little unfair. It was borne more out of Susan's shackling of Dave to his work duties, hardly leaving him space to breathe. Dave was the hero, Hans Solo, and she was the mass of evil ready to thwart his every move.

'She's offsite this morning, but don't worry she'll be back this afti to wish you bon voyage,' Mel replied in a matter of fact way.

'So glad to hear it,' Dave was extremely sarcastic.

The rest of the morning went quickly as Dave effortlessly checked detail after detail on all the unit trust certificates submitted to him. He intermittently checked his e-mails, taking more time over the jokey messages from his mates rather than concentrating on the firm's business. There were even a couple of mails from Phil and Tony, building up the excitement for the Campaign. And there was the usual one from Bill in redemptions, eager for assistance with *The Express* crossword. Doing the crossword seemed to be Bill's job description, and it was all he ever talked about. Before the advent of e-mail, he would be forever wandering the office looking for help with three down or whatever. Now he just saved his old legs and mailed the entire office.

The afternoon was flying by, when Dave smelled the distinctive odour of Jabba's sister's breath as he typed away at his keyboard. A warm gust of air touched his neck at the same time.

Dave swung round to be greeted by Susan's plump face growling back at him. She was dressed in a heavy, dark black suit from head to foot, even though the day was hot and sunny. But something was different. Her hair was not all wild and abandoned as usual, but her jet-black locks were tied back in a ponytail.

'Wow! Very sexy, Sue.' Dave could not have been more insincere.

'Watch it, Dave. HR is only a floor away and they are pretty hot on sexual harassment at the moment.' Susan was totally sincere. Her face then turned even more severe, 'Have you finished your batches?'

'Not quite, only about thirty certs to do.'

Susan tutted loudly and raised her eyebrows almost to her hairline. 'Time management, that's the key. I'll see what courses are available and get you on one, as soon as possible.'

Dave was quick to remind her. 'Sue, I've been on "Time Management one" twice, "Time Management two" and "Time Management three". They are all the bloody same. You must use your diary more… complete a "to do" list every morning and stick to it… a tidy desk is the key. Total bollocks presented by a prat who has never worked in an office in his life.'

Susan was taken aback by Dave's rant. He usually just grunts at her and then accepts her managerial advice. 'Well, I found them all useful. You could do far worse than use me as a role model if you ever want to get on. I'll be aiming to be on the board by the time I'm your age. Take a look at me and what do you see?'

A fat, unattractive badly dressed trout, with breath from the depths of Hades, who has probably never had sex and probably never will. She thinks that she's well liked and respected by her staff, but so does Saddam Hussain. She thinks that management adores her, but they all call her 'that lesbian'. That's what Dave truthfully wanted to say, but instead he just grunted and said, 'I'll have to look at courses when I get back from holiday.'

'Too right, and isn't it about time that you started taking some more sedate vacations instead of always ha'way wi' the lads?' The last few words were delivered in a very poor, mock Geordie, accent.

'I like to stay young at heart, Sue. Keep myself fresh for the job.' Dave wished she would walk off now.

'Is that rude, fat lad going with you?' Susan had met Phil in a local pub. He had constantly ripped into her, alluding to many lesbian themes from shot putting to facial hair. A very uncomfortable twenty minutes for Dave, but most of the comments seemed to go over her head. She was powerless to retort on the spot, away from the comfort of the office. Instead, she delivered considered jibes about Phil to Dave back at work 'Well he seemed to think I was fat, but he's not exactly Mr Bean himself... so what if I don't always shave my legs, does he always shave the bum fluff on his fat cheeks?' And so it went on.

'Er, yeah, Phil will be going. He asked to be remembered to you the other night.' Dave was not lying, although Phil had actually said, 'Tell the dyke that if I don't pull in Crete, I will happily give her one. Release all me sexual frustration and she loses her virginity into the bargain.'

'Did he? He was a bit of all right, actually,' Susan walked off with a wry smile on her face. Dave looked on a little stunned.

'So is it last minute packing tonight? Leopard skin thong, baby oil and that?' Mel interrupted Dave's stupefied trance as he watched Susan walk away.

'No. Did it all the other night, including the thong.' Dave wondered if this was the start of another breezy chat with strong sexual undertones.

'Wow! That's impressive for a bloke to be so organised. No Time Management course needed at home, obviously,' Mel quipped at Susan's managerial chat with Dave.

Dave chuckled. 'It's the first time ever. I'm normally a throw-it-all-in at the last minute merchant. But tonight, Dave Holliman has a date with a gorgeous young lady.'

Mel seemed shocked by the revelation. 'Seriously?'

Dave has noted the reaction. 'Too early to tell if it will be serious. I'm sure to blow it true to form. Never been very good at relationships.'

Mel had recovered her composure. 'Well, I should hope so. You're meant to be saving yourself for me.'

Mel instantly returned to her work, totally embarrassed by her last remark. Ditto Dave.

Five o'clock came. Mel told Dave to 'have a good 'un' and not to forget to send a filthy postcard. Even Susan wished him 'happy holidays' and added 'regards to Phil' accompanied by a very large wink.

Dave's rueful smile broke into a massive cheesy grin as he jumped into his Golf GTi. He pressed play on the car stereo to trigger a blast from 'School's Out' by Alice Cooper. He had placed the cassette ready that morning and now the time had come.

'Schhooools out for ever.' Dave sang loudly as he pulled out of the company car park, flicking Vs at the office of Mutual Life as he went.

'...And then I told her to get out of my face. She sheepishly muttered sorry and went back to her desk. Any neutral observer would have sworn blind that I was the boss and not her.' Dave's speech was all gung-ho as he recounted to Sally his confrontation with Jabba's sister. The truth had been totally twisted of course, to make Dave sound much more like Hans Solo than... well, Dave.

Sally looked sweet and radiant, but with a cheeky lilt to her smile as she giggled along to Dave's heroic tale. It wasn't an immature girly giggle but a cute intellectual chuckle. Sally was bright, even if she did like Steps, and Dave was starting to wonder if she had been joking about that all along. He also wondered if she had really been taken in by his tall tale.

The romantic couple, albeit one with quite an age gap, looked casual and relaxed as they enjoyed their meal at Amalfi's, the town's best Italian restaurant. It was owned by a family from Naples and was truly authentic, definitely not a crap theme restaurant. Dave loved all things Italian; the food, the style and the women. He once went out with a girl from Florence. Her name was Anna-Maria and the relationship lasted the summer of '93. Weller released 'Wild Wood', Shaggy sang about 'Carolina' in a ragga-crazed summer and Meatloaf would do anything for love but he wouldn't do that. Dave tried but failed to explain the concept of *Groundhog Day* to his Italian beau, but made a better selection with *Jurassic Park* as they both cuddled in awe at the huge dinosaurs. They parted on good terms when Anna-Maria returned to her homeland, leaving Dave with some great memories and even a smattering of Italian.

Sally did seem genuinely interested in everything that Dave said. 'I bet your boss will be glad to see the back of you for a couple of weeks. You're like a naughty schoolboy playing up the teacher. Were you naughty at school?'

'I was very cheeky,' Dave was not lying this time. 'I went to an all-boys grammar school, where everyone was so bright. You know, the type who takes their 'O' levels before they are thirteen, and are better read than the teachers by the time they are fifteen. I felt really thick and became impudent to hide my intelligence.'

'But you went to uni though,' Sally offered some support.

'Well polytechnic, but they are all unis these days. It was funny as none of the teachers gave me a hope of getting any 'O' levels, never mind 'A' levels. But I was just good at exams. I was crap in class all year, but would do a bit of revision when it came to it and passed everything put in front of me. Really pissed them off.' Dave allowed himself a smile that showed conceit.

'So GCSEs wouldn't have been any good for you, what with the course work.' Sally brought the education system up-to-date.

'How many GCSEs did you get?' Dave was guessing at five or six in his mind.

'Twelve. All As, plus three A levels, all As again. Not bad eh?' Sally was nonchalant about her educational prowess.

'Fuck. Is that what you need to be a midwife these days?' Dave was shocked, but suitably impressed.

Sally chuckled, and in the process accidentally spluttered out a crumb of garlic bread on to her plate. 'Of course, that's just to make sure that you pull the sprog out of the right hole. Seriously, my dad was an attorney. He's retired now, but he was desperate for me to go to law school.'

'So you chose midwifery to piss him off. The rebellious daughter and all that.' Dave was confident that he had sussed her.

'Nah. I've just always fancied doctors. There's something about a white coat and a stethoscope,' Sally smirked.

'I shall be purchasing both items upon my return from the Campaign.' Dave was pleased with his off the cuff riposte. 'Would you like some more wine, young lady?' The main course was still to arrive and an empty bottle of Orvieto Classico already sat proudly on the table between them.

'I'd love one, old man.'

'*Scusi camereri, un botielle de Orvieto, por favore,*' Dave impressed her with some Italian, he had brushed up with a phrase book earlier that evening.

'*Prego!*' the waiter smirked at Dave's pronunciation as he tried to impress the pretty girl.

'Very impressive. Are there no ends to your talents?' Sally's eyes widened as she looked alluringly at Dave. He raised his eyebrows in response.

As Dave finished his tagliatelli, the third bottle of Orvieto stood half empty next to its two wineless brothers. Sally was struggling with her lasagne, and her words.

'So, what's the story?' she slurred.

'Morning Glory. Cracking album. Top band, mad for it,' Dave interjected, concluding with a passable Liam Gallagher impression. He was totally mellow and pissed.

'No. Let me finish,' Sally gave Dave a weak slap on his shoulder. She was almost struggling to speak. 'The Campaign thing, or crusade or whatever you call it. Your mates, what's it all about? How come you're all still single and not sprogged up and wearing slippers and a cardigan waiting for retirement.'

It was a question that Dave had mulled over many times before, and he answered quite soberly. 'Fate, I think. That and wanting to hang on to our youth. I mean we've all put it about a bit in our time, apart from Tony that is. I think he's only ever had one girlfriend, which is pretty sad. But the Campaign, it seems to reaffirm our youth. It's something to aim for. A bond, an adventure, call it what you will. Fate conspires to ensure that we are all single by the time of the Campaign.'

'Mmm. Accept that you have a girlfriend this time around,' Sally looked serious.

Dave was a little stunned. 'Yeah, you're right, and the others don't know it. It does feel really different somehow. I mean we're just starting something off I guess.'

'I didn't mean to get heavy. I mean who knows where you and me will end up. Fate as you say.' Sally tried to lighten the serious conversation that she'd started.

'Yeah. I always think that life is like one of those "you are here" maps that you see in the city centres. It shows you where you currently are, and then you light up bulbs for any selected destination. And then you go there if you chose. Life's like that, choices to be made and bulbs to be lit on the way.'

'Very philosophical. Well this bulb is flashing like crazy. Shall we go back to yours?'

Dave hastily requested and settled the bill. '*In bocca al lupo*' he muttered with gusto and then exited Amalfi's hand in hand with Sally.

'*A lupo e crepi.*' Dave's colloquial Italian genuinely impresses the waiter.

Even sleeping with so many women, Dave still experienced that odd moment of pre-coital embarrassment in initiating the rampant desire to discover every curve, find and stimulate every erogenous zone, and be at one with the gorgeous girl before him. She looked even sexier after three bottles of Orvietto, and she was definitely up for it.

Dave had left Sally sitting on a sofa in his lounge whilst he popped to the bathroom, both to empty his bladder and to retrieve a condom concealed in a soap bag. His hands were shaky and sweaty as he fingered the ribbed rubber sealed inside a mauve foil wrapper. 'X-tra sensitive' was the promise in silver letters on the simple packaging. Dave's whole body gave a little shudder of excitement.

Take it real slow, and be cool, thought Dave, as he calmly walked into the lounge. The sight that greeted him touched every nerve end of his body. Sally had made the first move for him, as she lay naked on his sofa. Her petite frame was superbly proportioned with ample breasts, silk smooth skin and a cute, neat, bush of pubic hair peeping from her crotch, masked in part by her pose. She was elegantly sitting with her back against a cushion at one end of the sofa, with her knees shut together and pulled slightly towards her pierced naval.

Sally slowly moved her knees apart to reveal two soft gaping lips below the neatly trimmed bush. 'Come on in the water's lovely.'

Dave did not need a second invitation. He instantly dropped to his knees and buried his head between her legs. He just could not help himself. Not all girls appreciated that kind of attention, and it was not Dave's usual approach on a first shag, but it just seemed right. Sally's whole body shook and she moaned her approval. Dave continued to caress her with his tongue with gusto and relief.

The passion lasted for an intense hour. Sally had slowly removed Dave's clothes, massaged him from head to toe with her delicate hands, and then followed the same route with a salacious darting tongue. Dave entered her twice and they both wildly shuddered in unison as he climaxed. The only interlude was for Dave to go and retrieve another condom from his packed suitcase for the second shag.

Dave and Sally fell asleep on each other in the cusp of Dave's comfy sofa. A white sheet covered their elated and exhausted bodies. Even in sleep, Dave's face had a constant and firmly fixed smile.

A Big Red Bus and Una Stubbs

Dave's face was stuck firmly to a cushion, as he lay prostrate on the sofa. His tired eyes flickered open and he took a gulp of stale air through wine parched lips. Slowly his head eased upward and turned away from the back of the sofa. His eyes focused on Sally's skimpy white knickers seconds before her hoisted trousers hid them.

'Time to get up, lover boy. Saddle up your steed and rape and pillage Europe, or whatever else you do on these crusades.' Sally's voice was lilting, and reassuring.

'It's the Campaign, and drinking beer and talking bollocks is what we do.' Dave's voice sounds gravelly. 'What time is it?'

'Seven-thirty,' replied Sally, after a glance at her slim blue watch.

'Fuck! Fuck!' Dave leapt from the sofa in a scene reminiscent of the opening of *Four Weddings and a Funeral*. He stood totally naked before Sally, and felt a little awkward as he frantically searched for his boxer shorts.

'I'm meant to be picking the lads up in fifteen minutes. No time to shit, let alone shave. Good job I'm packed.'

'Well, I'll get out of your hair in a minute. I've called a cab as I've got to be at Tesco's by nine.'

'Don't you want any breakfast, a cup of tea before you go?' Dave forgot his panic for the moment, as he didn't want Sally to leave thinking that the previous night had been a casual thing.

Sally put her hands on her hips. 'Dave, you have fifteen minutes to get out of here,' she looked at her watch. 'Make that ten.'

Dave gave Sally a long and lingering kiss before she sidled into the yellow cab. 'Send me a postcard,' she uttered through the open window. 'And have fun.'

'I will, and I'll call you. I promise.'

Sally smiled. Dave was not sure if it was a 'yeah right' sarcastic smile or a genuine 'can't wait' smile. And then the cab pulled away and Sally and Dave exchanged cheerio waves.

Dave snapped instantly into action. He grabbed his case and travel bag and loaded them into the boot of his car. The apartment was locked. He slid into the driving seat, slipped on his shades, allowed himself a grateful smile for the previous night, and then accelerated away.

The M25 traffic moved efficiently and uncluttered as the sun's rays sank into the pale yellow tarmac. Dave's silver GTi glimmered in the morning sunshine, as it traversed effortlessly toward Gatwick Airport. Traffic jams allowing, it would be pulling into one of the airport's many satellite long-stay car parks in about thirty minutes.

Inside the car, Dave and Phil occupied the driver's seat and front passenger's seat respectively. Both were wearing near identical dark black shades. Gavin was slumped in the back half asleep. He was groggy and hung over after enjoying a few too many pints of Guinness with Patrick the night before. Tony was sitting upright and daydreaming as he stared at the fast-moving vehicles all around him. The roof was raised. It was down for the first fifteen minutes of the journey, but Gavin complained so much about the breeze, or hurricane as he labelled it, making him feel ill, that Dave relented for a quiet life. He could not hear the music above the moans, and counter debate from Phil, and music was important to Dave. He attuned to the beat reactive to his mood. The Campaign 2001 was underway, and he had just had one of the best shags of his life. The rhythm and vibe were upbeat in the extreme.

Dave and Phil nodded their heads in unison as 'Do You Know What I Mean' by Oasis boomed from the car's speakers.

'This is it, man. This is what makes it all worthwhile. The open road, heading for the sun, four desperados on a mission.' Phil is on a real high. The Campaign was his zenith, despite its ephemeral nature.

Dave smiled. 'Yeah, it's going to be cool.' He glanced back at the sedate Gavin and thoughtful Tony. 'Not sure about the desperados bit though, more like desperate saddos.'

Phil ignored the last comment. 'You can't beat it, though. Going on holiday and escaping life's mundane routine, taking time out from the rat race. Even as a kid I used to get such a high as we headed on the annual jaunt to Butlins. A family of four packed into a small red Mini, with bulging suitcases tied to an overloaded roof rack. Shit, we didn't even have a car stereo. I used to sit in the back with one of those really old flat tape recorders with large red and white function keys, playing badly recorded tunes from *Top of the Pops*. Because you had to sit in front of the telly with a microphone trying to pick out your favourite song, whilst encouraging your dad not to speak too loudly or he would ruin all your hard work.'

Dave laughed and nodded to concur relative to his own childhood memories.

'Shit, I remember, "You're The One That I Want" from *Grease* including my dad on vocals,' Phil continued. 'John Travolta was just telling us about his multiplying chills when you could hear "how long until tea, I'm starving" and then Olivia Neutron Bomb would tell him that he had better shape up.'

'You see you should have asked for one of those big grey boogie boxes that came with scart leads. Just wire it into the back of the gramophone for Sunday's top forty countdown and Bob's your uncle. No dad on vocals,' Gavin interjected without moving an inch from his slumbered position.

'Yeah, all right if you could afford one, or if your parents could afford one more like. I bet you were one of those little sods who never bought any albums or tapes but just pirated everyone else's.' Phil looked over his shoulder at Gavin to see if his mocking hit home.

'Correct,' was Gavin's arrogant reply.

Dave mocked them both. 'So who had the best gramophone? The amplifiers were always so right for blasting out "Never Mind The Bollocks". Revolution, I really mean it, maaan.'

The comment was ignored.

'Wake Up Boo' by the Boo Radleys is just fading out on the stereo. It is replaced by the twanging guitar of Hank Marvin followed by the boyish vocals of Cliff Richard, exclaiming that he and the gang were going on a summer holiday, going where the sun shined brightly.

'Brilliant.' Phil was pleased that Dave had included the

timeless feel-good tune on his compilation tape. 'This would really set the mood.'

Dave, Phil and Gavin, who were now sitting up, sung along loudly. 'No more working for a week or two…'

Tony didn't join in.

The song drew to a close. Phil chuckled. 'One of my all-time fantasies you know. A double-decker bus as a travelling home, hit the road to anywhere, pick up some tasty hitch-hikers and head for the nearest beach.'

Dave nodded in agreement. 'And Una Stubbs of course.'

'Of course.' Phil would not have it any other way.

'Well, your fantasy is almost there. Just substitute the double-decker with a spotless Golf GTi and we're on the way,' Dave offered.

'Just need to track down Una Stubbs and make some room and who knows where it will end.' Tony at last joined in with a dry comment on the proceedings.

'There's more than enough room for her to squeeze in up front,' said Phil, wildly slapping the top of his thigh. 'So what are we waiting for? She's probably waiting around the next bend with her three most gorgeous flatmates. So put your best foot forward my good man.'

De Plane, De Plane

Tony sat alone in the Sports Bar at Gatwick after a hurried check-in and saunter through passport control. He was pondering the précis description on the back of one of the paperbacks he would read on the Campaign. The first few chapters would be read by the time he boarded the plane. Gavin was getting the beers in. Dave and Phil were off scouring for some last minute CD bargains to enjoy by the pool. Tony was official bag minder.

The lads were used to Tony's thoughtful moments and his need for personal space, but they'd all noticed that he seemed more distant than ever, even quieter, and even more considerate. They all remembered him being like it once before, just prior to the Campaign of nineteen ninety-five.

As Dave had casually remarked to Sally, Tony had only ever had one serious girlfriend. He had been an awkward and shy teenager and had never recovered to confidently pursue the opposite sex by the time he'd reached his twenties. Tony was most comfortable in the company of men, with whom he had learnt to drink and banter as good as the next man. His mum soon tired of waiting for her son to bring home that prospective daughter-in-law. She compared him to Cliff Richard and joked about her eternal bachelor boy. Inside it tore her apart as she wondered if he would grow old alone. His three younger brothers were all married by the time Tony was twenty-five. Tony enjoyed each of their weddings, performing the duties of best man at them all.

Despite what some suspected, Tony had no inclination or aspiration to forge any erotic bonding with his own sex. Talk of footie, beer and girls was all he wanted from his male friends. He enjoyed the odd drunken snog on some Campaigns and took solace in his time with the lads, and solitude alone with his books. He remained a virgin until the age of thirty-two, and the year was nineteen ninety-five. The year he met Carol.

Carol was a divorced mother of three, aged forty and struggling to raise her young offspring after the complete disappearance of her philandering husband. The divorce and disappearance was inevitable, particularly when the new babysitter turned out to be an eighteen-year-old pretty blonde, whose body and mind were maturing at a rate of knots. An impressionable teenager and a philanderer is a concoction that will always ignite.

Carol took a job at the local bookies to earn some valuable pennies, coupled with her other job as a barmaid at the Greyhound. With a career in alcohol and betting, her path was bound to cross with Tony's eventually.

The couple became friends, and then lovers, after meeting at the bookies. Carol was loud and overpowering, and swooped on Tony for a date before he could even try to register any shyness. She took him under her wing and tutored the virgin in the ways of sex. Tony would spend most of his evenings at Carol's. He had his tea made for him, the fridge stacked with beer and sex on tap. The kids called him Tone and would jump all over him at every opportunity, even as he lay in bed with their mum. When Carol worked at the Greyhound, Tony would renew his relationship with the lads. Carol's mum looked after the kids. A perfect life for Tony, and this paradise lasted for eight months.

Tony had a cousin called Martin, who was everything that he was not. He was athletic and a keen bodybuilder. He only drank bottled lagers, was a smooth talker and a real hit with the ladies. Tony was sure that Feargal Sharkey's cousin, Kevin, was a doppelganger as they were both so perfect. And yes, Martin did thrash him at Subbuteo when they were younger. The reality was that Tony liked and admired his cousin and always put him on a pedestal. He could never be Martin, but he could share in the stories of his sexual conquests and tales of heroics lad's escapades.

On that fateful day, Tony went on a pub-crawl with Martin and Carol. Before, he had always taken Martin along with the lads, who tolerated him for Tony's sake but they all thought him a prat of the first order. He was constantly either on his mobile or on the prowl for anything female. Phil labelled him the 'wanker with brains in his cock', although not to Tony.

Carol could drink as well as Tony, and matched him pint for

pint that day. Martin stuck to a few bottles of weak Mexican lager before moving on to Red Bull. They ended the night back at Carol's watching a video. The next thing that Tony could recollect was waking up on the sofa at about two-thirty in the morning, gasping for some water. He staggered into the kitchen and almost tripped over Martin's arse as he vigorously shagged Carol on the floor. Paradise was lost. Carol never contacted Tony to apologise or ask him to come back. Tony hadn't spoken to Martin since.

It took two months for Tony to admit to the lads what had happened. He had been so cold, so quiet and so distant. He got over it, but now, in August two thousand and one, his sullen mood was replicated again. He felt that his life had reached a crossroads, and that he needed the courage to drive it in a new direction or forever be affable, likable Tony, always good for a pint and a chat. Tony could see himself sitting in the pub in twenty years time with grey hairs and a few wrinkles, and they would be the only things that distinguished him from today. He was still alone, and Carol would have been his only love, being the cruellest irony of all. Even Shakespeare would have steered clear of such a tragedy. And at the end of this lonely life, his epitaph would say 'Fuck! I blew it.'

Tony knew he had to take a chance. Did he persevere with his crappy job, from which he could be sacked anyway? What about a change of image? What about risking his heart, and overcoming his shyness to find real love? He could get a new job, buy new clothes, enter the lottery of love by putting himself forward to talk to, and meet, the opposite sex. Show them he was really interested. If he wanted to win the lottery he had to buy a ticket.

Tony's mind was clear now. He was content in the knowledge that it was time for the new Tony to step out of the shadows. This Campaign would be the start of the rest of his life.

'There you go, Tone. I would say penny for them, but you'd have bankrupted me this week,' said Gavin, as he placed four pints of Boddingtons on the high, round table, interrupting Tony's thoughtful, but now uplifting, trance. Around him the pub was packed with pale expectant holidaymakers wearing their recently acquired surfing T-shirts and shorts.

Tony answered with the glee of a newfound optimism. 'Cheers, mate. Wondered where you'd go to.' He took a couple of large devouring gulps of the smooth bitter, and sighed his appreciation as it hit the spot.

'Yo, tossers,' Phil loudly heralded the return of himself and Dave. He grabbed one of the pints and drank nearly half of it in one go. 'Ah! Needed that, the party start here.'

'What did you buy?' Tony noticed Dave's small CD bag.

'John Lennon's "Rock 'n' Roll" album. I've been after it for ages. Wasn't cheap though. Fourteen bloody quid. Bring back duty free and European borders, I say.'

Tony laughed loudly at Dave's comment, registering the big change in mood immediately with the others. 'You've been gone a while?' Tony suddenly realises how long he'd been pondering.

'You too, mate, but glad to see you back. I thought we'd brought along some miserable bastard, but I now trust I am mistaken.' Phil was as tactful as ever.

'Yeah… I think so. I've already ditched the Radiohead CDs, just needed to make a decision, and it took a while to get there.'

'And?' Dave was inquisitive.

'Nah… all you need to know is that this boy is ready to party on down, so Crete better watch out and make sure that there is enough women and beer to take the job on.'

The lads looked on stunned.

Tony brings them to. 'So, anyway, where were you all this time?'

Phil was quick to respond. 'Did you miss me, Tone? I never stopped thinking of you.' He mocks Tony by fluttering his eyelids whilst tilting his head and imitating a lover's gaze.

'Just concerned that you might have wandered off and boarded the wrong plane or something. That you might have been heading for Peru instead of Crete,' said Tony, now in the mood to fight back.

'Yeah, Peru sent us Paddington Bear and we sent them Phil Mockley in return. A sort of cultural exchange, although they both have big bellies and the same fashion sense.' Dave loves to jibe his oldest friend.

'Fuck off!' was Phil's unconsidered response. It was his only response when the girth of his stomach was raised.

There was a pause, and then Gavin broke the silence. 'Fancy a game of cards?' He produced a small deck from his travel bag.

'Fuck off,' the lads gave a unified response followed by spluttered laughs. Gavin was laughing too. He knew the others hated cards. This particular deck would only be used for solitaire in the next two weeks, unless Gavin was fortunate enough to meet another like-minded poker fanatic.

'Phil and I went over to watch the planes coming in.' Dave finally explained to Tony why they had been so long. 'Some old couple thought that Phil was a retard when he did his tattoo impression from *Fantasy Island*. Got down on his knees, the lot.'

Phil was quick to spot an opportunity and repeated the performance for the lads and the surrounding tables. 'De plane, de plane,' he shouted with a poor South American accent. It brought a roar of laughter and approval from all in the immediate vicinity.

'I wonder what it would be like to be a jet-setter. Flying from airport to airport, your passport bulging with visa stamps, your wallet stuffed with cards from your favourite restaurants in every major city. I think I'd like that. Life would never be mundane or dull with a whole world to explore.' Tony was thinking about a radical change of lifestyle.

'Actually, a mate of mine from Poly works for some big American bank and flies all over the world. He loved it to start with, used to send me postcards from wherever he was. Now he's just bored with the endless airports and he reckons you only see a bit of the place if you're lucky enough to stay for a weekend. Otherwise it's just the view from the taxi, hotel window or the inside of a restaurant or hotel room. Business class is meant to be cool though. You get your own little telly to watch the latest films on, booze is free and on tap from some top floozy, and they always give you those cool little soap bags to keep. He's got hundreds.' Dave de-glamorised the image, although not totally.

'Has he been to any weird or exotic places?' Tony hadn't been put off by Dave's description.

'Yeah, and dangerous. He caught Malaria in Swaziland, was shot at in Pakistan and had to be given an armed escort in

Nigeria.' Dave now made his friend sound more like James Bond than a banker.

Tony nodded and decided that maybe international travel was not for him. Far safer to be a hero in his dreams, or enjoy the scenery in a Bond film, from the comfort of his sofa or the local cinema.

'Never mind, Tone. Perhaps the airport is full of international terrorists and you can be Bruce Willis instead of a secret agent. *Die Hard 4*, the thoughtful estate agent.' Phil put his arm around Tony's shoulder.

'Or how about *Die Lard*, starring portly Phil Mockley?' Gavin puts the joke back on Phil.

'Fuck off,' is the familiar response.

'Shit!' Gavin suddenly jumped up. 'The plane leaves in ten minutes. We should have boarded by now.'

Gavin's realisation triggered a stampede for gate twenty. The lads had somehow been oblivious to the calls to board the flight, and nobody, not even Gavin who was normally so meticulous, had bothered to check the screens.

As luck would have it, the lads arrived just in time to join the back of the remnants of the boarding queue. There had been a slight delay. They hastily gathered their composure and breathing, and handed over their boarding passes.

Tony sat across the aisle from the other three. Dave always had the window seat, and Phil always sat by the aisle in order to catch the drinks trolley at every opportunity. Gavin was stuck between them, and silently studied the safety card, learning what he needed to do in case of a crash landing. In his mind he pictured the chaos and fear, should the plane come down in the ocean, and shudders as he is overcome with a ghostly chill.

The plane soon taxied and the flight attendants, or stewardesses/stewards to the lads, sprung into action to deliver their best semaphore representation of how to use the oxygen masks, where to find the life jackets, and how to locate the nearest exits whilst crawling on the floor. Gavin observed and noted the steps as he again pictured the plane crashed, and taking on gallons of water. The blonde flight attendant is in his daydream, soaked from head to foot, and looking damn sexy with it. Fear has turned to erotica in a second.

Tony looked on and wondered if he was too old to become an air steward, or whatever they call themselves now. Phil and Dave leered unashamedly at some of the gorgeous female forms before them, dressed in spotless, bright-red jackets and three-quarter length skirts, with tanned and shaped legs to complete the perfect pose. These were the girls of Rainbow Airlines, the airline responsible for today's chartered flight to Heraklion in Crete.

The 737 was soon up in the clouds and en route for sunnier climes. There was a mixture of people on board: families, couples, groups of lads and groups of girls, all chomping at the bit to start their holidays.

'Good afternoon, this is Bob Cruthers, your captain speaking. This is flight RA18 from Gatwick to Heraklion. Please sit back and enjoy your flight with us today. The journey should be smooth and we hope to reach our destination in just under four hours. We are scheduled to arrive at 5 p.m., local time. If you have not already done so, please adjust your watch, as Crete is two hours ahead of the United Kingdom. The flight attendants will shortly be serving drinks followed by lunch, which today is a delicious fish pie... mmm, you lucky people.' The lads laughed at the captain's sarcasm, backed by Phil mockingly sticking his fingers down his throat.

The captain continued. 'In order to allow the flight attendants to deliver a tip-top service to you scrumptious people, it is Rainbow Airlines' policy not to show any films or videos during the flight. I am sure that this meets with your approval.' Captain Bob was now sounding like John Cleese. The groans of disappointment from the passengers did not concur with Bob's last statement, and he knew it was coming. It was his little game, toying with the oiks whose expectations were so limited in respect of life's pleasures. In the cabin, Bob flicked the microphone off but continued to speak into it. 'So up yours, you bloody little poor people, and I truly wish you the holiday that you all deserve. Next week, however, I shall be sipping marguerites whilst enjoying the Mauritius sunshine... ha ha ha.' His co-pilot, Jack, grins with disdain. One day the bastard was going to get caught out and broadcast his little joke for real.

'Anyway, sit back and enjoy the flight to Heraklion, where the current ground temperature is twenty-nine degrees Celsius. You're in good hands.' Captain Bob goes back on air for real and signs off with his own well-groomed catch phrase.

'No film! Fucking typical,' Phil was pissed off. He aped the captain. 'So everything can be tip-top, old fruits, for a first-class service. So fucking cheap skate that they can't afford it more like. And as for fucking fish pie…'

'You never eat the airline food anyway,' Gavin was quick to remind Phil.

'Yeah, but it's the principal. Airline food is always shite, but this sounds like the shitiest of the shits.' Phil sounded almost poetic.

'Oh well, it will help your diet,' Tony added, from across aisle.

Phil reached out to slap Tony, but ended up brushing the backside of the male flight attendant as he backed up the drinks trolley.

'Well, hello, you're an eager beaver. I shall deal with you personally,' came the camp response, confirming the lads' misconceived stereotype of all male flight attendants.

Phil's face turned bright red. 'Uh, sorry mate, didn't mean to do that.' His voice was gruff and deeper than normal.

Through tears of laughter, Tony ordered some beers and small bottles of wine. His recent mid-life crisis was almost a distant memory. Pete the trolley dolly, winked at Phil as he moved down the plane. He was having fun too.

Phil was still smarting when the food arrived, or slop as he called it.

'Nah. You're all right, mate. I'll give it a miss.' Phil's voice was still deeper than normal as he addressed his newfound friend, Pete.

'Well, your mother wouldn't be pleased. A big boy like you needs feeding up.' Another camp response from Pete.

Phil did not respond, but slowly shook his head and whispered to Gavin. 'Is this guy for real or what?'

Gavin had already devoured half of his slop, a big mound of white slush, also known as fish pie and mashed potato, with some green and orange flecks on the border, which were probably green beans and carrots but no one could be certain. 'I think you're in, mate. Just think if he'd been one of the beautiful young girls whose arse you'd felt? You'd be as happy as Larry's happy brother with a reaction like that.' Gavin took another gulp of slop, almost holding his nose as he did so, like a dose of bad medicine.

'Yeah, maybe I'll give it a go,' Phil looked like he was seriously contemplating the idea.

'Don't you fucking dare,' Dave was concerned, he knew Phil too well.

'Mmm,' Phil pondered. 'Okay then, I'll save the magic hands for Crete.' He held his hands out in front and moved his fingers backwards and forwards like a pianist about to tenderly manipulate the ivory keyboard at a major concert.

'Oh yes, very Paul Daniels.' Tony glanced with scrutiny at Phil. 'Come to think of it, there are similarities.'

'Yeah, Phil, seeing as we haven't got a video, maybe you could put on a magic show for the passengers.' Dave had just finished his slop and joined in the fun to take his mind of the pending indigestion.

Phil smiled. 'Actually a puppet show would be better.' He'd noticed a large empty white screen near the cockpit entrance and pointed it out. 'A sort of Punch and Judy in the air. More violence than *Reservoir Dogs* guaranteed.'

After a few cups of tepid and tasteless coffee, the small plastic trays were whisked away from the slop-fed passengers. Tony had just started chapter three of his paperback. Dave was listening to his CD Walkman and enjoying Weller's artistic rebirth on Stanley Road. Gavin and Phil were relaxing and enjoying a plastic beaker of red wine. All the lads looked calm and almost tranquil in their own way. There was a gentle hubbub of noise throughout the plane, rising just above the humming pitch of the aircraft's engines. Dave glanced out of the window and could clearly see an expanse of blue water below, through faint wisps of cloud. The opening bars of 'You Do Something To Me' stirred his senses through the small earpieces amplifying the sounds from his Walkman. He swore he could see a couple of small fishing boats glistening in the sunlight. They must be near Greece now, he thought, so maybe they were local fisherman. Dave conjured up images from the film *The Guns Of Navarone* when Gregory Peck and friends disguised themselves as fishermen. He was sure that all the crew below looked just as hardened and grizzled as Anthony Quinn.

Tony was really into John Grisham's latest masterpiece. His mind was buried so deep into the depths of the plot and the complex lives of its characters, that he was far removed from the concerns of his mundane life. His body was no longer taut but slackened as his imagination took control. Tony was oblivious to those around him. A couple in their fifties enjoyed a loving cuddle and whispered sweetly to each other on his left.

Gavin enjoyed the distinctive grapes of the fruity Merlot as he sat back in his chair and relaxed his mind. He wondered if they served any ale in Hersonissos, or whether he would have to stick with gassy lager for a fortnight. Usually when it was time to come home he couldn't wait for his first real pint, although he didn't mind the odd bottle of cold lager as a refresher. It was the fizzy stuff from the pump that he couldn't take too much off. By the end of the Campaign he normally felt so bloated, just like a fairground balloon ready to fly. He might have to stick to Guinness, because that was sold in all four corners of the earth.

Phil's taste buds were not discerning enough to distinguish the Merlot grapes, but he had reclined his chair and was also totally at peace. He was dreaming of a perfect holiday, of finding romance on a deserted golden beach, and enjoying a bottle of cold, crisp white wine from an ice bucket as the waves tickled his feet and those of his curvy companion. In his dream, Phil was a couple of stone lighter and his beau looked uncannily like Britney Spears.

'Yeeees!' A loud chorus jeer broke the tranquillity. The lads all jumped up startled out of their respective trances, and looked back to the source of the commotion. It continued as a drunken ramble of a song. 'He's fat and round and sleeps with sluts, Davie Hoft has puked his guts la la la la la la.'

A group of about seven twenty-year-olds were mocking a fat member of their brood, who had drunk too much lager and had thrown up in the aisle. Most of the liquid had been hurriedly consumed at the airport as the young chubby lad tried to live up to his nickname, the Barrel.

The flight attendants hastily rushed to attend to the runny

puke as the other passengers in the vicinity looked away. The Barrel was hastily ushered towards the toilet at the rear of the plane, to further cheers from his erstwhile mates. They all had identical mauve T-shirts on, with the words 'Bramsgrove Boys On Tour 2001' emblazoned in white letters on the front.

The lads settled back down. Phil spoke for them all. 'Fucking kiddies! Just can't hack it these days.'

Hot, Hazy and Daisy

The 737 touched down on the faded tarmac at Heraklion with the slightest of bumps. In the cockpit, Captain Bob Cruthers gave an arrogant glance to his co-pilot to reaffirm his brilliance as a pilot. Jack had seen that look so many times before, especially when Captain Bob hit a heavily top-spinned passing shot on the tennis court as he whopped him again. Captain Bob was not just good at everything he tried, he was brilliant. He knew it to.

A slight click of the microphone and Bob was back on air from the cockpit. He coolly stated that flight RA18 had been smooth, and had landed two minutes ahead of schedule. The outside temperature was down to twenty-seven degrees Celsius in a nice late afternoon breeze.

'We at Rainbow Airlines truly hope you all have a wonderful holiday and look forward to when you fly with us again. I have been your Captain, Bob Cruthers, you've been wonderful passengers, good night,' Captain Bob ended his flight finale speech sounding like Ben Elton, almost believing that there were ripples of expectant shouts of 'encore' behind him.

The strains of Vivaldi's 'Spring' piped out as the plane gently taxied to its parking slot. Dave gazed from his window at the hazy layer of heat hovering over the tarmac of the runway. A plain white airport building stood in the near distance, and a patch of pale green vegetation lay in-between, beyond was the Cretan landscape.

A sudden bustle heralded the plane coming to a standstill, as all the passengers desperately sought their hand luggage ready to make a quick getaway. For some it was as if their lives depended on it. The lads took it calmly, although Phil was quick to gather up their duffle bags from his advantage position in the aisle. He interrupted Tony with a jolt as one bag fell on his head, whilst he was buried in a paperback.

The sun was still bright as the four thirtysomethings

descended the aircrafts steps, with the sharp glint of its rays making them squint and the intense heat hitting them hard in the face with the force of a boxer's persistent jab.

The luggage carrousel was like a game as each of the lads jostled and dodged to snaffle their suitcase first. Passport control was quick and easy, now it was time to find a holiday rep with a bright banner showing the name 'SunRay'. Gavin was first to spot the sign, held aloft amongst a sea of competition. It was proudly held by a tall Amazonian like brunette, overdressed in a SunRay uniform of a long floral gown. Zoe, the area manager, gave them a beaming smile and ticked the Holliman party off her list. They were beckoned to join several couples and a family behind her.

Nearby, a rejuvenated Barrel and the mauve T-shirt brigade headed for the plump peroxide blonde holding up the Club 18–30 banner. Behind, groups of kiddies of both sexes gathered like cats and dogs on heat. The air was dense with the omission of expectant pheromones.

Zoe led her crowd to bay twenty-one, where a dusty, almost decrepit bus, awaited them. The driver ungraciously piled all the luggage into the underbelly of the rust-ridden vehicle, whilst not once removing the half-smoked cigarette from his mouth; it was mostly molten ash, delicately balanced. Dave led the way onto the bus that proudly declared itself air-conditioned. The seats were both flimsy and uncomfortable.

As the bus trundled out of the car park, a petite young female rep stood nervously hunched at the front of the bus, in the centre of the aisle. She was beautifully tanned and wore the more flattering SunRay uniform of white polo shirt and red skirt, with the company logo emblazoned on both. The logo was a simple drawn sun, as if taken from a nursery school painting.

The anxious small brunette clicked on her large microphone and blew into it.

'Hi, everyone,' she mewed like a mouse, before clearing her throat with a manufactured cough and speaking with more clarity and confidence. 'Welcome to Crete, I trust you all had a pleasant flight. My name is Daisy and I would like to extend a warm welcome to you all on behalf of SunRay holidays. We are now heading for Hersonissos, which should take about thirty minutes.

We are in the trusty hands of Kavos, our driver.'

Daisy glanced over at Kavos for a reaction, but he didn't flinch.

'Kavos speaks very little English,' Daisy explained. 'Anyway, sit back and relax, and as we near our destination I will give you some more details.' Daisy abruptly concluded her speech, which was punctuated by Kavos shouting loudly out of his window at a couple on a scooter, who he had come close to decapitating.

As the bus chugged down the central road leading into Hersonissos, Daisy once again nervously fumbled the microphone. The passengers all looked up from their tired travel daze.

'Hello again, we are now about to enter your holiday destination, the famous harbour town of Hersonissos. The good news is that it has been hot, hot, hot... so make sure that you splash on that lotion. If you like your nightlife, then there are bars in plentiful supply all around the harbour. I look forward to sharing a metaxa or two with you if you spot me in my favourite taverna. "Where's that? you cry." Well it's the Dia Sands, about one hundred yards past the beach. I have cards with directions for everyone.'

'Blimey, we even get a commercial with the speeches now.' Gavin is bemused by Daisy's blatant publicity. 'And finally a word from our sponsor,' he concluded in a mock American accent.

Daisy had paused, but soon continued with a concentrated glance at Gavin. Had she heard him?

'For the shopping addicts amongst you, there are some excellent shops here, mainly specialising in jewellery and furs. There is also every opportunity to hire cars and bikes, and explore more of the wonderful island of Crete. Please see the SunRay approved list of dealers, and don't drink and drive.' Daisy's voice rose like a teacher warning some unruly pupils, before she once again softened her tone. 'We are now approaching our first drop off, the Hotel Garden Imperial. The rep is Jo, and the welcome party is at nine-thirty tomorrow morning. Enjoy!'

This was the lads' stop and they were amazed and relieved; usually they were the last on the bus, having toured the cobbled streets of some Mediterranean resort at dusk. But this time they were the first to shuffle down the aisle, which they did swiftly and with equally false smiles as they passed Daisy at the front. She mirrored a brief and faint smile in return. A thirtysomething couple followed behind.

The new arrivals retrieved their luggage from the indelicate offloading service offered by Kavos. Daisy then led the party past the pool, and its customerless bar, and into an unmanned sparse reception. She smacked her hand down hard on the counter bell.

'Maria will appear shortly. She is the owner's daughter and will check you in. See ya,' and with that Daisy was gone.

The lads and the couple waited for the appearance of Maria as the SunRay bus's ignition spluttered into life, and Kavos moved swiftly away without a signal or a care.

Five silent minutes passed, and still no Maria. Phil smacked the bell again.

'This is no good, boyos, do you think that Daisy has made a mistake, perhaps?' The thirtysomething man spoke with a Welsh accent straight from the valleys, as he put a comforting arm around his dour-looking partner.

'Could be right, mate. She was bit dizzy. You from Wales?' Phil did not need to ask.

'That obvious, eh? Swansea born and bred, me and the missus. Childhood sweethearts we are; married now for eighteen years, since we both hit twenty-one. Isn't that right, my lovely?' The Welshman glanced over to his beloved.

'If you say so,' was the unconvincing reply.

'I'm Gareth and this is Cheryl.' His wife's cold response did not register.

Phil introduced the lads just as a small stout Greek lady appeared behind them.

'What you want?' grunted the mean looking receptionist.

'And you must be the lovely Maria?' Dave spoke with mocking sarcasm.

'Yes, I am. What you want?' Maria really needed to learn the value of good customer service.

'We want to check-in please,' Dave remained cheerful.

Maria looked puzzled. 'Then you go to restaurant in town. Now please go, I am busy.'

'Eh?' Dave is also puzzled.

'You want check-in, you go and order at restaurant. This hotel!' Maria was coming across like a Greek female version of Basil Fawlty.

Gavin quickly realised where the confusion lay. 'No, no... we would like to *check* in to the hotel. We are from SunRay. We do not want to eat chicken.'

'Why you not say? English joke I suppose.' Maria shrugged her shoulders and beckoned for the SunRay booking confirmation. After a few grunts she handed over two sets of keys and pointed the lads to some stairs around the corner. The foursome lifted their bags and begun to 'cluck' like chickens in unison as they headed for their rooms.

The two double rooms were situated below the ground floor at basement level. Dave and Phil took the first room, Gavin and Tony the other. Inside the walls and floor were pure white, with two single beds placed on each side. At the other end there was a basic rickety wooden wardrobe and an equally tardy chest of drawers, placed either side of the door to the bathroom.

'This is well basic, mate, but it'll do.' Phil remembered far more luxurious apartments from previous Campaigns.

'Yeah, it's not exactly the Ritz, but it beats a tent. Remember Blanes?' Dave slumped on to one of the beds.

Phil smiled as he remembered the Campaign of eighty-nine in a large tent on the Costa Brava.

'Yeah, but that was fun and this will be too.' Phil was determined to retain a buoyant holiday mood. 'Mind you, I think the communal campsite bathrooms had more to offer than this.' Phil had opened the bathroom door to reveal a space not much bigger than a large cupboard containing a basic shower cubicle, and a small basin and mirror squeezed in between the door.

Dave shrugged after moving over to view it for himself. He put on a posh accent. 'What, no bidet? Well really, I think we'd best go and see what the veranda has to offer.' And with that Dave unlocked the external door at the base of his bed and pushed it open. Outside was a small patio with a plastic table and two chairs that could have come straight from the local DIY store. Beyond was miles of shrubbery leading to some kind of vineyard. The air was filled with the sound of crickets.

'That's a mating call, hundreds of horny Jimmies shouting "I want a shag – give me a shag,"' Phil could empathise.

'That's very good, and after a few pints tonight you'll be pining for the very same.'

Phil smiled and raised his eyebrows. 'So very true,' he then echoed and joined in with the insect crescendo.

Opening Night

Dave had connected some speakers to his personal CD player and the rocking sound of Oasis filled the air. In anthem-like fashion Liam sang 'Cum On Feel The Noise' for a gritty update of the Slade classic.

Phil was both keen and ready to hit the bars and sat uncomfortably on his bed, vigorously flicking through FHM. His twitching feet betrayed his eagerness to sup that first cold lager, and he so wanted Dave to finish grooming each individual hair on his head.

'I knew I should have washed it.' Dave was having a bad hair night.

Before Phil could offer a crude expletive, a knock at the door heralded the arrival of Gavin and Tony.

'Glad to see that your room's shite too.' Tony glanced around the identical abode.

'Yeah, even more reason to get out of here, but we have to wait for Mr Ponce, here,' Phil sternly nodded towards Dave. 'He's like an actor on opening night preparing for his adoring public, But, oh no, horror of horrors! Hair D-nine is out of place, better cancel the whole show.'

'Bloody hell. You really are desperate for a beer. Come on, let's do it,' Dave jumped up, quickly checked his reflection, grabbed his wallet and switched off the music before leading the posse to the nearest watering hole.

One and half minutes later the lads were sitting on bar stools by the hotel pool, faced by four pints of ice cold Amstel.

'Hey, you English guys? You like AC/DC? I play for you.' Within seconds the bartender had conjured up 'Whole Lot Of Rose' from his impressive music system. He was very dark skinned, slightly chubby and with long, black curly hair.

'My name is Theo and I like good rock 'n' roll.'

'Yeah. Good stuff. I've seen AC/DC twice.' Gavin was a fan too.

Theo was stunned and stood open-mouthed. 'No shit. Was it Bon Scott or Brian Johnson?'

'One of each, but Scott was the best.'

'Shit, you are so right. Hey, I'm gonna play you some good music for your stay. I've got stacks. Rainbow, Whitesnake, Black Sabbath... one big party man.'

Gavin smiled politely and the others groaned heavily.

Theo went to serve a couple of pale-looking English girls.

'How come on every Campaign you always get pally with the bar staff, Gav? And you usually end up either squaring free beers or shagging the barmaid. Or both in fact!' Phil spoke sternly.

'Dunno. I must have an aura that keeps on shouting "I love beer, I love beer" as well as the odd "and I'd love a shag too", although that normally comes after the beer. The only drawback is it never conjures up any real ale in these hot places.'

'Here we go. He's off already. First night and it's the whole lager vs. bitter debate once again. Some routines simply must live on.' Dave had always drunk lager and nothing else.

'I think Gav will be buried by the side of a bar, haunting anyone who dares delay getting a round in. Mind you, this is the man with a framed black and white still of Norm from Cheers in his bedroom. So bar life is almost a religion.' Tony put his arm around Gavin.

Gavin seemed quite taken aback by the comment. 'You can bloody talk, Mr Mandatory two pints of Guinness every night man.'

'So, anyway, I don't mind the odd bit of metal, but I think a quick beer here each night will suffice, lads.' Dave thinks it might be a lost cause to get Theo to play any Britpop.

Phil gulped down the remainder of his beer and chuckled. 'Do you remember that German girl in Kos who asked Gav if he knew Status Quo and he went – "Yeah, I know them".' Phil's impression of Gavin on the night was very accurate. 'They looked so stunned it was, "Wow, then you get them to come here and party with us?"' His German accent was also pretty good.

Dave remembered the incident well. 'Yeah, your face, Gav. It was a picture. And then you committed the lads' cardinal sin and tried to explain the misunderstanding instead of playing along to get inside her knickers.'

'Philistines,' Gavin mockingly stuck his nose in the air. 'Anyway they weren't pissed enough.'

'Let's have another quick one here, and then get something to eat.' Phil beckoned Theo over before Dave could raise any protest.

Theo expertly filled four glasses of fizzy beer, and declared them on the house as a welcome present to his new friends. Just as he laid the pints on the bar, his attention was diverted to the main road. Theo forced two fingers into his mouth and let out a piercing whistle, before shouting, 'Albert, my man!'

An old man of about sixty, with a baldhead and short grey beard, waved back and then marched towards the bar. He was wearing a Manchester City shirt from the late seventies, and khaki knee-length shorts.

'Ay up, man, give us five,' Albert raised his hand in the air, looking like a granddad trying to play it cool with one of his grandchildren. His thick Lancashire accent made the scene even more amusing. Theo gave his hand a slight smack.

'Hey, Albert, these guys are from England too.'

Theo poured Albert a lager and beckoned for him to take a seat. He then turned towards the lads, 'My man, Albert here, is almost, how you say, a bit of the furniture in Hersonissos as he has been here so long now.'

'Is that right?' Dave raised his eyebrows at Albert, as the trendy pensioner took a large gulp of beer, half soaking his grey moustache in the process.

'Oh aye, lad. Left Blighty in eighty-one. Watched City get dumped by that Argentinean guy in the cup final at Wembley, went straight to the airport and I've never been back since.' Albert gulped the remainder of his beer.

'Wow! I was pissed off when England was knocked out of Euro in ninety-six, but I never contemplated fleeing the country.' Dave was almost impressed.

'Nah,' Albert grinned. 'That weren't reason lad. I went to Wembley for my last taste of Blighty. I'd already decided to go.'

'Why was that? Broken heart, or just pissed off with the weather?' Tony could sense a soulmate.

Albert smiled. 'Let's just say that there were people who

wanted me from both sides of the fence. Staying would have meant propping up a motorway or staring at bars. So if anyone asks about me, I'm just here on holiday. All right?'

And with that, Albert nodded at Theo and went off in to the night. The lads all looked at each other and simultaneously began giggling like school kids.

'You ain't seen me, right?' Phil immediately broke into one of his many fast show character impressions. 'I mean what a load of bullshit. I was just waiting for him to say that he'd slipped back to Blighty for Ronnie Kray's funeral.'

'Is he serious or what?' Dave asked Theo.

Theo laughed. 'Who knows? Albert has more stories than anyone I've ever known.'

The lads bade farewell to Theo and headed on to the main road. The traffic was busy, restricting the foursome to a single line convoy along the dusty gravel at the roadside. Night had fallen and the path was not well lit, but in the near distance they could see the flickering lights of small shops and bars marking the turning that led to the beach and the main strip of Hersonissos nightlife.

Phil was cheered at the thought of what lay ahead. Another chilled out Campaign adventure. Unfortunately he held the thought a little too long and did not see the road sign inches from his head. The top of his temple smacked against the corner of the sign.

'*Fuuuuuuuck,*' was Phil's knee jerk response to the pain that ensued.

Phil was still rubbing his head and moaning about his misfortune as the lads were ushered to their table in a half full basic restaurant. It was the first one on the strip and offered a billboard of wholesome fare that negated the need to shop around. Four hungry Brits filed in before the suave Greek on the door could even crack a smile and use his charm to entice them.

'Good guys. The best table in the house for my friends, right by the road; watch all the pussy go by, the best show in town.'

And the new customers were ushered to a table by the entrance. The 'enticer' shuffled four menus and expertly opened them at the page headed with a Union Jack.

'Four beers coming right away,' this time the enticer struck before anyone else could speak.

'I reckon I might be concussed. I didn't 'arf smack my head,' Phil shook his head vigorously, like a boxer trying to recover from a heavy punch. He then bowed forward towards his mates to assess the damage. 'Can you see a cut?'

'Not even a scratch, mate, so just down some beers and forget about it.' Tony knew that Phil was a total hypochondriac and wanted to nip his moaning in the bud before he declared the possibility of a brain tumour within the hour.

The waiter arrived with four pints of lager on cue, along with a basket of very stale bread. He nonchalantly took the order without a comment or change in expression and headed back to the kitchen. He weaved in and out of tables that were placed with no set pattern on the cold concrete floor. The roof above was a simple red and white awning, stretched, and attached to a beam and six wooden pillars, covering the length of the plot. The kitchen was separate from the seating area, the interior hidden from the eyes of its clientele. At the rear of the restaurant were three tables occupied by couples enjoying a moonlight romantic view of the sea. On the opposite side four Englishmen were enjoying a very different view.

'Look at that!' Phil excitedly nodded towards a couple of dark skinned swarthy brunettes walking by, wearing identical white mini skirts and loose, skimpy, pink sleeveless tops. The pain of Phil's head was forgotten. 'I think I'm in love.'

The others purveyed the scene as droves of gorgeous continental-looking girls strolled by. A trance enveloped all four and they almost failed to notice the waiter efficiently returning with the food. Instead loud whistles and a laddish roar broke the trance. All eyes looked down the strip to see a group of about fifteen lads, identically sporting skinhead haircuts, stripped to the waist and blowing silver referee whistles with vigour. The shrill of the whistles was interspersed with loud grunts and out of tune chants. It looked like a Hari Krishna march on acid. The lads looked at each other, baffled by the spectacle.

Two German girls stood aside on the road outside as the rabble passed, and in earshot of the lads. 'Hollander,' the taller of the two girls confirmed to the other.

Gavin smiled knowingly. 'Did you know that the Dutch now have a worse reputation abroad than us Brits? Makes you proud, eh?'

The strip was buzzing amidst the warm glow of the evening. People were at ease and milled around with time on their hands. No bar or restaurant was empty, and there was no one without a smile. Clothes and styles were diverse, but with an overwhelming continental feel. This was a display of European culture from Milanese chic to Swedish cheek. Even four thirtysomething Brits fitted in with smart chinos and light pastel shirts. There was no Union Jack shorts or English football shirts in sight. No British mock pubs and no cheap offers of traditional English breakfasts or stodgy Sunday roasts. This Campaign was unlike any other, with only the cosmopolitan Italian jaunt of eighty-eight, to Lido De Jesolo, coming close for sheer panache.

Dave nodded with satisfaction at the passing fashion parade as he led the others towards the first bar. This was a man who loved style and was prepared to pay hard cash for the right designer label. Tony was his opposite, looking more for comfort than fashion. He was still ribbed by the others for owning a cardigan and some dodgy brown moccasin shoes. But this time he made the effort and spent over the odds to catch up with the basic trends. Style had helped the others get noticed, so why not him.

The inaugural bar had an all-glass shop-like front, displaying a central oval bar surrounded, but not crowded, by a partying throng. A DJ enthusiastically plied his trade as several French girls danced with flowing rhythm in the small dance area. The sound of Destiny Child's 'Survivor' filled the air, with a pumped up heavy base line.

Dave and Phil had spotted the bar in unison, making an instant beeline for the entrance without consultation from the other two. Gavin and Tony knew that their turn to choose would come later.

Tony elbowed his way to the bar and returned with four bottles of Red Stripe. From that moment on it was a relay as everyone took their turn to collect four of the same. Each bottle was emptied swiftly and effortlessly. Dave and Phil both started moving their bodies in time to the endless beat. The DJ had moved on to 'It wasn't me' by Shaggy, and pumped up the volume a few more notches, attracting more customers to the party. Tony and Gavin were mellow and relaxed, content to stand motionless, enjoying their beers and soaking in the atmosphere.

Phil glanced around the bar to scan for any stunning looking girls in the vicinity, perusing every female form like an art connoisseur patiently viewing the contents of a major gallery. He turned suddenly to be greeted by the cherubic faces of two girls still clinging on to their teens. They both smiled sweetly back at him. Phil was now drunk beyond care and marched over to greet them like two long lost friends.

Phil strained to shout above the music. 'Where are you from?' was the uninspired introduction.

The sweet-looking brunette turned to smile at her sweet-looking blonde friend. 'We are from Germany, Dusseldorf. Do you know it?' The blonde spoke in a soft tone, with a light accent. Uncannily she was audible without shouting.

'Yeah, I know. Auf Wiedersehen Pet. Well cool.'

The girls looked puzzled for an instant, before giggling at their total miscomprehension of what Phil was referring to.

'So, you're on holiday, yeah?' Phil instantly felt a prat. Nigel Paxman he was not.

'Uh... yes,' was the predictable reply from the brunette. 'You too?'

Dave had moved alongside Tony and Gavin so that they stood three abreast, and all watched Phil like spectators at a park watching two sides in a Sunday football match.

'Do you think he'll score?' Tony half wished it was he under the spotlight, doing the chatting-up.

The lads looked over to see that Phil was now jigging around in front of his prey in time to the music, and looking like Muhammad Ali waiting for an opening to strike. So Solid Crew's '21 Seconds' now provided the backbeat.

Gavin replied. 'Nah... they're too young. They'll get bored soon,' the comment was cynically based on Phil's recent track record, particularly on Campaigns.

'Yeah, Gav's probably right, but Phil's having his fun. The

thrill of the chase, as he would say,' Dave felt a little hypocritical in respect of the girls' age, baring in mind the new secret girlfriend at home.

Phil downed his beer, gave the girls a big smile, and briskly headed back to his mates.

'Oh, well. Bad luck, mate. Got to admire your cheek though,' Tony was about to suggest that they should now maybe call it a night. He felt shattered.

'Quite the contrary, Tony, my friend. We have been invited to accompany the gorgeous Nicole and Anna to their favourite club to dance the night away.' Phil's mood was both radiant and calm.

'Seriously?' Dave wondered if this was yet another of Phil's wind-ups.

'Totally. They're well cool, and gorgeous to boot. And the beauty is that you can talk total bollocks and they couldn't care less.'

'So that's how you did it!' Gavin was not far from the truth.

The two German girls walked over to Phil's side. Nicole, the brunette, tapped his arm. 'We go now. Your friends, they come too?'

Phil looked inquiringly at his mates.

'I'm knackered, mate, I got to get some kip. Anyway, I don't want to crowd them.' Tony saw a way out.

'Yeah... me too... we'll leave them to you and Dave,' Gavin was quick to follow the lead.

Dave hesitated before nodding slowly. 'Okay, mate, let's go.' Phil's pleading puppy eyes were just too much to bear. And then they were on their way, with two very young German girls in tow.

Gavin couldn't resist a parting shot. 'See you daddies later, and remember, not too much ice cream and sweeties.'

Phil and Dave looked back with a fixed grimace as their young beaus predictably giggled.

Gavin and Tony began their walk back down the strip, which was still a hive of activity as the next day officially dawned. Just as they were about to take the turning back to the hotel, the glint of an inconspicuous green sign caught Gavin's eye.

It read 'The Harp – A Real Irish Welcome'.

'*Yes!*' Gavin almost punched the air. 'Excellent. Tone, I think we need to have a nightcap. They are bound to serve Guinness here, at least. It's the first night, and I'm gassed out already on lager. This is the only known cure.' Gavin no longer felt tired.

Tony knew Gavin too well. It was pointless to refuse.

The Harp was only a few yards off the strip. 'In The Name Of Love' by U2 boomed out as the two friends approached. They entered to a scene of sheer revelry, with the majority of the clientele dancing on either the bar or the tables. It was like a rowdy scene from a Wild West saloon as two strangers made their entrance. Gavin nodded with satisfaction, heightened by the sight of a Guinness pump. He jockeyed a quick route to the bar, and hastily ordered two pints of the black stuff. As the white froth touched his lips, Gavin felt almost orgasmic. Tony laughed at his friend's reaction as they both leaned back on stools by the bar, and began to soak in the atmosphere.

'This is better. Much more like it. Better than that last poncy place. Reckon we should just come here every night.' Gavin was serious.

Tony was more realistic. 'It is good, but remember... no routines. Variety is the spice of life and all that.'

'Okay, but at least I know where I can get a good nightcap. Same again?' Gavin had downed his pint, but Tony's was nearly full.

'Nah. You're all right. You have one though.'

Gavin was quick to draw the attention of the nearest barmaid. She was a raven-haired woman in her forties, with a full figure and classic gypsy features.

'There you go, my lovely. I hope it does you proud,' the barmaid's accent had a quiet Southern Irish lilt.

Gavin acknowledged her with a friendly smile. He then turned to Tony. 'This place is the business in every way. I just love everything Irish, and especially the girls. It's the Gaelic outlook and as for the accent... Here's to a bloody brilliant Campaign mate.'

The two friends raised and clashed glasses as the pub once again erupted into manic dancing to the sound of 'Come On Eileen' by Dexy's Midnight Runners.

Nicole and Anna walked several yards ahead of Dave and Phil as they set a course for their favourite club.

'So how old do yer reckon they are, mate? I mean I could swear that the blonde could still be at school, or have I finally just become an old bastard?' Dave half wondered if the German girls were on holiday with their parents.

'Trust me, they are old enough, and they seem to be looking for the more mature man. Anyway, I thought you'd taken to fancying younger birds after your infatuation with that supermarket girl. And I hasten to add that you did sod all about that one. Holliman, you've lost your touch.' Phil feels that he is now king of the chat-ups following tonight's success.

Dave hesitated. 'Uh... that's not strictly true.'

'Eh?' Phil stopped briefly and awaited more of an explanation.

Dave decided he had no option but to tell his mate all. 'Well, the supermarket girlie is called Sally, she's twenty-two and we're an item, for now, I suppose. I promised to call her tomorrow, so at least I won't have to lie to you about where I'm going now. But not a word to the others, Phil.'

Just ahead, Nicole and Anna were in the doorway of a very large detached building. It was very grey in colour, and would have been mistaken for a bank back in England, or at least one of the many pubs and restaurants that so many disused branches had now been converted into. The German girls beckoned their new English friends to follow them.

Phil waved to acknowledge that he and Dave were on their way. 'Wow, man, you did well to keep that quiet, but it will now have to wait until later, 'cos I want to know all the gory details.'

Dave followed Phil into the club, wondering if he should have kept his mouth shut for the sake of wounded pride.

A wall of sound hit them as they entered the club. It was an incessant repetitive drumbeat turned up to maximum volume, interspersed with an almost melodic burst of music. The dance floor was heaving so much that there was barely enough room to dance, but still swarms of kiddies were frantically moving their arms in the air. It was like an acid version of the Eton wall game, equally lacking in purpose or meaning to the observer. Dave looked around for a bar, but could not spot one.

'You like techno, yes?' Anna broke Dave and Phil's transfixed glares.

'Uh… Yeah… It's not bad.' Phil's hesitancy almost revealed his blatant lie. Dave stared hard at him as a traitor to all things musical.

'Good. Nicole likes techno, but I like hardcore techno much more. It is much harder and faster.' Anna's eyes lit up like a demon, and Phil suddenly felt quite aroused.

'Anyway, come on, let's go.' Anna pulled Phil's hand to follow Nicole in amongst the dancing throng. Phil in turn grabbed Dave and gave him a look to say please do not leave me here on my own.

Nicole had managed to secure a dancing space for them all, equivalent to the floor dimensions of a telephone box. She and Anna immediately began to frantically move their young fit bodies to the beat, as if suddenly charged with a high voltage jolt of electricity. Dave and Phil awkwardly tried to follow their lead, but looked like they were dancing to Abba more than serious rave music.

Twenty minutes on the beat was still the same, and the dancing throng still retained exactly the same moves. Whistles shrilled out from all corners of the floor. Suddenly Phil jerked forward, knocked by a blow to his back. He turned to see a large German teenager with very black spiky hair, matched in colour by the shades he was ludicrously wearing. The boy was frantically moving his arms and shoulders, oblivious to the pain and bruises he was causing to anyone who came near. Space suddenly appeared on the floor as the Teutonic whirlwind picked up even more speed.

'Fucking kiddie… fancy a bit of pogoing, Dave?' and with that Phil launched into a non-finesse style of bobbing rapidly up and down that was the plain genius of Punk's one and only dance craze. Dave laughed before joining in. The duo began crashing into people and making their own space, before launching an invasion of the one created by the whirlwind. A few glancing body checks against the German's bulky form soon put him off his pattern. So much so that he very quickly disappeared to look for a softer part of the floor to target. Phil and Dave laughed to each other and then proceeded to pogo even more frantically. Both were now sweating profusely.

Nicole brought the 'old time' dance exhibition to a halt when she suggested that they all get a drink. She led the way to a very small bar in a separate room at the back of the dance floor. Only water and soft drinks were on sale.

The ice-cold water felt good on Dave's parched lips. He felt exhausted, but had actually enjoyed the dance. Some pent up work tension and stress had been released.

'We are going to go from here now and go to the beach. Would you like to come?' Nicole's offer was not in danger of being rejected.

Nicole led the way to a small area of beach at the end of the strip. The greyish sand was cluttered with small groups of people huddled in conversation. Anna picked a plot for the foursome to set up camp.

The night was calm and peaceful, with a clear sky shining above. All around there was the punctuated murmur of conversation in many different accents and languages. The world was being put to right with a calm beach life philosophy.

A few yards behind where Dave lay in the sand was a small group of Danes. Two of the boys in the group were tuning their guitars in between smoking a spliff that was doing the rounds. Both had the classic beach bum look of tousled hair and goatee beard.

Dave was just wondering if they would play any actual tunes when they answered him by launching into a very mellow version of 'Patience' by Guns 'n' Roses. The chubbier of the two goatee boys took vocals and sang superbly. So much so that he soon had the attention of everyone on the beach, almost like a surreal moment from an Elvis movie.

'Hey, they're cool,' Dave broke the conversational silence halfway through the rendition.

'Ya... very good.' Anna was also impressed.

'A bit more tuneful than techno, eh?' Dave decided to jibe the girls for their musical taste, or lack of it. He only received a polite smile in response. Phil gave him the hardest stare as if he had killed any chance of a shag.

'So what do you do in the Fatherland, sorry Germany, girls?' Phil's unconscious remark could have put another nail in the shag coffin, but fortunately the war reference went over the girls' heads.

'We are students at university,' was the short response from Nicole.

'Wow, what are you studying?' Phil sounded genuinely interested.

'Psychology.' Anna's response made him feel more cautious and uneasy. Maybe he and Dave were a social experiment for inclusion in the last chapter of a dissertation.

'And you? What do you guys do?' Nicole turned the tables.

'Um… we both work in finance. A bit boring really.' Dave felt that their jobs were too tedious to expand on. Also, he was bored with throwing a line as a chat-up, like the time that he and the lads were a famous rock band on tour. That one nearly worked, until one of the girls had them announced as such in a pub. There were instruments at their disposal and a now expectant audience waiting in anticipation. A sharp exit out the back door soon followed, like a scene from a 'Hard Day's Night'. The big difference being four untalented and un-musical individuals.

'Are you married?' was the next question from Anna.

'Uh, no… are you?' Phil bounced that one back.

'No. But we have boyfriends… back in Dusseldorf,' Nicole's statement was very matter of fact.

Phil was tempted to say, 'Does that mean a shag's out of the question then?' but instead just said, 'That's nice.'

And so the chat went on, and in the background the Danes carried on playing their music. In some groups, couples and even trios lay down together, affectionately kissing and caressing. Above, the sky grew lighter and lighter until the sun came into view to herald the dawn. Dave shook his head to gather his unrested senses, before marvelling at the glory of nature in the sunrise. Viewed from a beach, it was all the more special.

'I think we go to bed now.' Anna stood up quickly and helped her friend up. Phil jumped up with speed too, not believing his ears. Dave slowly followed suit.

'Will you be out again tonight? More techno?' Anna's words at once clarifying that 'we go to bed' was limited to the girls going their separate ways and was not a very forward proposition.

'Eh…? Yeah maybe. Have to check with our other mates.' Phil was now both deflated and knackered. The girls gave the boys a peck on the cheek each and wished them 'Guten Abend'.

Phil and Dave began the walk back to the hotel, and the girls went in the opposite direction down the strip. Phil was very quiet and it did not take Dave long to realise that his friend had been under a momentary misapprehension.

'You really thought she was inviting you to her bed, didn't you? I wondered why you were suddenly so energetic and looking pleased with yourself.'

'Yeah, all right… I'm obviously getting too old and misreading all the signs. I mean they were just kiddies anyway, hanging out with two old 'uns for a laugh.'

As the duo walked past the hotel pool and into reception, the sun had thrown out all its rays and the sky was a deep blue. The room was cool, as the curtains remained closed hiding the light of day. Dave and Phil both slumped simultaneously onto their beds. They both looked over at each other and said in unison 'We're too old for this shit a la Danny Glover in *Lethal Weapon*.' Both heads then hit the pillows and sleep instantly followed.

The 2001 Campaign: Week 1, Day 1
– an Alarm Call

A few hours after Dave and Phil had gone to sleep they were suddenly woken by loud thuds on the door. Dave managed to raise his head a few inches off the pillow and checked his watch. It was 9.15 a.m. He was shattered beyond belief and felt like he had been asleep for all of five minutes. More loud thuds at the door rang through his head. The fist making the noise may just as well have been pounding him personally.

Tony's voice then boomed from the other side. 'Oi! Lazy bastards. Have you got birds in there, or what? Well put them down and get your arses in gear as it's time for the welcome party.'

Dave pulled himself up and slithered across the room, just finding enough strength to unlock the door. Tony and Gavin burst in without hesitation. Both were wearing garish Bermuda shorts and surfer T-shirts, and smelled strongly of suntan lotion. They also had beaming grins and were full of energy after a good night's sleep. Tony marched over and flung open the curtains, bringing instant light to the room. Dave instantly raised his hand to protect flinching eyes. Phil pulled a sheet over his head, and hid like a vampire retreating to a coffin at dawn. Gavin went over and sat on Phil's bed.

'So, late night was it, lads? I s'pose Mockley's spent all his energy for the week?' Gavin pulled Phil's sheet away to reveal his tubby frame, dressed only in a pair of very old black boxer shorts.

'Fuck of, Carter. What is all this shit? Why are you up so early?' Phil grabbed his sheet back. The reversion to calling each other by surnames made the scene seem like something from an old-fashioned boarding school.

'Well, the words bear and sore head spring to mind.' Gavin had seen Phil like this so many times before.

'More like a sore with a bare head,' Dave could not resist a dig at Phil's receding hairline.

'Fuck off!' Phil was in no mood for jokes.

'Anyway, we'd better get cracking. The welcome party is about to start. Are you two up for it?' Tony was eager to go.

Dave scratched his head and yawned. 'Yeah, give us a minute. Let me throw something on.'

Phil did not move or answer.

Dave sat semi-motionless in the hotel bar, taking the occasional sip of sparkling water. His head felt full of sawdust through lack of sleep, and he just wanted to get the welcome party out of the way and go and sleep by the pool. Tony and Gavin were both bubbling with enthusiasm, eager to enjoy the atmosphere.

Gareth and Cheryl, the Welsh couple, arrived and sat at the table next to the lads.

'Hey, boyos. Settled in all right? Got the shags in yet?' Gareth's voice boomed around the bar and Cheryl gave him a gentle prod to tell him to be quiet.

The lads all grimaced and laughed nervously as the eyes of the bar were upon them.

'Where's your other mate? Lost him already then?' Gareth had noticed the absence of Phil.

'Nah. He's still asleep. Too much dancing last night,' Tony answered.

Dave noticed that Gareth was wearing an old Alarm tour T-shirt from the eighties. It was badly faded from the wash, but still recognisable.

'Cool band, used to really like them. Saw them a couple of times. Great live.' Dave was keen to talk music.

'Oh, the Alarm,' Gareth looked down at his own T-shirt. 'They were the business, man. Wales's most successful export ever. Even bigger than the Manics.'

The retro music chat was brought to an abrupt end by a young SunRay rep grabbing the bar's attention with a methodical thud on a nearby table. She was about twenty, beautifully tanned and with long blonde golden hair. The attention of all the males in the room was guaranteed.

'Thanks, everyone, I promise not to keep you long, as I'm sure you want to get outside and make a start on those tans. I'm Susie, and I'm your SunRay rep here at Hotel Garden Imperial. I have to my left, Nicholas, the hotel owner who will shortly serve you with some free bubbly to get your holiday off on the right track.'

In a real surreal moment, the big fat balding Greek owner shouted 'Ole!' and did an impression of a Spanish flamenco dancer before laughing loudly, and then proceeded to distribute glasses of cheap sparkling wine around the bar.

'You'll get used to Nick's sense of humour,' Susie continued.

'Yeah, after some serious drugs,' Tony whispered to himself.

Susie continued and gave some spiel about the cosmopolitan appeal of the area, before giving a less than subtle soft sales pitch on all the wonderful trips and events that SunRay had to offer. Dave's tired mind managed to register the highlights of what was said, whilst his eyes and the large part of his brain reserved for sexual thoughts gave full attention to every firm muscle and tender curve of Susie's extremely fit body. The slobber from his mouth would have flooded the floor had he not been so dehydrated.

The lads opted for the booze cruise and the evening barbeque at the hotel. Gavin signed up for a trip to Archanes, and rather easily persuaded Tony to join him.

'So, are you boys not up for the pub crawl in Malia, then?' Susie had made her way over to the lads to take their order. She was even more delectable close-up.

'No. We've decided to go off our own backs,' Gavin replied.

Susie looked around as if to check that the head of SunRay was not standing behind her.' Don't blame you. It's only a short cab ride away, and you'll have just as much fun.'

'Archanes,' Susie noticed Tony and Gavin's day trip selection. 'You'll have a good time there. It's really nice. I actually live just outside with my girlfriend.'

Dave was forced to speak. 'Uh, do you mean girlfriend in the sort of American, my buddy sense, or in the I like women's tennis and listen to K D Lang sense.'

Susie laughed and was obviously not insulted by Dave's remarks. She winked. 'More the latter, but no stereotypes, please.

For example we're both vegetarian, but can murder a bacon sarnie now and again.' And with that Susie moved over to talk to Gareth and Cheryl.

'I think I need to jump into the pool to cool down.' Dave pulled himself up.

Tony and Gavin sniggered and stood up next to him. Gavin was keen to see the sights. 'We're going off for a bit to explore. We'll see you back by the pool later, when hopefully Mockley will have risen from the dead.'

Dave managed to find a free sunbed in a corner of the pool area, in the full glare of the sun. He put his beach towel down to claim it and wrestled his T-shirt over his head. A bottle of factor fifteen lotion was selected from a small plastic carrier bag, and Dave smeared it thickly onto his body. His frame felt reasonably trim as he massaged the oil into every knot of skin. Dave was proud of his physique and subconsciously used the opportunity of rubbing in the lotion to proudly display himself to any observing females, like a peacock would display his array of feathers.

With the lotion applied, Dave put on his shades and selected a CD for his personal stereo. He chose 'The Hush' by Texas, with its constant summertime feel. The opening track 'In Our Lifetime' was perfectly breezy in mood as Dave perused the pool area for any resplendent female forms. Unfortunately, most of the women were mothers on the wrong side of forty who chose to act cool by going topless in front of their kids. Their breasts were either shrivelled or heading south towards rolls of fat on their middle-aged tummies.

Dave spotted Gareth and Cheryl on the other side of the pool. She wore a brilliant white bikini that almost faded as one into her extremely pale body. Gareth sat reading *The Sun*, still wearing his faded Alarm T-shirt over baggy shorts and topped with a large safari sun hat.

Dave smiled and eased his head back on the sunlounger, relaxed and at one with the music, his mind drifting into a soothing daydream. His first thoughts were of Sally and the sex they had enjoyed just before Dave left for the Campaign. Dave quickly grew conscious of a growing bulge in his shorts, as the erection of the moment was re-enacted from the images he recalled in his mind. Paranoid that everyone in the pool area would suddenly stop and stare in disgust at his groin, Dave swiftly moved his thoughts on to other things. First it was the upcoming football season and the World Cup qualifiers. Did England really have any chance of getting a result in Germany and making it to Japan next summer? Would the summer of two thousand and two be another embarrassing write-off like nineteen ninety-four? Dave's erection subsided immediately at the thought of Graham Taylor.

Dave's mind then wandered back further in time to nineteen eighty-four, the year of Live Aid and when he was a first year student at polytechnic. He was a real rebel back then, fighting every cause that needed to be fought. He proudly wore his 'free Nelson Mandela' T-shirt, whilst picketing Barclays with the local anti-apartheid group. He marched for the preservation of student grants, shouted loudly to save Britain's coal industry, and stood shoulder to shoulder with Billy Bragg on the left wing Red Wedge tour; and standing proudly next to Dave was Sarah.

Sarah was Dave's college sweetheart. They shared the same philosophy of life for whatever came their way. They were a unit. They got pissed together, ate curries together, and marched together. And when they were not doing all that they simply shagged. The bedrock to a great relationship, remembered Dave, but really the partnership was totally superficial. They went out together for nearly a year, and Dave never really got below the surface to find out what made Sarah tick. She never talked about her family and he never met them. Sarah was a very outgoing girl from Newcastle, who was simply fun to be with. And that was all Dave wanted at the time. That was why they remained a unit.

Dave and Sarah went to Wembley and saw the Live Aid concert, after winning a fixed student union raffle. It was an awesome day, with so many stars on show, and the atmosphere just got better and better as the day, then night, went on. Dave remembered Quo opening, followed by the slick performance of the Style Council. Elvis Costello sang 'All You Need Is Love', and Queen and The Who were awesome. Dave held Sarah throughout, but had eyes only for the stage.

Soon after Live Aid, Dave returned home for the holidays and spent the summer with Phil. The early incarnation of the Campaign was a budget driven camping holiday in north Cornwall. The routine was exactly the same – the days were spent sunbathing and the nights getting pissed. Sarah was forgotten, and Dave did not think of making any contact, even when the holiday was over.

Dave arrogantly returned to polytechnic at the end of the summer, and just expected to pick up his tempestuous love life where he had left it. But Sarah's life had moved on. She had found a flash and rich new boyfriend, and Dave was history. He felt that his pride had been injured, but felt no great loss of love at the time. Consolation came in the shape of shagging every impressionable fresher in sight. In the present Dave smiled at the drastic cure for the pain of his loss. He then smiled again as he remembered his last night at polytechnic, when Sarah was hammered and succumbed to a final night of passion in his lodgings. A block away her boyfriend dutifully packed her belongings into boxes as he excitedly prepared to take her home for good.

Sarah's view of life soon changed as she became quickly bored with the constant pampered whims of her rich man. Dave moved on to many new relationships, but was still drawn to think of Sarah now and again. Through the naivety and brashness of his youth he was blinded to the fact that she may have been the one. If he had made more effort to get to know the real Sarah, where would they be now? Where is she now?

Dave felt the sun blot out as a shade moved across his body. He opened his eyes and looked up to see Phil's large frame before him, acting as an impressive guard.

'Managed to get out of bed, but I'm still totally knackered. Thought I'd catch some rays and then go for a fry up,' Phil loudly scraped a sunbed along the floor and positioned it alongside Dave's. He then removed his T-shirt to reveal a pale blubbery torso. The rolls of fat around his naval were extenuated as he sat down. Phil took out some suntan lotion and tapped it sparingly over his body, before laying back and shutting his eyes.

'Yeah, I'll come with you and grab a cappuccino or something. Give it about half an hour.' Dave could never face a full English breakfast in the heat of the Med. He noticed that Phil was already asleep and so reached out and changed his CD to 'Head Like A Rock' by Ian McNabb, the former Icicle Works' frontman's collaboration with Crazy Horse. The twining guitar of 'Fire Inside My Soul' soon filled his earphones, and Dave was in a relaxed mode once more.

Whilst Dave and Phil were resting, Gavin and Tony were tirelessly exploring the area. Gavin had meticulously searched for hidden beaches, interesting restaurants, and alluring bars. He painstakingly noted the best of each in a little notebook to share with the others. Tony ambled along behind him and took more interest in the array of lavish villas on display. He had reached the stage of hating his job, but Tony could not resist trying to value each of the properties in his mind. The busman's holiday was complete when he stopped to view the displays in several agent windows. He wondered if the Cretan Estate Agent was like its English counterpart. Was there a Greek Karen running the shop? What if he got a job out here, made a mint, and lived in one of the villas for himself. Tony half hoped to see a 'Situations Vacant' card in one of the windows, and use his understated charm to seal the job. Giving in his notice at Elson & Smythe would never be so much fun.

Tony was brought back to the real world by a rough yank to his arm by Gavin. Next part of the whistle stop tour was a stroll around the local gift shops. Most were pretty identical in terms of goods on display, with ornaments, pictures and artefacts that would seem perfect gifts to buy for older relatives on the last day of the Campaign. Amongst the endless cloned displays, Tony spotted a shop that openly sold counterfeit goods. It was the main boast of the signs outside. The shop sold everything from aftershave to football shirts at ridiculously low prices. Tony and Gavin each purchased a pair of 'Armani' sunglasses for about five pounds a time, and proudly wore them straight away. They felt naively cool.

With all the walking and the intense heat of the day, the wandering duo decided to find somewhere to eat and enjoy a cold beer. As they walked down the strip, Dave and Phil were spotted at a table in a small shaded café. Phil was eagerly tucking into a disgustingly unhealthy full English breakfast. The whole plate was swimming in fat that glistened in the sun, but Phil was devouring the food like it was gourmet cuisine. Dave sat alongside him wearing expensive sunglasses with a genuine label, and nonchalantly enjoying a cappuccino and a croissant.

'Fuck, I feel ill just looking at you, Mockley.' Gavin led Tony over to the table.

Phil looked up from his plate of grease to see his two friends proudly wearing their new identical shades.

'Bloody hell, it's the Blues Brothers. Chicago's that way boys,' Phil pointed out to sea.

Gavin and Tony pulled up chairs to join their friends, and ordered sandwiches and beers. Gavin recounted some of the treasures he had found from his notebook, and managed to get the others to agree to visit a restaurant up on the cliff that evening.

A girl sitting in the corner of the café suddenly took Dave's attention. She was stunningly pretty, with a very smooth silky complexion. Her hair was golden brown and left naturally unbrushed and wild. She wore a tight black T-shirt that proudly displayed the frame of large ample breasts. Her legs were athletic, slightly hidden from view by large baggy walking shorts. She sat alone drinking coffee. She was a vision.

'Earth calling Dave. Are you Tony in disguise?' Gavin brought Dave out of his trance.

Dave smiled. 'No, just letching as usual.'

The lads returned to the poolside at the hotel. All four dumped their gear on a row of spare sunbeds, and jumped into the pool. The sensation was revitalising as the cool clear water doused each sun-dried body. Gavin swam a few lengths as the others bobbed up and down under a cloudless sky. Dave noticed Gareth and Cheryl sitting in exactly the same positions as before, right down to the rigid body language.

The rest of the afternoon was spent sunbathing. Phil slept. Dave and Gavin listened to music. Tony all but read his first book. Tired from doing nothing, the foursome then retired to their rooms for a siesta, and a chance to recharge the batteries for the evening onslaught. It had always been that way on every Campaign.

The chilled air of the shaded room, and the coolness of the clean, white sheets on the beds, was the perfect refuge from the intense Cretan heat.

All slept soundlessly out of sun-drenched exhaustion. All except Dave. He had decided to make his first call home to Sally, and felt awkward. Ironically the heat of the island had somehow chilled Dave's feeling for his young lover. The sex had been great, fantastic even, but there was something missing. Dave had thought long and hard but could not fathom what it was. In defeat, he tried to convince himself it was probably the age difference.

'Hi, is that you, Sal? It's Dave. Dave Holliman.' Dave had purchased a phone card from Maria, and then wandered down the road to make the call. He was conscious that one of the others might wake and stop him on his task.

'Hello. Dave Holliman? As opposed to all the other Dave's I've shagged recently,' Sally's impish sarcasm never waned.

'Okay, okay. Anyway, the Campaign has begun. It's hot; I've drunk lots of beer, eaten, danced, and sunbathed. How's life with you?'

'Oh you know. It's August in England, it's overcast, I've stacked hundreds of boxes of cereal and helped deliver at least ten babies. Apart from that, pretty dull.'

The conversation lasted another five minutes, with a typical English emphasis on the weather and what the respective partners planned to do that evening. Sally had bought a microwave meal for one, and was going to study. Dave was going to eat in a cliff top open-air restaurant, and then get pissed.

As Dave walked back to the hotel, he already knew that this was one relationship that was not going to grow. Sally was a great girl, but she was not *the* girl.

All the lads were spruced and ready to hit the town by seven. Tony was slow in getting ready and met the others at the poolside bar. Theo had brought along some Metallica tapes especially for the lads. Even Gavin was ready to move on quickly after a swift beer.

The cliff top restaurant was quite a trek, and Phil insisted on a halfway house drink in a small and very empty bar. Once again the four thirtysomethings sat watching the girls go by on the strip. Life seemed grand, when suddenly standing out like a large thorn amongst roses, an old balding bearded Brit in a T-shirt and shorts appeared. It was Albert and he honed in on his new pals like an exocet.

'How're doing, lads? 'Aving a few chilled ones? Managed to pull any pussy yet? I tell you, I don't do badly myself. Never lost the knack you see.' Albert spoke rhetorically as he had no real interest in the answers.

'Just chilling out, mate, then we're off for a bite at the restaurant up on the cliff.' Dave was spokesman.

'Ahhh, I know it. It's owned by a guy called Antonio, but it's just a front for his real business if you know what I mean.' Albert tapped his index finger several times on his nose. 'Yeah, he's a good lad, done a few jobs with him in my time. He calls me the Rock, because I never let him down. Hell of a temper mind you. Just steer clear of anything with mince in it. Anyway, best be going, things to do,' Albert walked swiftly away with his left hand aloft.

'Wanker!' Phil was not impressed.

Unsurprisingly, none of the waiters at the cliff top restaurant knew of an Antonio when asked.

'Maybe he just wants to retain anonymity,' Tony half-believed Albert's yarn.

'More likely that Albert's a sad old tosser with more fables than Aesop.' Phil hoped that they could avoid him from now on.

The cliff top restaurant was plush, and presented a great view of Hersonissos at dusk as the nightlife began to twinkle into action. The food was of high standard, and plentiful, with several bottles of wine to compliment the occasion.

'So, here's to us. Another year older, another year wiser and another year where we are all sad single bastards desperate for a shag.' Phil's toast lacked all eloquence as he raised his glass of white wine. 'Well, apart from Dave... oh shit! I never said that.'

Dave glared at Phil as he tried to mask his *faux pas* by taking a large gulp of wine. Gavin and Tony smirked heavily.

'You twat, Mockley. Can't tell you anything, you've always been the same, even when we were kids.' Dave was not amused.

'So who's the lucky lady? Could we be looking at the first Campaign boy's wedding?' Tony made a joke of the situation, which really masked his envy. He had always aspired to be like Dave, a magnet to women with his looks and charm.

'She's that young, sorry, very young checkout girl at Tesco. Come to think of it, is she old enough to get married?' Phil spoke with foot firmly in mouth once more.

'She's actually twenty-two, and she's not a checkout girl. She's a student midwife, who just supplements her wages by stacking shelves. Her name is Sally and I called her earlier when you were all kipping. She's a great girl... but...' Dave hesitates.

'But what?' Tony had followed Dave's every word.

'But, I don't know... actually that's it. The whole relationship lacks that *je ne sais quoi*. It could be the age thing. Maybe it was just lust, and now that I've shagged her, there's nothing else.' Dave noticed his admission of having recently had sex raised three pairs of envious eyebrows. 'Yes, we had a great shag, brilliant in fact. And it's almost like we should leave it there as a defining moment, because it can't get any better.'

'So did you end it today?' Tony continued as quiz master.

'No, but I know it's just going to fizzle out. I'll call her again at the end of the week just to make sure.'

At that moment, four large ice cream dishes were placed on the table, and at the same time a couple of stray dogs came over and lay close by. The focus was suddenly off Dave, and the desserts were quickly devoured.

'Look at that. The so-called best restaurant in Hersonissos and they let dogs just stray around the premises. Nobody gives a toss. Imagine if that happened back home, the environmental health would be straight on to it. Even if it was Zak's kebab shop,' Gavin was not angry, but just found the experience a bit surreal.

'Actually, I think quite a few dogs wander into Zak's. How else would he get all that meat for the Zeniths? He then makes them so spicy, that you could be eating anything and wouldn't notice,' Dave's image made the others turn white as they though of all the ZZs they'd consumed over the years.

In a merry and mellow state, the four friends strolled back down the hill towards the strip. The wine had nicely numbed the senses in preparation for a full alcoholic onslaught.

Tony spotted a bar with an overspill patio at the back that overlooked the beach. Inside, a disco was in full swing with pumped up retro tunes. In celebration of his choice being approved, Tony bought the first round of four very large Metaxa's with coke.

'I think I might stick with this, better than bloody lager.' Gavin was serious.

'Shut up.' Phil was not enjoying the spirit so much, and was desperate for a pint. He knocked it back quickly and headed off to buy another round. Gavin trekked off to find the toilets.

'Sorry it didn't work out... with Sally, that is,' Tony wished that he had the luxury of being in a relationship, let alone being confident enough to end it and move on to the next one.

'No worries. She was a nice girl, but it's not fair stringing her along just so I can get my end away.'

'I wish I could be you sometimes, but I think if I found a girl that remotely liked me, I'd never let her go,' Tony was suddenly full of pathos.

Dave was hoping it was not the start of a drink-induced unlucky-in-love speech. 'Mate, you'll find someone soon. Maybe on this very holiday.'

'Yeah, maybe you're right. I've made a decision on this Campaign. I'm going to take a chance for once. Not just drink into oblivion whilst I letch. No, I'm going to take action. If a girl tells me to piss off, I'll move on to the next one.' Tony was now in determined mood.

Dave is pleasantly shocked. 'Yeah, that's the way to go. A toast,' Dave raised his glass and Tony did likewise. 'Go for it, because it won't come to you.'

The two friends clashed glasses and then drained the rest of their drinks. As they did so, Phil approached carrying four large litre pitchers of frothing lager. Gavin followed behind with a look of horror and disdain.

'I wanted another Metaxa, you wanker,' Gavin still took the massive long glass from Phil.

'Shut up you twat. No more women's drinks tonight,' was Phil's unsympathetic response.

The music from the disco seemed to be turned up a few decibels after every other song. The DJ put on an ABBA medley, which started with the Eurovision success 'Waterloo'. The small dance floor was suddenly packed, but only with girls. Most were frantically dancing and singing along in English, but with a multitude of different European accents. All the men in the bar looked on with lust, picking out their favourite gyrating body to focus on.

The four English lads were part of the admiring throng, silently letching and less than subtly pointing out any girl who caught their eye. As they did so, they all struggled to finish the never-ending beers. ABBA hit followed ABBA hit. The girls carried on dancing and the boys carried on watching. In the end Phil could not resist the urge to dance himself. He took a big gulp of his beer and pulled Dave's arm to follow him as he headed for the floor.

The two only dancing males moved with a basic rhythmical shuffle from side to side, grinning broadly as they perused the female talent close up. Gavin and Tony continued to observe from the sidelines.

Fifteen minutes later, Dave and Phil returned to join the other two. Both were sweating, but Phil's extra weight had made him perspire so much that he looked like he had just climbed out of the swimming pool fully clothed. Phil grabbed his beer and devoured it like a man taking his first drink after crawling through a desert for days.

'Hey lads, I'll be back in a minute. Just need to go and cool off and make myself look presentable, 'cos I ain't ever going to pull like this,' Phil looked down at his sweat soaked T-shirt before heading for the toilets.

'Actually, I need another waz. This lager is going straight through me tonight, especially now that I've already broken the seal,' Gavin set off in pursuit of Phil.

'Wow. That was a good boogie. You should have been up there Tone. Remember, go for it, take no prisoners.' Dave was determined to spark his friend into action.

'I will, I will.' Tony tried to reassure himself.

Dave savoured his cold beer as he scanned the bar. He noticed two very tanned attractive brunettes sitting at a table just behind Tony. They were both sipping long glasses of vodka and Red Bull, but there seemed to be no conversation. One had long hair which cascaded halfway down her back, and framed a pretty round face with extenuated cheekbones. Her friend had very dark skin that almost merged into her brown bob. She was pouting with a sad refrain, looking like a moody young Natalie Wood posing for a black and white still in the sixties.

'Right mate, follow me,' Dave passed Tony, tapping his arm to beckon him.

Tony looked around in a daze and observed with sheer nervousness as he saw Dave head over to the two brunettes. Dave smiled and spoke confidently to the girls. He immediately brought their attention to Tony and signalled for his friend to come over. Tony wanted to just run away, but he took a large gulp of beer, uttered the words 'go for it, that's my motto' under his breath, before moving over to join his assured friend.

'Here he is. This is Tone. Come and join us, mate, this is Adele and Barbara,' Dave respectively introduced the smiling and grimacing friends. 'They are both form Vienna, and before you say anything we've already done the whole Midge Ure and Ultravox thing to death.'

Tony would not have even made the connection; he was too busy concentrating on giving a sincere smile and saying 'hi'. He managed the 'hi' but with a false overly nervous smile. He sat down next to grimacing Barbara, who raised her eyebrows to acknowledge him. In return, Tony gave a large boyish grin that stretched his cheekbones so much that he gave a passable impression of Stan Laurel.

Dave had turned to face Adele and they were already deep in conversation. Tony was to all intent and purpose alone with a girl.

Meanwhile, Gavin and Phil had returned from the toilets. Phil was the most stunned to see Tony partnering Dave in chatting-up two very attractive foreign girls.

'What the hell's Tony been drinking? I'll be well pissed off if he pulls before me.' Phil wondered why Dave had not waited for him before making a move. Surely Tony would just cramp his style.

Gavin shrugged his shoulders with disinterest.

'So, um, Vienna... I've never been there myself. I bet it's lovely though,' Tony stuttered but tried to start a conversation.

Barbara pursed her lips. 'It's okay,' she said with the faintest of smiles.

'Have you been to England before?'

'Yeah. Twice.'

'Ah right, where did you go to?'

'London. Twice.'

'Did you like it?'

'It was okay.'

'Right... so how do you know Adele?' Tony glanced over to see Dave and Adele chatting intimately almost face-to-face.

'From work. We are beauticians.'

'Ah, that must be an interesting job.'

'It's okay.'

Barbara's face remained emotionless as she responded curtly to Tony's eager questioning. Tony smiled and tried to think over what to say next. Barbara half smiled but remained silent as she glanced over Tony's right shoulder. Tony suddenly jolted when he felt a vigorous tap to his left shoulder. He turned to see Gavin and Phil.

'Tone, I'm taking Phil to the Irish bar, just in case you move on later. Otherwise, see you in the morning.' Gavin gave a subtle wink.

Phil pointed straight at him. 'You bloody dark horse.'

Dave and Adele obliviously continued their romantic tête-à-tête. Tony almost rose to follow his friends, but held back. No, he would give Barbara another half an hour and if the position was still the same he could always move on then.

'Can I get you a drink?' Tony noticed that Barbara's glass was empty.

'Uh yeah, a vodka and Red Bull, that would be nice.' Barbara at last gave a full smile, as though De Vinci had told the Mona Lisa that the session was now over and she could lose the pose.

Tony shouted to the other two. 'Drinks?'

Dave raised a thumb. Adele echoed her friend. 'Vodka and Red Bull. That would be nice.'

Tony was served quickly, but still almost expected Barbara to have gone upon his return. She was still there, albeit with the same relentless pose.

'Thank you. You are a nice person,' Barbara's comments made Tony feel good.

'No problem.'

'I am sorry if I am quiet, I am a little annoyed,' Barbara at last started to open up.

Tony looked over towards Dave and Adele. 'What, with your friend?'

Barbara smiled. 'Oh no, no... I have been taken for a ride by a bastard. He used me and he thinks he's so cool. I hate him because he has the upper hand on me. He is the tall French bastard at the bar wearing the Armani shirt.'

Tony looked around without any subtlety to observe the focus of Barbara's angry stare. He had no idea what an Armani shirt would look like, unless it had the word Armani printed across the chest in big letters. He was the same with cars, only naming a BMW if he spotted the badge. Dave was the total opposite, spotting designers labels, all makes of car or anything with style, with unerring ease and indomitable accuracy.

In the corner of the bar stood a very tall, dark-skinned man, with Latin looks. He was wearing a tight, white T-shirt that moulded to the contours of his chest. Tony guessed that this was the bastard, particularly as he was nonchalantly chatting to two stunning blonde girls.

'Aha. Oh well he must have been mad not to treat you right and run the risk of losing you.'

'Thank you. You are so nice. So very English, and such a gentleman. Sorry, what is your name?' Barbara was suddenly interested in the man beside her.

'Tony.'

'Hey, Tone, me and Adele are going for a boogie so you take care of young Barbara there.' Dave had stood up and was leading a giggling Adele towards the dance floor.

Tony went quite red and still felt a little awkward. 'Will do.'

'So, um, are you having a good holiday? Apart from the bastard of course.' Tony's eyes were now starting to peruse

Barbara's full figure, which was clothed in a low cut grey summer dress. Every time she leaned forward her ample cleavage would look up at him and he felt very aroused. Since Carol, his one and only sexual conquest, Tony had reverted to soft pornographic magazines to satisfy his relatively low sex drive. Barbara sparked his libido into life in the real world.

Barbara pulled her dress up slightly to cover her cleavage as a reaction to the subconscious feeling that Tony's eyes were burning in that direction.

'Yeah, sure. How about you? Have you uh... shagged yet?' Barbara searched for the word 'shag' and then delivered it with indifference.

'Uh no... not yet,' Tony went red again, and then immediately worried that Barbara would read the 'not yet' as a confident come-on. He was out of his comfort zone.

'What do you want? Have you tired of your little girls?' Barbara had suddenly started a conversation above Tony's head.

'Hey babe, you're so cool. That's why I love you. Come, let's dance my sweet, Barbara,' a strong French accent replied.

Tony turned around to see the bastard standing there looking the epitome of cool and suave. He turned back to see Barbara on her feet. 'Oh, let's go' was a response that he did not expect given the previous vitriol. Barbara smiled in Tony's direction before linking arms with the Frenchman and walking away.

Tony sat open-mouthed before composing himself to quickly finish his beer. He uttered the word 'girls do truly love bastards' before standing up and heading for The Harp and solace with his mates.

Phil looked up from his stool just as two girls kicked their legs high in the air as they danced on the bar just inches away. The circular bar that stood proudly in the centre of The Harp was swamped with revellers dancing without rhythm or sense. All were ecstatic, inebriated on both alcohol and the atmosphere. Phil shook his head and felt uncomfortable. This was just cheesy. It reminded him of the student bar at Dave's polytechnic, when he used to go and visit. He felt uncomfortable then.

Gavin sat smugly beside Phil, soaking in the atmosphere and

thoroughly enjoying his pint of Guinness. It had been a task in itself to get served through the sea of legs that shielded the bar staff.

Phil downed his beer and stood up as if to move on.

'Same again?' Gavin made his position clear.

'Nah, let's move on. Try another bar on the strip,' Phil was really eager to go.

'You can. I'm just going to have a couple more here and then call it a night. Besides, Tony might turn up looking for us.' Gavin took another gulp of the black stuff and then raised his hand to get the attention of the barmaid.

Phil was not happy. 'Come on, Gav, this place is sad. We ain't ever going to pull here. Let's go and find somewhere stylish. Somewhere with a bit of class.'

Gavin ignored Phil's pleading and smiled at the barmaid as she came over to take his order. It was the same fortysomething barmaid that Gavin had admired the night before, and on whom his eyes had been transfixed all night.

'Hello my lovely, glad to see you back. Don't need to say a word as I'm going to pull you a pint of what I know you fancy.'

Gavin watched as the barmaid slowly and delicately drew a pint of Guinness in front of him. The bar was now clear of revellers as people had either clambered to rest or attempted a slow dance as the DJ played Westlife's version of 'I Have A Dream'. Once the pint was ready, the barmaid placed it delicately in front of Gavin, then sensually collected some frothy residue from the pump on her finger, and slowly licked it off.

Gavin gulped. 'Wow, that's great. I think I shall come back here again.' He looked around, only to realise that Phil had gone.

'Lost your friend?' the barmaid's smile was warm.

'Yeah... oh well, I can enjoy this pint in peace,' Gavin said, as he paid for his drink. 'What part of Ireland are you from?'

'Cork. Ever been there?' The soft lilting accent was unmistakable.

'No. Only ever been to Dublin. Loved every minute of it though, my favourite city.'

'Ahh, but you've never been to Cork. What's you name?'

'Gavin, and yours?'

'Annette. Nice to meet you, Gavin. I must go and serve now. See you around.' Annette moved to the other side of the bar, with a glance and a smile that made Gavin shiver with excitement.

Gavin's dreamy disposition was interrupted by Phil. 'Didn't you get me one?'

'I thought you'd gone.'

'Nah, just to the bog. Couldn't be bothered to hit the town solo.' Phil ushered a young barman over and ordered a bottle of lager. 'What was all that stuff with the barmaid?'

'Her name is Annette, and she's the woman I love.'

Phil looked at his friend with disdain. 'Fucking hell!'

As Tony wandered into The Harp, the music was still slow and there were now more people sitting outside than inside. It made spotting his friends easy.

'Hi lads. Thought I'd join you for a nightcap,' Tony raised his hand to order a beer.

Phil bear-hugged Tony like a long lost relative. 'Mate, were you blown out? Fair play for having a go though. She was a right looker.' The speech was totally insincere, as Phil no longer had to be envious of his shy friend.

'Thanks, mate,' the insincerity went over Tony's head. 'I gave it a shot, but I'll just move on to the next one and the lovely Barbara will never know what she missed.'

Phil re-enacted the disdainful look he had given Gavin. 'Fucking hell.'

What had become of his two introvert friends?

Dave was pissed. He could hardly walk from the effect of constant beer and a multitude of spirit chasers. Once Tony had disappeared, Dave had endured a conversation with the bastard; he only spoke in sentences of three or four words as if it was uncool to say more. This guy was truly up his own arse, he loved himself that much. Barbara stuck by his side all night until she left to go to the toilet. She returned to find the bastard with a full-figured blonde girl on his knee. Barbara stormed off and the bastard did not flinch.

Now Dave was really drunk, and so was Adele. They propped each other up as they staggered towards the beach. Dave found some secluded small rocks and fell to a seating position, followed by Adele as she fell on top of him. Adele had been good fun. She had been easy to talk to, matched Dave drink for drink and danced with sheer sexual energy. The couple were now shattered, and too tired for conversation. Instead Adele simply pressed her lips to Dave's and initiated a snog that soon developed into vigorous French kissing. It lasted for about fifteen minutes before Adele lifted herself off Dave's body. Dave remained on his back, relaxed and with no energy to move. He was faced by the stars above and raised a wry smile.

Although numb from alcoholic abuse, Dave could just register a tugging movement around his groin area. Adele had unbuckled his belt and unzipped his fly. She released his semi-erect cock, which soon became fully erect as the sea breeze blew gently against it. Adele placed her mouth to engulf the erection and sucked with gentle precision. Dave's eyes opened wide and he again looked at the stars as Adele lovingly caressed him with her mouth. The moment of ejaculation was pure ecstasy when it came.

Adele lovingly cleaned Dave with her mouth and redressed him. She then cuddled him without saying a word. The couple lay there for a while before Adele signalled that she was going back to her apartment. They walked up the strip and Dave gave Adele a goodnight hug and kiss. Still no words were spoken. Dave headed for the hotel, looked up to the night sky and said, 'Thanks, mate.'

Week 1: Day 2 – Sunday Roast

Dave woke at 9 a.m., once again after only a few hours sleep. This time his eyes opened without hesitation and he felt strangely wired. The sound of Phil's rasping snores suddenly grabbed Dave's attention and he glanced over at his friend lying in an untidy heap on top of a crumpled white sheet. Phil's clothes had been unceremoniously dumped on the floor, bar an old pair of red underpants that had badly faded and worn over the years, and were now the sole protector of his dignity.

Dave dressed himself quietly in baggy surf shorts and T-shirt, brushed his hair and gabbed sunglasses, money and a Ben Elton paperback before slipping out the door. Phil snored on in oblivious ignorance.

The sun was already glaring down on the pool area as Dave strolled by. There was a nice crispness to the morning heat that felt warming without the intensity of the midday furnace. The poolside was already densely occupied with parents watching their offspring splash excitedly in the water.

Dave ambled his way down to the strip and found a comfortable-looking café called 'Sunstrip' close to the beach. He ordered a double espresso and croissant before sitting back to start his book. Breakfast was quick in arriving and Dave had only managed a few pages. His eyes were now tired and so the paperback was placed to one side whilst Dave looked out onto the beach. Again, families dominated the scene interspersed with the odd reveller sleeping off the night before. Dave rolled his head on his shoulders as his body relaxed against the backdrop of the sea gently lapping on the shore.

Back at the hotel, Gavin and Tony were both up and sharing a large bottle of mineral water, as they sat outside their room enjoying the morning sun. Like Dave, they were relaxed and content as they read their respective books, stopping only to either look up and soak in the sun or to drink some cold water. Phil still lay snoring.

Once Dave had finished his breakfast he was quick to signal to the waiter that he was ready to settle the bill.

'Hey, my friend, there is no rush. Have another espresso, on the house,' the waiter was in no mood to be hurried. 'Besides, you'll do me a favour. Having a customer attracts more customers.' Dave was the sole patron.

Dave accepted the offer with a wry smile. He was enjoying the solitude, and the espresso was good. It was a decision that was to change his life for ever.

The second double espresso arrived with compliments, and sure enough along with it came more customers. With a large grin, the waiter honed in to greet two young couples. Dave followed his movements, and that is when he saw her. As the waiter shared a joke, which brought overemphasised laughter from his audience, a girl in her late twenties wandered in alone. She wore no make-up, but her face was so pretty and her complexion so faultless that no one would have actually noticed. No male anyway. Her hazel hair was tied back revealing high but proportioned cheekbones that lay the foundation to a model-like beauty. She wore a scruffy black T-shirt and long khaki hiking shorts that were plain in the extreme, but on this girl they could have been paraded on the catwalks of Milan with style.

Dave glared spellbound as the waiter moved over to the girl. She smiled and greeted him as a friend. Soon she sat alone on the opposite side of the café, mirroring Dave right down to the double espresso. His heart started to beat a little faster as Dave outwardly retained a cool and relaxed pose. It almost slipped a little as the girl glanced around, stopping for a few seconds to stare directly at Dave. He was sure he detected a slight smile at that moment.

The café started to fill rapidly now, but Dave was so transfixed that he hardly noticed. It was only when the waiter came over to thank him for helping to draw in the crowds that the spell was broken.

'Um... do you know that girl over there?' Dave nodded towards her as she delicately sipped from the small coffee cup.

'Ah, yes, my friend. That is Elsie and she is English too.' The waiter held his hand to the side of his mouth. 'Very attractive yes?'

'Uh, yes, very. Does she come here often?'

'Every morning at the same time,' the waiter gave a knowing smile.

'See you tomorrow then,' Dave raised his eyebrows to punctuate the statement, before rising and slowly walking towards the exit. As he walked past Elsie, Dave nodded slightly as if greeting a casual acquaintance in the street back home. She reciprocated and Dave felt that the first contact had been made as he strolled on to the strip. *Elsie?* he thought, *whatever.*

Tony and Gavin had tried to wake Phil with large thuds on the door, but to no avail. They guessed Dave was not inside, but though that he was most likely still with his conquest of last night than simply gone to breakfast. Phil lay sound asleep. It was now half past ten.

Unperturbed by their friends' absence, Tony and Gavin ventured to the beach. The sun was now intense and the sand was awash with sunbathers. The two mates managed to find a small gap on which to lay their towels. Gavin proceeded to plaster his body in factor twenty suntan lotion as Tony sat with his shirt on, perusing the scene. Everywhere he looked there were young, topless beauties sunbathing or splashing around in the sea with liberal abandon.

'Look at that! God, they'd keep you warm in the winter,' said Tony, as he pointed out an extremely large-breasted girl frolicking in the surf.

Gavin looked over. 'Oh yes, indeed. What would you give, eh?'

'I'm not that lucky, mate. The opposite in fact,' Tony sounded pensive.

'Hey, what happened to the new "go for it" Tony of last night?'

'Oh he's still here, and raring to go,' Tony smiled. 'No, it's just that I've really wasted a lot of time on my own, when really, with a bit more luck and application, I could have probably shagged into double figures. I've let life pass me by in that sense, and been too happy with my lot... now I'm pissed off about it. I mean look at us four; we're all so different. Dave is Mr Cool who can get a shag without trying, Phil gets totally pissed and asks so many girls out that he always scores in the end, and then you...

well you never seem to go out to actually chat a girl up but you always end up attracting some female like a magnet. And she's always dying for a shag.'

Gavin acknowledged his own particular skill. 'But girls like you, Tone, you're a good-looking bloke; you've just got to be you. Don't try and put on an act. Don't try to be Dave, Phil or me. Just be you, just like you are with the lads. And by the way, I don't actually fancy you myself.'

Tony looked up as a group of four topless Swedish girls walked past. 'At the moment I feel fine. Beering it with the lads, letching, and having a crack. It's only when I think on to when all this is over. When I get home with autumn on the horizon, followed by the dark nights of winter. I either meet you guys down the pub once a week or just stay in and watch the telly more often than not. And I like the evenings in – I even watch all of the bloody soaps, bar *Brookside* of course. And then Christmas comes and I go shopping for my family and spend every Christmas day with my folks. Suddenly a new year begins and by spring I feel good and full of hope that it will be my year. And so the routine goes on my old chum.'

'I trust that you are not getting all morbid on me, my friend. Not in this sunshine.' Gavin had now lain down to soak in some rays.

'Oh no, I'm determined to find someone and so I can't afford to be morose. Oh yes, I will find that special girl, and then I can share my Christmas with her, and of course watch all the soaps with her on the dark winter evenings. Still lead the same bloody life, but share it with someone. Know what I mean?'

'Oh yes. And then kids of course.'

'Of course,' Tony smiled before removing his shirt and standing up. 'Time for a dip.' Sand splattered Gavin's face as Tony sprinted past on his way to the sea.

Once he had negotiated the rocky seabed, Tony fell into the warm water. It felt invigorating as he floated on his back with the bright blue sky in full prominence above. Tony felt better than he had done in a long time, in fact for many years. For so long he had hidden in the shadows of his friends, and felt so lonely inside. He had never shown his true feelings before and bottled up his emotions. To everyone he was just quiet, unassuming and harmless Tony. Now he had acknowledged to Gavin that he no longer wanted to hide from life, he felt like a weight had been lifted off his shoulders. Like an alcoholic declaring his addiction as half the battle won. Tony had drawn a line in the sand and was ready to truly challenge his one-dimensional existence. He suddenly jumped out of the water and fell back in with a large splash and a whoop of joy. A few nearby onlookers observed his display with pitiful mocking stares, but Tony was oblivious and would not have cared anyway.

Dave returned to the hotel to find Phil still asleep, and no sign of Gavin and Tony. In fact, he had just passed his two mates in the street, but all parties had been distracted at the opportune moment when their paths would have crossed. Tony and Gavin's attention was taken by a small gift shop display, whilst Dave looked on with lust as two large-busted American girls walked by in ill-fitting bikinis.

Dave gathered up a towel and prized personal CD player, selected a couple of CDs and prepared to head back to the beach. He decided against waking Phil, who was in such a deep sleep that it would have taken him a good hour to come around. Instead he left him a note.

The sand on the beach was now soaking in the late morning sun and had become too hot to linger on, for more than a few seconds. Dave had put his towel down and stripped to his shorts. He then made a mad dash for the sea as if running over hot coals. The cool water felt even more relieving on his blistering feet. Dave looked down half expecting steam to be rising up around him. He then waded out until the seas touched his waist before diving in.

Ten minutes later Dave emerged from the water, holding in his stomach and extending his shoulders to impress any watching females with his physique. The sand suddenly felt boiling hot against the soles of his feet, but this time he grimaced and momentarily bore the pain as he walked past three girls sitting on their towels. Once out of vision, Dave sprinted for his towel and delicately massaged the pain from his soles. He then lay back after selecting 'London Calling' by The Clash for his CD player. The opening vigorous chords of the title track roared into his ears.

As Dave lay back, sweat began to swamp his face, stinging his eyes severely. It was as Dave sat up to wipe away the acid like perspiration that he spotted Gavin and Tony just ten yards away. In unison Tony noticed Dave and waved.

'How long have you been here?' Dave moved over to join his friends.

'Well over an hour. Where's Phil?' Tony checked his watch and it was now eleven forty.

'Asleep. I left him a note to say I'd be here.'

'Did you score last night then, stud?' Gavin smirked.

Dave felt slightly embarrassed before bragging. 'Just a BJ, not bad though. In fact it was just over there,' Dave nodded towards some rocks at the rear of the beach.

'Lucky bastard. I had no such luck with the lovely Barbara,' Tony chuckled.

'Nah. Although she thought you were lovely. A real English gentleman. Said she'd really enjoyed talking to you. And the French bloke blew her out.' Dave spoke sincerely.

'Really?' Tony looked pleased with himself. 'Well, yeah, she was all right. But she didn't put out, so on to the next one.'

Gavin sniggered. 'Easy, tiger, I think that we had better cancel that Viagra prescription now.'

Dave had once again lain back to enjoy The Clash's finest hour, when his face was suddenly splattered with sand. He jumped up to wipe the small particles from his eyes, whilst spitting grit from his mouth. As the perpetrator came into focus, Dave was half expecting a large thug intent on starting a fight. Was this to be the scene out of some 1970s retro bullworker advert? It was not, and instead both the face and voice were instantly familiar.

'You bastards. Why didn't you wake me?' Phil looked angry as he stared at his friends. He stood tensely in just a pair of shorts, with a T-shirt draped over his shoulder. His stomach spilled out over the waistband of the shorts.

'If you turn green now, you'll be like a really fat Incredible Hulk.' Dave opted to try and enrage his friend further rather than look to appease.

'Fuck off.' Phil self-consciously held his T-shirt over his paunch and sat down on Dave's towel. He did not say another word but stared solemnly out to sea.

Gavin tutted and raised his eyebrows. 'You eaten?'

Phil ended his sulk instantly. 'Nah, I'm starving.'

Within minutes Phil was leading the others off the beach in the errant search for food. In fact just as they left the sand a large green sign almost impeded the way promising a full roast dinner at The Harp.

'Just the job, follow me.' Phil began to almost march with military precision as the others huffed but reluctantly followed; anything to avoid more sulking.

Phil ordered roast beef and all the trimmings, followed by apple pie and custard to take advantage of the pub's offer of a free dessert with every roast platter. The others all opted for an assortment of baguettes with light fillings.

'How can you eat all that in this heat?' Tony felt queasy just thinking about it.

'It's tradition mate. Part of our fine English culture. I've always had my Sunday lunch right from when I was a nipper to these days when I pop round to my mum's.' Phil felt a surge of patriotism and half expected the opening chords of 'Jerusalem' to strike up in the background. 'You must have been the same, brought up to appreciate one fine routine. Bloody Gavin will tell you, he's such a creature of habit.'

'We had whatever was going. My dad was always down the pub and my mum was off shagging whatever lover she was with. So my elder bother and me cooked whatever we liked. It was usually chips. That was until we knocked the fryer over and set fire to the kitchen. Had to get the fire brigade and the whole works. My dad came home so pissed that he didn't even notice the kitchen was gutted as he staggered through it. And my mum, well she couldn't say a word, could she?' Gavin nodded as he shared the memory.

'Well at least you turned out a well-balanced, intelligent adult despite your upbringing,' Dave interjected with a hint of shock at the childhood revelation.

'Absolutely.' Gavin then mockingly performed with a pronounced psychopathic twitch of the head whilst growling like a dog.

Dave turned back to Phil. 'Anyway, we always had a Sunday roast, but my mum was a shit cook and it tasted bloody awful.'

Three fresh baguettes were placed on the table with a crisp colourful salad as a side garnish. In contrast, Phil's roast was a mound of potatoes and big thick Yorkshire puddings. Thick dark brown gravy cascaded from the top, trickling down to the overcooked vegetables and slices of tough beef hidden below. Steam billowed into Phil's smiling face, causing him to wipe instant sweat from his brow.

'Shit. I feel bloated even looking at this. It will knock me out for the afternoon,' said Phil.

Tony shook his head and delicately fingered his tuna filled baguette.

'And that's just it, another part of the tradition. That's what Sunday's are all about, full stomachs and sleeping it off in the afternoon,' said Phil, as he shovelled a mound of food into his mouth.

'You're living in the past mate. For most that's just Christmas these days. It was just that when we were kids there was bugger all else to do on Sundays. All the shops were shut, even the supermarkets. Everything on TV was geared towards religion for just about the whole day. Alternatively people actually went to church. I even had to go to Sunday school up to the age of ten. Even had to wear a bloody tie.' Dave recounted the memory like it was a major punishment.

'You sound like a member of the *Waltons* or the bloody Ingle family from *Little House On The Prairie*. I can just see you now, heading for church on the back of a horse-drawn cart in your very best suit.' Gavin painted a scene of innocence and purity.

'Except that I was sitting in the back of a Ford Cortina in flared trousers and a kipper tie, whilst my dad played Slade at top whack.' Dave painted the real picture. 'And besides, it was *The Waltons* and *Little* bloody *House On The Prairie* that were the only TV respite from *Songs Of Praise*.'

'Aha. That is where you are wrong, my friend.' Phil looked up from his now nearly empty plate. 'You see, as you settled down to digest your Sunday roast, there was one hour of truly heavenly television in the shape of *On The Ball*, as presented by the god-like Brian Moore.'

'Oh yes. The icon of seventies' football. I always remember that Frank Worthington goal at the start when he chipped the ball up and back-heeled it in. I used to practice that for hours, but could never do it.' Tony was a walking football encyclopaedia.

'I don't think I ever stayed in on a Sunday afternoon. Once Dad got back pissed from the pub after last orders, my brother and me used to bugger off down to the amusement arcade. We'd play Space Invaders and Lunar Rescue and all that stuff. We got so good we could make a ten-pence go last for an hour. And it was my name that was always listed up there as the best score.' Gavin had shared stories of his unstable upbringing before. The unpredictability of his parents' fiery and alternative relationship meant he often found ways to occupy his time and stay out of the way. Time was often passed in mundane and repetitive tasks. A former girlfriend who had practiced psychology told him that his childhood need for distraction had manifested into the comfort and need for routine in adulthood.

Phil would not be budged from his fond memories of childhood Sundays. 'But, you see, you also had the late afternoon serials. *Black Beauty*, *The Black Arrow*, *Just William*… kids just don't get that today. It's just all soap omnibuses now.'

'I always remember when I was really little, the highlight of Sunday night was staying up to watch *On The Buses* after my bath. With a cup of Ovaltine of course.' Dave continued the cosy scene setting before changing tact. 'Although I also remember *Love They Neighbour*, which even then I thought was racist propaganda shit.'

'I'm sure that the young seven-year-old David Holliman reviewed the programme with the exact same words as he sat in the lounge in his kung fu pyjamas and tartan dressing gown.' Tony transposed Dave into his own childhood scene.

'Absolutely, except I had *Star Trek* pyjamas.'

The thick wedge of apple pie and equally thick custard was devoured in minutes. As the last drop of dark yellow liquid was savoured, Phil tapped his bulging stomach, 'Now I'm full.'

Phil glanced to his left and was startled by the sudden appearance of an equally protruding gut, badly hidden under an ill-fitting seventies football shirt. The others quickly followed his stare.

'Albert!' Dave exclaimed for the rest.

'Ay up, lads. How's it hanging? Good nosh in 'ere, eh?'

'Yeah, not bad.' Phil spoke as the only true connoisseur of such cuisine.

'Ay, I tell you, do I look really white? 'Cos I bloody should do. Just had the fright of my considerable life.' In reality Albert looked as he always did.

Tony looked puzzled. 'Why, what happened?'

Albert needed no further enticing to tell all. 'Well I was down at the Olympian you see. Nice hotel. Quite often I pop in for a free beer and a natter with the owner, Michael. Well you see, Mikey introduced me to a young English couple and they seemed nice enough. Pried quite a bit like, but nice enough. Anyway, I says what do yer do? And you'll never bloody guess but they're only a couple of bloody coppers. Married and that. Well, anyway, I tried to act cool and made me excuses and left. But I'm sure that the girl clocked me. She kept looking at me all funny and asking what I used to do back in England. I reckon someone from the yard'll be on a plane tonight. Better lay low for a while?'

Dave tried hard to keep a straight face. 'Maybe she just fancied you.'

Albert stroked his beard and reflected. ''Appen you're right, lad, 'appen you're right. Her husband was an ugly mug, so she probably appreciated my fair good looks. Let's 'ope so,' he then walked away.

'Well hello again, Gavin. Back to see us once more.'

Gavin's eyes darted from the departing Albert to the source of the greeting. 'Annette. Hi. Yeah, I just can't stay away.'

Dave looked slightly puzzled. He had not been updated on Gavin's new vision of perfect womanhood. Tony had heard talk of nothing else all morning.

'So, what's all your names? I saw you two last night,' Annette nodded towards Phil and Tony. 'But the handsome one over there I definitely haven't seen before.'

Gavin introduced his mates, although gritted his teeth with a hint of jealousy when it came to handsome Dave.

'So what did old Albert want? More tall stories to tell, no doubt,' Annette knew him well.

'Yeah. Is he for real?' Gavin remained as spokesman.

'Nobody truly knows, but I tell you, whatever Blarney stone he kissed, it's had some really weird effect. Anyway I expect you're all back out to enjoy the sun, so I'll get on and hope to see you in here for a jar later tonight.' Annette then walked away after giving the slightest of winks and accompanying smile.

'Would you like to join us?' Unfortunately Annette was still in earshot when Gavin muttered the words as he immediately felt a fool for making the suggestion.

Annette turned and smiled. 'No thanks, Gavin, but cheers for the offer. Me delicate Irish skin is no good in the midday sun. God knows why I moved out here.'

The lads left the dark shade of the pub and winced as the glare of the sun hit their eyes.

'Would you like to join us?' Phil mimicked Gavin's saddest moment. Tony and Dave laughed loudly as Gavin turned a deep shade of red.

'All right, all right. It was a spur of the moment thing.' Gavin was still annoyed with himself.

Phil continued. 'You're losing it, mate. I reckon you've blown any chance. Besides, she fancies Dave anyway.'

The last comment hit Gavin hard, shattering his dream that he was Annette's perfect man. He said very little as they walked back to the hotel.

A hot Sunday afternoon was spent either in the pool, or for Phil by its side as he slept off and digested his large lunch. It was not long before the others were asleep on adjacent sunbeds. At four, they all moved from the pool area to their rooms and slept even more.

Dave woke to the sound of loud anthem-like singing coming from the small bathroom. It was six-thirty in the evening and yet Phil was up and for some reason giving an excited rendition of the Queen classic 'We Are The Champions'. He soon appeared with a white hotel towel wrapped around his ample waist and looked deliriously happy.

'Why all the sudden delirium?' Dave got up and started to select some clothes for the next night on the town.

'Because tonight I am going to give it large. Because it is time for the...' Phil reached into a drawer and whipped out an old dark blue faded T-shirt '...*the* pulling shirt.'

Dave sighed. 'What already? It's only the third night. And we ain't staying out that late tonight because it's the boat trip tomorrow.'

The pulling shirt had been on every Campaign with Phil, and had derived its name from some successful chatting up performed in its owner's younger years.

'Aha, you see the power of the pulling shirt can call at any time. I have to be ready when it calls.' Phil pulled the shirt on and admired himself in the mirror. It was still nice and baggy, sufficiently covering his increased frame.

'You tosser,' Dave headed for the shower as Phil preened himself like a peacock.

Phil was still beaming and proudly displaying his 'magical' shirt as he stood with the others by the poolside bar. Tony and Gavin both groaned with the realisation that the rather sad annual ritual was under way once more.

'I mean you slag me off for being habitual, but every year you re-enact the same desperate routine. And I tell you what; it's bloody falling apart. The power of the shirt will soon erode into a heap of rotten fibres.' Gavin pointed to Phil's underarm.

Phil lifted his arm and saw a gaping hole. 'Shit, I'll have to stitch that. Like Connor McLeod of the clan McLeod, this shirt is immortal. It must live forever.'

'Yeah, and you're the sad bastard who'll be still wearing it when he's sixty-five.'

Led Zeppelin's 'Whole Lotta Love' suddenly drowned Gavin's words out.

'Hey, you guys. You'll like this,' Theo grinned and began to play air guitar.

Dave noticed that the lads were once again the only customers at the bar. 'Why is this bar always so quiet? It seems to be the same very night.'

'Oh yes. Most people go to the strip and don't bother with the bar, apart from the barbeque night that is.' Theo did not seem to care.

'Do you play your heavy rock music to everyone, or are we just the privileged few?' Tony knew the answer already, but probed like Sherlock Holmes making a point to the simple Watson.

'Oh yes, apart from barbeque night. Nik makes me play tunes for the young ones. I think that they would love real rock, but Nik says no.'

'Aha,' Tony laid out the facts in the case of the ghost bar for even the less bright juries to grasp.

The hotel residents had now started streaming by the bar on their way to the strip, many grimaced at the loud guitars and screaming vocals that greeted them. Gareth and Cheryl walked past and Gareth gave a smiled 'hello'. Cheryl in contrast retained a blank soulless expression. The couple walked alongside each other but did not speak or hold hands.

The lads quickly finished their mandatory starting beer and hastily followed the throng towards the strip. They found a small restaurant serving simple food, but despite his heavy lunch, Phil still found room for three courses.

It was decided by a majority of three to one that this was not to be a late night. Phil, the minority, truly believed that part of the fun would be to stay out as late as possible and then just sleep off the effects on the boat the next day. The others were never going to be convinced.

In order to appease him, Phil was allowed to choose the main bar for the evening. He chose a basement dancing club called 'The Underground'. As it was only about 9 p.m., the club was barely a third full.

Phil bought the first round of beers as his friends stood motionless in a corner by the edge of the dance floor. They purposely stood out of the beams of the constant strobe lighting that circulated from above. When Phil joined them he could not stand still through anticipation and nervous energy. He started to move robotically to the melodic beat of Destiny's Child's

'Bootylicious', whilst glancing over his shoulder for any sniff of talent.

'Come on, all you gorgeous girls. Come on and succumb to the power of the shirt. It is futile to resist.' Phil's mocking plea masked some true sincerity.

The others just smiled patronisingly.

'Can we try The Harp next?' Gavin's motive could not be clearer.

The request riled Phil instantly. 'No. Fuck off, Mr Routine. We only have a short night tonight because you tossers want to go to bed early. So I say fine, but we stay here and have some fucking fun.'

Gavin couldn't be bothered to argue.

After a few more rounds of beer, Phil began to put more movement into his dancing. He had now edged onto to the dance floor, but was still facing towards his motionless friends. The club was now more than half full. With his back to the other dancers it was inevitable that Phil would collide with someone eventually, especially as the number of dancers grew rapidly.

The collision came with a large thump of someone's body pounding into Phil's backside. He turned to see two short, but very fat, girls smiling back at him. Phil offered the slightest of grins as an apology and turned back quickly to face his friends.

The two fat girls moved swiftly in front of Phil and beckoned for him to dance with them. Phil's face was now a picture of horror.

From their position at the side of the floor Phil's mates had quickly realised what was developing. They all instantly roared with laughter, becoming more animated than at any other point in the evening.

Gavin shouted over. 'I take it all back. That shirt truly has magic powers.'

Phil grimaced back at him. The two fat girls were now grabbing at his hands and chanting at him in German. Phil kept trying to exit but was constantly pulled back by both girls.

It became all too much when the lads started heading for the door, abandoning Phil and waving cheerily as they went. Phil finally made a frantic break.

Dave was chuckling to himself, thinking of all the mileage he would get from this situation, when Phil suddenly barged past and through the doorway. He had almost knocked Gavin and Tony over in a desperate surge of speed. Once outside, Phil just kept on running. Behind him, the two fat girls were in hot pursuit like a surreal parody of a Benny Hill chase scene.

'I'm fucking burning that shirt tomorrow,' was the last audible comment from Phil as he disappeared into the night.

Week 1: Day 3 – All Aboard the Skylark

At eight-thirty in the morning the air was surprisingly fresh and chilled as it circulated around the small Cretan harbour. A gang of half-awake holidaymakers huddled in small groups having endured an extremely short ride in a rickety old bus.

The lads moved around the edge of the group, taking it in turn to yawn and stretch before individually gazing over the side of the jetty into the water. Each remembered the plan of good intentions from the night before. After Phil's comical escapade at 'The Underground', it had seemed a good idea to have a quick nightcap with Theo before turning in. The nightcap quickly, and far too easily, became a plural to the backdrop of some classic rock ballad album. An early night was finally drawn to a close at about two-thirty.

A sudden bustle as the crowd scooped up their bags heralded the swift arrival of a compact but ageing cruiser. It quickly docked, and an excited young, male SunRay rep, emerged, and beamed the biggest of smiles to the waiting throng.

'All aboard the Skylark,' he shouted with avid enthusiasm that would have secured a Red Coat position at Butlins without hesitation. The Skylark of 'Captain Pugwash' fame was doing the TV rounds long before his effervescent personality was conceived.

The crowd shuffled onto the boat like dumb animals beckoned by Noah before the flood.

'Dunno if you realised, mate, but this boat's called the *Olympian*, not the *Skylark*.' Phil's dry and bemused comment brought only loud hoots of laughter from the young rep.

'Very good, very good. I like your wit and style, my man,' the rep had obviously been watching too many Jim Carey films.

Once on board, everyone quickly grabbed a space to crash, with the majority of girls occupying the front deck for prime sunbathing space. The lads found a section of shaded bench towards the front as the sun began to break through and rapidly warm the air.

The young rep introduced himself as James via a microphone and then announced that Susie, the rep from the Hotel Garden Imperial, was his co-host. The captain went by the name of Hercules. He was a youngish man with a severe face and cultured George Michael stubble. James warned everyone that Hercules had a bit of a temper if anyone should abuse his ship, before talking through the day's itinerary. It was very simple. A leisurely cruise out to some clear deep water, when the boat would stop and then anyone who wanted to could dive in to the sea. When everyone was back on board, they would set sail for a delightful sandy cove. The anchor would be weighed and all would go ashore for a barbeque. After lunch, the return journey would include another dive stop, but of course allowing time for all the 'wonderful food' to be digested. Susie then took the microphone to go over some housekeeping in terms of where the toilets were located, how refreshments could be purchased and what the drill would be if the boat sank. Nobody listened to the last bit, assuming that it was every man or woman for themselves. Susie finally warned of the perils of sunbathing without lotion, particularly as the sun was even more severe at sea.

The boat then set a course and quickly motored out of the harbour. As it did so, the light of the sun lit up the deck with a hot intensity. Simultaneously there was an orchestrated 'ping' as bikini tops were discarded by the dozen, revealing a sea of breasts in all colours, shapes and sizes. The lads half shut waking eyes suddenly grew in size, focussed in glaring satisfaction.

Twenty minutes later, Tony stood looking out over the calm sea, as the others sat with their heads resting against the side rail, with their eyes firmly shut once more. Each one took it in turn to suddenly jolt, with their head flopping forward, as sleep took over from a restful daydream. Tony captured the moment with his camera for posterity.

'Can't your mates handle the pace then?' Tony swung around to be faced by a beaming Susie.

''Fraid not. We're getting too old for this lark,' was Tony's honest reply.

'Eh? Speak for yourself, mate, I'm just resting my eyes, preparing for another twenty-four-hour party mood.' Phil was almost shouting as he jumped up after hearing Susie's voice through his sleepy haze. He instantly stirred both Dave and Gavin.

Susie looked gorgeous in a flimsy red company T-shirt and matching shorts. Her deep blonde hair glowed under the bright sun and her visible body was a consistent golden brown. As she stood next to Tony, Susie's large chest was thrust out so far that it was in danger of hitting his chin.

The lads looked on in awe before Tony finally broke the brief silence. 'So, how long have you been a lesbian?'

All heads immediately rotated to face Tony. Each face was filled with shock and disbelief that he has asked such a question.

'Uh… yeah, right… you'll have to excuse our friend. He's been going through a rough time recently. Really stressed at work and that… in fact the stress has brought on tourettes syndrome, so he just keeps saying the strangest things without thinking. So, um, please don't hold it against him,' Phil's unrehearsed babble brought a hard stare from Tony.

Susie flicked her hair and laughed loudly. 'No, actually I like that question. It's much more interesting than the usual, "So, what part of England are you from?" or "How long have you been a rep?"'

'Don't feel that you have to answer it, though,' Dave said, really hoping she would.

'No, it's okay, I will.' Susie now had everyone's undivided attention. 'It was when I was twenty-three, three years ago now. I'd been living with this guy for about two years. He was a sexual animal, always wanting to try new things. He pushed and pushed me until I agreed to a threesome for his birthday. He set it up with a friend of his sister's who was always gagging for any kind of sex. We all got pissed and got down to it. Only trouble was, us girls had a great time and didn't let him get a look in. Within two weeks I'd moved out and had gone to live with Cheryl. She's still my partner to this day. So there you have it.'

The lads were speechless as imaginations ran away with themselves.

'Anyway, looks like we're coming up to the first swimming stop, so I'd better go and help out.' Susie started to walk before glancing back with a smile. 'Oh, sometimes just to keep things fresh we snare a hapless male and treat him to a Susie and Cheryl sandwich. Better than any other late snack you'd care to mention.' An exaggerated wink punctuated the statement.

The boat came to a gradual halt and James announced that it was safe to enjoy a swim.

'Well, I don't know about you lads, but I need to cool down and fucking quick.' Seconds later a large thudding splash heralded Phil's desperate dive into the sea.

Numerous loud splashes followed in quick succession as the day-trippers abandoned ship into the clear warm water. Soon the vessel sat motionless, devoid of everyone but the crew. Excited heads bobbed at different locations around the hull like bees buzzing around a honey pot.

Phil let himself slip under the surface before bouncing back up in a wave of spray, drenching his mates in the process. They shook their heads of the excess water and grimaced at Phil's juvenile antics.

'Wow! That's good. Now you see, guys, no matter how old you are this will always feel the same. The grind of everyday life is lifted and you feel young again. Carefree. For this moment nothing else matters. Do you agree or do you agree?' Phil was on a high.

'And then you get home, the feeling wears off with your tan after two weeks and you wait for a bloody year to capture it again,' Tony said, dampening the mood.

'Spoilsport. You see, Tony, with an attitude like that you'll always be alone. You need to lighten up, let yourself go and then the good life will come to you.' Phil was determined to find a happy consensus to support his belief that everything was right with the world.

'Yeah, right, I'll follow you mate 'cos your life's so perfect. You get pissed ... and that's it. Otherwise it's just a shite job and a routine life for an eternal bachelor boy. I mean we've even started going to the bloody pictures together now. Lads only do that when they're fourteen or fifteen. You told me that the last film you took a girl to see was *Shakespeare In Love*... I mean how many bloody years ago was that? So I'm sorry. The power of the

Campaign is starting to wear thin and become as mundane as the rest of our existence. I need a life beyond it.' Tony starkly stated his new realism.

Phil was stunned. His joyful spirit was crushed. 'Yeah, cheers for that, mate.' He swam slowly away from the group to be alone.

'What's going on, Tone?' Dave was stunned by the outburst.

'You know me, Dave, I think too deeply. I just wish we could find a new direction in life; change the routine. Because all we do is go to a different country every year and get older. Maybe this is the year we can aim higher and look beyond the bloody Campaign.' Tony then swam off in the opposite direction to Phil.

Gavin and Dave looked on in silence.

The silence continued back on the boat through a wall of tense atmosphere between Phil and Tony. Tony eventually broke it. 'Sorry, mate, didn't mean to come across as a miserable bastard.' Tony offered his hand. 'Really I was just worried that you might go to the pictures with someone else.'

Phil smiled. 'What, and not be able to nick your popcorn. No chance.'

The barbeque was prepared and served by the crew on a small, sandy, secluded beach, neatly located in the curve of a rounded cove. It was idyllic, but felt so familiar like every cove visited on each and every Campaign for the mandatory cruise. And the routine here was also the same as every other year, as various bits of meat and fish were cooked until dark black, and placed alongside a heavy olive-oiled salad, dominated by ripe beef tomatoes and feta cheese; a pile of stale bread completed the feast. When the call to eat was made, a stampede ensued that complimented the cuisine far beyond its worth.

The lads ate quickly to satisfy their hunger more than their palate. In particular, the charred sausages were not to be savoured for long. Phil bemoaned the quality, but still went back for seconds.

Before the food could even begin to settle, a game of beach football was quickly arranged and underway. Phil found the going tough and decided to goal hang throughout. When he finally managed to score he gave it the full Marco Tardelli treatment, mimicking the emotion the Italian generated when he scored in the World Cup final.

When the game was over, sheer heat-drained exhaustion followed suddenly as most of the players either dived into the sea or flopped down under the nearest shade.

'Did you like the Tardelli? Magic, eh? I remember that so well, I mean the emotion in his face; it was pure poetry without words. You could almost feel and hear an orchestra rising to a crescendo in his honour,' said Phil. He had never forgotten that moment.

'Yeah, true, but it was very Italian. I suppose the closest we have is Gazza pulling faces and blubbing,' said Dave. Dave thought about performing his Gazza impression, but did not have the energy.

'Do you think England will make it to the World Cup next year?' asked Gavin, almost sounding disinterested in the answer.

'Nah! I doubt it. We won't beat Germany *in* Germany. Might get through the play-offs though, but anyway it's in Japan. All the games will be at breakfast time. It won't be the same,' said Dave. But he still hoped and prayed that England would make it never the less.

'We'll be there. I can *feel* it. Just trust me,' Phil sounded more confident, but he just hoped they would make it against the odds, without really believing they would.

'And of course a year later it's the rugby World Cup. That's going to be in Australia, so more beer at breakfast,' said Gavin. 'And England has a chance of winning that.' Gavin preferred the fifteen aside game.

'Yeah, let's hope it has a better ending than the bloody Lions' tour,' said Dave. Dave thought back to the recent defeat in the deciding test that silenced his local pub.

'Don't remind me. I prefer to remember the glory of ninety-seven in South Africa and the sweet boot of Jerry Guscott.' Gavin pursed his lips as he visualised the drop goal that won the series.

'You see, guys, you're all dreamers. Now I support Arsenal, who will of course win the league again. Most of the Arsenal team play for France, who will of course win the World Cup. As for rugby, an All Blacks Australia final is already written in the stars.'

'Fuck, that's why I hate Gooners.' Phil pushed Tony from his perch on a rock.

The cruise back was slow, and included another brief stop for a swim. A dishevelled set of passengers disembarked at Hersonissos, parched by a constant combination of dry sun and sea breeze.

The hotel pool was like an oasis in the dessert and all the lads had no hesitation in running and plunging into the cool water as soon as it came into view. The baked in sea salt, sand and sunburn were all dealt with in one swoop.

Refreshed on the outside, the foursome quickly changed and devoured several ice-cold beers to regenerate and oil the rest of their tired bodies. The chilled lagers were raised and drunk in unison as Theo marked the moment with a blast of Whitesnake.

A bar crawl was out of the question that night. Dinner was taken at the first restaurant that came into view, before moving to the bar next door, securing a table and slowly savouring and drinking a few beers. Conversation was slow and muted before drying up to be replaced by a chorus of yawns. The strip was emblazoned with colour and full of vigour and life as four tired thirtysomethings headed back to the hotel for an early night.

Week 1: Day 4 – The Early Bird...

The muffled bleep of the concealed travel alarm clock was sufficient to pull Dave out of his early morning slumber. Once open, his eyes were wide and alert as he quickly killed the sound of the alarm. Across the room a deafening snore emanated from Phil, signalling the oblivious ignorance to the early morning call. It was eight-thirty.

Dave swiftly, and covertly, shaved and dressed himself before slipping out the door. He breathed a sigh of relief in the corridor and headed for the morning sunshine.

One minute later the door to the next room opened and out stepped Gavin. He had mirrored Dave's routine to perfection, right down to the sigh of relief.

Five minutes later Dave was sitting in the Sunstrip café awaiting a double espresso and croissant. He was the only customer. Gavin was also waiting for his breakfast, which was a full Irish fry-up in the Harp. The pub was packed, with the majority being revellers filling up after an all-nighter.

Dave sat back, enjoyed the jolt of dark coffee beans, and slowly began to peruse the copy of *The Sun* he had purchased on the way. It was Monday's edition.

Gavin sat reading a copy of *The Mail on Sunday* he had pulled from a rack of papers left for customers. A large plate of overfried food sitting before him suddenly took his attention. He looked up expectantly but the waitress's face was not the one he had hoped to see.

Thirty minutes later *The Sun* and *Mail* had been thumbed to death respectively. Dave was now wired on espresso and Gavin was on his third refill of coffee. Both were ready to leave, with a sense of disappointment.

Dave raised his hand to hail the bill. As the waitress came forward, Elsie came into the café and took a seat right on cue. Without hesitation, Dave changed his mind and ordered another espresso.

Gavin counted out his money to settle the bill and was about to call the waitress over when he suddenly spotted Annette's beaming smile. He still hailed the waitress but ordered another coffee.

Elsie was dressed in a baggy black T-shirt and equally baggy brown shorts. Her hair was tied up and she wore no makeup, but her beauty was so natural and striking that she had no need to emphasise it any further. She was alone and the only other customer in the café.

'Enjoying the solitude?' Dave finally broke the silence with an almost subdued line. Elsie smiled and nodded. There was a pause but he persevered.

'I think you were in here the other day, we must have similar tastes,' Dave said, already subtly trying to pry for more information.

Elsie smiled again and said, 'Yes, it was probably me. I always drop by when I'm down this way.' She was very posh.

Dave stood up with his espresso and moved over next to Elsie. 'Mind if I join you for a few minutes?'

Elsie shrugged nonchalantly.

'So, where are you from and how come you're in Crete?' Dave cringed at his own over-eager teenager act.

Elsie laughed. 'Whoa! Less of the Gestapo act please. My name is Elsie, I originate from Cornwall, but now I just travel from place to place.'

'Good answer!' Dave thought for a moment. 'So are you running away from something or trying to find yourself?'

'Now that's more like a question,' Elsie pondered before answering. 'I'm running away from mundane conformity to find the freedom to be different. And I can truly say that I have found it.'

'Cool. Life's a beach and all that. Actually I thought *The Beach* was an excellent book. The film was a bit dodgy though.'

Elsie did not look impressed. 'So, my turn. Who are you and why are you chatting me up?'

Dave was slightly taken aback. 'Um, my name's Dave, I'm on holiday with my mates and you looked like a good person to shoot the breeze with. We are actually very alike. I hate conformity. I've always been a free spirit, striving to make sure I don't just become another middle-aged statistic.'

'Ah! What's your life about then? Do you travel? Sing in a rock band? Act?'

Dave went a shade of red and realised he could not lie. 'Uh no, I work for an insurance company.'

Elsie laughed out loud. 'Excellent, so nowhere near the pipe-and-slipper brigade then. No pinstripe suit and make sure you're home in time for *Coronation Street*.'

'Certainly not, I've never owned a pipe in my life.' Dave decided that the best tactic was to mock himself.

'Well, Dave, it's been great speaking to you but I must fly. Have an exciting life, and don't lose that rebel spirit.' Elsie then threw some coins on the table and swiftly got up.

Dave smiled. 'Yeah right.' He was thinking 'snooty cow' and almost wanted to snap some insult back, but he just knew that there was something about her that had him smitten. This was a challenge and Dave liked a challenge. He would return and try again.

After a dozen expectant glances and false smiles, Gavin finally caught Annette's eye.

'Hello there, smiler. Come to be fed?' Annette sounded warm and welcoming.

'Yes, I've already tasted your fine fare. I'm just recovering now.' Gavin actually felt quite bilious.

Annette sat beside him. She was wearing very tight blue jeans that clung firmly to her ample bottom and wide thighs. Over her jeans hung a large black shirt that tactically hid a couple of love handles that just spilled over the waistband. The baggy shirt could not mask the profile of her large breasts. Jet-black hair cascaded over her shoulders framing a plumpish but very pretty face.

'No, come on! We haven't killed anyone yet. A few hospitalisations sure, but they all pulled through.'

'Glad to hear it,' said Gavin, feeling so at ease.

'I desperately need my caffeine injection,' said Annette. She signalled for a coffee to be brought over. 'So where are you friends?'

'All asleep without a doubt,' Gavin stated, oblivious to Dave's early rise.

'Aha. Have you all been mates long?'

'Yeah, we go back a long way. We've been coming on holiday for years, each year somewhere different, but always together. It's almost like a marriage, which is ironic as none of us have actually come close to the real thing.'

'Wow. And such good-looking lads too.'

'You mean Dave, the dark haired smooth one,' Gavin stated with a dismissive tone.

'Yeah, he's nice, but too pretty for my taste. I like a man with a bit of a beer belly, who likes his morning fry-ups.'

Gavin pondered. 'What, Phil?'

Annette gave him a playful punch. 'No, you, stupid.'

Gavin looked down at his belly and breathed in. 'Thanks. I'm flattered. You're pretty hot yourself.'

Annette laughed. 'So what are your plans today?'

'Sunbathing, eating, and then drinking; pretty much the same every day. Although we did go on a booze cruise yesterday. And on Thursday me and one of the lads are going to Archanes.'

'Wow! Would you believe it,' Annette suddenly looked surprised. 'I live in Archanes and Thursday's my day off.'

Gavin was worried for a moment. 'You don't share a place with a girl called Susie do you?'

'No,' Annette was puzzled. 'I live alone.'

'Uh, no, it was just that our rep lives there with a mate and I put two and two together.'

'Ah, you mean Susie and Lynda, the lesbians. I think I can see what your two and two was adding up to.'

'No, no. Not at all,' Gavin was not convincing.

Annette suddenly laughed loudly. Gavin laughed along with some relief.

'Anyway, back to Thursday. It's my day off and if you like I could meet you and your friend and show you the relaxed nightlife. You can kip on the floor at my place and I'll run you back in the morning.'

Gavin was already excited. 'Yeah, great. That's really good of you.'

Annette described a good meeting point and then left Gavin to get on with her work. Gavin headed back to the hotel plotting how to persuade Tony not to join him on Thursday evening.

Phil and Tony had both realised that they were missing a roommate at about the same time. Bemused, they met up and shared a hotel breakfast by the pool. They took it in turns to work out where the others had gone, and both concluded, rightly, that women were involved.

Dave was the first to return and face the questioning glares of his mates. He coolly deflected every query and guess as to his early morning intentions. The bombardment soon abated and the response of waking up early and going for a quiet breakfast was finally accepted. Dave then headed in to collect his personal stereo and then settled down to sunbathe. As he clicked on some music, Dave now joined the curiosity as to where Gavin had gone.

Gavin soon returned, wearing a large grin and walking with a confident swagger. After a couple of tame questions, he revealed all. He had the smell of victory in his pursuit and was happy to share it.

Within ten minutes, the four lads were lying on aligned sunbeds and soaking up strong rays. From the left there was Dave's athletic semi-muscular frame, followed by Phil's podgy and pale body, followed by Gavin's tallish flat frame punctuated with an out-of-synch mound of beer belly, and finally there was skinny non-descript Tony with matchstick legs. Dave listened to music; Phil read *Viz*; Gavin lay dreaming and Tony read a book.

'What are you listening to?' Phil prodded Dave.

Dave awkwardly, and frustratingly, stopped his CD and removed the earpiece. 'Some compilation from the eighties, it was free with the *Mail On Sunday*.'

'Brill,' Phil sat upright. 'It's amazing, isn't it, that you can get a free album with a newspaper. I mean it would have been a bit impractical in the age of vinyl. The bloody thing would have been bigger than the paper. All the delivery boys would have ended up with hernias.'

'Yeah, true. Things are certainly different since I was a lad. Why, I used to live in a hole in the ground, go to bed when it was time to get up and then work a seventeen-hour shift for nowt down pit.' Dave's strong Yorkshire accent perfectly represented his Monty Python delivery.

Phil laughed. 'It's true though. You think when you're young that the trends and the time itself will never be old-fashioned. I mean twenty-five years since the Sex Pistols and now it's granddad music.'

'Yeah, it's the Queen's golden jubilee next year and they'll probably re-release "God Save The Queen" in her honour, whilst in seventy-seven it was totally anarchic. Hey, I wonder if they'll have street parties next year. I still remember the one we had for the silver jubilee. I was only eleven and got pissed on homebrew ale.' Dave remembered his first hangover like an old friend.

'I doubt that they will. Everything was so much cosier in nineteen seventy-seven, even in the midst of punk. There was a real national identity. Everyone listened to Radio One, watched *Top Of The Pops* and believed in family values to the extent that the country was almost one big happy family.'

Dave was not so sure of Phil's summary, and said, 'I think that punk changed all that; it just generated a new way of thinking. The seventies were dull until the end and then you had the eighties when it was a time to party and not care about your identity, followed by the harsh nineties when it was suddenly dog eat dog to survive. Now the new millennium is here and we've gone all high tech and dull. Manufactured is the name of the game from the monotonous conveyor belt of drab TV programmes to soulless pop bands, modified food and boring careers.'

'Lighten up, lads. You sound like a couple of old men. Time moves on, things change. Just deal with it.' Tony was losing the thread of his book.

'Ooh, get her. The new forward-thinking Tony.' Phil's camp accent was totally over-emphasised.

Dave laughed. 'He's right though, we're starting to sound like those old friends that Paul Simon once sang about. Time to stop.'

He pressed play again on his CD player and fell back into oblivion.

Gavin lay deep in thought, having also picked up his personal CD player to drown out the inane chatter around him. The twanging guitar of Neil Young resounded as he dreamt of himself and Annette playing out a love scene, culminating in a hot, sex session. The latter aroused him considerably, and it was a while before he opened his eyes to the realisation that he was in a very public place. Quickly he shifted to mask the considerable mound in his shorts, hoping that it had not been noticed.

Gavin decided to park his lustful thoughts about Annette until he was alone in bed. Instead his mind wandered and for no rational reason he thought back to his first real love. Her name was Carol and she was the main part of Gavin's life when they were both seventeen. Now and again Gavin would think of Carol, not just because she was his first love but for a more desperate turn of events.

Gavin went to an all-boys grammar school and had very little knowledge, or experience, of the opposite sex, during his adolescence. Carol went to an all-girls grammar school and ditto the previous. This left two shy and awkward teenagers feeling out of place at the sixth form link disco. They were two amongst a crowd, with the girls on one side of the dance floor and the boys on the other. Teachers were on hand to provide soft drinks and strained mono music from an outdated disco unit.

The cocky confident lads made their move first, honing in on the best looking up-front and arrogant girls. Gavin chatted confidently to his schoolmates for most of the night, avoiding the issue of talking to the girls. And then came the call for the last dance. The cocky lads and arrogant girls danced closely and sexily like they had known each other for years. Some of the shyer lads plucked up the courage to request a last dance, but most were rejected by arrogant girls who thought themselves pretty, but in reality were not. The cocky lads had made no move on them.

Gavin nervously drank some Cydrax and glanced around the room. His eyes moved past and then back to a gawky brunette with glasses standing alone. Her clothes were so plain that they almost blended into the dingy grey décor. This was Carol.

Gavin closed his eyes for a second, took a deep breath, and then walked over to his selected target.

'Would you like to dance?' Gavin spoke faintly and was only just audible.

Carol giggled and then took Gavin's hand and allowed herself to be led on to the dance floor. 'Dance Away' by Roxy Music provided the slow rhythm. The young inexperienced couple moved slowly and awkwardly in jittering rotation.

Over the following weeks, Gavin and Carol became an item. They gradually became more confident with each other and with life in general. Gavin got on famously with Carol's parents, and would spend most of his spare time at their house. They even had a special room put aside for the young couple in their large Georgian mansion, complete with sofa and television.

Carol was an only child and her parents were so immensely proud of her, wanting only the best for their golden daughter. She was sure to go to a top university, which would be the pinnacle of her father's life. It was the very evening after Carol had sat her final A-level exam that marked the change. Filled with elation, Carol felt carefree and uninhibited. Gavin fed off the mood and they both lost their virginity after nearly a year together, and in their special room.

Sensitive Gavin had no idea that his luck would be in that night and did not take precautions as the usual innocent fumbling escalated to a passion beyond return. Two shy ex-virgins were soon to become two shocked parents to be.

When Carol's dad discovered that his precious daughter was pregnant, his world suddenly collapsed. Carol had even been accepted at Cambridge and her bright future was now in jeopardy. Gavin was sent into exile and an appointment was made with a top physician. Too frightened to challenge or upset her father, Carol was soon an ex-mother to be. Gavin was powerless to act. The next time, and last time, he saw Carol was during a chance meeting at a railway station, just before she left for Cambridge. She was quiet, pale and forlorn. The same gawky Carol that Gavin had asked to dance for the first time over a year before.

Gavin did hear several months later that Carol had dropped out of university and instead left for America to be a nanny. Her father was a broken man.

Gavin thought briefly of the unborn child before flickering his eyes open to the full glare of the Cretan sunshine. His friend still lay alongside him, totally relaxed and oblivious to each other. He had never shared the secret with any of them, and probably never would.

That evening, the four friends stuck together as a unit, drinking, laughing and dancing. Nobody else mattered. They had stumbled across a small club that played anthem-like, stomping tunes. The small dance floor was soon dominated by a formation routine that basically involved lots of jumping up and down and swaying from side to side as classics such as 'Come On Eileen' and 'Whole Of The Moon' inspired a raucous sing-a-long chorus.

The only intrusion during the whole evening was the arrival of Albert, spruced up with a Hawaiian shirt undone to the navel to reveal a massive gold medallion. The sour aroma of Old Spice aftershave completed the look.

'Hey, lads, like the gear. My pulling shirt this. No matter the age, twenty-one to forty, it never fails me.' Albert had the look of a proud peacock.

Suddenly all eyes turned on Phil, who immediately looked totally indignant at the implied suggestion that Albert's pulling shirt was a parody of his own. Roars of laughter ensued, with even Phil succumbing in the end.

Albert was soon to exit after unwittingly being dragged into the lads' huddled circle as they stomped vigorously to 'Whiskey In The Jar' by the Pogues. Once the song had faded out, Albert made his escape gasping for air from a bright red face.

Week 1: Day 5 – Trying to Stay Out of Trouble

Dave rose bright and early once more and headed for breakfast at his new, already accustomed, regular café. The aromatic espresso and doughy fresh croissants were a small percentage of the attraction compared to another chance meeting with Elsie.

As Dave made his way to the Strip, another was taking the very same route. That other was Phil.

The light bustle of noise made by Dave as he steadily prepared himself to leave the room had been just sufficient to stir Phil from his sleep. With one eye flicking from open to closed to observe, Phil did not let on he was awake. Instead, as the door shut behind Dave, he quickly threw on his shorts and a T-shirt, brushed his hair and headed off in tactical pursuit and surveillance of his best mate. The tactics, however, were more Inspector Clouseau than *The Professionals* as Phil darted in and out of cover bringing puzzled looks from curious passers by. Luckily Dave was oblivious to the bumbling comical efforts in his wake.

Dave settled down at his usual spot in the café and the waiter reconfirmed his regular patron status by shouting 'the usual?' Dave nodded with a smile. He then looked expectantly towards the entrance, hoping that Elsie's heavenly body would soon be in view. Instead he did a double take as Phil's ample frame darted across and tried to find cover. Puzzled, Dave walked quickly to the entrance, and found Phil crouching by a bin.

'What the fuck are you doing, Mockley?' Dave was totally taken by surprise, and already feeling miffed that he would no longer have a free uninterrupted solo run at Elsie.

Phil knew the game was up. 'It's a fair cop,' he said whilst raising his hands up in surrender. 'Just thought I'd have a laugh and see where you were going. I didn't think it was just to have some bloody breakfast. But seeing as I'm here, I might as well join you. I could murder a coffee.'

Phil made his way into the café as Dave sighed in defeat. He could not tell him to get lost without arousing suspicion.

'I tell you what, I should be a private eye, mate. You had no idea I was following you.' Phil took a bite into a large toasted sausage and egg sandwich. 'Blimey, this is wonderful.'

Dave tutted. 'Anyway, you weren't that good 'cos I spotted you in the end. Phillip Marlow can sleep easy tonight.'

It was just then that the gorgeous Elsie walked in. She was alone as usual. Today she was wearing a very short denim mini-skirt and sleeveless white T-shirt. Her smooth tanned arms were almost as toned as her equally brown legs. Dave took a deep breath before almost deflating into a constant drool.

'Fuck me, look at that. Now would I give that one.' Phil had also spotted Elsie and was less subtle in his appreciation. Dave closed his eyes momentarily in frustration and embarrassment.

Phil was not to be shaken off, and continued in the same laddish and lecherous tone. Dave realised that this would not be the time to try and hit again on Elsie, so instead he settled the bill and ushered Phil towards the exit.

As the two friends walked out, they passed Elsie. Dave could not conceal an acknowledging smile. Elsie nodded with a mouthed 'hello'. Phil noticed the exchanged glances out of the corner of his eye, and was about to comment before Dave shoved him out of the exit and followed behind.

Phil grinned broadly. 'So that's why you come here. You were going to hit on that bird. I know you too well, Holliman, you old sly bastard. Well, don't let me cramp your style, mate. Get back in there and have a shot at goal.'

Dave shook his head. 'Nah, that would be desperate and uncool. Tomorrow, my good friend, I shall return alone. Capice?'

Phil nodded in agreement.

Gavin and Tony had ventured to a small café over the road from the hotel for breakfast. It was not a typical tourist haunt but catered more for the locals with simple fresh cuisine.

A few hotel workers were enjoying a hot drink of some description, but there was no sign of anybody to take an order. The two mates sat at a rickety old table adorned with a plastic red gingham tablecloth. A small, dog-eared menu lay in the middle of the table. Gavin identified the word omelette amongst the scribbles and both he and Tony were sold on trying the local version.

Ten minutes passed before a young Cretan girl appeared through a thin curtain at the rear of the café. She smiled at everyone individually before placing a small pepper mill on one of the tables. Gavin tried to subtly catch her eye but she did not notice him. In the end he had to 'cut her off at the pass', before she disappeared back through the curtain. After a few minutes of trying to explain what he and his friend would like to eat, the young girl finally cracked a smile and said in very shaky English, 'No problem, please sit, please.'

As Gavin turned to go back to the table, the girl laughed loudly before descending through the curtain. The other locals also began to laugh, without looking away from their newspapers or beverages. The two Englishmen were obviously the butt of some joke and had absolutely no idea why.

Fifteen minutes passed before the girl appeared again, but she did not make any move towards Gavin and Tony's table. Once again Gavin had to move quickly to intercept her. 'Will be very soon,' was the giggled polite response.

A few more locals filed in and sat huddled together at the table opposite. The girl appeared as if by magic, brandishing drinks for the new arrivals.

Gavin once again was moved into action, pleading for at least some coffees as Tony sat nonchalantly reading his book.

Fifteen minutes passed and Gavin was about to suggest giving up and moving on, when suddenly the girl re-appeared brandishing two large plates. She placed them in front of the hungry Englishmen with a sweet smile and uttered quietly, 'Enjoy.'

As she turned to go, Gavin almost screamed 'coffees' startling everyone in the vicinity. 'Very soon,' was the light giggled response.

Gavin was now feeling really stressed as he at last prepared to satisfy his hunger. In contrast, Tony gently laid his book on the table, picked up his cutlery and began to eat. He smiled at Gavin's perplexed state and shook his head. 'You see it's all manyana in the Med. Everything can wait. For once you'll just have to go with the flow.'

'Yeah, sure,' Gavin snapped as he tackled the omelette aggressively. 'Well, as you lot always remind me, I like my routines. You order, you get, you eat, you go. Simple.'

'Mmm, nice though. Worth the wait,' Tony had almost eaten everything on the plate.

Gavin nodded. 'Maybe that's the ploy. Keep you waiting and you enjoy it even more. Mind you, imagine if Mockley had been with us.'

Tony shook his head once more. 'Mockley, kept from his food! Very dangerous; lives would have been lost.'

The coffee did arrive, but ten minutes after the food was cleared. It then took another fifteen minutes to get the bill and pay, with Gavin almost thrusting his money into the girl's hand.

Wednesday was soon becoming a carbon copy of Tuesday as the four friends were reunited and soon lying by the hotel pool on parallel sunbeds. Retro music was listened to, books and magazines were read and dreamy lustful thoughts were made.

Tony volunteered to fetch some food at lunchtime from the bar and returned with four burgers and four large one-litre ice-cold lagers.

As a Campaign rule, long lunchtime drinking sessions had been avoided over the years. The idea was to conserve any energy and be ready to give it all in the evenings.

'Thought that one beer would do us no harm,' Tony was quick to excuse his weakened resolve. 'And besides, let's be different for a change and sod the rules.'

Despite some concerned grimaces, there were no outright complaints as each beer was taken.

Dave took a large gulp of beer as the hot sun simultaneously caused him to perspire. 'Ahhhhhhhh... heaven. This is a rare treat on a Campaign. The only time we've ever gone for some serious daytime beers in the past was when we caught the start of the footie season in some bar with satellite.'

There was a muffled agreement as the others devoured their beers.

'Same again?' Phil had the taste now and wanted more. Again, there were no objections. And so it went on until each had bought their round.

The alcoholic effect was quick to touch the senses, bringing on a state of over-relaxation followed by a mood of total silliness. It was then that Dave slipped from his seated position on the sunbed and crashed to the floor. Tony laughed so much that he did the same. As Dave stood up, Phil rugby tackled him firmly into the pool. Their combined weight caused such a splash that Gavin was totally drenched. It did not stop his persistent laughter as he watched Tony struggling so badly to get to his feet that he resembled Bambi on ice.

To the four inebriated Englishmen it was a perfectly normal affair within their oblivious drunken cocoon. The rest of the pool looked on as an audience, either laughing at the comedy show or through reserved English eyes tried to mask their disdain for the typical loutish Brits abroad.

Once the silly period was over, tiredness came and it descended quickly. Once more the foursome lay out in the full glare of the sun. The intense heat took no prisoners, irritating the tired numb bodies like a persistent child constantly prodding a younger sibling. Soon the mad dogs were out of the midday sun and asleep on the cool darkness of their rooms.

The early evening drink at the poolside bar was not enjoyed with the usual verve of the first drink of the day. An afternoon nap to recharge the batteries had become a slumber induced by alcoholic need.

All of the foursome were tired and jaded, but Tony was suffering like never before. He felt like he was trapped in the shell of a body with no life or spark. He had instigated the early drinking session and he was suffering the most, hardly speaking a word since getting up. Even that act had been a momentous task. The others assumed that he was just taking a long, quiet, Tony moment.

Theo was playing The Quireboys on the stereo, and giving an ecstatic and lively display of air guitar in between serving beers.

'Hey guys, maybe we should all get in a line and play air guitar. We'll look just like the Quo. Crazy.'

The sad plea was ignored and only answered with dazed expressions.

It was not until some food was eaten, at the first available beachfront restaurant, that life began to return, except for Tony. Conversation became more than a few muttered words. Tony remained silent. Colour began to return to faces. Tony remained white. Beer tasted good again. Tony stuck to coke.

As the meal was finished, Tony excused himself and headed for the toilets. Inside, he looked in the mirror and felt even worse. Suddenly he had to steady himself, as the floor seemed to rush towards him. Then it happened again. If possible, Tony turned even whiter.

'Lads. I'm going back to the room. I feel like shite, just totally dehydrated. Just got to drink water and take it easy. I'll be fine tomorrow.' Tony stood before his friends like an unsteady apparition.

'Nah, mate. You'll be all right. Have some beers and you'll soon forget about dehydration.' Phil's unsound medical advice was not heeded.

Tony left some money for his cut of the bill and walked away very slowly.

'Do you want me to walk back with you?' Gavin was concerned at Tony's unsteady steps.

'No worries, I'll be fine. Just don't be late. Early start in the morning my dear.' Tony smiled as he walked on with more confidence.

Dave and Phil were quick to find a second wind as they drank round after round of vodka and red bull. Highly energised, they both felt like dancing and headed for the first small club, called Sunbeach. Gavin left them to go for an early nightcap in the Harp, saying that he just wanted to check the details of his rendezvous with Annette.

The atmosphere inside Sunbeach was muted, as dire house music filled the air. The repetitive, annoying beat grated on Dave as he stood by the bar with Phil. As they looked around, the place was almost awash with Germans. Large Bavarian lads with sad mullet haircuts and a uniform of white T-shirts and jeans jumped up and down with no rhythm or purpose. From the sidelines a group of miserable Teutonic girls looked on with blank expressions.

Dave's eyes moved across the scene, before he suddenly blinked and refocused on an approaching figure. A man dressed in bright orange knee length shorts and matching orange vest was waving at Dave and Phil as he came to greet them. It was Gareth, the Welshman from the hotel.

'Hi guys,' Gareth's voice boomed above the house beat. 'I've had a bit of a barney with the missus. Thought I'd best get out and let things cool down. So I thought why not have a bit of fun with you boyos.'

'How did you know we would be here?' Dave's surprise was as genuine as his concern.

'Well, see I really just went for a pint at the Irish bar. I bumped into your mate. He was chatting up the barmaid good and proper and I think he thought I was cramping his style like. He said you'd be down here and would be up for a laugh. Anyway, let me get you boyos some beers,' Gareth shot over to the bar.

'Gavin. *Bastard*!' Phil whispered.

Dave looked concerned. 'Yeah, this is going to cramp our style. I mean what's he bloody wearing. Let's drink this beer pretty lively and get out of here somehow.'

Gareth was quick to return with three bottled lagers. 'Down your necks, boys.'

Despite good intentions, Dave and Phil found it almost impossible to flee form Gareth. They even felt pity at proposing such a cruel trick, although that pity was severely tested as Gareth vigorously threw himself about on the dance floor whilst performing some early Wham dance moves at frantic speed.

Phil shook his head at the remnants of a dire evening. He suddenly felt a finger prodding his shoulder and his night was about to get a lot worse.

Phil turned to be faced with two of the very large German girls who had chased him in his pulling shirt on Monday night. His eyes almost shut tight in agony.

'Hello,' said the small dark haired fat girl. Her accent only just coped with the simple English pronunciation. Her equally small fat friend giggled. Together they looked like a pair of oversized weebles.

The giggling continued as Phil and Dave responded with awkward smiles. A language barrier was not about to be broken. The standoff ended when a very sweaty Gareth came barging between his two new friends, flaying a wet encompassing arm over each of their shoulders. Dave and Phil spun to grimace at the same time.

'Hey boyos, who's the totty?' Gareth licked his lips as Dave and Phil's faces contorted further.

'Come and dance my lovelies,' Gareth reached out two sweaty palms and took the two weebles' small round hands. He led them to the dance floor, but glanced back. 'Hey, you don't mind do you? Not stepping on your toes, am I?'

'*Noooooooo*,' was the emphatic chorused response as both Phil and Dave raised their hands to concede.

Gareth danced with vigour once again as the weebles literally rocked from side to side. Phil and Dave looked on dumbfounded. Shock was soon to take over as Gareth winked at them both before waving goodbye and herding the weebles towards the exit.

Almost to the second that they disappeared from view, Phil felt another tap on his shoulder. He turned to be faced by two even fatter and taller German weebles.

'Where your friend go with our friends?' the largest of the two new weebles adopted a very aggressive interrogation mode.

'Uh… not sure. Fresh air, I think, very hot in here, isn't it?' was Phil's reactive reply.

'He will not touch them,' the stern weeble got even sterner.

Phil reassuringly shook his head. 'Oh no, he's married.'

The weebles looked puzzled.

'You know, married!' Phil slotted his right index finger through a looped finger on his left hand to signify a wedding ring.

The big weeble suddenly became so infuriated that flames almost came out of her nostrils. With great speed and accuracy she suddenly punched Phil flush on his left cheek. He toppled backwards with the force, and the weebles set off in pursuit of Gareth and their friends.

'What the fuck was that for?' Phil was rubbing an already glowing red cheek. The Mullets suddenly cheered and jibed as an audience to the scene from the dance floor.

Dave calmly explained it from his viewpoint. 'Well you were never any good at charades. The finger and the ring was very good... I got it... but I think they might have just been thinking cock and fanny... only a thought... maybe they thought you were saying that Gareth was off for a good shag... could be. Either that or they just hate weddings.'

Week 1: Day 6 – Didn't We Have a Lovely Time

Dave and Phil both woke later than usual. Dave had opened his eyes on a few occasions and checked the time through blurry eyes. He contemplated getting up and heading for the café and another crack at Elsie but decided to grant his energy-less body some needed recuperation. Phil slept soundly on the other side of the room.

It was nearly eleven before the two friends moved from their beds to the poolside for a full English breakfast. Two large plates of fried delights were devoured under the constant burning morning sun.

Tony and Gavin had left the hotel some two and a half hours ago, en route for the picturesque town of Archanes. Although it was the beauty of Annette, rather than the backdrop of fruit trees and quaint houses, that was at the forefront of Gavin's mind.

Dave and Phil soon took respite out of the morning humidity and instead supped cold mineral water under a large parasol. A couple walked past.

'Hey, Gareth, you all right, mate?' Phil suddenly recognised the man wearing garish and worn Bermuda shorts and top.

Gareth did not reply but gave an awkward smile in recognition, turning a little red with embarrassment in the process. Cheryl glared at him like an owner would view a chastised dog. Gareth was quick to be called to heel and followed his miserable wife to a couple of sunloungers on the other side of the pool. They both sat down and looked ahead without uttering a single word, or turning to acknowledge the other.

'Marriage, eh? Who wants it? You just end up trapped. A real prison without bars,' Phil smacked his lips.

'Not all couples end up like those two. It just means it has to be right. You can't seriously ever want to get married.' Dave was ready to put the case for the defence.

'Not yet, not by a long shot. When I'm much older maybe.

Just want to live a little, not get tied up in some bloody routine life. I don't want my life organised. I just want the freedom to make my own choices.' Phil was sounding almost passionate.

'Bollocks.' Dave discarded the eloquent approach. 'Your life is already in routine. You work, you eat, you drink, you have the odd, very rare, shag.'

Phil was now affronted. 'I do all right and I can choose. I don't have to stick with one girl.'

'Okay, when was your last shag?' Dave pointed sternly at Phil.

Phil was taken aback. 'Quite recently... Mmm, can't even remember her name.'

Dave grinned. 'You haven't done it for ages, have you? I know 'cos you used to brag about every fucking conquest you ever made.'

Phil looked beaten. 'Okay, okay, it's been a while. Just going through a lean spell.'

'And that's it, mate. You ain't the old go and get 'em, Mockley. You're now thirty-five. We're all heading for forty. We should all be bloody married with kids and just meeting up down the pub on a Sunday lunchtime. Yes, we all have the freedom to live our lives, but the thing is we do sod all about it. And for that reason we can't be that critical of the married blokes whose lives are supposedly over.'

Phil shook his head vigorously. 'Now come on, where's the old rebel Holliman, ready to take on the world? What about the Campaign? Isn't that a sign of our extended youth?'

Dave flung his head back momentarily and looked upwards before re-focusing on Phil. 'Mate, the Campaign is now the very epitome of our sad lives. Four thirtysomething men, with dreary monotonous lives, trying to recapture their youth for two weeks every year. Haven't you noticed, we're just old men in kiddie territory. If we carry on we'll end up like Albert in his sad disco gear. In fact, come to think of it, we're probably already there in the eyes of some.'

Phil was now speechless.

Dave continued in a calmer voice. 'I think that we should all take stock of our lives and challenge where we are going. And if we are all together on another bloody Campaign next year, then I suggest that we have failed.'

Dave stood up and headed for the sunbeds, armed with his trusty personal stereo. Phil pondered. He knew Dave was right. In fact the anti-marriage talk was a total façade. A real front. In reality Phil wanted nothing more than to settle down and find security. He just feared that it was getting further from his reach now.

Tony and Gavin were also chatting over a coffee at around the same time, as they sat outside a small café in a tree-shaded terrace. The day had so far been relaxing in the extreme away from the cosmopolitan beach life and bustle of Hersonissos. Archanes by comparison was quiet and sedate, inviting a gentle stroll around cobbled back streets to look in small shops and to enjoy the picture-postcard look of the small houses and tavernas. Clusters of small vineyards, prompting Tony to buy a bottle of local wine as soon as he spotted one, had highlighted the short journey in. The busload of holidaymakers had been given a very brief tour of the village with running commentary. Most of the guide's speech, delivered by a local man in pigeon English, had completely by-passed Gavin and Tony. Although, Gavin did become more attentive during a stop at an archaeological dig. He had become an avid viewer of *Time Team* at home.

'Blimey, this guy can talk for England and Crete put together. I wish he would give it a rest and let us go our own way now,' Tony wiped some sweat from his brow as he spoke to Gavin with his back to the group.

'Uh, yeah… but all very interesting never the less,' Gavin looked flustered and grimaced hard at Tony.

Tony swung around to see the guide grinning at him.

'Anyway… time to let you explore. You have one and half-hours before we meet here at 1 p.m. Then we have lunch. A wonderful local lamb dish. Enjoy.'

Tony now felt guilty, but surely the guide had not heard him.

At the café, Gavin felt totally at ease. Even Tony had forgotten about the worries over his job and his burning desire to change his life's direction.

'Mmm… I wonder what it would be like to really settle here. Buy a nice little house, become accepted by the locals, get a job as a guide maybe. Of course I'd have to kit out my house with satellite so I don't miss home too much. Wonder if I'd have the balls.' Gavin was comfortable with the dream more than if it was reality.

'Yeah, maybe, with the lovely Annette by your side. You could carve out a niche. A nice little easy going routine.' Tony could never see it happening.

'What about you, Tone? Fancy it? You could become an estate agent out here.' Gavin already knew the answer.

Tony did think for a moment. 'Nah. Funny enough I did seriously think what it would be like to work out here, but I think if I were to live abroad it would have to be either New York or Dublin. A sort of English lifestyle and snow at Christmas.'

'Sad Muppet. And I'm the one who gets slaughtered for being set in my ways,' Gavin stopped and grinned. 'Maybe I'll change all that and move out here just to prove a point,' he said.

Tony wanted to take time out from this conversation. 'Yeah right... let's see how you get on tonight first.'

Back in Hersonissos, Dave and Phil had moved from just lolling around to actually taking some exercise. Dave had got talking to a young couple in the pool, who mentioned that they had played tennis at a nearby hotel. To break the routine, and to sweat out a deluge of alcohol, Dave had persuaded Phil to take him on. They subsequently wandered down to the hotel with the court on the off chance, although Phil felt confident that someone would be playing. If Dave then managed to book for another time, he would have the chance to come up with a suitable excuse. Fane a twisted ankle, claim sunstroke. Anything to escape serious exercise.

Unfortunately for Phil the court was free and the hotel receptionist was happy to oblige with the hire of rackets and balls.

'Superb, I really though that it would be booked out,' Dave almost snatched the rackets in his eagerness to play.

The receptionist laughed. 'This time is always very quiet. We do not have many English guests, but I now know it is true what Noel Coward sang yes? Mad dogs, eh?'

'Eh?' Phil was lost.

The penny had dropped quickly with Dave. 'Phil, I think it's going to be hot out there, mate.'

Sure enough the parched red clay court sat out on its own without any shade or cover. The sun was high in the sky above, and it was almost as if it was concentrating all of its efforts on this one small patch of land.

Phil was already sweating by the time he had walked to the back of the court. The heat made him feel tired as he made feeble efforts to play some practice rallies. Dave, on the other hand, was a more natural player. When he was younger he had even played to county level. Although Dave had not played for a while, all the natural ability was still there. And it was going to have a chance to really shine against the unhealthy and unathletic specimen that faced him.

Phil could now feel the sweat dripping from his face, stinging his eyes and blurring his vision in the glare of the day. As he looked down the sweat was dripping on to the ground, but was drying up instantly as it hit the burning clay. The Noel Coward statement was now clear and replaying in his mind.

When a game finally ensued, Dave wiped the floor with his unfit opponent. Phil's only weapon was to cheat with the odd dodgy line call. Dave knew the truth but just ensured that he won the point straight after. A younger, although fitter, Phil had been just the same during their adolescence.

With the match over, and Dave having won without dropping a game, the two players offloaded their hired rackets and ran straight into the nearby sea. The feel of the cool water on very tired and sweaty bodies was relief in the extreme.

Refreshed, Dave and Phil sat by the water's edge.

'Tennis is such a great game. A real icon of summer. I should play more often,' Dave felt much healthier after some exercise.

'Yeah, well you can play one of the others next time.' Phil felt knackered.

Dave laughed at his friend's almost permanent bright red complexion. 'The thing is I love playing the game but there's just so much snobbery attached to it. I used to play for a club but to earn the right to play on the top court was all about social standing rather than just being a good player. I wanted to play at school but you could only do so if were bad at cricket or athletics. No wonder it's taken so long to produce any decent English players.'

'I played at school,' the underlying meaning of his statement was lost on Phil. 'And I enjoy watching Wimbledon. Well, actually I used to but it's a bit boring these days. They're all bloody robots. We need more players like Borg, Connors and McEnroe.'

'Yeah, you're right. Sport relies on characters. I remember trying to serve like Roscoe Tanner. He was like Steve Austin.' Dave stood up to try and mimic the action.

'All sports need icons. I mean rowing got major interest because of Steve Redgrave. The decathlon got loads of focus when Daley Thompson was going strong. Beckham's a superstar and can sell the game because he's a great player and has got an image. Guscott did it for rugby and even Hurricane Higgins made snooker exciting to watch. Tennis just doesn't have it now. You might as well watch crown green bowls.' Phil could have been on a soapbox.

'You sound like that guy from *The Royle Family*, and of course you are the ultimate armchair fan. Pity that they didn't teach that at school. They could have called it sport appreciation.'

'And I would have got A plus, mate.' Phil raised a clenched fist.

The arranged lunch in Archanes was pleasant enough. Tony and Gavin mingled with couples and families, inclusive of very bored pre-teen children. A lamb dish, as promised, and a fresh colourful salad were enjoyed on a small picturesque terrace.

Once the time arrived to meet Annette at the designated spot, Gavin ensured that he was there without a minute to spare either way. He had already checked the location several times and almost knew every feasible route within Archanes to the destination. Tony joined him for now as he still had an hour before the bus would take him back to Hersonissos.

As it is every woman's prerogative, Annette was a few minutes late. It was literally that but had still prompted several nervous glances from Gavin to his watch. Tony smiled as his friend squirmed.

'Well there yer are. And hello, Tony,' Annett beamed her usual welcome.

The trio enjoyed a drink in a nearby bar before Tony was sent on his way to the bus with a less than subtle wink from Gavin. Tony boarded and took a seat at the front. He then watched Gavin stroll away with Annette, and although he wished his friend well, he longed for a similar break in fortune. Instead he pulled out a personal stereo and sat back to enjoy some upbeat music to lift his mood. A collection of reggae full of summer vibe.

Gavin and Annette returned to the same bar that they had just left with Tony. This time, instead of sitting up at the bar, they found a secluded table in the corner. Both drank Guinness and were provided with constant refills by the barman, who was a friend of Annette's. In fact everyone in Archanes seemed to be a friend of Annette's, from the locals who greeted the couple en route to every customer venturing into the bar for a drink.

'So what prompted you to live here?' Gavin was keen to know more about Annette's background.

'Why not?' Annette's responded with her usual deep smile. 'And I suppose that has always been my philosophy. Let me ask you a similar question. What's prompted you not to live in a place like this?'

'Now that's a good question,' Gavin searched for a suitable answer. 'I guess because I've never had the nerve. Part of me would love to jack it all in and change everything. A bit like that film with Tony Hancock when he goes to Paris to become an artist. But it's the fear of change, I suppose. My mates all think that I'm stuck in one big routine and I'd be tempted to do it just to shut them up. Just to see the look on their faces.'

'And then they would remain in their own routines. What makes them any different to you?' Annette signalled to settle the bill.

Gavin nodded his head. All his mates were stuck in a rut and tied to a routine. 'Yeah, you're right. We're all the wrong side of thirty-five and stuck in jobs that will simply take us to retirement, with no real thrills on the way. None of us are married and every year seems to merge into the next without change. Bloody hell, we're like those hamsters running on a continuously moving wheel. In the words of David Byrne, on the road to nowhere.'

'Easy, tiger. I think we should away and have something to eat.

Come and try some real Irish cooking and hospitality in my little Cretan home.' Annette stood up and motioned towards the exit.

Gavin's whole body felt electric with anticipation and excitement. 'Not 'arf.'

In Hersonissos, Tony had reunited with Dave and Phil. All three smirked as they downed a beer by the pool and toasted Gavin's proposed night of passion.

'Where's your friend?' Theo was puzzled and a little concerned.

'He has a date with a beautiful lady.' Dave framed the statement by raising his eyebrows.

Theo smiled. 'I see. A beautiful lady. You say in English lucky bugger, yeah?'

The lads stared back with a slight grimace.

'Albert, he teaches me some odd English sayings from oop north.' Theo added the final words with an awful attempt at a northern English accent. 'Anyway, he may have a beautiful lady but he has missed out on Kiss, hey. But I play for you and we can rock this joint.'

Theo turned to set the music system in motion and within seconds 'Hotter Than Hell' was blasting into the night. He turned as if he was Gene Simmons, sticking out his tongue and holding a high air guitar pose.

The lads had gone.

Annette's small villa was a chic but cosy abode, mixing European style and precision with the warmth of an Irish welcome.

Gavin had made himself at home in the lounge, sprawled on a large deep sofa. To his right the French windows opened into the clear night, revealing a small but adequate balcony. The sparse lights of dotted small villas shone brightly below sharp glowing stars. Gavin was nicely full after a good helping of chicken salad and a bottle of red wine. Annette was fixing him her very own special Irish coffee.

The smell of strong Irish whiskey far outweighed the aroma of coffee as Annette appeared with two very large glasses. Gavin breathed deeply as he looked beyond at an ample display of cleavage heaving from Annette's low cut blouse. This night was going to be special.

'There you go, my man, that will put lead in your pencil,' Annette sat alongside Gavin, sliding her body against him as she did so.

Gavin blushed very slightly at the sexual reference. The Irish coffee was incredibly potent, with the strong aroma not betraying its strength. Gavin felt warmed, relaxed and totally confident in an instant. His back unhunched any tension and settled back into the sofa. Annette just smiled.

'This is great. Wow, I feel so good,' Gavin looked straight into Annette's hazel eyes.

'That's good. You enjoy. There's no rush. We have the night,' Annette sunk back into the sofa.

The couple took their time enjoying each strong mouthful of whiskey infused caffeine. Gavin was well known for being able to hold his drink. He could drink as many pints as the next man and hardly change mood or expression. But right now he felt very drunk. He didn't want to eat fast food, go to a club or try some ridiculous stunt. He just felt really good in the wonder of the moment.

Annette reached over and took Gavin's glass just as he nearly slid on to the floor. Gavin looked across into a valley of cleavage as the edges of Annette's large breast moved with regular motion of her heartbeat. As he looked up, Annette's face was now inches away and her ruby red lips made first contact seconds later. Another rush of sexual anticipation swept through Gavin's body.

The couple kissed and cavorted for an eternity, but no clothes were removed.

Annette finally moved her lips away. 'Want to make love under the stars,' she nodded towards the balcony and Gavin followed her gaze. 'The sunbed mattresses saves you from the cold floor and the neighbours mind their own business.'

Annette led a dumbstruck and non-resistant Gavin towards the night. His crotch was so tight he almost could not walk.

On the small dimly lit balcony an almost silhouetted Annette laid two large blue mattresses on the floor and delicately placed some fluffy large towels on top of them. She then beckoned

Gavin forward whilst remaining on her knees. As he moved next to her, Annette slowly undid Gavin's belt and lowered his trousers. A huge erection almost stretched his grey boxer shorts to breaking point. Annette moved up Gavin's body, rubbing against his proud and unrelenting cock. She instantly pulled off his T-shirt and kissed his chest before pushing him down towards the makeshift bed.

As Gavin lay down, Annette performed a slow and voluptuous striptease. First she removed her blouse to reveal a very low cut white bra that just about contained two huge breasts. The bra soon went to reveal a pair of tits that were large but well proportioned to Annette's curvy full figure. Gavin's eyes became so fixated on the large brown aortas that he hardly noticed as Annette removed the rest of her clothes. As she moved forward, Gavin's eyes moved to a very dark and bushy mound of pubic hair. He almost had to catch his breath as he felt the warmth of her pussy move down his chest.

Annette expertly removed Gavin's overworked boxer shorts and pushed him down. With great dexterity she placed a conveniently produced condom on his stiff cock and instantly perched herself on the erection, sliding her pussy lips down the shaft. Gavin looked up in ecstasy and placed his hands on the large warm breasts. Annette began to jerk and moan as the stars looked down.

The moment seemed to last forever, and Gavin so much wished it would. As he finally climaxed, his loud moans chorused in time with Annette's scream of passion. Both then collapsed in drunken and orgasmic exhaustion. Annette pulled a blanket from the patio table and covered their naked bodies. The couple huddled together and fell asleep without uttering a word.

Week 1: Day 7 – Anyone for a Barbie?

It was mid morning before Annette drove Gavin back to Hersonissos. A satisfying morning shag, followed by a full Irish breakfast, had preceded the journey. Gavin now felt calm and relaxed as he gazed out of the window at the sparse Cretan countryside. Annette was chatting away as an Irish folk compilation played on the stereo.

Annette dropped Gavin at the hotel and they agreed to meet again on Sunday night for a meal. Gavin decided to keep this next date to himself for now. Anyway, there were three of them and they would have done okay without him last night.

The other three were strewn across sunbeds at the usual location by the pool. 'Bloody routine,' Gavin muttered to himself.

Dave was listening to a Jam compilation CD on his personal stereo. Once again he had meant to rise early for breakfast and have another crack at Elsie. Once again he had fallen back into slumber after being momentarily woken by the faint beep of a travel alarm clock. When he awoke again it was too late. Even Phil was up and singing Janet Jackson's 'All For You' badly in the shower.

The song was stuck in Phil's brain from the previous night. Gavin had missed a very uneventful evening as his friends mooched around a few half-filled clubs. As Gavin and Annette reached an orgasm in unison, the three friends sat in subdued silence gazing into space as techno dance tracks filled the air. By the time they turned in for the night, they all felt sober and bored. It was only midnight, and so an early night at that. Even Phil did not push for more. Given the early night, Dave was even more miffed at missing his chance at going for Elsie.

Phil was writing postcards home. He was already on number twelve. This was an obsessive ritual with Phil as every year he would send in the region of twenty postcards to let everyone he knew know what a great time he was having, even if he was not.

Tony was reading book number three, *The Man On Platform Five* by Robert Llewelyn. He was totally lost in it and oblivious to the other two as they were to him. In fact, they were all oblivious to the beaming Gavin as he stood with a large smile on an obviously unshaven face.

Dave spotted him first and stopped his stereo as 'Town Called Malice' faded out. 'Hey, lover boy, how was it for you?'

Dave's shout alerted Tony and Phil, who both looked up to greet the returning conqueror. It was as if Gavin, the man of routine, was now their saviour to break the routine. He was the man of the moment.

There was a smugness written all over Gavin's face, but he was not the type to betray his elation further by verbally boasting of the previous night's passion. The others knew that, and respected him for it, but it did not stop the odd hopeful stab at gleaming some juicy titbits.

Gavin found himself a sunbed and flopped onto it, relaxing every taut and excited muscle as he laid-back squinting his eyes in the morning sun. Dave settled back down whilst Tony looked on in awe and Phil with pure jealousy. It was the end of the first week of the Campaign and only Phil and Tony were yet to taste any kind of carnal pleasure. With Tony that was just as expected.

Gavin stood up briefly and positioned a parasol to create some cooling shade. Once it was firmly in place, he fell back on the sunbed, closed his eyes, and thought back to the night before. Annette's face and her full naked figure filled every inch of the imaging part of his brain. Deep and pleasurable sleep followed within minutes.

Phil gritted his teeth as Gavin fell into carefree sleep. He decided to concentrate his mind on something else and go back to the obligatory postcards home. Of all the lads, Phil was now the only one to retain the urge to dispatch numerous postcards back to Blighty. In the early days it was a regular Campaign team exercise to sit and scribble short, very unliterary classics to all and sundry. The passion had waned over the years until even Dave could barely be bothered to send a rude postcard to the office. In fact that pleasure had already been long removed by new political correct times and a stringent HR department.

In the early nineties there was an annual competition as to who could send the filthiest postcard back to Mutual Life. Anyone who ventured abroad, or even on a family holiday to Devon, would join in. As Europe became even more risqué, the scenes and intimation of the cards became more pornographic. Full nudity and slogans like 'save mice, eat pussy' became as common as 'wish you were here'. It was not long before cards started arriving in brown envelopes, censored by executives concerned at unsettling diverse sensibilities. Soon the day of the smutty card was over. Dave even innocently sent a card showing a couple of pretty girls lying on a beach as a donkey paddled by the shore. It took a lot of explaining as to how he had not actually spotted the donkey's large and obvious erection. A verbal warning was very narrowly avoided.

To Dave the tradition of the postcard was no longer any fun. No longer rebellious or juvenile. It was just like the rise and fall of the strip-a-gram. So normal and commonplace in the late eighties that there was hardly a bar, pub, or office reception, that did not have someone of either gender removing every inch of their cheap costume. Camera's clicked as everything from baby oil to whips came into play. At Mutual Life they even had a senile-a-gram for a secretary on her twenty-fifth birthday. The sight of an eighty-year-old withered and wrinkly naked man was not a sight that Dave chose to remember with fondness. Particularly as it included a semi-erection. Political correctness, and common taste and decency, soon condemned such sexual exhibitionism in the workplace to the past.

The smut of the postcard had been replaced by the technological efficiency of the e-mail and the pure voyeurism brought out by the strip-a-gram has been substituted by the never-ending supply of porn on the Internet. Dave now regularly received e-cards from colleagues making use of global cyber cafés.

For a man of ritual, Gavin had never really shared a passion for sending cards. He had no strong family ties bar his brother, and would often just follow tradition for the sake of it by telling his workmates that the weather was great and he was constantly pissed on lager, but could not wait to get home for a real pint. Tony had always written to his parents, but his mum constantly joked about how he was always home before the card and kept telling him not to bother. In the end he decided to heed the advice.

Phil was the extreme opposite and by some way at the other end of the postcard-sending spectrum. From the very first Campaign he had sent numerous cards from everyone to his hairdresser to his Nan to Zak's kebab shop by proxy from all the lads. By this, the fourteenth Campaign, Phil was not going to change his ways.

A large wad of carefully selected cards lay under Phil's sunbed, chosen with each recipient in mind. Zak's showed several bronzed bikini clad gorgeous women and would soon take pride of place in the shop, and give Phil something to ogle at every Friday night when he ordered his Zenith. Jo, his hairdresser, would receive a nice romantic shot of Hersonissos bay. It represented his desire to score with the outgoing crimper, who cheekily listened to the ups and downs of Phil's one-dimensional life with apparent interest. Down to earth quips delivered with a big smile was all the tonic that Phil needed during his monthly cut. The lads at work would get a party scene full of gorgeous girls once again. And so it went on, right through to the boring scenic view of Crete for his Nan.

Like the pictures on the front, the narrative on the back was edited for its target audience. Basically the message was the same to all, telling of Phil's capacity to party non-stop, his constant magnetic attraction to every pretty girl in town and all against the backdrop of a tropical climate. The last bit was pretty much true.

With complete poetic licence, Phil became the ultimate stud to every male friend, the hopeless and faithful romantic to his hairdresser and the cheeky chappie to his Nan. Life delivered by post was rose-tinted on arrival but a dead-end and mundane in reality. The pathos was completed by the fact that every reader knew the truth.

Friday soon melted away under the ever-increasing furnace of the Cretan climate. Sunbathing, swimming, reading, eating and listening to music were the simple components of a programme called busy doing nothing. No one complained. The late afternoon siesta was the one remaining formality before the evening's festivity and the final break in business as usual.

Dave was the only one to break ranks and ditch his regular nap. He had decided that it was only fair, and much easier from afar, to tell Sally it was over before it had ever really begun. As he stood in a small open phone kiosk, Dave did contemplate abandoning the idea. Maybe he should just not call at all and ignore her upon his return until the message was clear. Trouble was Dave was no bastard and that meant he could not be a coward either.

The phone rang for an age and the call was nearly abandoned altogether until a familiar chirpy voice almost shouted 'Hello' down the line.

'Oh hi, Sal. It's Dave. I was just thinking that you might be out.'

'Oh hi... no... but I have just got in,' Sally sounded equally as coy as Dave.

After a few shared niceties comparing the awful English summer to life in the Med, Dave decided to move the conversation quickly on to their relationship.

'So, are you missing me or have you had time to think that maybe the older guy's not for me.' Dave closed his eyes as he tried to soften the words and the blow as best he could.

Sally gave a little nervous giggle. 'Um, well Dave, you're a lovely guy right. And we had a breeze right? But...'

Dave's eyes opened wide. Maybe Sally was going to dump him first. 'But... please go on.'

'Well, don't take this the wrong way,' Sally breathed heavily, 'it's just that I want to go out and explore life. Live it to the full. That's why I chose midwifery. I can qualify, and then I can go anywhere. That's the beauty, every country needs midwives.'

'And I thought that it was because you fancied doctors,' Dave interrupted.

'Uh, well that sort of leads into part two.' Sally paused and then delivered a blunt report. 'There's this new Australian doctor called Brad started at the hospital and we've just clicked. He's a real surf dude with curly blond hair. We're the same age and...'

'It's time to give the old man the heave-ho. Message understood,' Dave felt relieved, but also now slightly pissed off.

'I knew you'd understand,' Sally also sounded relieved. 'You're a great guy and fun to be with, but your youth is sort of over and mine's just begun. You're happy with middle-aged conformity and I'm nowhere near ready for it. We had great sex and… now I'm rambling. Listen I'll send you some cool postcards from Bondie to keep you going through the English winters.'

The call ended amicably, just like the short-lived relationship. However, Dave now felt low. It was not the fact that he had been dumped as he was going to do the same. It was the fact that in so many words he had just been labelled a middle-aged fart whose life was now destined for nightly cups of Horlicks enjoyed in a cardigan and slippers.

Dave did not head back to the hotel but instead went and sat on the beach. The crowds had now departed as the sun began to set in the clear evening sky. The air was nicely warm and the sea rippled gently to the shore. From where he sat Dave threw the odd pebble into the clear water.

'Well if it isn't the conforming rebel.'

Dave was shaken from his dreamy disposition and turned to see the angelic Elsie standing above him. She almost looked glamorous in a mauve blouse and knee-length black suede skirt. Her tanned brown legs and arms once again held prominence, topped only by a flawless cherubic face. Elsie's hair looked like it had just been washed and had an almost golden tint within the brunette tussles that cascaded down the side of each pronounced cheek. The early evening sun lit up and framed every inch of Dave's idyll.

'Oh God, don't you start.' Dave reacted with an apparent disinterest whilst his eyes remained fully focussed on a slim pair of brown legs as they crouched beside him. His body tingled with a rush of full-blooded excitement as Dave caught a glimpse of bright white knickers as Elsie completed her position to sit down.

'Oooh, do I detect a little holiday frustration? Maybe the young girls aren't taking the bait these days and the handsome boy cannot get a bonk, wondering if his pulling days are finally at an end. Time to settle down with the bank manager's plain and simple daughter or the secretary desperate to have kids. Am I right?' Although she was obviously mocking Dave, for all it was worth, Elsie seemed ready to genuinely shoot the breeze.

'Claire Rayner you are not.' Dave decided to hit back with a child-like jibe by adding 'hippy girl' like a fourth former irritated by the teacher's pet.

The approach worked as Elsie almost fell backwards as she laughed. 'Oh I take it all back. I would even assume that you must be the offspring of Oscar Wilde's love child if he had been that way inclined. You are at least a well-read man who can debate with the best of them.'

'Oh yes, I'm known as Dave the great orator down our way... or was that Dave the great orang-utan on account of my legendry body hair?'

Elsie grinned. 'So anyway. As one anteater said to the other anteater, why the long face?'

Dave had to think quickly as he did not want to come across as some saddo about to have a mid-life crisis. 'Uh, no reason. Just chilling out. Maybe I'm just bored of the usual lad's holiday routine... just looking for some personal space.'

'Aha, fair enough. You seem to like a lot of personal space, what with the solo breakfasts. Not a mid-life crisis is it?' Elsie noted Dave's rueful reaction. 'Sorry, shut up Claire Rayner,' a mocking self slap of the wrist followed.

'No, the breakfasts were just so I could tap off with you,' Dave truthfully showed his lads' colours.

'Oh that's fine, fair enough,' Elsie laughed, thinking he was joking. 'So what are you all about... Dave isn't it?'

'Yeah, Dave Holliman.' Dave was impressed that she had remembered 'and you're ... Elsie,' Dave thought that the hesitant pause would be cool.

'Yeah, Elsie Roundbottom... but it's not true,' Elsie slightly lifted her backside to prove a point.

Dave sniggered like an impressionable schoolboy learning about reproduction in biology. 'Wow, are you sure that you're not a Charles Dickens character?'

'Ha, ha, very funny. So anyway, what makes you tick, Dave Holliman?'

'Well,' Dave hesitated and searched hard for a suave but poignant response before opting for the truth. 'As the Irish say, I just want to have a good craic. Yes, my job and my average week is pretty mundane, but whose life is any different really? I'm not rich and need to work to earn the money to have the good craic. It's the most common life syndrome. One big eternal circle.'

Elsie gently bit her upper lip. 'Well, you see if you were married with kids, I could agree. But you're not, are you?' Dave shook his head. 'And that is the mystery to me. If you really wanted to attack life then go and see the world. To quote a cliché, it really is your oyster. And to sound all "hippy girl" for a moment, you're as free to roam as those waves that visit the world's shores. Life really is a beach, man,' Elsie held up each hand to demonstrate a stereotypical victory sign of love and peace.

'So what about Elsie Roundbottom? What's your background and what gave you the guts to challenge conformity?'

'Well actually,' Elsie grimaced as if about to make a confession. 'Would you believe I'm a bank manager's daughter who trained to be a secretary?'

Dave looked incredulous and intrigued. 'And…'

'Well,' Elsie continued. 'I got a job as a holiday rep to be different. I was teasing about being a secretary, which was just my ambition as a kid for some odd reason. Stupid what you dream of when you're young.'

'Yeah, I wanted to be an astronaut. Anyway, so I suppose being a bank manager's daughter was also bollocks.' Dave was disgruntled at being gullible.

'Oh no, that's true… well sort of; he was a chief executive of a high street bank. Mr Anthony Roundbottom. A cool guy actually, despite the job.' Elsie thought for a moment as she visualised her loving dad. 'I was a real daddy's girl and he was a real rebel despite his pin stripe, but family life and my mum brought country estate conformity. Anyway, as you would doubtless say, I copped out of all that and studied media studies rather than languages or literature. My mother was appalled, but got used to it, so I jacked it in and became a holiday rep. Getting the job was like taking a showbiz audition, so the media studies came in handy. I passed and was posted to the Costa Brava. It was a real laugh. The money was awful but that's not why I did it. It was just one big party in the sun, with hardly any sleep and people living life like the world was about to end.'

Dave interrupted sarcastically. 'Not to mention the important paperwork, airport duty, and never-ending customer service duties. Right on,' before raising a Citizen Smith type fist in the air and just falling short of shouting 'power to the people'.

Elsie nodded to concede. 'Okay, okay, very true. But the point is, I met people wanting to see life. They travelled the world working the bars or any old job they could find. Or they moved from resort to resort, including the ski centres, only returning to the UK for a quick hello to jealous friends and relatives.'

'So you decided to become one of the wandering people and what did chief executive Mr Roundbottom make of his daughter's escapades?' Dave thought he had found just another rebel daughter defying her dad's wishes.

'Oh he was so jealous, and so cool about it. Unlike Mummy. Poor upper-class, conservative with a capital C, Mummy. Her weekly highlight has always been a coffee morning circle with her friends from the WI.'

'And so you are destined to travel the world for eternity. A free spirit never to be tamed.' Dave was now very sceptical.

Elsie screwed her face slightly. 'The free spirit can always be reigned in a little, and I know I will settle down one day. I do not know where or with whom because my life is not predetermined. I might even have children. And when I die I'll be there with this big knowing grin on my face to say, "Yeah, I did it all."'

'So you think I should just give up my job and see the light. The gospel according to Elsie Roundbottom. Give it up, grow a goatee and travel the world.'

'In a word, yes,' Elsie could not see any argument against.

Dave was far from convinced. 'So what next? I go home, resign, sell or rent my flat and then…?'

'Well,' Elsie moved closer to Dave and almost whispered. 'Before you buy, try the goods. Meet me at the Sunstrip café on Sunday at 8 a.m. and I'll think of a little taster of life on the road. Don't ask me where we'll go because I do not yet know. Exciting, yes? That is the beauty of this life,' Elsie considered for a moment. 'To think I only came over to take the mickey out of an ageing gigolo for a bit of sport. Maybe you'll prove to be all right after all. First appearances, eh?'

'Thanks for that. I feel great now,' Dave stared into Elsie's wide and enthusiastic eyes. 'Well, as long as you're not some serial killer hell-bent on murdering all ageing gigolos, you've got a deal.'

Elsie stood up to go, pulling her stretched skirt back down over two tanned thighs. 'See you on Sunday, then.' She turned to go before adding 'promise not to be too upset if I do stab you in a passionate clinch and leave you by the roadside. Decapitated penis in hand is my usual calling card.'

Dave shivered slightly, 'Bloody hell.'

By the time Dave returned to the hotel, the SunRay reps were already preparing the poolside for the weekly barbeque. The unmistakable scent of burning charcoal already filled the air as smoke bellowed out from the far corner. Patio tables and chairs had been hastily arranged in clusters around the pool.

Four or five male reps were goofing around by the pool as they prepared a large bucket of punch. One particularly loud Cockney rep was acting like the haphazard concoction had gone straight to his head. Every few seconds he would try and push one of the other male reps into the pool, or announce in a loud voice that he was 'really up for a minger tonight'. The others seemed to barely tolerate him, whilst the female reps stayed out of the way.

As Dave walked by, the loud Cockney fell into him. Dave gave him a slight shove to send him back towards his fellow reps.

'Easy tiger, nah offence geezer,' was the response as the Cockney felt a little venom in the push.

Dave did not respond but wished that he had now pushed that little bit harder and sent the tosser into the water.

As Dave reached the room he was uncertain of his mood. So much had happened in a short space of time. He had heard in stereo from two girls how he was basically leading an old fart's life and had been dumped by one and pitied by the other because of it. Dave decided to take hope from his Sunday date and just have a good time with the lads tonight.

Inside the room was empty, but the patio doors were opened and Dave could hear voices from beyond. Gavin and Tony were already up and ready and were sitting with Phil, sharing a large bottle of Amstel. All were mellowing in the remains of the evening sun.

'Yo! Holliman. Is the dirty deed done?' Phil sounded as upbeat as ever.

'Uh, yeah. No sweat,' Dave could not be bothered to share the whole story. 'She was cool about it.'

'You best get ready, mate, the Barbie kicks off shortly.' Phil was savouring the rare occasion that he was up and ready on time.

'Yeah, I'll grab a shave. There's a whole load of kiddie reps chomping at the bit out there already.'

'Any fit birds amongst 'em?' Phil sat up from his relaxed pose. Gavin groaned.

'Uh didn't really look properly. Maybe,' Dave had, for once, been too preoccupied to eye up the talent.

'Wow, you are losing it, Holliman. We'll need to put bromide in your tea next to re-ignite that legendry sex drive,' Phil was genuinely incredulous.

'You're absolutely right. I'll order the Stenna lift as soon as we get home, and I'd better order some incontinence pads for the flight,' Dave was now really getting a complex.

'If not, we'll see if we can get some large nappies and hire a nurse,' Gavin interjected without moving an inch from his laid-back pose.

'No, that's just your personal fantasy, Gav,' Dave chuckled, before removing his T-shirt and heading for the shower.

'Absolutely,' was the motionless Gavin's response.

By the time the lads joined the barbeque, the poolside was already almost full to capacity. A few young couples were interspersed with numerous average model families. The music was bellowing out from behind the bar, where a motionless and grim looking Theo stood unimpressed by Geri Halliwell's version of 'It's Raining Men'.

Young teenyboppers of about nine or ten were jumping up and down or spinning around enthusiastically on a makeshift dance floor, as reps put on false smiley faces as they gyrated amongst them. A few keen mums also joined the fun, already tipsy from the potent punch. Some of them were beckoning for their embarrassed and disgruntled teenage offspring to join them, or even their bored husbands.

Tony managed to find a table as Gavin secured some chairs. Phil fetched some beers.

'I think Theo is in mourning for some heavy metal,' Phil said, as he placed four large lagers on the table. 'He could hardly speak and I'm sure I saw a tear in his eye.'

'Mind you I think Geri Halliwell does that to most people over the age of ten.' Gavin nodded towards the mini pops giving it their all, 'At least they're happy.'

'What, the kids or the reps? I'm not sure who's got the higher IQ. Look at that prat there.' Tony huffed before picking out the Cockney wanker doing an over enthusiastic impression of a young George Michael miming to 'Wake Me Up Before You Go Go'.

'Probably popped a few too many Es to keep him wired throughout the season. It's a rep's main staple diet, I believe.' Dave was totally cynical.

'Yeah, sad really. The chemical generation. What's wrong with a good natural pint of bitter? Some real ales could do strange things with your mind, believe me.' Gavin took a gulp of lager and winced. 'Mind you, if I had to drink this shit all the time then the chemical generation could have a new convert.'

'Hey, guys,' Phil suddenly looked startled. 'Have you clocked some of the girls? Remember when we devised that points system in Spain for tapping off and it was top score of ten for a rep?'

Dave looked over at three blonde SunRay reps dancing with three equally blonde little girls of half their age.

'Not bad, but what was the point of mentioning the scores as none of us have actually tapped off with a rep?'

Phil gave a false cough. 'Uh hu, excuse me, the very same Campaign I believe I scored five for getting a snog and tit fondle with posh Liz.'

'So you say, but there were no witnesses and you had plenty of chance to go and finish the job, but didn't,' Dave was not going to concede this one. 'Besides if it was true, even then that would have been your only score, placing you third behind me for ginger Lucy, eight points, and Gav in first place with nine for two ton Carrie the fat minger.'

'She wasn't that bad, you bastard, although I'm pleased that you acknowledge me championship year,' Gavin sounded self-satisfied.

'So, do you think that you might score a rep tonight then, Phil?' Tony enquired with total innocence.

'Watch me go, old boy,' was the confident reply as Phil took a large gulp of seemingly Dutch courage.

The alcohol continued to flow, and Theo remained totally glum as pop hit after pop hit resounded in the night. The char grilled over-cooked meat and over-baked potatoes earned no great marks as barely edible cuisine, but sufficed to satisfy rampant appetites like a bad bucket of fried chicken after a Saturday night on the beer.

The younger kids grew tired as their mums got even more pissed. Dads sat quietly enjoying a pint of lager, whilst young couples sat observing but saying very little. With the food out of the way, the reps decided that it was time for a cabaret of drinking games. The Cockney wanker took the microphone after requesting Theo to kill the music. Theo gave his first smile of the evening.

'All right, geezers and geezettes. Are we 'aving a good 'oliday?' Cockney wanker shouted into the microphone like he was about to introduce U2 at Wembley Arena.

High-pitched screams of 'Yeeees' came from the mums and kids, with a muted bassy background acknowledgement from the dads. It was far too uncool for the teenagers to say anything as they grimaced at their embarrassing parents.

'Good stuff, good stuff. Well for those of you who 'ain't met me yet, me name's Darren and I'm from Laandan. I'm gonna be yer main compère as we play a few little games. That all right with you all? All up for a bit of fun, eh?'

The crowd gave an identical response as before. What followed were the usual British drinking shenanigans as played out weekly in most rugby clubs. It started with a boat race, when various males were picked out to form teams of five, plus one token female. Gavin and Phil were amongst those selected to knock back a pint of lager and stick the empty glass on their heads. The female in each team was last to go with half a pint. Gavin's team came last and he bemoaned the fact that they all 'drank like bloody women, sipping rather than supping.'

Next up was the broom game, with teams of five again, going in relays at the poolside after drinking a glass of punch and running the length of the pool. Each team member then picked up the broom and aimed it at the night sky, before spinning around ten times. From then as they headed back to the start it was like the end of the London Marathon where some of the less fit runners had lost all power in their legs and were desperately trying to get to the finishing line. Numerous mums ended up in the pool and were promptly rescued as sodden giggling wrecks.

Throughout it all, Cockney wanker gave a Stuart Hall style commentary in true 'It's A Knockout' fashion, laughing loudly at everyone's misfortunes and always finding some way of ridiculing all the contestants. Phil was particularly affronted when his bright blue and red Hawaiian shirt brought some comment about *Magnum PI*.

The knobbly knees and gorgeous legs competitions were straight out of Butlins or Pontins and gave Cockney wanker some really good material for his comedy routine. It was all completed with a rowdy group game of fuzzy duck.

'Just need the yard of ale and I'll be convinced that I'm back at my old rugby club,' Gavin was really enjoying himself.

'Yeah, but without the knobbly knees and that Cockney tosser,' Phil was not having a good time and had failed to get anywhere near the pre-occupied female reps.

'Actually no, we did have the odd knobbly knee competition,' Gavin pondered for a moment. 'Or was that a knobbly cock competition. Anyway, every rugby club has a Cockney tosser. Usually plays on the wing.'

'Shall we go down the strip shortly for a real boogie?' Phil made the last of several pleas to move on.

'Nah, I'm far too knackered,' Dave spoke for all.

Gavin was keen to continue with his old rugby club stories. 'I remember we used to have this game at my old club called the ocky ocky, and we had this Australian bloke who was world champion. Basically you had two cones spaced a few metres apart. You then had to take all your clothes off and a line of three sheets of toilet paper was delicately placed in the crack of your arse so that it hung down. You then had the other end set fire to and it was then a case of how many times you could go round the cones before the flames touched your arse.'

'Lovely. I'm surprised that they don't televise it. John Motson would give a great commentary with some obscure arse burning stats and Alan Hansen could give a real expert view by actually talking out of his arse,' Dave laughed at his own wit.

'Where's Tony gone?' Phil had just noticed that one of the party was missing.

'Dunno. He's normally so quiet and I hadn't even realised he was missing,' Dave looked around but Tony was nowhere to be seen.

Meanwhile, Cockney wanker had still not given up the microphone and was now attempting some kind of stand-up act with really poor and smutty jokes.

'Fucking hell, I'm going to smack that tosser in a minute,' Phil was agitated by the incessant Cockney whine coupled with the fact that he was now stuck at the hotel for the evening.

Gavin suddenly leaned forward as though hit by a moment of inspiration. 'I know, what about the three-man lift. Do you guys know it?'

Dave nodded, whilst Phil shook his head. Gavin went to coerce with a couple of the other reps, whilst Dave explained the concept.

Cockney wanker's fellow reps were more than willing to assist Gavin in his plot, mainly because they were as miffed with Darren as anyone else. Mark, the head rep, managed to grab the microphone although he almost had to wrestle it away.

'Ladies and gentlemen. To end the festivities tonight, we have something of a treat. One of our party is a champion strongman and he has agreed to demonstrate his strength by lifting three male adults with one hand before your very eyes,' Mark gave it the full circus ringmaster act. 'We have two gentlemen here and I wondered if Darren would mind being the third?'

Cockney wanker nodded, 'Yeah, all right,' as Phil and Dave stepped forward. Gavin was then introduced as the strongman.

Gavin positioned Cockney wanker to lie on the floor and then got Phil and Dave to lay either side of him, interlocking their arms.

'Sorry, but I'm going to have to loosen your trousers to get a good grip,' Gavin undid the buckle on Cockney wanker's three quarter length shorts. He then pulled the waistband up high to fully reveal a pair of white Calvin Klein underpants. As Gavin did so, and appeared to take the strain for one big lift, another rep ran into view with a bucket of iced water and threw the contents into Cockney wanker's shorts. The crowd roared with laughter as Cockney wanker jumped to his feet, red-faced with anger.

The lads returned to their table after several pats on the back from the other reps for a job well done. Some free beers followed from Theo.

'Excellent. Tony will be well pissed off that he's missed free beers.' Phil took a large gulp of cold lager. 'He must have gone to bed.'

'Uh, not quite. Look over there,' Gavin pointed to the side of the bar. Tony was sat on a small wall with a gorgeous female rep sat on his knee. They were snogging vigorously.

'That's five points to Tony then,' Dave said with a 'get in there' approving grin.

'Fucking hell,' added a very jealous Phil.

Week 2: Day 1 – From Vienna to Barnsley

As the sharp blast of the shower hit Dave's body, it relieved the tension of his first real hangover of the Campaign. He shook his head to loosen the final cobwebs and felt revived in a very short space of time.

With the image of Elsie vividly held in his mind, Dave contemplated a quick wank as he turned off the shower and stood dripping a constant stream of water. His cock was just moving to a full erection when incessant female giggling could be heard coming from the room. It was interspersed with some mumbled comments from Phil. Dave quickly wrapped a towel around his waist and waited for his erection to subside before going to investigate.

Phil was lying in bed with his arms behind his head as a maid scurried around talking in Greek and laughing out loud. She laughed even louder whenever Phil said anything at all, even mumbled acknowledgements. Phil spotted Dave and shrugged his shoulders as if to say, 'don't look at me'. The maid looked up and smiled at Dave. She was about fifty with very dark sun-drenched wrinkled skin and jet-black hair. After a final swish of the mop on the floor, the maid mumbled something else in Greek and tugged at the sheet covering Phil's body. It was nearly enough to pull it from the bed had Phil not made a last minute effort to retrieve the thin white cotton cloth preserving his modesty. The maid laughed out loud before exiting with one swift motion, tugging her mop and bucket behind.

'Well, Phil, I'll happily award you fifty points if you score an old maid,' Dave smirked. 'And I reckon they're in the bag there mate.'

'Ha, ha, very funny. Mind you she does that every day, just laughs and cackles on in Greek. She seems to think that I can understand her.' Phil prised his large frame out of bed displaying a cultured potbelly overhanging an old and dirty pair of brown Y-fronts.

'I tell you, you're in there mate. She was even trying to take a sneak peak at your gorgeous body,' said Dave.

'I think you'll find that she was actually commenting on the disgusting state of the sheets. She's not had a chance to wash them yet,' said Phil. He then looked down at his podgy frame before breathing in as hard as he could and assuming a bodybuilder's pose. 'Mind you, I can't blame her if she did want a piece of that. What self-respecting female wouldn't, eh?'

Dave chose not to comment.

Dave and Phil sat in the shade from the morning sun, contemplating the very greasy-looking omelettes they had ordered from the poolside bar. They suddenly shook as though rocked by a small earthquake, as a loud shout with a strong Yorkshire accent bellowed around the pool area.

'*Aaaaaaalistaaaaaaaair*,' shouted a very pale-looking gruff man with glasses, as he looked up from his paper. His very large and equally pale wife did not flinch as she sat alongside him simply staring at the pool. A small boy of about six came running to his dad's call with a cheeky grin all over his face. 'If I see you do that again I'll 'ave yer, boy,' was the equally loud welcome from the dad with almost perfect Geoff Boycott diction.

'New arrivals,' Dave correctly commented on the one pale family amongst several others who had arrived the night before.

'Yeah, I forgot to tell you. Gareth and Cheryl went home yesterday and passed on their regards. Well, he did anyway!' Phil raised an exasperated eyebrow at the less than sociable Cheryl.

'De da, de da, dedada da,' Gavin screamed out a mock fanfare as he and Tony arrived. 'I give you Tony Johnston, master stud extraordinaire.'

Tony looked suitably embarrassed as he and Gavin sat down. Gavin lurched forward for the menu.

'So. Give us the gory details then, Mr Johnston,' Dave pretended to hold a microphone.

Tony leaned forward as if there was a microphone. 'No comment.'

'No, come on, what happened?' Phil was more forceful.

Tony decided to tell all. 'Well it was so bizarre. I was feeling really pissed and needed to go and clear my head. I actually thought I was going to throw, so I went and sat on that wall over there. I was just sitting staring into space when this rep walks past. I remember that she was really fit with luscious big lips.'

'Are you sure that it wasn't Mick Jagger?' Dave's interruption was only greeted with hard stares from the others.

'No, she was definitely very female. Well she suddenly sat down next to me and started chatting away. To be honest I never said a word but just mumbled at times. The next thing I knew she was up sitting on my knee and sticking her tongue down my throat. It was really sweet,' Tony paused for a moment, before adding, 'but bloody brilliant.'

'And?' Phil wanted more. 'What happened next?'

'Nothing,' Tony pursed his lips. 'We had a snog and then she went into the night.'

'Like the Lone Ranger,' Dave held his hand up. 'No, make that the Lone Snogger. Who was that masked snogger?'

'Well, I'm disappointed,' said Phil. He actually seemed relieved. 'You flunked it mate. I mean, what more of a come-on do you need.'

'It's still five points,' Dave pointed out. 'And I reckon you'll have to shag that maid to beat him.'

'Who's this?' Gavin was very inquisitive.

'Aaaaaaalistaaaaaaaair!' came the loud Yorkshire roar to punctuate and end of the discussion. A little lad with a cheeky grin was once more trotting over to his irate and glum-looking father.

Another day was spent routinely lounging by the pool in the Cretan sun. The premise this time was that it was relaxing preparation for the evening jaunt to Malia. It had already been agreed to skip the afternoon siesta and instead catch an early taxi to the local resort town.

It was no problem finding an air-conditioned but battered old Ford to ferry the lads to a change of scene. A small dusty taxi rank on the edge of town marked the spot for three or four identical vehicles, driven by equally doppelganger drivers. All had moustaches and designer stubble.

En route, Phil acted like a giddy child being taken on a day out to a theme park by his parents. Malia was a Club 18-30 destination and Phil was sure he would find plenty of girls to finally provide the elusive shag of Campaign two thousand and one. In fact, if successful, it would be his first since a quick knee-jerker way back in nineteen ninety-seven on a Campaign to Majorca. He was already chuffed that the ride was only a few drachma and if Malia turned out to be that hot he would certainly be investing in a few more trips.

For most of the journey Phil enthusiastically interrogated the taxi driver to gain confirmation that Malia was going to live up to expectation. The others all looked out of their respective windows admiring the Mediterranean landscape, trying to remain oblivious to the constant questioning. Phil sat in between Dave and Tony on the back seat as Gavin took the front seat.

'So, is Malia really made for it then?'

'Uh?'

'You know, a party place with lots of pretty girls'

'Uh?'

'Um… very English. Lots of English people having a good time.'

No reply but just a raise of the shoulders and contorted face.

'Do you recommend anywhere to eat?' Phil tried a less enthusiastic stab.

Another raise of the shoulders and contorted face.

'Any good pubs?'

'Uh?'

'You know, bars… for a drink.'

'Uh?'

'Um, anywhere we should avoid?'

'Uh?'

'Have you been to Malia before?' Phil was now showing signs of exasperation.

A raise of the shoulders and a contorted face.

'Oh well, we'll soon find out for ourselves,' Phil thought, and decided to abandon any further questioning. As he did so, the taxi suddenly ground to a halt in view of a beach of fine golden sand.

'Wow, they certainly score better marks for beach quality,' Gavin glanced at the back seat. 'And I don't know if it's an optical illusion but I swear the sea is bluer.'

The taxi driver grunted and pointed to his meter, which displayed 3,200 drachmas. Gavin paid as the others shuffled onto the sidewalk 'Speak English?'

'No,' came the reply with a shake of the head as Gavin smirked at Phil just before he stepped out of the car.

'Well, where to boys?' Dave stood by a sign that pointed the way to Dolphin Beach.

'We could always get Phil to ask the taxi driver,' Gavin was still smirking.

Phil gave a hard stare but did not reply.

Suddenly a large roar went up from the other side of the road as a group of lads in T-shirts and Bermuda shorts loudly performed a conga to the total disinterest and bemusement of a few locals. It was Barrel and his mates, who had come across on the same flight.

Dave spotted and recognised them. 'I suggest we follow the conga.'

A couple of hundred yards later the remnants of the conga turned right into a street lined with bars. Barrel was amongst those waiting for others to catch up, having either stopped to throw-up or take a leak in some of the small alcove alleyways.

The main street was not greatly populated with people but the bright flashing lights of the numerous bars against a constant tempo of remixed pop tunes offered a good taster of what was to come. After all it was only 6 p.m. and the night was very young.

Gavin spotted a Mexican restaurant and persuaded the others to try it out. Like the majority of restaurants it was open air and provided the feeling that you were almost eating out on the road itself. By the time the fajitas were served, along with another round of Corona beers, the main part of Malia had suddenly become a hive of activity. The restaurant and the surrounding bars had filled up effortlessly. The music pumping out of the bars grew louder as the sky grew darker and the neon lights of the town shone brighter. A hubbub of noise filled the air fuelled by singing, chanting, screaming, and shouting, as groups of late teen and twentysomething kiddies appeared. Each group seemed to have their own uniform from the collective 'on tour' T-shirts of the boys to the short white mini skirts and flimsy tops of the girls.

The contrast to easy-going cosmopolitan Hersonissos was very marked.

'Bloody hell, there's just kiddies everywhere,' Dave watched as a group of about fifteen girls of all shapes and sizes walked past. 'I feel like a bloody granddad.'

'Oh shut up, old man. Just look at all that lovely bare flesh, and all gagging for that experienced, mature approach.' Phil's eyes followed the party of mini skirts as they disappeared down the road.

'Phil, mate,' Gavin looked serious. 'These young girls are not interested in the likes of us. They're all dreaming of finding some young Westlife or Backstreet Boys clones.'

Phil was not to be dissuaded. 'Listen to you lot. I always say that you're as young as you feel, or rather what you feel. Ain't that right, Tone?'

'Uh… yeah… I s'pose so.' Tony looked up from his food after unexpectedly being brought into the debate.

'Well, look at Dave. He's just been out with a kiddie and found out that they had nothing in common, so just moved on.' Gavin looked to rest his case.

'True,' Dave nodded and agreed.

'Well he still got a bloody good shag out of it,' Phil pointed at Dave.

'True,' Dave nodded and agreed.

Gavin decided to give up.

'Oh, by the way, I've got something to tell you guys,' Dave grabbed everyone's attention. 'You know that bird I told you about. The one from the café… actually Phil's seen her.'

'The hippy,' Phil confirmed.

'Uh, well yeah,' Dave decided not to challenge the title. 'Well, I'm off for the day with her tomorrow. Just bumped into her yesterday by pure chance and we got chatting and now we're sort of on a date.'

'You kept that bloody quiet.' Phil appeared hurt.

'Well, you ain't going to believe this but I'd almost forgotten about it.' Dave had truly cast the arrangement to the back of his mind.

'Oh, so blasé, Mr Holliman.' Gavin sounded like an art critic. 'Where are you going?'

'Uh… dunno… a magical mystery tour,' Dave shrugged.

'Well I hope it's not that mad serial killer who's being leaving playboys dead at the side of the road with decapitated penis in hand.' Tony suddenly piped up.

'Eh?' Dave looked really worried and almost grabbed Tony for more information.

'Joke,' Tony looked alarmed and surprised at Dave's reaction.

Gavin and Phil looked at each other as Dave sighed heavily.

'I'll call for the bill.' Tony broke the silence.

Phil led the way on to the now crowded main street of Malia. He was almost knocked back on his feet by a swarm of Club 18–30 teenagers as they breezed by in the same logo'd T-shirts and under a cloud of rampant hormones.

Tony looked down the road with an almost timid hesitation, blinking at the now vivid lights before staring like a rabbit caught in a car's headlights. A sudden loud engine roar caused everyone's heads to turn in the imminent vicinity. A large chopper style motorbike came into view, as the crowd parted with gusto, almost like Moses parting the Red Sea. Its rider performed several Evil Kineival showman wheelies and then headed by at speed to large cheers. As he passed, it became obvious that the majority of the cheers were due to the fact that he was stark naked.

Gavin instinctively led the others onto the first moderately uncrowded bar only yards from the restaurant they'd just left. It almost felt like a place of refuge. A sigh of relief at escaping an agoraphobic nightmare turned to elation as Gavin spotted the Worthington's pump at the bar. He volunteered to get the first round in with pleasure.

After returning quickly with some cold beers, Gavin noticed that his mates were all transfixed by the buzzing nightlife.

'Oi… you fooking muppet, that's me stool, gerroff.'

The trance was suddenly broken. Dave turned from his half-seated position on a high stool to see a small squat girl of about nineteen giving him an aggressive shove. She was wearing an extremely short white mini-skirt and loose sleeveless white blouse. Her hair was deep ginger and her skin red raw as if she had been boiled alive. Several other girls of similar stature and attire stood aggressively behind her.

'Sorry?' Dave was taken by surprise.

'My fooking stool, gerroff, if you know what's good for you, lad.' The ginger midget shoved home again.

Dave relented. 'It's all yours, my dear. Do you need a hand up or shall I call for a ladder?'

'Keep your fooking hands off me, Muppet, or I'll slap yer.' Ginger midget climbed up the stool, straightening her short skirt as she sat down.

'Hey, don't you realise that this is the captain that you're talking to. Captain Shag, every girl's dreamboat.' Phil put his arm around Dave.

Ginger midget eyed Dave up and down. ''E's all right like, do you fancy a shag later, mate?'

Dave stuttered. 'Uh… thanks… but I'm saving myself.'

'Your loss, lad,' said Ginger midget, as she took a big swig of some orange alcopop.

Dave turned his back to close off any more conversation, but Phil decided to persist.

'So where are you girls from?'

The reply came as a collective football style chant. 'Barnsleeee, Barnsleeee, Barnsleeee, Barnsleeee. We are, we are the Barnsley girls,' An accompanying group pogo was performed in synch.

Phil gave a big grin. 'Excellent. I've never been myself. What's it like?'

Gavin quickly finished his pint and patted Dave on the arm. They both grabbed hold of Phil and marched him out of the bar. Even the attraction of another pint of bitter could not entice Gavin to stay any longer. Phil's feet almost left the ground and he felt an urge to kick them like a toddler throwing a tantrum.

'You're wankers and you know you are, wankers and you know you are,' was the less than melodic tune sung by the Barnsley girls that sent them on their way.

'I tell you, that would have been like taking sweets from a baby.' Phil was still feeling quite disgruntled as he was presented with a fresh pint of beer in the corner of a small bar. 'The slags were up for grabs and no mistake.'

'You might be right, but did you seriously want to go there?' Gavin grimaced like he had just sucked a lemon.

'Yes, actually, a shag's a shag, Mr Picky.' Phil remained indignant.

'Would you have gone there?' Gavin turned to Dave.

Dave shook his head. 'Maybe a few years ago, but no, not now. I think that you look for a bit more class with age, like enjoying good wine instead of cheap supermarket plonk. Your taste buds will try anything when you're young.'

'Mind you, Phil is as desperate as a teenager looking for his first shag.' Gavin's comment brought a hard stare from Phil. In the background Tony seemed to be just staring into space.

'Well, guys, I think that we may have totally lost him this time.' Gavin nodded towards the motionless Tony. He showed no sign of reacting as Dave waved a hand in front of his eyes.

'Yo, earth calling Tony.'

Tony suddenly moved his head to look at his friends, appearing like a child caught in a naughty act. 'Uh, sorry lads... miles away.'

'We could see that. Daydreaming as usual?' Gavin was very used to his friend's odd comatose moments.

'Well... no. You see that girl over there,' Tony nodded towards a thin, pale brunette in her mid-twenties.

'Which one, the gawky one or the fat one?' Dave unkindly described the two girls opposite.

'She's not gawky,' Tony confirmed the object of his affection.

'Uh... no. Very nice actually, mate,' Dave tempered his view. 'Is she the one then? The dream girl?'

'Well actually, I think I know her.' Tony's admission brought some semi-startled stares. 'On Saturdays I quite often go to Capper's coffee house and read the papers, and I'm sure that she's one of the waitresses. I've always quite fancied her but never had the nerve to ask her out,' Tony turned a slight shade of red as he confessed his crush.

There was a slight silence before Dave put his arm around Tony and in a very poor Eamon Andrews accent said, 'Well, tonight Tony Johnston, this is your time.'

As he said it, as if by cue the larger girl got up to go to the toilets leaving a shy, gawky brunette supping a glass of white wine. Dave saw this and quickly stood up.

'Right, mate, it's now or never. Just go over and say, "Hello, can I have a cappuccino?" or something.'

Tony hesitated before gulping hard and moving forward, slightly propelled by Dave. As he approached the table, Tony felt like his whole body was going to start shaking uncontrollably and his legs stiffened up so that they could barely support him.

'Uh… hi,' Tony desperately tried to calm his voice and sound cool. 'This may sound corny, but I think I know you. Do you work at Cappers Coffee House?'

The girl looked up glumly for a second before breaking into a big grin. 'Yes… and I know you. A cappuccino, a bakewell tart and you always read *The Mirror*. Every Saturday.'

'Very good,' Tony remained standing. 'Um, my name's Tony Johnston.'

'Kim Cookson,' was the response.

There was a slight awkward pause before Kim spoke. 'Please, take a seat.'

Tony sat down and felt like he had convincingly won the first round of a major title fight. He took a good look at Kim, who was wearing sensible plain light blue trousers and a white T-shirt. Her face was very thin, and almost hidden by her long brown hair, but pretty despite the presence of numerous spots brought out by the sun. 'Who are you here with?'

'Oh a friend, Gill. She's just popped to the loo. And you?'

'A few mates. They're over there,' Tony pointed out his friends, who all gave a thumbs up accompanied by a heavily mouthed 'get in there'.

'Um, I think they're a bit drunk.'

Kim went a little red and sat coyly, making sure that she did not make any more eye contact with Tony's laddish mates. Her friend Gill then returned and sternly enquired 'Who's this?'

'Oh hi, Gill, this is Tony. We sort of know each other from back home,' Kim giggled as Tony looked up at the bulky frame of Gill. She wore similar clothes to Kim, but they looked to be a size too small and stuck to her body extenuating her overweight bulk, whereas Kim's clothes hung from her so loosely that you could have sworn she had the build of a wiry coat hanger. Gill's fat cheeks puffed out like a large guppy fish from beneath a bleached blonde crew cut.

Gill continued to stare at Tony before finally deflating her cheeks and giving a handshake before offering to buy him a beer. Tony was starting to feel comfortable and ready to relax. There were still a few more awkward silences and the conversation remained as general small talk, even when Gill returned.

Across the bar the others had watched as Tony settled down and encamped with the girls.

'Good boy, good boy,' Dave gave his approval. 'I knew he wouldn't let me down.'

'Guys, this place is a bit dead. Shall we move on for some real Malia action?' Phil stood up to go.

'What about Tone? We can't just leave him,' said Gavin. He remained seated and Dave nodded whilst glaring at Phil.

'Well, can't we come back for him? Tell him we're moving on.' Phil remained standing.

'Phil, if you want to go, then go, but I'm staying put.' Gavin finished his beer. 'Want another, Dave?'

'Sure,' Dave was not moving either.

Phil sat back down in a sulk and looked over at a now laughing and relaxed Tony. He viewed the scene with envy and realised that the night he thought was to be his was now to be Tony's.

Tony had now totally won the confidence of Kim and even Gill. They were sharing holiday experiences, and the stories of Phil's pulling shirt had really tickled both girls. It had transpired that Kim and Gill, who were both twenty-seven, were lifelong friends and almost in the spirit of the Campaign had been away on many summer jaunts as a pair. This year they had chosen Malia, but found it a bit too wild.

The time moved on to ten o'clock. The girls were booked on a boat trip the next day and with regret said they would have to go. Tony wished them both a good night as they stood up to go.

One final awkward silence was broken by Gill. 'Well, Tony, I could do with an early night tomorrow. I need to read my book as I've hardly dented it, so why don't you take Kim out.'

'Oh, what are you reading?' was Tony's innocent response.

'Never mind that. Yes or no to the date?' Gill nearly threw her hands in the air in despair.

'Yes, yes. Definitely. What time would be best?' Tony suddenly sounded assertive.

'Um, how about six-thirty? I could meet you on the front, by the sign pointing to Dolphin Beach. It's where most of the taxis drop off.' Kim also sounded more confident.

'Six-thirty, by the sign for Dolphin Beach, it is,' Tony was now elated.

'Now, Tony, take good care of her 'cos I pack a mean punch! All right?' Gill held up a fist.

Tony mockingly grimaced. 'Absolutely.'

'And it's Marian Keyes *What She Wants*, by the way. See you soon,' Gill pushed Kim forward as she looked back with a coy smile.

'See you tomorrow,' Tony mirrored the smile.

Just as they disappeared from view, Tony felt like hurdling the tables between him and his friends like Colin Jackson, before breaking into 'What A Wonderful World'. Life could get no better at that moment.

Despite Tony having the appearance of a mouse who had just acquired his body weight in cheese, Phil's opening comment summed up his own flagging mood.

'You've been blown out then, mate?'

'No,' was the quick and straight response from Tony. 'Far from it. Tomorrow night, gentlemen, I shall be meeting the very gorgeous and delectable Kim in Malia for a date at 6.30 p.m. precisely.'

Dave and Gavin both thumped the air like England had just won the World Cup.

'What about her fat mate?' Phil continued with the cynical approach.

'Uh, well, actually she's free tomorrow night apart from reading a book. I could try and set you up. Her name's Gill and she's really nice.' Tony was completely genuine.

'No, you're all right, mate. Standards and all that. She looks a bit bloody frightening to me. Anyway, just don't blow it and make sure you get the shags in.' Phil stood up in a determined mood.

'Anyway, can we move on now and find a better bar?'

'Actually, I think I've had enough of Malia. I'm going to head back for a swift one in the Harp,' said Gavin, as he stood up.

'Yeah, I think I'll join you. To be honest I've become a bit of a European boy thanks to laid-back and cosmopolitan Hersonissos.' Dave held up his hands to mimic a set of scales. 'Girls from Vienna versus girls from Barnsley,' the right hand representing Vienna fell to the floor in an exaggerated movement.

'I'd rather go back too. Sorry, Phil,' Tony confirmed the obvious.

'Fuck!' Phil exclaimed and then said very little as he sulked all the way during the cab ride back.

The Harp was lively and raucous as usual, but without the banality of the typical Brits abroad atmosphere of Malia. Annette greeted Gavin with a full long lingering kiss on the lips and then gave a warm peck on the cheek to the other three.

Gavin hardly spoke to his mates after arriving but divided his time between his Guinness and chatting to Annette over the bar. Dave listened to Tony recounting his joy at fixing a date with Kim, whilst Phil sat as a loner in abject silence.

A decision was made to have some nightcaps at the hotel, and Annette agreed to come along after her shift.

As usual the hotel bar was empty except for Theo, who was amusing himself by playing air guitar along to Status Quo.

Theo greeted the four English lads with all the enthusiasm of Annette, bar the kissing, but provided some free beers. One nightcap became several and it was not long before Annette joined the group as promised. She brought along a couple of middle-aged barmaid friends. This at least ignited Phil back into action for a while as he tried his best to chat-up an attractive forty-year-old brunette from Cambridge. The initial enthusiasm soon waned however as it became obvious that the brunette, and her heavily made-up friend, had a major crush on the handsome Dave.

The night ended with Dave being dared to strip to his boxer shorts and dive into the pool. He did this without question or hesitation but was very promptly told off by Maria, the hotel owner's daughter.

Annette gave Gavin a number of signals that she was willing to stay for the night. In turn, Gavin awkwardly asked Tony if he minded sleeping in Dave and Phil's room. The in-love and on-a-high Tony did not object and even made a beeline for some sunlounger mattresses to form his bed for the night.

As the clock hit two, a half-dressed Gavin and Annette were already in mid passionate shag on his single bed. Dave had set his alarm and fallen asleep instantly, briefly wondering what the next day would hold. Tony lay staring at the ceiling with a large smile upon his face, his mind too occupied to welcome sleep. Phil also lay awake in a sad trance, trying to understand why the Campaign two thousand and one was going so wrong.

Week 2: Day 2 – Players and Spectators

The faint beeping of the travel alarm was just enough to stir Dave from a deep sleep. It was 8 a.m.

Dave was not due to meet Elsie until nine, but he was determined to get up early and clear his head. He staggered out of bed clutching a tight and throbbing forehead, instantly regretting all the extra nightcaps. As Dave moved into the bathroom an awake Phil felt an instant pang of jealousy for his friend, who was about to embark on some wild romantic adventure. He remained silent and tried once again to close his eyes and clear his mind to bring the deep sleep he had lacked all night. Alongside Phil's bed, Tony lay blissfully asleep on top of a blue sunlounger mattress covered by a white sheet.

Dave showered quickly before dressing and gathered a few essentials in a beach bag. Elsie had told him to basically bring himself and little else for a traveller's adventure. He wondered for a brief moment what lay ahead and whether it was worth blowing out his date whilst contemplating going back to bed and spending the day lounging by the pool. There were plenty of far less complicated girls to pursue. Then he thought of Elsie's angelic face and perfect slim, tanned figure, and her jibe that he was a man on the road to steady middle-aged security.

The door closed behind Dave with an unintentional loud bang, and he grimaced hoping not to have woken the others. Dave then strode on confidently and defiantly.

It was nine-twenty as Dave sat staring out to sea from the Sunstrip café. He was on his third double espresso but was once again starting to feel jaded and frayed around the edges as the initial enthusiastic feelings waned. Maybe he should have gone back to bed after all. Perhaps this was all some joke and Elsie had no intention of turning up. She had probably already left the island and was doubtless trekking through Borneo by now. Dave considered how he would explain this one to the lads.

At nine thirty-five, Dave was going to call it a day before agreeing to allow yet another five minutes. He looked back out to the calm sea and focussed on a small yacht gliding across the horizon. As Dave turned back he was no longer the only person sitting at the table.

'You look knackered. Been waiting long?' Elsie beamed a cheeky smile before signalling the waiter for a coffee.

Dave shook his head slightly to wake himself. 'Um... well since nine o'clock actually. That's when you told me to be here,' Dave tapped his watch.

'Ah,' Elsie held up a finger. 'First rule of the day, time is of no consequence.'

Dave stared at her in disbelief and frustration. 'Oh, fucking hell, I hope this is not going to be some David Carradine, Kung Fu, ah grasshopper meditation shit. How many fucking rules are there in the Roundbottom guide to a better life?'

'Only two: swearing is evil, being the second,' Elsie fixed a stare at Dave for a second before laughing.

'Except that I am now talking fucking bollocks.'

Hearing Elsie swear with precise posh elocution really turned Dave on. He had always yearned for a posh wild child after reading about the exploits of upper class society girls in the tabloids, as well as lusting after Elizabeth Hurley since she wore that dress to the *Four Weddings* premier. Elsie certainly had the accent and the perfect English rose looks. Even wearing three-quarter length tartan shorts and a large baggy lilac T-shirt, Elsie still allured style. Her hair was tied up allowing Dave to soon get lost in her deep hazel brown eyes.

'So what shall we do today?' Elsie once again brought Dave out of his semi-hypnotic trance.

'I thought that was your call. You mean that nothing's planned?' Dave suddenly had thoughts of just crashing out on the beach for the day.

'Rule number...' Elsie paused, 'I never plan anything. Now let's have a think and then just go wherever we please.'

'Ok, but what would you like to do?' Dave did not want to have to think too hard.

Elsie was hit with some quick inspiration. 'I know, Mr office boy, wide boy. We've taken the boy out of the office, so let's take him to the wide open countryside.'

Dave thought for a minute. 'Sounds like bullshit to me, and I'm not an office boy or a wide boy... posh girl.'

Elsie laughed out loud. 'Oh you and your childish taunts. They are so cute and quaint,' she reached out and grabbed his hand. 'Come with me my bit of rough.'

Dave was now totally turned on.

Elsie held Dave's hand all the way out of the café and down the road as she led him with a childlike excitement. The destination was a scooter hire shop called Effy's, run by a large glum Greek lady.

'These things are bloody death traps, aren't they?' Dave was nervous and a little horrified as he looked around the old rusty machines. 'Our rep told us to stay well clear of this place.'

'Oh, they're okay, Effy's never let me down yet. Trust me, you'll have fun,' Elsie patted two scooters - one red and one blue - standing side by side. 'We'll take these.'

Dave pulled out some drachmas to pay but Elsie insisted that it was her shout and pulled out a large wad of notes. 'Father still sends me the odd allowance.'

Elsie slowly drove her scooter on to the main road and waited for Dave. A few minutes later he appeared chugging unsteadily around the corner, and wearing a bright green old-fashioned helmet that could have been worn by Stirling Moss.

Elsie jumped off her scooter and broke into fits of hysterical laughter. 'I'm sorry, but if you're going to wear that then we are going in different directions. Nobody in Crete wears a crash helmet and that includes grannies. Come on, where's this supposed cool? Have you never seen *Quadrophenia*?'

Dave indignantly removed the helmet. 'It's my favourite film.'

'Well, now's your chance to live it,' Elsie took the crash helmet and threw it aside. 'Without going off any cliffs of course.'

Shortly after Dave had closed the door and embarked on his adventure, Phil had got up in a mood of resignation that he would not gain any more sleep to alleviate his restless night. At first he sat on the patio in the morning sun, mulling over his lot and feeling self-pity as the only member of the group to be failing to pull any women.

Phil soon tired of wallowing in his own misfortune under the bright rising sun and decided to go for breakfast. When stressed or feeling down at home, Phil would find comfort in either food or drink as he sat alone during long winter weekday evenings. A large fry-up was now surely the best solution to clear the morose black cloud from his head.

With Tony still in deep slumber, Phil made his way to the other end of the strip from Dave's rendezvous, buying a copy of *The Sun* on the way.

As he devoured the incredibly greasy platter and lost himself in an array of oddball kitchen sink journalism, Phil began to feel more relaxed and uplifted. He looked out to sea and tried to clear his head to think more positively. However, the vastness of the water made him feel even more alone. As he looked around it became apparent that the entire café was now full of couples as he sat on his own.

Phil had always believed that the Campaign would go on forever, oblivious to the advance of time and the need for change. It had always been his escape and the only true highlight of his year. Now it had turned into a personal nightmare, reminding Phil of his own fragility and mundane life rather than helping him forget it.

After a nervous and shaky start, which saw more brake testing than any real acceleration, Dave had grown in confidence in controlling his machine. Outside of Hersonissos he finally caught up with Elsie, who had made no allowance for Dave's novice status by moving at a brisk pace with the odd teasing glance back. Spurred on by her mocking, Dave decided to open up the throttle until he rode in parallel down a dusty coated road.

The road was almost deserted as it forged a path past Malia into the wilderness of the Cretan countryside. Symmetrical tree formations aligned and dotted an expanse of green and grey plateau between lolling hills and mountains. Above, the sky was a rich dark blue as the sun lit up the whole scene.

A cool steady breeze engulfed Dave ruffling his hair and

bringing relieving respite from the heat. As he exchanged glances with a smiling and composed Elsie, Dave felt a total adrenalin rush. He pushed on ahead of Elsie and yelped like a young teenager. 'Yeeeeeeeeehaaaaaaaaar.'

To his surprise, Elsie mirrored his cry and accelerated to join him.

As the journey continued, the scenery was diverse and constantly changing from an often harsh and barren landscape to areas smothered in luscious greenery. Old stone farmhouses and small villages were perched on the sides of hills not far from vineyards and lines of olive trees.

With Malia now firmly in the distance, the road began to climb up and away from the coast and became engulfed like a large ravine. The two scooters began to struggle until the road widened and the slope eased off.

Instead of following a smooth, and now quite busy, highway, Elsie signalled for Dave to follow her down a smaller and much less modern road. The road continued to climb and Dave started to long for a flat wide open space. In consolation he thought of the ride back down the hill and a real chance to test the brakes. At the summit stood a small town called Vrakhasi, Dave slowed expecting to stop for a respite but Elsie continued on and waved for him to follow. She took him through a mountain pass and a descent on the other side.

Looping back round, Dave found himself again on the much busier road. In the distance he could see another town and hoped that this was an intended destination. With the scooter's small engine a short trip had started to feel like the Isle of Man TT.

The town came rapidly into view and to Dave's relief Elsie signalled to stop on its outskirts. It seemed very old and steeped in history, with some grand old buildings and churches. The main road was busy but the inhabitants were generally milling around at a leisurely pace.

'This is Neapolis,' Elsie held out her hand to demonstrate, as if there were other towns to distinguish from. 'It's a lovely quaint little town, but I just want to stop for a little refreshment and then on we go.'

'So this is just the halfway house,' Dave was really starting to think this was the end of the road. 'What, are we doing a lap of the island?'

'No silly,' Elsie gave him a little slap. 'We really have to put some adventure into you don't we?'

'Oh lead on Ellen McArthur,' said Dave, as he prepared to follow on his scooter once more.

'Ha, ha, but I think that you'll find that she just treks across the sea. Deadly dull, nothing to look at. Almost like working in an office it's so mundane.' Elsie then slowly pulled away.

Elsie made her way down some back streets, following a defined route that would normally have been familiar only to a local. She also expertly weaved in and out of wandering pedestrians, waving to a few as obvious acquaintances. Dave tried to copy the line and almost ran down a handful of locals, waving only to warn them of his oncoming vehicle.

Eventually Elsie drew up outside a grey and drab-looking terraced building, with a very old man sitting outside. The man smiled and waved in an ecstatic manner, before Elsie reached down to kiss him on the cheek. She then beckoned Dave to follow just as the old man reached up and pinched her bottom. He laughed and then cheered.

'Oh, Cyrus, you are a randy old devil.' Elsie wagged her finger in mock scorn.

Cyrus laughed even more with the delirium of a naughty schoolboy.

'Am I safe to have a go?' Dave held up two fingers in a pinching movement.

'No, you'll get a large slap,' Elsie pushed Dave's hand away. 'Now come and meet Nick.'

At the end of a dark and dingy corridor was an old dusty room containing several leather settees and small wooden tables. Two old men sat playing chess in one corner adjacent to a small bar, behind which stood a young Greek man. He had dark Mediterranean looks and a very slight black moustache. His clothes had the appearance of a manual labourer more than a bar owner.

'Hey, Else, my baby,' the barman put down the glasses he had been cleaning and moved quickly over to greet Elsie with a large bear hug along with kisses to both cheeks.

'Nick, this is Dave.' Elsie provided an introduction that was followed by a vice-like handshake. 'I'm showing him the sights of Crete.'

'There is no better guide my friend, you shall have much fun, believe me.' Nick put an arm around Elsie and squeezed her so hard that the colour drained from her face. 'Every time I see her beautiful face I must ask one thing…' Nick suddenly dropped to one knee and looked up at Elsie. 'My dear English lady, will you marry me?'

Elsie screwed up her face and puckered her lips as if in deep thought. 'Um… no, I don't think so.'

Nick jumped up. 'Oh well if you don't try, eh?'

'Uh… yeah,' Dave raised his shoulders as if to commiserate.

'Anyway Nick, two of your finest Soumadhas, please.' Elsie signalled for Dave to sit down. 'We can't stop long as we have a way to go.'

Dave sat down on the dark brown leather sofa, which was cooling and surprisingly comfortable. Elsie sat beside him as Nick returned quickly with what appeared to be two glasses of milk. Elsie grabbed a glass and took a large gulp before savouring the taste. Dave tentatively tasted the drink, which was chilled and as milky as it appeared but with a very sweet almond taste.

'It's called Soumadha,' said Elsie, as she took another large gulp. 'It's a local speciality, made from pressed almonds. Isn't it great? Just the ticket to refresh and revive.'

'Yeah, it's certainly different,' Dave was finding it a bit sickly, but at least it was cold. 'I'd prefer a beer though.'

Elsie emptied her glass. 'Come on, Mr Brit abroad, we still have a lot to do if there's to be any hope for you. Drink up.'

Dave downed the drink quickly. 'Oh, so I'm some kind of patient now. A hopeless case no doubt.'

'I don't know about hopeless,' Elsie stood up and pulled Dave after her, 'helpless maybe.'

Elsie bade Nick a swift farewell and then received another pinch on the backside from Cyrus outside. To Dave's horror, he also received an affectionate pinch on his right buttock, which Cyrus acknowledged with a subtle wink.

A startled Dave remounted his scooter and once again set off in pursuit of Elsie as she trekked back down the side streets.

It was mid morning before Phil made tracks back to the hotel, having moped in the café, daydreamed on the beach and occupied his mind by wandering around an array of shops. Just as the hotel came into sight, he spotted Tony and Gavin sitting outside a small roadside café.

'Yo!' Phil put on a bright and cheery face 'Good night, Gav?'

'Faaaaaaaantastic,' Gavin gave a thumbs-up. 'Annette is one routine that I could seriously stick with.'

'Hey, well find somewhere else to do it next time. My bloody back's killing me this morning,' Tony arched his upper body to stretch all the stiff muscles.

'Well, Tone, he owes you, mate. Just need to get Kim back and Gav can sleep on our floor.' Phil raised his eyebrows but Gavin did not respond. 'Anyway, d'ya reckon Holliman will have shagged by now?'

'Oh yeah,' Tony spoke confidently of his ultimate role model. 'He'll probably be back within the hour and ready for a new conquest tonight.'

'Well actually, he told me that he won't be back tonight,' Phil signalled to order a coffee, his fifth of the morning. 'Looks like it's just me and thee tonight, Gav, now that Tone's getting the shags in as well.'

Tony looked embarrassed and felt a little pressurised, whilst Gavin had a sudden shocked frown.

'Shit… I thought Dave was just out for the morning. Shit,' Gavin was now quit perplexed.

'Don't worry, mate, Dave's a big boy now,' Phil gave a puzzled look in exchange. 'I'm sure he'll be touched you're missing him so much.'

Gavin's serious demeanour did not alter. 'Um… well… oh, I'll have to cancel. Don't worry about it.' Gavin was obviously hiding something.

'Cancel? Cancel what?' Phil was now really curious.

'Annett wanted to take me to this restaurant out in the sticks. Apparently it's her favourite one in the whole world.' Gavin sounded excited about the place before altering to a more sombre tone. 'But I'll cancel as I can't leave you on your own. I only agreed as I thought Dave was around and that you two would want to go out on the pull.'

For a few seconds Phil looked like a lost child before noticeably transforming with a large false smile. 'No, mate, you shall go to the ball. As it happens, I might be on a bit of a promise tonight, so you'll only cramp my style.'

'Oh right, who's this then?' Gavin asked tentatively.

'Oh, some bird who keeps giving me the eye,' Phil lied. 'And I just thought that I'd steam in there tonight. So you go for your meal, Tony can get his leg-over at last and Dave's doubtlessly shagging already. I just need to complete the set. What a team.'

'Okay, right.' Gavin was still not convinced. 'Are you sure?'

'Positive.'

'Hey what about Gill, Kim's mate?' Tony was suddenly animated. 'I'm sure that I can get you in there.'

Phil mocked a bout of nausea. 'Thanks, mate, but I'd rather have a shot at this other bird. She's a right babe, looks a bit like Tamsin Outhwaite.' Phil's lie was turning into a developing fantasy.

'Oh well the offer was there.' Tony felt some nervous twinges in his stomach and was half hoping that Phil would provide some moral support on a double date.

'Cheers!' Phil raised his cup of coffee like it was a pint of beer.

Elsie led Dave out of the shaded side streets of Neapolis into the glaring heat of the day. Dave was now feeling surprisingly revitalised, which helped him relax and take in the surroundings. Instead of being stuck behind a desk in some stuffy drab office, obeying the orders of a fat ugly woman, he was totally free. There was no weight of daily grind on his shoulders but just the freedom to roam. He was a dot in an open landscape rather than an employee number on the company's books. Dave took in all the sights and fresh country smells, savouring every new scene. A row of strange-looking windmills provided another in a line of unexpected sights, before another small village came into view. Elsie stopped again and Dave pulled up behind her.

'Stopping already. Don't tell me, we can have another milky drink. You're taking me on a kind of pub crawl, but it's a milk crawl... or even a milk round.' Dave was full of high spirits.

'Very funny,' Elsie pointed down a small side road. 'We're

going to head down there towards a place called Elounda. You're going to love it, trust me. It's a little village on the coast, where we can spend the rest of the day.'

'And night?' Dave was hoping that the return journey was not going to be today.

'Not planned that far ahead,' Elsie winked. 'It would just be a mundane touristy thing if I did. Live by the hour with the excitement of the unexpected.'

'Let's go, Grasshopper.'

'You should be Grasshopper. I'm the old wise master, except that I've got more hair and better legs,' Elsie pulled up the right side of her shorts to reveal a slim and tanned thigh.

Dave drooled as the beauty of the Cretan landscape suddenly paled into insignificance.

The road was smooth and fairly straight as Elsie powered on ahead without hesitation. After a few miles and with no sign of other traffic, Dave accelerated to move alongside Elsie and they rode in parallel.

'Wow, the office boy is letting go,' Elsie shouted over.

'Hey, I've never been your Mr Average office stiff. The rebel has always been there. Just needed a bit of stirring up.'

'Good job that you met me then, bell boy,' Elsie threw a cheeky grin as she referenced the double life of Sting's character in Quadrophenia.

'Oh, my saviour.' Dave took his hands from the handlebars and pretended to pray, before quickly reaching out to regain control of the scooter as it severely wobbled.

'Bell boooooooy,' Elsie laughed loudly as she accelerated away.

Defiantly, Dave took off after her, determined to create a race and win. Elsie already knew that the race was on and gesticulated back to her opponent like an arrogant boxer teasing his foe. The challenge continued through several villages as pedestrians cleared the way and waved as though this was some major sporting event. Dave was slowly catching Elsie, spurred on by male pride and daring to take a few chances. He could sense that he was at some altitude, surrounded by a very rocky terrain and a mountain range dominating the horizon.

Suddenly Elsie slowed as she negotiated a sharp bend and

Dave moved into her slipstream. As the road straightened he saw his chance and gave the scooter full throttle moving with ease past his opponent. Dave raised a triumphant fist in the air and moved at great speed down the home straight, as he saw it. As he looked back Elsie had almost come to a standstill and was waving for Dave to stop, pointing to an acute fork in the road. Dave's scooter was no longer hurtling over a winding dusty grey road but a smooth, straight and very white surface. He applied gradual pressure to the untrustworthy brakes, slowing sufficiently to master a sudden tree-lined bend. Almost immediately around the corner, Dave was faced with a large white villa. He reacted quickly and swerved to the side of the building and through an open side gate. A more forceful applying of the brakes brought him to a skidding and screeching standstill inches from the edge of a swimming pool.

Dave sighed with relief before looking up to see a group of people staring with open mouths from their al fresco lunch on the patio.

'Anybody order a pizza?' Dave spluttered to break the silence.

Dave drove back up the drive slowly, unchallenged by the shocked villa occupants. Elsie met him halfway.

'Don't say a word,' Dave held up his hand as he slowed down.

Elsie bit her lip to badly mask her inward glee. 'No, no. That was great. You've just explored a part of Crete that I've never been to myself. Way to go,' She gently punched the air before roaring with laughter.

Once back on the main road, Elsie slowly led Dave down to a small track. They parked the scooters and clambered up a small grass bank. The view from the top was wonderful. A large expanse of blue water flowed around a rocky undulating coastline that led to the distinct white buildings of a small coastal town.

'Awesome, eh?' Elsie crouched to relax and enjoy the view. 'I love it here.'

'It's fantastic. Where are we again?' Dave had no idea how far he had travelled or even in which direction he had been going.

'Well that's the Gulf of Merabello and that town is Elounda. That's where we are heading for.'

'Wow, how did you first discover this place?' Dave sat beside Elsie and scanned the panoramic view.

'Well, actually it's a bit of a traveller's secret. You know like the book, *The Beach*,' Elsie looked very serious.

'Really?' Dave was excited. 'Now this really is an adventure.'

Elsie fell back laughing. 'No, you wally. You're so gullible. Elounda is a top resort in most travel agents brochures.'

Dave briefly closed his eyes with embarrassment before focussing on Elsie lying in the grass. Without hesitation he moved alongside her. After a brief silent pause he gently kissed her on the lips. Elsie smiled and then pulled Dave to her and they began to kiss passionately, bodies entwined on the floor.

The kissing continued for about ten minutes, intertwined with affectionate stroking and the occasional lustful grope.

Suddenly Elsie sprang up and away from Dave. 'I don't know about you but I'm starving. Time to move on lover boy.'

Dave wearily got to his feet, knocking the dried grass from his clothes whilst waiting for his erection to subside. He then gingerly pursued his energetic and unpredictable companion.

The descent down to the small town took Elsie and Dave past numerous luxurious villas, perfectly placed to capture the view of the bay. Dave briefly thought of his lottery ticket sitting at home and the minutest of chances that he was already a multi-millionaire. The first million was quickly earmarked for a stylish new white villa set in the hillside, with a pool and jacuzzi in the foreground.

Elounda itself was equally as chic as the properties that adorned its main road. A small beach in amongst the rocks marked the entrance to the town, enjoyed by a large number of people but without appearing crowded. Beyond the sand, several speedboats moved gracefully through the water. Dave mentally spent a little more of his hopeful lottery windfall.

Elsie moved on into the town, passing dozens of hotels and tavernas. Finally she pulled up by a side street, signalling for Dave to park alongside.

'How about a picnic?' Elsie dismounted. 'A Roundbottom special.'

Dave nodded his agreement as he climbed off the scooter. Although the ride had been exhilarating, he was now happy just to walk at a slow leisurely pace.

'Shit, I feel like John Wayne after some bloody cattle trek out west.' Dave reached down and aligned his shorts. 'I'm sweaty and frazzled and need a drink.'

Elise led Dave to a small supermarket, where she bought bread, cheese and a few salad pieces along with a bottle of chilled white wine. Throughout Elsie remained oblivious to Dave's requests for beer and crisps, single-mindedly picking from her own mental shopping list.

Clutching a couple of thin and unsupportive shopping carrier bags, the couple returned down the road past the scooters and on towards the beach several hundred yards way. Dave clung tightly to the ice-cold wine bottle, holding it to his over-heating and travel-weary chest.

Once on the beach, Elsie pulled out a long thin towel and laid it on the sand. Dave sat down instantly and removed his shoes, before lying back as the sun's rays magnified upon him to open up every sweat pore on his face. He felt tired now, both from the exhilaration of the journey and the delayed alcoholic effects from the previous night.

Elsie continued to unpack numerous items from her small rucksack, including fold-up plates and cutlery before triumphantly brandishing a tiny compact corkscrew and two plastic glasses.

'Da da,' Elsie handed the corkscrew to Dave, who was still clinging to the cold wine bottle.

'Shit, is that bag some kind of Tardis or something?' Dave tried to peep into Elsie's rucksack to see what else was inside.

'Travel light and essential, that's my motto,' Elsie held up the glasses, egging Dave on to open the wine.

'You must have a book of bloody mottos in there as well. You keep quoting so many,' Dave obliged and squeezed the cork out with a strain from the bottle.

The wine tasted superb as Dave savoured the slight tang of the grapes, without giving in to temptation to down the ice-cold liquid to ease an extremely dry and parched throat. Elsie too closed her eyes and enjoyed the wine's flavour, before efficiently cutting up and dividing the food onto the plates.

'So the Roundbottom special is basically a cheese and tomato salad sandwich, topped with a bit of lettuce,' Dave smirked.

'Oh yes, but enjoyed on Elounda beach, the most essential ingredient,' Elsie took a large bite from her sandwich.

Dave nodded and took in the surroundings once more. 'Yes, yes, you've got me. This is the life all right. So how does one become a traveller? You've still got to have the dosh to get places and to do that you have to work, or have it given to you on a plate by Daddy.'

'Oh yes, Daddy does give me the odd bit of pocket money, but I don't really need it. I do work, but all over the place, in bars, on farms, on beaches… but no offices and no set career, which equals no worries. I earn the money to move on,' Elsie leaned back on her elbows, holding her head up to feel the full force of the sun.

'Very nice, too,' Dave looked at his carefree companion with envy. 'Just wish I'd had the balls to do it myself. Should have done it when I was younger.'

Elsie jerked back to a seating position. 'Are you married?'

'No,' replied Dave instantly.

'Any kids?'

'No.'

'Love your job?'

'No.'

'Planning for your retirement?'

'No.'

Elsie took a big sip of wine. 'No excuses then. A toast to Dave the retired office boy-cum-lad-about-town to newly fledged travelling philosopher staking his claim to the world.'

'You're mad,' Dave clashed glasses none the less.

The impromptu picnic and wine were savoured as if expensive and high quality cuisine. As the last drop of wine disappeared Dave yawned and stretched as the combination of heat and alcohol took full effect.

'Shit, I could crash here for the night. Can't say I'm looking forward to the return journey,' Dave threw a worried look. 'We're not intending on heading back today are we?'

Elsie smiled. 'Enjoy the moment and the future will take care of itself.'

Dave exhaled loudly and stared hard as Elsie's life philosophy took its toll. His attention was then fully drawn to his companion as she stood up and slowly stripped down to a bright purple bikini, which fitted perfectly with the slim contours of Elsie's toned body. The top supported a large bust, revealing ample cleavage for Dave to ponder over before his eyes moved down to the bottoms, which equally supported a firm rounded bum and provided just enough cloth at the front to guarantee the need for extensive attention to any bikini line.

Elsie lay down on the long towel and wiggled her toes against Dave's thigh. 'There's some lotion in the Tardis, be a love.'

Dave grabbed Elsie's bag and located a lotion spray with fumbling hands. He then stretched both sets of fingers before spraying the lotion on to Elsie naval area. Elsie gave a little squeal as the cold spray tickled. Dave then gently began to massage every contour of her body, momentarily lost in the moment and oblivious to being on a crowded beach. Several guys looked on with envy in the immediate vicinity as their girlfriends sunbathed. A middle-aged German man sat transfixed before gazing down at his very overweight and very pale wife in a jumbo black bikini. She had fallen asleep and was snoring loudly. Her husband reached out towards the suntan lotion but instead picked up a personal stereo, which he promptly put to use.

Once Dave had covered and caressed every inch of Elsie's body he really was ready for sex to the point of painful desperation. He stripped off his T-shirt and made a dash for the sea to cool his travel-weary and lust-ridden body.

Throughout the massage, Elsie had lay with her eyes closed and secretly enjoyed every second of the experience. The odd bite of the lip and repressed sigh went unnoticed as Dave's nimble fingers almost enticed a full orgasm.

Elsie opened her eyes and smiled as Dave sprinted away.

Back in Hersonissos, the day had seemed to drag. Tony nervously noted every passing hour as he mentally prepared some key conversation prompts for his date with Kim. Gavin gave the same recurring tips that Tony should be himself and relax. At the same time, Gavin eagerly awaited his next date with Annette, regarding the ritual sunbathing by the pool as a mundane obstacle before the event. Phil spent the whole afternoon on a sunbed, wearing his personal stereo and constantly mulling over his solo evening to come and really remaining oblivious to the endless spooling tunes. He now just wanted the night to come quickly so he could get it out of the way and then look forward to the rest of the Campaign with renewed vigour and determination.

Late afternoon once again heralded the move from poolside to a cool, darkened room. Phil lay alone and awake, as Tony and Gavin got ready for their respective dates. Once they were showered, casually but smartly dressed in almost matching designer polo shirts and white chinos, whilst strongly smelling of the same aftershave from the same shared bottle, Tony and Gavin visited Phil.

'Are you sure you're okay with this?' Gavin checked to allay his nagging guilty conscience.

Phil looked at his friends wearing their best holiday clothes like teenagers going on a date. Tony even jigged with nervous anticipation.

'No, actually you're right. Let's go out on the lash instead,' Phil's response brought immediate startled and worried looks. 'Only joking, it's good for morale. You two get going and don't do anything I wouldn't do.'

Gavin gave Phil a pat on the back whilst Tony mimicked him in a scene of pure pathos before they disappeared out of the door.

Phil looked around the small enclosed and darkened room. He thought of his mundane and lonely life at home. He slumped down on his bed as his eyes welled up before burying his face in his hands.

The early evening heat was still intense as the glowing seafront of Malia bade farewell to the day and the large populous crowds who had covered the shore.

A full expanse of sandy beach could now be seen, dotted with the occasional couple enjoying a romantic stroll. In the foreground stood a single girl in her late twenties, gazing down the road with a frequent nervous glance, interspersed with the odd shiver despite the warmth around her. Her freshly washed brown hair shone under the sun's rays as she constantly adjusted a new white cotton shoulderless blouse that complimented a creaseless knee length cream skirt.

Kim Matthews was ready for the evening although daylight kept the remains of the day clinging on. She had changed into at least ten outfits that afternoon before going with her initial choice. Kim had her dream man to impress and she did not want to make any mistakes. She was an old-fashioned honest girl who was the pride and joy of her hard working middle-class parents. Only Mr Right was going to do for Kim, but as she headed for her thirtieth birthday the concern over his existence had grown stronger and stronger. Most of her school circle was married with children and enjoying the life that Kim so wanted for herself. Her only single friend was Gill, who had endured so many bad experiences with men that she had come to almost detest the opposite sex. Gill was the eternal trophy shag that drunken men prayed on and then quickly dumped without a second thought. Kim saw sex as sacrosanct and only a bond of true love. She was not a virgin and had been persuaded between the sheets by one time fiancé Nigel. The first time came after eight months of courting and an expensive engagement ring. The bank he worked for then gave suave, posh Nigel a post in Asia, but Kim could not bare to go with him and be parted from her mum and dad. The engagement stayed intact for several months after Nigel left, until an aggressive career-minded manageress seduced him.

These days Kim would read her romantic novels and watch every chick-flick as it did the rounds. Man-hating Gill was her only real companion acting as friend and protector. This time even Gill had backed off and given her blessing to the man on his way to meet Kim. The same man that Kim had observed on so many cold, wet Saturdays at home as he silently read his newspaper alone in the café that she waitressed in. The times that she had prayed for a golden romantic moment to bring them together in true Hollywood tradition. And when she had given up all hope, the same man turns up thousands of miles from home. Incredibly he not only recognised her, but he wanted to be with her.

The nerves were now getting too much as Kim stood by the sign for Dolphin Beach as agreed, her eyes anxiously following the increasing number of taxis passing by. A glance at the watch revealed it was now six thirty-five and her date was five minutes late. Perhaps he wouldn't show at all.

'Hi, sorry I'm late. The taxi dropped me in the wrong place,' Tony had taken several deep breaths before coolly announcing his arrival.

Kim looked up, amazed that she had not spotted Tony sooner, having studiously watched the road for over twenty-five minutes. She giggled. 'Oh I didn't realise... I mean that you were late.' She giggled again and tried to collect some composure, 'Um, shall we go and have a drink?'

'Excellent idea,' Tony had already drowned a couple of quick whiskeys at the hotel in the name of Dutch courage.

The shy, awkward couple walked along the front with a slightly nervous swagger. Kim led the way past the main street, which was already showing signs of effervescent rowdiness, and on to a quiet bar in amongst some small restaurants. The décor was traditional and topped off with the mellow strains of local music. White tablecloths and glowing candles finished off the romantic ambience.

The bar had been selected specially by Kim and she smiled with joy at the perfection of the scene, as she began to relax more and more. Tony nodded with a satisfied air and congratulated Kim on her choice. This was a true date in every sense of the word.

To start with, the conversation was coy and gently probing, with the loud waiter interjecting more words than the nervous couple. To fill each nervous silence Tony and Kim simultaneously drank their wine until the bottle was quickly emptied. With immediate empathy they both began to laugh and freely acknowledge their parallel nerves. The ice was now broken. Another bottle of wine was ordered and this time it was the conversation that flowed freely.

Once the wine was gone, the now confident and slightly intoxicated couple moved on to a small restaurant called Analpsi, where Tony persuaded his beau to share a large swordfish platter.

Complimented by more wine and candle-lit conversation, the food seemed to taste all the better.

With a full life history and philosophy well and truly shared by the end of the meal, it was time for a full cabaret as traditional dancers energetically went through their paces in the centre of the packed dining area.

It was not long before unsuspecting diners were selected to be part of the show. Tony's arm was grabbed and he was thrust on to the main floor. Initial efforts to mimic the dancers bore more of a resemblance to a Norman Wisdom routine as the alcohol took over. Kim clapped and laughed loudly, wiping away drunken tears of joy and ecstasy.

In all the Hollywood films that Kim had seen, none could have compared to the pure romantic spectacle that she was now part of. This was old-fashioned love, founded on a Greek night, on a Greek island only yards from the bars and clubs that hosted the animalistic pursuit of sex and revelry that was the modern day holiday norm.

As Tony's night began with first date nerves, Gavin strode over to the Harp with the calm disinterested air of a man meeting his wife for lunch. Although he had known Annette for less than a week, it already felt so cosy and within Gavin's need for structured security, it felt so right.

The fact that the relationship was already on such a familiar even keel had distracted Gavin's thoughts from beyond the imminent future. Unless the lives of one of them was about to drastically change then the couple's perfect union could be over as quickly as it had begun.

As he neared the rendezvous, Gavin at last gave a thought to beyond Friday. Like the theme of his life it was one-dimensional and focussed on familiar territory. He would bring the girl home and make her part of his normal everyday life, supporting her whilst continuing with a career at Maxies. Annette could then find work too and eventually they could get married and have two lovely children. Gavin smiled at the simplicity of his dream and the notion that it was not a demand for the world.

Annette gave Gavin the now customary all encompassing bear hug of a cuddle, accompanied by a large sincere welcoming grin. Gavin put his arms around Annette's full figure feeling the full warmth and comfort of her curves, happy to stay in an eternal clinch and die happy. Eventually they both prised their bodies apart and after an equally lingering and satisfying kiss Annette led Gavin to her car.

With her usual effervescence, Annette chatted incessantly as she turned her attention to Gavin almost as much as she observed the road. Indeed, the car seemed to run on autopilot as each individual bend was expertly navigated and every large pothole somehow avoided. Annette's enthusiasm bubbled and boiled to melting point as she spoke of the destination for the evening, from the culinary delight of the food to the colourful staff and unique location. Gavin was already beginning to feel in awe of the place before Annette soberly added 'I just so love J'alopex... but I hope I'm not building it up too much.'

The journey retraced part of Dave's epic scooter trek, following the winding hill that rose above the coastal plane beyond Malia. Just as the hill began to rise steeply, Annette suddenly took a sharp turn down what looked like an old disused track.

A bumpy ride over another mile during which Gavin was convinced on several occasions that Annette's car would simply collapse and leave them stranded. Finally the track led to a proud, old stone building that blended into its surroundings as if camouflaged from view. A small wooden sign announced that it was J'alopex restaurant, betraying its function to those not in the know. The windows were lit up by lanterns and gave an eerie welcoming glow.

The inside of J'alopex was like a cavern, sprouting into numerous breakaway rooms. Simple old wooden tables, with large dark carver chairs, were the only furnishings on a cold, grey concrete floor.

A youngish half-shaved man appeared and immediately embraced Annette. Gavin went to shake the man's hand, expecting a typical warm welcome.

'So who's this fecking gobshite then, Nettie?' the man held a stern face as he spoke with an authentic Irish brogue.

Annette slapped his shoulder. 'None of your games, Niles. I told you when I booked that this is my fella.' The final statement gave Gavin a little shiver of pride.

'Nah,' Niles turned in astonishment. 'But he looks like a right eejit of the first order.'

'Niles,' Annette shouted with a disdainful stare.

Niles looked even more aggressive before breaking into a smile and then roaring with laughter. He leaned forward and hugged Gavin like a long lost brother. 'I was only slagging you, man. I do it to everyone, just to see their faces. Follow me, let's get you a jar.'

As Niles led the way to a cosy small side room, the sound of twanging guitars struck up filling the air with unmistakable Celtic melodies. Niles lit a small lantern that barely illuminated the room as another man entered with two pints of Guinness.

'Cheers,' Gavin took a large gulp of the black stuff.

'No problem,' came the waiter's reply in another strong Irish accent.

'Is everybody here Irish?' Gavin looked up at Niles.

'Oh yes. Now let me know when you're ready to order,' Niles then walked off down the corridor.

Gavin looked around in the semi-darkness. 'Where's the menus?'

'There aren't any,' Annette announced. 'You just have to tell Niles what you fancy and if he's got it, you can have it.'

'What if he hasn't got it?' Gavin looked concerned.

'Then you try again until you find something that he has,' Annette leaned forward. 'Ordering has been known to take a while before now.'

'Wow, I can see why you like this place,' as Gavin spoke some roars and shouts echoed down from another room. 'I was expecting some bog standard Greek place, especially with the name.'

'Ah, you see, even that has an Irish connection,' Annette sat back as if to tell a long story. 'Well the word alopex is Greek for fox and so J'alopex translates as J fox.'

Gavin thought for a moment. 'Right, like Johnnie Foxes in Dublin. I've been there actually.'

'A gold star to the man. Johnnie Foxes in the village of Glencullen, high in the Dublin Mountains,' Annette looked lost in thought. 'I love it there too.'

'Do you think you'll ever go back to Ireland?' Gavin hesitated before adding, 'or even England maybe?'

Annette gave a big smile. 'No, this is my home now, and with J'alopex I have my own little piece of Ireland.'

Gavin suddenly realised that his plans to take Annette home were going to be totally unilateral. 'What... what about us? Do we have a future?'

'I hope so, fella, but that's going to be down to you and whether you're ready to change.' Annette leaned forward again, 'Let's eat and I'll tell you more.'

Niles returned with impeccable timing and was able to instantly confirm that he could meet Gavin's request for a steak and ale pie. Annette ordered the same.

Dinner was now a slightly anxious affair, although the food was fantastic and the conversation remained free flowing. During every short silence and every mouthful of food, Gavin pondered with anticipation just what Annette's announcement would be.

When the meal was over, Annette ordered two large goblets of port.

'Well?' Gavin held up his goblet. 'I would propose a toast to us, but... um... what next?'

Annette suddenly looked uncharacteristically serious. 'I have a proposition for you and I want you to hear me out. I know that at home you have a very ordered life and that you're happy in all that you do. Well... then there's me. I'd be no good being the little wife in your nine to five world, and it wouldn't work no matter how much I'm falling for you. Now you could come and live in my world and enjoy all this, and perhaps that wouldn't work too. Maybe you can't give up your structured life. So... well I've had a word with Niles here. You see he has this place and a very large vineyard down the road. He won the Irish lotto two years ago and used some of the funds to start a new life for himself and his friends. Well, I told him that you like computers, and the

Internet, and all that, and he's agreed that you can have a job making a website, or whatever, to advertise this place, market his wine, organise wine tasting, and all that.'

Gavin was stunned.

'Now I don't want an answer from you tonight, but I want you to think about it and let me know on Thursday. If it's yes then you can come and live with me. If it's no we'll kiss goodbye with a tear in our eye.'

'Well…' Gavin went to speak but Annette put a finger to his mouth to stop him.

The drive back was very quiet, although punctuated with the odd shout on account of Annette's slightly shaky drunken driving. During the short journey, Gavin mulled over the proposal. He made and changed his mind at least ten times. This was going to be tough.

Annette dropped Gavin at the hotel and gave him an affectionate kiss. 'Now I don't want to see you until Thursday, when what will be, will be.'

After the departure of Gavin and Tony, Phil's night began on a total low. By himself and feeling lonely and vulnerable, Phil knew that he had to get out and be with the crowds. From wallowing in self-pity, he suddenly snapped into an assertive and vibrant mood. The evening was not to be wasted and Phil was determined to enjoy himself. With uplifting music blasting from the stereo, a revitalising shower and carefully selected go-getting clothes, coupled with splashes of strong aftershave, the metamorphosis was complete. Phil Mockley was ready to take on the world, single-handed.

First stop was the pool bar and the now familiar company of Theo, who himself stood alone as the strains of Guns 'n' Roses filled the air.

'Yo, a nice long cold one please, Theo.' Phil sat down on a bar stool as a gentle breeze wafted the strong aroma of his aftershave.

'Wow, man, you really going for the ladies tonight.' Theo handed over a lager. 'Where are your friends? Still preparing themselves for the ladies?'

'Uhhh,' Phil hesitated and took a sip of beer. 'Nah, they're all having quiet ones tonight, so I'm holding up tradition and making sure that someone gets the shags in.'

'Somebody talking about shagging?' Albert suddenly appeared from nowhere dressed in customary baggy shorts and a polo shirt. 'Now that's a subject for which I am the master. In fact, you could put me on Mastermind with that Scandinavian fella, and I'd have shagging as my specialist subject. I wouldn't pass on anything.'

Theo handed Albert a lager and he took an instant swig, soaking half of his beard as well as his palate. He then continued, 'Up to nearly a thousand notches on the bedpost now. That's why I look so old. From always getting me end away. I'm only thirty-five really.'

Albert roared with laughter and gave Phil a gentle dig to the kidneys. Phil grimaced from both the punch and the tall story.

'So, what's the secret mate?' Phil asked sternly.

Albert pondered. 'Two things: one, I've always lived life on the edge and women like a man of danger; two, I make 'em laugh… best route to the sack.'

Phil nodded as a token gesture. 'Wise words. I can certainly learn from you.'

'Are you and your mates getting your ends away?' Albert looked around. 'Where are your mates?'

'They're taking it easy,' Phil kept to what he had told Theo. 'And yes, we're doing all right.'

Albert cracked a big smile. 'And you just keep on going, looking for pussy whilst they're flagging. Not the marrying type, eh?'

'Definitely not. Life's for living. Too much pussy to be had. I'll sleep when I die and all that,' Phil began to convince himself.

'Bon Jovi. Cool man. Sleep when I die,' Theo suddenly interjected and began to sing the song badly as he played air guitar. 'I have the album somewhere here. I will find it and attract all the ladies here to the bar for you.'

'Thanks,' Phil sarcastically curled up his top lip.

'You know young 'un, you remind me of me. When I was your age like,' Albert stood up next to Phil. 'And just to think in thirty years time you could still be in your prime like me. Seeya lads, keep it hanging,' Albert once again disappeared into the night.

'You Give Love A Bad Name' by Bon Jovi, began playing as Theo started to slowly headbang unrhythmically. 'Check it out, ladies, come and meet the boys.'

Phil finished his beer. 'Right, I've had enough of being a spectator, time to be a bloody player.'

Phil managed to find a small quiet café, where he was able to eat, without feeling too conspicuous for being on his own. He then moved on to a large and very dark club, where it was easy to mingle with the crowds, get pissed and letch.

At first the club was relatively empty, but started to fill up as Phil began to relax after a few beers. Soon the dance floor was heaving, and with a diverse selection of girls from all over Europe. Phil had danced alone when his mates had been around so he convinced himself that it would be no different now that he was actually by himself. Moving to the edge of the floor he began to dance in an apparent trance, lost in the rhythm of the music. Gradually Phil began to look around him, staring with lust at the scantily clad and tanned fit female bodies, as they gyrated to the never-ending beat.

As subtly as he could, Phil tried to infiltrate some of the small circles of dancing girls. On each occasion backs were turned and bodies strategically manoeuvred to repel the foreign invader. Eventually Phil gave up and returned to the bar.

With another beer ordered, Phil once again surveyed the now crowded bar. Trying to find a hint of friendly eye contact was starting to seem impossible, when his eyes suddenly held a static position. A girl with curly, peroxide blonde hair, and wearing a very loose cotton dress, caught his attention. She sat alone, looking lonely, several yards away and Phil was sure that he detected a slight welcoming smile, as the girl stared in his direction.

Phil took a large gulp of beer. 'Here we go,' he whispered to himself.

Once by the girl's side it was clear that she was nonchalantly staring into space and looking beyond Phil. He still decided to give it a go.

'Hi, thought you looked a bit lonely there so came over to say hello.' Phil jigged from one foot to the other as he stood in front of the blonde.

'Hello,' she looked up with a false smile and fluttered her eyelashes before changing to a very stern expression. 'And fock ov,' was added in a very strong east European accent.

From momentarily thinking he had scored, Phil was now shocked. He quickly turned on his heels, drank his beer, and decided to call it a night.

Heading past an empty hotel bar, Phil had no way of avoiding Theo.

'Hey, man, where are you going? The night is young,' Theo said, holding up an empty beer glass, offering to fill it.

Phil could not face returning to a lonely room once more and chose to drink himself into oblivion in the company of Theo and his stash of soft metal.

Phil stayed until the alcohol had almost knocked him into sleep. As he returned to the room, he missed the return of a thoughtful Gavin by literally seconds, followed closely by an ecstatic Tony.

After a day on Elounda beach had left Dave feeling tired and extremely sun drenched, he longed for the cool hotel room and much needed siesta. Instead he was marooned miles away, and with no fresh clothes to change into, from the sweaty T-shirt and shorts that he had worn all day. On the other hand there was Elsie.

As they walked off the beach, Elsie had an exaggerated spring in her step. 'Come along, David, let's go freshen up and eat.' She pulled Dave by the hand and led him back towards the main town. He followed with a slight drag of the heels, puzzled as to where they were going next.

Elsie led Dave straight past the scooters and to the white glossy steps of a posh hotel.

'Don't tell me, you've booked a double room for the night,' Dave joked, whilst hoping at the same time.

'Not quite, that would be no fun,' Elsie pulled Dave close. 'Now just follow my lead and all will be okay,' Elsie then motioned a bewildered Dave up the steps.

Once inside, the décor and ambience of the main reception area was very suave. Several people stood in front of the main desk as Elsie remained in the background unnoticed.

Elsie moved over to the concierge and said in an even posher voice than normal. 'Excuse me, when is breakfast first served?'

'Seven-thirty, madam,' the man replied.

'Thank you,' Elsie then motioned Dave towards the lifts, and into the first one to arrive.

'What was all that about? Are we room crashing or something?' Dave was now wondering if he was going to get arrested.

'No, silly, I just needed to get past the main desk and check if any keys were hanging up. I think we'll be number one five three three.' The lift stopped and Elsie marched off down the corridor until she came to the health suite. 'Come along, darling, I desperately need my sauna.'

A young man in reception looked up from his magazine to see a coy English girl with her bedraggled partner.

'Could we use the health suite please, had a beastly hot day on the beach,' Elsie fluttered her eyelashes.

'Sure, what's your room number, please?' The man took out a pen whilst still focussing on his magazine.

'One five three three,' Elsie stated quickly and confidently.

'Sign here, please.'

Elsie signed the book and bounded into the club, followed by a disbelieving Dave.

Inside the club, Dave was able to enjoy a sauna, shower and shave, whilst using an extensive range of toiletries to spruce himself up. As the woman's sauna was separate, Dave agreed to rendezvous with Elsie after half and hour, by which time he felt revitalised beneath the same travel weary clothes. Elsie also looked cleaned and refreshed, choosing to clip her hair back into a ponytail.

The indignant couple swiftly left the club and the building before any questions could be asked.

Dave looked down at his ragged attire. 'Well I still don't think we can eat at the Ritz. Don't tell me, another Roundbottom picnic under the stars.'

'Oh no, something far more civilised. Follow me my good man.' Elsie strode on at a pace once again.

She did not walk far, as round the next corner stood a small basic pizzeria. Inside, Dave was a little startled to be confronted once again by Nick, the bar owner from Neapolis.

'Hey, man, good to see you again,' Dave held out his hand. 'Do you own every pub and restaurant around here?'

The owner looked baffled and glanced at Elsie to explain. She chose to laugh first. 'Dave, I'd like to introduce you to Paul... who has a twin brother called Nick.'

Dave grimaced. 'Sorry, mate.'

Paul cracked a slight smile and then squeezed Dave's hand like a wrench as he finally greeted him.

Dave shook his fingers vigorously after escaping the handshake and whispered to himself. 'Obviously a family trait.'

Dave and Elsie were taken to a basic table in the corner of the small half-filled room. The kitchen area stood in the opposite corner, where a fat chef prepared pizza in front of a roaring clay oven.

Elsie ordered two pepperoni specials and a bottle of Chablis before Dave could even mention the word menu. When the pizzas arrived they were huge and stacked with thick pepperoni, almost hiding the cheese. They looked good and tasted superb after a long day in the sun.

'So, Elsie Roundbottom,' Dave poured them both another glass of wine, 'tell me a bit more about yourself.'

'What more is there to tell. I'm just a free spirit from a wealthy family who just travels the world,' Elsie seemed indifferent.

'Well,' Dave persisted. 'What was your childhood like? Is it the answer to why you do what you do?'

'Okay, you asked. Let's get it out of the way then,' Elsie took a deep breath. 'I was born in nineteen seventy-one as the first daughter but third child of my very wealthy parents. Mummy and daddy were fine and upstanding, although Daddy shagged every secretary he had. I was educated privately at a god-awful boarding school. As I told you, I studied media studies. The trouble was I went to Norwich poly, when my three brothers and little sister all went to university in Edinburgh. As did Mummy and Daddy.

Mother was outraged when I became a holiday rep and immediately stopped my allowance.'

'But I thought that you still got money from your parents?' Dave remembered a previous conversation.

'Oh yes, Daddy never cut me off. He's got oodles of money, so Mummy never notices the odd direct debit to an offshore account,' Elsie gave a cheeky smile.

'Aha… and that's just it, rich girl,' Dave pointed indignantly. 'This lifestyle is so easy for you. You've never really had anything to give up, and you've got an inheritance to fall back on. If I just dropped everything and travelled, I'd be searching for scraps wherever I went and most likely return home to be a tramp in the local precinct.'

'Rubbish, office boy,' Elsie mimicked the indignant tone. 'You just invest your money and rent out your flat to pay the mortgage. Yes, then you have to live on your wits, as I have to. The trick is that you only spend what you earn on your travels. I invest most of what Daddy sends me. When I return home one day, I'll have a nice little nest egg, and so could you if you did it right.'

'Simple,' Dave said sarcastically raising his glass, and totally unconvinced.

'Simple,' Elsie reciprocated the toast, realising that there was still some converting to do.

Elsie settled the bill and ordered another bottle of wine as a takeaway. She swore the money was some recent wages. After another knuckle crunching handshake, Dave followed Elsie once more.

This time Elsie did head back to the scooters. 'Just a short ride to our accommodation for the night, and we can then polish this off,' the bottle of wine was held aloft.

The ride back up the hill felt a little eerie as night had now descended and the majority of flickering lights were being left behind in Elounda. The road was deserted and hard to see, lit only by the stuttering lights of two struggling scooters. Dave felt a slight chill as the cooler night air brushed his exposed knees. He now longed for a big warm bed, preferably sharing with Elsie.

Elsie forged a route to the crest of the steep road before taking a sharp turn without warning down a small side track. Rather than continue down the track, she immediately dismounted. Dave followed suit, wondering once more what lay ahead.

'Follow me. The next bit is a little climb,' Elsie grabbed her bag and handed Dave the wine. 'And don't drop this.'

'Uh!' before Dave could ask any questions, Elsie had disappeared into the darkness up a wooded bank.

Dave made haste to follow, but continuously stumbled through the undergrowth, scratching himself frequently on the sharp vegetation. After a couple of minutes he came to a steep slope that inclined up to a clearing. Elsie stood above and lowered a hand to usher Dave up. With only a little effort, Dave was able to squeeze his frame onto a well-kept lawn. He then gazed up to see a small summerhouse several yards away, which marked the boundary of the grounds of a lavish villa, whose lights glowed some distance away in the background.

'Shit, if we're staying in some posh villa, couldn't we have arrived in a more civilised way,' Dave dusted himself down and made to walk towards the lights.

'No, no, no,' stressed Elsie emphatically. 'The deal is we sleep here.' She pointed to the wooden structure of the summerhouse, just shaded from view on the edge of the moonlit lawn.

'Why?' Dave shrugged. 'Don't you even want to say hello to your friends?'

'Oh no. I see them lots anyway. The deal is that I can use the summerhouse whenever I'm passing,' Elsie walked over to the door. 'Come and take a look.'

Dave followed once more as Elsie opened the door. Inside was very dark, but as Dave's eyes adjusted he made out the outline of several cane sofas and chairs. 'Is there a light, or do you have a torch?'

'No, but don't worry, your eyes will soon get used to the dark.' Elsie walked over and looked out of the front of the house. 'See that, Elounda at night in all its glory. I love it.'

Dave looked out on the glowing beauty of a small bay town at night, lighting up the beach and the odd wave moving towards the shore. In the sky above, the moon and stars also shone brightly from a dark blue and totally cloudless sky. For a few seconds Dave was caught in a trance, broken by the popping of a wine cork.

'Come and join me,' Elsie had sat down on one of the large cushioned settees.

Dave moved over and sat alongside her in the darkness. 'You are one big surprise, aren't you. They just threw away the rule book when they wrote your destiny.'

'Oh yes, great isn't it?' Elsie once again retrieved two small glasses from her bag and filled them both with wine.

The more wine that was drunk, the more both Elsie and Dave sunk back into the soft cushions, bonding their tired bodies together in the process. Throughout, they looked out on the night sky as if sitting in a lounge at home, fascinated and encapsulated by a movie on TV.

It was not long after the final glass of wine was gone that the couple simultaneously fell asleep, seated and leaning against each other.

About an hour later, Dave woke with a jolt and through bleary eyes looked down on Elsie cuddled against his shoulder. He carefully laid her down on the full length of the sofa and crept over to lie on another across the room. Just as he reached it, Elsie's voice struck up. 'Don't you fancy a bonk then?'

Dave looked back over to Elsie's crouching silhouetted figure just as she lifted her top and flashed her boobs. Even in the twilight they looked magnificent as they almost bounced into view. An exhausted Dave soon found a second wind.

As Dave moved closer Elsie whipped her top off to fully reveal a pair of large ample breasts. Dave sat down and immediately began to gently caress each nipple in turn, before cupping Elsie's right breast firmly in his left hand and pulling her into a passionate kiss.

The gentle caressing quickly turned into a wild and frantic tugging of clothes, before a naked couple fell back into the soft cushions. Dave lay underneath as Elsie straddled him and began to ride him with vigour. Through ecstatic eyes Dave looked up as Elsie's breasts bobbed up and down with carefree abandon, alternating against the rest of her body as it thrust towards orgasm. Elise threw her head back, staring at the night sky through the glass-panelled roof, almost yelping in delight.

Dave lay completely still, not having to move his tired body but instead savour every moment until Elsie finally brought him to a shuddering climax, twitching her own body in orgasmic union.

That was Dave's final memory of the evening.

Week 2: Day 3 – Where do we go from here?

Dave's eyes were firmly closed and his brain at least ninety-five percent shut down, but there was a thumping shrill beat somewhere in the distance.

A cool breeze brushed over the hairs on his naked body as Elsie lifted herself from the sleeping embrace. Dave slowly twitched his eyes open to see the full-figured naked Elsie stood up with her back to him, as the sun rose up in the background. Dave gazed at her firm buttocks and immediately felt the urge to jump up and initiate more rampant sex.

Elsie, however, began to dress herself, and quickly. 'Come on, lover boy, we've got to get going. We haven't got time for that,' Elsie pointed at Dave's obvious erection.

'Shit, it's only six,' Dave wondered if his blurry eyes were misleading him as he picked up his watch. 'What's the bloody rush?'

Elsie threw Dave his clothes and was now fully dressed. 'I'll explain, just keep moving.'

Dave prised himself up from the sofa and dressed as quickly as his tired body could muster. Elsie then dragged him by the hand and led a sprint across the lawn, which almost resulted in the couple falling down the steep bank on the other side.

The two scooters still sat side by side, just as they had been left the night before. Elsie climbed aboard her machine and gave a deep sigh, followed by a large grin.

'So what's going on then?' muttered an unshaven and bedraggled Dave, who was feeling a bit naïve. 'You don't actually know the people who own the summerhouse, do you?'

'Well,' Elsie thought for a second, 'I've been staying there for so long, I almost feel like I know them. Besides, no harm done and we had some fun, Mr Stud,' Elsie pushed out a hand and tweaked Dave's groin, causing him to take a small jump back.

Dave was exasperated. 'I don't know... you're bloody mad.'

'But bloody good fun,' Elsie interjected.

Dave jumped onto his scooter. '"So where do we go from here, is it down to the lake I fear.", to quote the Haircut boys.'

'Well that would be telling, and deadly dull.' Elsie moved off from the small track and headed up the hill, closely followed by Dave.

Phil woke relatively early and was dressed and shaved by nine. He felt surprisingly cheerful, as well as rested, after a deep sleep. With a slight chuckle and mocking curse towards Dave's empty bed, Phil headed out in the bright Cretan morning.

After collecting some chocolate and a copy of *The Sun*, Phil settled down by the pool and felt relaxed. The poolside was already very crowded as numerous young British families set up camp for the day.

As more families ventured out, a crescendo of noise began to build as the children splashed enthusiastically in the water. Concerned young mothers watched their young offspring's every move as the fathers either read newspapers or dozed in complete ignorance.

'*Aaaaaaalistaaaaaaaair!*' suddenly boomed out from the hubbub of activity. Phil looked up to see the cheeky young lad being hotly pursued by his dad. 'Come 'ere, I'll tan yer hide for yer.'

How could the lad refuse an offer like that, thought Phil, as the rest of the poolside wondered what the mischievous mite had done this time? With perfect comedy timing, just as the dad reached out for his son, he slipped on a small pool of water and fell heftily onto his backside. A spontaneous roar of laughter followed.

Phil considered the family lifestyle briefly, and convinced himself that the young, carefree single life was still the best option. After all, what could beat the lads' holiday, even if this one was not going strictly to plan; surely it was just a glitch.

After about an hour Gavin and Tony appeared and ordered some breakfast by the poolside.

'So studs, I take it you both got the shags in last night?' Phil raised his eyebrows suggestively and waited for detailed accounts.

Instead there was muted silence.

'Come on… you didn't get blown out, did you?' Phil tried again.

'No… I had a lovely evening,' Tony replied before innocently adding 'it was very romantic and it wouldn't have been right to have pushed for sex.'

Phil tutted loudly. 'Well, Gav, you must have got the shags in. You're on a constant promise there.'

Gavin turned slightly. 'No, not last night. We just had a meal and some beers.'

'Blimey!' Phil was amazed. 'Well at least we can be guaranteed that Holliman will have scored last night.'

'I take it that he hasn't returned then?' Gavin already knew the answer.

'No. Probably shagging as we speak.' Phil nodded to affirm his thoughts.

'So what about you … and Tamzin Outhwaite.' Gavin reached out and playfully slapped Phil's leg.

Phil looked totally puzzled for a moment. 'Eh? Oh, no joy. Had a go, but just found her boring.'

Elsie continued to trek down a good quality road out of Elounda. For a stretch it almost resembled a grand prix course, with a series of hairpin bends.

Once again the road descended to a colourful scenic backdrop and directly towards another small coastal town. As Elsie led the way into the town, she suddenly took a left fork in the road and headed for the harbour.

Dave had expected another marathon journey under the burning Cretan sun, and so was amazed when Elsie pulled up by the harbour's edge. The morning was still breaking and they had been on the road for barely twenty minutes.

'Don't tell me we're stopping already,' Dave said, waiting for the catch.

'Absolutely. I'm starving and need some breakfast,' Elsie held out a hand to present the picturesque harbour town. 'Where do you fancy?'

Dave perused a seemingly endless stream of cafés dotted all the way down the road. 'Anywhere with food.'

The couple settled for an open-air café yards from where they had first stopped. Dave sat down and rubbed some delayed sleep from his eyes and looked out on the water as small boats glided along. The harbour's edge was becoming packed with tourists, milling but not rushing. Dave heard numerous German accents mingled with the odd snippet of English, with either a Lancashire or Yorkshire lilt.

'So where is this place? It looks all right.' Dave relaxed back in his chair as the waiter delivered two double espressos.

'It's called Agios Nikolaos. Very pretty, but a bit touristy really,' Elsie confirmed with a slight dismissive tone.

'Popular, you mean, and does that mean it's yesterday's news as far as you're concerned?' Dave challenged Elsie.

'In a way... I mean it's the same when everyone discovers the places you like. They then lose the mystery. It's a bit like discovering a really good band, who have a bit of a cult following. Then suddenly they top the charts and everyone's a fan,' Elsie gently bit her lower lip. 'A bit selfish really.'

'It doesn't stop you wanting to visit the places, though. I mean Hersonissos is well popular.' Dave's eyes widened as the waiter delivered a large plate of croissants and pastries.

'Oh, too right, I still know a good thing. Everyone loves these, but I'm not going to stop eating them,' Elsie took a large bite from a heavily iced Danish.

With breakfast finished, Dave would have been content to spend several hours in the café, soaking in the atmosphere and shooting the breeze with Elsie over many more double espressos. However, with another spurt of energy Elsie jolted up from her chair and once again beckoned Dave to follow.

Thankfully Elsie turned right and leisurely strolled away from the scooters. Dave walked by her side, relaxed by the calming coastal breeze brushing his face. He almost felt the romantic urge to reach out and hold Elsie's hand as they ambled. Just as he considered what reaction Elsie might give, she reached out to grab Dave's hand. It was, however, just to guide him down a side road and away from the harbour.

Elsie kept on walking until they once again came to the edge of water. A large inland lake stood majestically to the foreground of small rolling wooded cliffs. Like the harbour they had just left, the water's edge was lined with open-air cafés and restaurants, and the banks were swelling with people.

'This is one good reason why I always come back here,' Elsie had a satisfied smile. 'Welcome to the bath of Athena.'

'Wow,' Dave almost stood back in awe. 'That is what you call a bath, and I didn't even bring my rubber ducks.'

Elsie ignored the comment. 'This place is amazing. Voulismeni, to give the proper name, according to mythology, is where the goddess Athena used to take a bath. Hence the nickname.'

As Elsie stared out over the vivid blue lake, to Dave, she looked every inch a goddess herself. The sun lit up her golden brown hair and natural features to frame an idyllic scene. Dave suddenly remembered his camera and quickly retrieved it from his small beach bag to capture the moment. As the camera shutter clicked Elsie turned to smile, leaving Dave as much awe with her, as he was with the scene beyond.

The couple joined the multitude of tourists wandering around the edge of the lake. Numerous small fishing boats lined the shore as local fisherman tended to their nets.

'*Elseeee*,' a loud voice suddenly boomed from the water, several decibels above any other background noise. Dave looked around to see a very small Greek man, sitting in a speedboat moored amongst the fishing vessels.

The small man sounded a foghorn at full volume, causing everyone in the near vicinity to flinch and hold their ears. 'Everyone rejoice and sing your song for Elsie has returned,' the man shouted, with a deepness that betrayed his physical size.

'Eddie, come here so I can see you,' Elsie beckoned the small man to the shore.

With a sudden dash of speed, Eddie jumped from his boat to dry land and ran to hug Elsie. His head came up no higher than Elsie's shoulders and the embrace saw Eddie bury his face in her chest. As he came up for air there was a knowing smug grin.

'Dave, I'd like you to meet Eddie Large,' Elsie placed her arm around Eddie's shoulders.

Dave spluttered. 'Fuck off, I'm not that gullible, Roundbottom.'

Eddie looked serious. 'No, no, my good man, Eddie Large is my name. A cruel twist of fate, although I am blessed with a very large penis.'

Dave now stood silent as he pondered how his journey with Elsie was turning into 'Alice Though The Looking Glass'.

'Hey, Eddie, how about a quick jaunt in the boat. I'm trying to blow the cobwebs out of Dave the office boy here.' Elsie pointed over to Eddie's speedboat, which was called Goliath.

Eddie once again became excited and moved over to hug Dave. '*Yeeees*. It will be great. Dave, I will make you a better man,' his voice boomed out once again, forcing passers-by to turn and observe the commotion.

Conscious that he was becoming part of a sideshow, Dave simply nodded and willingly followed Eddie and Elsie to the boat. He went to take a seat at the back with Elsie as Eddie enthusiastically started up the boat and immediately accelerated out into the lake. The jolt of instantaneous speed almost sent Dave flying off the back. He managed to grapple to a position alongside a calmly seated Elsie, as the craft glided over the water at top speed, narrowly avoiding several fishing boats. Eddie swerved to and fro before heading for a small canal. The noise of the engine was loud and incessant, but it was not sufficient to drown out Eddie as he began to sing 'If You Want To Be My Lover' by the Spice Girls.

Elsie tried to shout above it all. 'Eddie's a big Spice Girls fan. He's convinced that he's destined to marry Emma Bunton.'

Dave nodded with a bewildered grin.

The boat passed through the canal and into the harbour, where once again Eddie, either skilfully or luckily, avoided all other sea traffic. From the harbour he headed out to the open sea and seemed to find even more speed, crashing into incoming waves. The sea spray was now a constant, almost soaking Dave and Elsie. Then suddenly Eddie spun the vessel at one hundred and eighty degrees and brought it to an immediate standstill.

'Zig a zig, ahh,' he boomed out over the silent water.

As Dave recovered his senses, he marvelled in the special view of Agios Nikolaos.

'Zig a zig, ahh, in fucking deed,' Dave echoed.

Thankfully the ride back was much slower and calmer after a special plea from Elsie. This time Dave savoured the ride like he was floating down the canals of Venice on a romantic gondola, albeit to Eddie's serenade of 'Viva Forever'.

'So, what next?' Dave took a sip of beer from the small open-air bar as he looked out over Lake Voulismeni. It was already lunchtime; the day had moved on whilst he and Elsie had sat motionless, shooting the breeze.

'Well. I'm afraid it's back to Hersonissos, and time for you to rejoin the reality of the lads' holiday,' Elsie punctuated the end of the sentence with mimed italics, whilst attempting a poor cockney accent.

'Yes, and what next?' Dave hoped for much more.

'Well,' Elsie paused. 'That's for you to decide. Only you can map your own destiny, but I think you'll make the right choice.'

'And us?' Dave finally asked the question he really wanted answered.

Elsie's face dropped a little to deliver bad news. 'Well, we've had fun. Both had a laugh. Had a bonk. And now we move on with the experience firmly in the memory banks… and you have a great photo to remember me by.'

'Right… okay,' Dave shrugged his shoulders. 'Shit, it's meant to be me who shags and moves on. Now it seems to always be the other was round.'

'Ahh… I'm sure that your broken heart will mend by the time you pull the next bit of stuff tomorrow night. At least you've had your wicked way with me, eh.' Elsie winked.

'Um, I think that maybe that was the other way round, too,' Dave pondered. 'So don't you think you'll ever stop moving and just settle down?'

'Will you?' Elsie deflected the question back.

'One day,' Dave answered immediately.

'Me too,' Elsie confirmed.

Whilst Dave had ventured out of Hersonissos, met new people and visited new places, his friends had not moved out of the boundaries of the hotel all day. Statically mingled within equally unmoving average families, the trio ordered food and drink and occasionally slipped from sunbed to pool. A few slow lengths, weaving in and out of eagerly splashing children, was the only time that any calories were burned bar a short walk to the toilets. Phil listened to music, Tony read and Gavin spent the whole day pondering Annette's ultimatum. Was it time to change his whole way of being, or just return to the simple comfort zone of normality? The day did not bring a conclusion.

The siesta came at four and by seven the trio were once again Theo's only early evening customers.

'I am playing this only as special treat for my very good friends.' Theo had declared that he would play the whole of Meat Loaf's 'Bat Out Of Hell', as if he was announcing that Elvis was alive and well, and popping round for a drink.

Gavin nodded. 'In my top five, definitely. Good album.'

Phil grimaced. 'Yeah, right.'

'Ah, now you see we all have different tastes. It would be a bit boring if all music was the same,' Gavin took a swig from his lager, wishing it was a dark ale. 'And actually, your favourite album and band tells you everything you need to know about all your personality traits.'

'Right,' Phil acknowledged, as if Gavin had lost his marbles before savouring the cold fizz of his lager.

'My favourite album is "Kiss and Crazy Nights", totally crazy man,' Theo stuck his tongue out and once more assumed the air guitar pose.

'See… totally nuts and couldn't care less what anyone thinks.' Gavin looked to rest his case like a confident lawyer.

'Okay, good start.' Phil was ready to put the case for the opposition. 'But more solid proof needed, methinks.'

'Tony, what's your favourite?' Gavin called the next witness.

Tony thought for a second. '"The Bends" by Radiohead.'

'Slow, unerring, methodical and thoughtful,' Gavin allowed himself a wry smile. 'And I know that Dave's is "All Mod Cons" by The Jam. Stylish, upbeat, assertive and going places.'

'Okay what about you?' Phil knew he was losing the case.

'Status Quo, "On The Level,"' Gavin quietly replied as if he was baring his soul.

Phil smiled. 'Repetitive, unadventurous and safe.'

'Okay, Mockley, what's yours?' Gavin looked for a quick return jab.

'"One Step Beyond" by Madness,' Phil said confidently. 'Try that one for size.'

Gavin pondered. 'Fun loving, larger than life, never to be taken seriously.'

A brief silence was quickly broken as Phil admitted defeat. 'Theo, pour us some more cold ones, mate.'

Just as the drinks were ordered, everyone turned to see a bedraggled, unkempt, and unshaven Dave standing before them. He had only been gone for two days but had all the hallmarks of someone returning from an endless trek through the Andes.

'David Holliman, I presume?' Gavin sniggered at the usual king of cool's rough appearance.

'Fuck, she must have been one good shag.' Phil also began to chuckle.

'What have you been up to?' added Tony with concerned innocence.

'It's a long story, my chum, which I shall recount over several of these this evening,' Dave took a large swig of cold lager like a parched crawling man dying of thirst in the desert.

Dave was shattered beyond belief and could have readily just crawled into bed as he returned to the cool hotel room. The scooter journey back had seemed long and uncompromising. Elsie spoke very little and simply gave him a quick kiss goodbye after they had returned the bikes. 'Good luck' were the final words she said before walking away.

After a shower, shave, and fresh clothes, Dave felt reborn and ready for action once more. Over a meal and several beers his story was recounted, with the odd moment of sheer dramatic licence. None more so than the ending as he coolly announced to Elsie that it had been fun, but it was time to move on.

Gavin and Phil hardly believed the bits that were true, whilst Tony was encapsulated. By the end of the evening, the four friends were once again standing in the corner of a small bar, drinking yet another beer. Phil had even offered Gavin the option of The Harp and was bemused by his refusal.

'Excuse me,' Phil tapped a tall leggy brunette on the shoulder. 'What's your favourite album?'

The girl looked bemused, preparing for some corny chat-up routine. 'Why do you want to know? Mr Saddo.'

'Um, just a little experiment. Give me an answer and I promise to leave you in peace,' Phil said very calmly.

'"Rio" by Duran Duran. Thank you, and good night,' the girl turned her back.

'Superficial, soulless and without significance,' offered Gavin.

Gavin and Phil roared with laughter as the girl turned to look in total bewilderment.

Dave was equally confused.

'I'll fill you in mate,' Phil put his arm around Dave's shoulder. 'You see it's like this…'

Week 2: Day 4 – Girls, Footie and Curry

It was Tuesday, but really it could have been any day. Time merged into a constant Campaign menu of sun and beer. There was no office slog to differentiate and highlight Friday nights or the weekend. Every day was work free and fun. Tuesday was now just a marker to show that there were three full days left before the return to reality.

This Campaign had raised more questions than any before, leaving decisions to be made and the catalyst for lifestyles to be changed. For now the Campaign still had a course to run. Was it to be the last? Would its end bring stark reality or true nirvana?

'A nice cuppa tea,' Tony said softly. 'That's what I look forward to most.'

The breakfast discussion point was the one thing that was sorely missed whilst away from English shores.

'Yeah, true. Never tastes the same abroad, does it? Maybe it's the water,' Gavin agreed. 'Mine would be a good pint of ale.'

'Predictable and bloody boring,' Phil jumped on the comment. 'With me it would be my bed. You can't beat your own bed.'

'Yeah, I can understand that with you. A big double bed with lots of space to accommodate your ample frame without any threat of having to share,' Dave grinned cheekily.

'Fuck off,' was the sensitive and predictable response from Phil.

Dave quickly moved on. 'With me it's my telly, DVD player, surround system and all.'

'I don't think you'll ever wander far from home, mate. The Campaign will be your lot,' Phil quipped. 'Mind you, probably true for all of us.'

Tony nodded as Gavin and Dave both stared blankly, lost in thought.

Gavin could not face another day mulling over the pros and cons of starting a new life. Taking a chance had never been in his nature, and it had been pretty easy to convince himself not to change the habit of a lifetime. And yet why did he keep challenging the decision as soon as it was made. Annette was the simple answer.

To help free his mind, Gavin chose to accompany Tony to meet with Kim and her friend Gill. A distraction was as good as a rest.

Kim and Gill travelled down to Hersonissos for the first time, and Gill was both relieved and concerned that Tony had brought along a friend. Relieved that she would not have to play gooseberry to the now sickening lovebirds, but concerned that she was on some kind of blind date with the serious looking mate. She thought that at least he might have brought the chubby cheeky guy. He was more her type.

Even as they shared a drink in a beach bar there was lovesick aura surrounding Tony and Kim. They stared passionately at each other, holding hands across the table, speaking in whispers and soppy facial expressions. The aura was like a barrier to the outside world and Gavin and Gill may as well have been in another bar.

Gavin began to wonder if he had really made the right decision as he started to feel almost nauseous with the sickly love scene. He looked over at Gill, who seemed to be watching with the same expression of disbelief.

'So, Gill, tell me about yourself,' Gavin tried to divert attention from the love scene.

'What do you wanna know?' was the grumpy, abrupt reply.

'Because I'm writing a book on my best friends' girlfriends' best friends. Do you mind if I take notes?' Gavin looked to the sky thinking that maybe the conversation was over.

'Yes, okay.' Gill at last smiled and gave a little giggle. 'Let's start again. Not much to tell. I'm single and live with my two cats. I work as a beautician and I'm crazy about George Clooney. Not much material for a book I'm afraid. How about you?'

'Oh, I'm single, work in an electrical store, I live with a mad Irishman and I'm crazy about Natalie Imbruglia. What a couple we'd make, eh?' Gavin gave a cheeky smile.

Gill had suddenly warmed to Gavin. He was not the best looking guy in the world, but he had something about him. He made her laugh. The conversation then flowed as Gavin finally stopped thinking about Annette and was distracted away from the loved-up friend to his left.

Eventually the foursome left the bar to head for the beach. Gavin and Gill both chuckled loudly as they shared a joke; Tony and Kim followed with their arms firmly around each other's shoulders. It was just then that Gavin spotted Annette out of the corner of his eye. He almost stopped in his tracks open-mouthed as he just longed to be with her. Obliviously she passed by and Gavin had to bite his lip to resist calling her name.

'Come on, Gav, let's go for a swim. I want to see some of that gorgeous bod,' Gill lifted the bottom of Gavin's T-shirt, and was now flirting for all it was worth, driven on by a couple of alcopops in the heat of the midday sun. She now longed for Gavin to reciprocate.

'Uh, right okay, after you,' came the subdued serious response from Gavin as if a switch had been triggered to instantly change his personality.

Gill stopped for a second, slightly taken aback, before sprinting towards the sea. Gavin stood still for a moment and then gave chase with a yell. Tony smiled at Kim in silent appreciation of the apparent bonding between their two friends.

'I think Gill likes your mate. It's very rare that she opens up like that,' Kim had hopes of more romance.

'Yeah... Gav's a great guy,' Tony said hesitantly.

'Uh oh, I detect a problem, he's either married or a bastard to women,' Kim commented with unusual assertiveness.

'No, neither actually. Just a regular guy. It's just...' Tony considered for a moment if he should just act dumb, but felt the need to be honest. 'He's been seeing this Irish barmaid who works in a bar around the corner. But suddenly he's not seeing her or even talking about her, so it's all a bit of a mystery.'

'Oh,' Kim looked over at her friend splashing flirtatiously in the sea. She had not looked so happy for a very long time. 'Oh dear,' a feeling of sadness overwhelmed her own happiness.

Dave and Phil had opted to go for a walk and explore a bit more of the town, with the premise of stopping for the odd beer.

The slow saunter of an afternoon bar crawl was halted almost before it had begun. As the duo passed a small hotel not far down the road from their own, they were attracted by some excited shouts and a general commotion. Unable to resist a look at the source of the noise, they both climbed a small perimeter wall to satisfy any curiosity.

Phil was sure that a fight was in progress in the best school playground tradition. Instead it turned out to be nothing more than an eager game of football. The poolside patio had been cleared and two small five-a-side goals erected at each end.

'Hey you guys,' came a shout with a strong European accent. 'Fancy a game?'

A young blond guy in a Liverpool shirt was looking up at the two spectators, and was soon joined by the other players, adorned in an array of premiership team shirts.

'Um... we're not very fit or very good, mate,' Dave replied.

'Hey neither are we,' the blond guy said with a big smile. 'But we play and then we have a beer.'

'I think that you've just persuaded us,' Dave clambered over the wall, closely followed by Phil.

'Great, we are now five on each side. Now one of you will be Finland and the other Denmark,' the blond guy looked carefully at the two English ringers and pointed at Phil. 'You look like a Jan Molby type, yes, so we will place you with Denmark. You look more like Jari Litmanen, so you are with my Finland team.'

It transpired that Dave really was lining up with four actual Finns, and Phil with four actual Danes. Introductions were made but soon forgotten in the commotion of the game, with a simple shout of 'over here' or 'give it' sufficing.

The game was a slow and silky continental affair in the furnace-like conditions, rather than the headless ball crashing mauls reminiscent of many British work yards.

With the score even at six all, Phil's lack of fitness was taking its toll. Breathing heavily and longing for the end and a well-earned beer, the ball landed at his feet. Dave instantly came over to tackle him, but Phil somehow fluked a nutmeg and then pushed the ball around a lanky Finn. Suddenly there was just the keeper to beat but the goal was still yards away. Rather than run another inch, Phil gave the ball a viscous punt with everything he had. It moved with unwavering speed and direction, passed a static keeper and went into the top corner of the net. The game was over and the winner had been scored.

Phil felt a rush of elated energy, flicking his sweat-soaked T-shirt over his head like Fabrizzio Ravenelli. His teammates ran to catch him and celebrate the moment, but were not quick enough to stop the hero from blindly crashing into the pool. Slightly dazed, but instantly refreshed, Phil's head bobbed to the surface. With a group cheer the other players then dived in to join him.

'So, you seem to be getting on well with Gill,' Tony had promised Kim he would quiz Gavin on his true intentions. Kim had conveniently taken Gill over to look in a small Cretan boutique, leaving the boys seated on a small wall by the beach.

'Yeah, nice girl and good fun. Thanks for bringing me along,' Gavin had managed to relax during the day, despite the brief interlude when he spotted Annette.

'It's amazing, but here we are enjoying a day with two girls from our hometown,' Tony knew he did not have long but was trying to be as direct as he could. 'A long way to come for a double date.'

Gavin looked over with sudden shock that gave Tony his answer. 'Hey, except that you're on the date with Kim and that's it.'

'Ah,' Tony half hoped that he had been wrong.

'Hang on a minute, you mean your real plan today was to match me up with Gill?' Gavin was now way off track.

'She's a nice girl,' Tony defended Gill's honour. 'And no, it was not a plan, it was just that you both seem to get on so well, and... well I think that she likes you.'

'Shit,' Gavin said calmly, leaning back against the wall. 'And you're right, she is a nice girl but I've just been having fun. Shit, and you think that she's misread that?'

Tony nodded. 'Possibly... and possibly Kim too... and even I was starting to wonder. I mean what the hell has happened between you and Annette?'

Gavin went a little white. 'I'll tell you very soon on that one, but we're fine.'

'Oh right,' Tony was now even more puzzled, but did not press any further. 'Well just think if you did go out with Gill, we could have a great laugh at home. It would be well cosy, slotting straight into relationships as soon as we get home to Blighty. Who knows where it might lead.'

Gavin thought for a brief moment just how easy a choice it would be but quickly shook his head. 'Sorry, mate.'

'Well listen, I'm going on a picnic with the girls tomorrow. To be fair to Gill just think up some excuse as to why you can't make it,' Tony slapped Gavin's shoulder as the girls came back into view.

Gill wandered over and teasingly prodded Gavin in the stomach. 'Have you missed me, cheeky boy?'

Armed with the facts, Gavin could now clearly see for himself the effect he was having on Gill. 'Uh yeah,' was the non-plus reply.

Gavin tried to keep the conversation short and simple, eager to escape at the first opportunity. Gill was fun to be with and it would be a simple choice to go out with her, but Gavin knew that it was not what he wanted.

When the topic of the picnic came up, Gavin acted suitably disappointed whilst stating how he had already arranged to spend the day with his friend, Phil. Tony backed up the story and Kim quickly realised that there was to be no romance for her friend. Gill could not hide her disappointment, but she still held out hope of another meeting, either by the end of the holiday or when they got home.

'So you could have shacked up with Miss Butch then,' Phil spluttered as tactfully as ever, as the lads once again enjoyed an early evening beer with Theo. 'I'll tell you, it would have been hats off there, mate, and double points to boot.'

'Shut up, Phil,' Tony snapped angrily. 'Beauty is only skin deep. Gill's got a heart of gold.'

'Still doesn't make her a good shag,' Phil continued crassly.

'Stop being a wanker, Mockley,' Gavin was also not in the mood. 'I'm sure that the girls say the same about you.'

Phil wobbled his head mockingly as if to say, 'Get you.'

'Anyway, I'm starving. Shall we go and find somewhere to eat, lads?' Dave looked to change the subject.

'Didn't you spot somewhere on your mega walk today?' Gavin asked curiously.

'Um,' Dave looked guilty. 'The mega walk was about one hundred yards down the road, where we somehow got involved in a Scandinavian footie match. Had a swim and a beer and came back again.'

At this point Phil jumped up with excitement. 'And guess who scored the winner? And what a bloody goal it was. Beat the whole team on my own, including Holliman, before rifling it past the keeper.'

'Slight exaggeration,' Dave said knowingly. 'But yes he did score the winner and I'm sure that we will hear all about it many more times this evening. Ronaldo will be quaking in his boots.'

Indeed, Phil even re-enacted his moment of glory as they walked along the strip, weaving in and out of passers-by with an imaginary ball, whilst providing his own stirring commentary. As the moment to score came he kicked a small pebble with some force to the other side of the road. It impacted with a loud crack against a small tin sign.

The foursome stopped in their tracks as they read the white lettered advertisement against the bright red background. It was only four words, but the message was clear 'Authentic Tandoori – Next Left'.

They had found an oasis in the desert.

The Tandoori Express certainly tried to capture the mood and feel of the standard English high street Indian restaurant. Piped sitar music and deep red flock wallpaper greeted the lads as they curiously entered, unsure of what they would find inside. From the outside the restaurant looked like a suburban town house, only betrayed by the small red sign baring its name above the door. The aroma of spices confirmed that it was right to enter.

'Ahh, welcome. Engleesh are always welcome,' a very tall white man appeared from nowhere with the appearance of Basil Fawlty and the heavy European accent of Antoine De Caunes. 'Please, please,' he beckoned them to choose a table in the completely empty restaurant.

Hesitantly, Phil led the others to a table by the only window.

"'Ere are your menus, but I will bring you poppadoms, no?' a large smile cracked below the man's bushy black moustache. 'Mai oui, always poppadoms, I am 'ow you say, 'aving a laugh.'

'Yeah, cheers,' Phil finally spoke for the group 'where are you from?'

'I am from France, from Paris,' the waiter almost stood to attention as if the Marseillese was about to strike up.

'Oh, so you naturally end up waiting in an Indian restaurant in Crete,' Gavin commented sarcastically.

'Oh non,' the waiter looked puzzled. 'It is actually very unusual. And I am the owner, and er... my boyfriend, he is the chef.'

The Frenchman then left to allow his customers to peruse the menu.

'Well this is certainly going to be no routine curry,' Gavin chuckled. 'In fact, the term "a whole new experience" comes to mind.'

'Yeah, it's bizarre enough meeting a gay Frenchman, let alone placing him running an Indian restaurant with his partner,' Dave looked around and spoke in a whisper so as not to be overheard.

'I didn't have you down as a homophobic, Mr Holliman,' Gavin spoke with some surprise.

'Oh God, I'm not. Live and let live and all that,' Dave held up his hands defensively. 'It's just that your normal French stereotype is some womanising sweet-talker. You just never hear of that many French gay icons.'

'What about John Paul Gautier?' said Gavin.

'Good point,' Dave conceded.

'I didn't realise he was gay,' Tony joined in the conversation and brought it to an abrupt end at the same time.

The French waiter reappeared with a large tray of poppadoms and the standard array of chutneys.

'Yes, these are good,' Phil quickly grabbed a whole poppadom and bit it with a large crunch. 'Although they've got that sort of bought-from-a-supermarket, out-of-a-packet taste.'

'Same with the mango chutney,' Gavin confirmed.

'Oh well, it's still a laugh eh,' Dave added cheerily. 'Who'd have thought it, a Greek ruby?'

'Made by a Frenchman,' the others said in unison.

With the food ordered, the conversation moved on to recounting curry-related stories, mainly focussing on the hottest dish that each had ever tried followed by vivid stories of the next day's after-effects.

'I think the need for extra strong curries sort of diminishes with age,' Dave spoke philosophically. 'I mean it's like when you're young you can drink nine or ten pints and happily order a vindaloo. At our age it tends to be three or four pints and a dopiaza.'

'True,' Phil nodded with a sad sigh.

'Bloody hell, I remember one curry sesh at poly,' Dave took a sharp intake of breath. 'I went to this Indian near Nottingham that did a special called Singapore Chicken, that was supposed to be even hotter than a phal. There were four of us sitting around the table shitting ourselves before we'd even had a curry, which is unusual in itself. We had all made a pact to eat this Singapore Chicken for a dare. The waiters acted like we'd just asked them to knife us all in the stomach. First of all they had a laugh and brought out a fish and chip supper from the chippy next door, as if it was the dish. One of the lads nearly tucked in. Then they went all serious and said that they would not serve any cold drinks whilst we were eating; the combination could make out throats bleed. Hot tea was all we could have. Anyway the dish arrived and we spooned it out as normal on to the pilau rice. Then we all stopped and stared like we were about to bungee jump, or parachute, or something. I agreed to go first and just placed a little bit of the curry in my mouth. After a few seconds I went, "It's okay, no worries" and just as I did so it hit me. My throat was like a volcano erupting from the bottom. Within seconds I couldn't speak and my eyes were full of water. The other three then followed and within minutes we were all crying for lager, water or anything. The waiters wouldn't serve us. One guy desperately grabbed a vase of flowers, threw out the flowers and drunk the water.'

'Did you manage to finish it?' Gavin grimaced.

'Did we fuck. None of us hardly touched it. A complete waste of money in the name of youthful bravado,' Dave spouted, before adding calmly, 'had to go to that chippy to get something to eat 'cos we were all starving.'

Three chicken madras and a korma arrived with a shout of 'voila' followed by 'Bon Appetite'.

'Is it just my taste buds or has this curry got no kick in it?' Dave nevertheless spooned in another large mouthful to double check.

'Yeah, it's well mild,' Phil concurred. 'I think we've all got Tony's korma.'

'Is everything okay, gentlemen?' the waiter ghosted in from nowhere.

'Actually,' Dave hesitated with a little English reserve. 'The curry has, how you say, no oomph.'

'It's not spicy enough, mate,' Phil added more bluntly.

'Oooh, I see,' the waiter pondered. 'I know, let me take your dishes. I will have Pierre spice them up until they are so hot that they will melt your bottoms, no.'

The curries were taken away forthwith bar Tony's korma, which he had all but eaten.

'Not sure about the "bottom melting" bit,' Phil looked concerned.

The waiter returned within five minutes. 'There you go, my Englishmen. Prepare your bottoms for Armageddon.'

The waiter stood by as Dave was first to sample the fayre.

Dave's face was apologetic before he even spoke. 'Mmm, it's a bit better, but sadly still not that hot.'

And so it went on.

The waiter would take the food away with a promise of spices drawn from the fires of Hades, only to return with mild offering after mild offering. In the end it proved too much and the waiter broke down in tears. Pierre heard the commotion and ran out to comfort his boyfriend.

'Look what you 'ave done,' spat an angry Pierre. 'You Engleesh 'ave no sensitivity. None at all. It grinds me to the bone.'

'Uh, look mate,' Dave was unsure how to gauge the scene in front of him. 'This is fine, absolutely fine. Lovely in fact.'

'Yes, lovely,' Phil added support before patronisingly adding 'mmmm' as he tried a mouthful.

Eventually Pierre was appeased and the waiter calmed him back to normality. The food was finished quickly and followed by a hasty exit.

After the meal, Gavin spotted a small karaoke bar, which became the base camp for the evening. He chose the bar after seeing a sign for English ale, and it was given the general approving consent of the others after they noticed how many starstruck attractive young females were heading the same way.

'Right, the deal is that after four beers we all have a crack at the karaoke. And whoever is voted the worst buys the fifth round. Agreed?' Phil made the announcement with genuine excitement.

'Fuck off, Mockley,' Dave did not agree. 'You just have a go and we'll laugh at you.'

'No, no, Dave,' Gavin surprisingly interjected. 'Phil's plan sounds like fun.'

Phil looked over smugly at Dave, whilst Gavin frantically signalled for him to play along.

'Oh, okay,' Dave got the message.

The beer then started to flow as a stream of teenage girls with flat voices insulted the bar's eardrums as they lived out their fantasies of being Madonna, Celine Dion and of course Gloria Gaynor.

'Mind if we sit at your table, boys?' a man in his sixties appeared with a lady of equal age. Both had silver grey hair but dressed with a style that was twenty years their younger.

'Uh sure,' Dave looked up to see that the whole bar was now packed to bursting point.

'Cheers. Alex Grimes,' the man held out his hand. 'And this is my bird, Marion.'

Marion immediately chuckled with delight.

'So, you boys having a good time?' Alex hailed a waiter to order some beer.

'Great, yeah,' Dave once more responded for the others. 'How about you?'

'Fanbloodytastic. We've found our second childhood, haven't we love?' Alex squeezed Marion's hand.

'Oh, yes my love, oh yes,' Marion replied with an almost innocent charm.

'Say no more,' Dave was about to add a comment about the effects of viagra, but decided against it.

'So are you two not married then?' Gavin asked.

'No lad,' Alex confirmed. 'We were, but to other people. She's a widow and I'm a widower. Our lives were nearly at an end and then we found each other. Now we're having the time of our lives. The kids don't like it, though. Sent to bloody Coventry right enough by both sets. And I thought it was the parents who were meant to disapprove of their kids' relationships.'

'Stuff 'em, mate,' Phil suddenly piped up. 'You should live to the full regardless of what others say. A toast to Alex and Marion.'

Phil's raised glass was clattered by everyone else's bar Tony. He was once more sitting in concentration with thoughts only of Kim and a pining to be with her and away from the crowd.

Alex and Marion quickly joined in all the banter as they bonded with the four English thirtysomethings. Alex told jokes and letched cheekily with the others at the array of pretty young girls giving their all on the karaoke stage. Marion giggled along and took a shine to the quiet lovesick Tony, lending a friendly ear to his romantic cravings that sent the rest rushing for the sick bags.

'Hey, Phil, it's time, mate,' Gavin announced with a tap of his wristwatch. 'Now I think we should all take it in turn to go and put our names down for a song.'

'Yeees,' Phil wholeheartedly agreed.

'Now you go first, mate, and then we'll all go up one by one,' Gavin moved aside to let Phil through.

'Okay.' Phil did not need any more enticing and duly strode over to the karaoke coordinator.

'Right the plan is this,' Gavin leant forward and spoke in a whisper as the other plotters huddled around to listen. 'We all put Phil's name down for whatever song he chooses. He's then bound to sing and we have a good laugh.'

Phil proudly announced that he had chosen 'Heartbreak Hotel' as his song, and so all the others, including Alex, went over to make the same selection. It was a matter of minutes before Phil's name was read out.

'Wow, looks like I'm first lads,' Phil looked a little stunned and instantly nervous. 'Watch me go.'

Phil stood anxiously by the compère, squeezing the life out of the large radio microphone. The fat announcer then roared an introduction that would have been worthy of the king himself. Phil stepped forward into the spotlight and waited for the music to strike up and the words to appear on the small screen in front of him. He could feel a flutter of nerves deep in his gut, which was compounded by the gurgling spices of the curry he had demolished. The build up was too much and just as Phil held up the mike aloft he let out an almighty belch that rang around the bar. Almost immediately the first bars of 'Heartbreak Hotel' struck up.

With a grimace at the laughter and applause that welcomed his impromptu intro to the song, led by his so-called mates, Phil tried to recover his composure and sing.

'Now since my baby left me, I've found a new place to dwell,' Phil heavily mumbled like a poor Vegas impersonator. 'Down at the end of lonely street, at Heartbreak Hotel,' he continued in the same vain. Then came the wiggle of the pelvis as Phil moved to a mumbled crescendo. 'I'm so lonely that I could die.'

And so it continued, with more wiggling and pouting lip curls as he lapped up the approving applause.

Phil returned to his friends with a beaming grin, as even the compère was lost for words. Even Tony was wiping the tears of laughter from his eyes.

'Beat that,' announced Phil, as if he had marked his stake in the long jump pit.

'And next we have… ' The fat announcer boomed across the bar. 'Phil Mockley and Heartbreak Hotel.'

'Eh?' Phil looked around.

'Eh?' spluttered the announcer. 'Surely a mistake, as good as Phil was. My God, he's the next one… and the next one. Were you desperate to get on, mate?'

'You bastards,' Phil had sussed that the joke was on him.

'Well, how could we really top that mate?' Dave conceded.

The announcer checked the next card. 'Ah, here we go. Do we have Alex Grimes in the house?'

'Here,' Alex shouted out as the lads turned their attention to him.

'Come up, my good man. Alex will sing the Tom Jones classic, Delilah,' the compère beckoned him forward.

Alex strode over with a cool air and took the microphone like a professional. Again the compère gave a roaring introduction.

The music struck up and Alex sang with perfect pitch and in tune. 'I saw the light on the night that I passed by her window.'

'Na na na na,' sang the whole bar.

By the time the chorus came everyone joined in with a percussion stamping of feet. 'My, my, my Delilah, why, why, why Delilah? I could see that she was just no good for me, but I was lost like a slave that no man could free.'

The lads sang for all they were worth, almost raising the roof with the climax to the song. Alex strode back over as coolly as he had walked to the stage, with rapturous applause and cries of 'more' ringing in his ears.

'Not bad mate,' was Phil's understated greeting.

'Thanks,' Alex shook his hand and then gave Marion a full-on kiss.

The compère returned to the stage. 'Well tonight ladies and gentlemen, there can be only one winner. Alex Grimes come and collect your champagne.'

Alex walked over to more rapturous applause and accepted the huge magnum.

'Well done, mate. The better man won on the night,' Phil conceded.

'Thanks, Phil, but I think that you must have come second,' Alex replied.

'Wow,' Phil turned to the others as if it was a fact. They all simply groaned.

Week 2: Day 5 – The Band Split Again

Tony was first up, and acting every bit the eager lovesick teenager, despite his thirtysomething years. It all came down to making up for lost time, for the man whose teenage years had been so shy and withdrawn that he had never enjoyed the experience of a real girlfriend. His schoolmates would enjoy dates at the cinema and adolescent fumbles at every opportunity. Tony read books and watched TV, and obviously masturbated a lot over streams of second-hand porn. The frustrated awkwardness manifested into his unconfident twenties and resigned early thirties, with an interlude for the cruel education that Carol brought.

Now at thirty-eight, Tony was ready to live his romantic dream and throw himself into everything it would bring. Who would have thought that his idyll had been staring him in the face the whole time in the shape of the shy, young, hometown waitress who had served him in his favourite coffee shop for so many years?

Tony had come to Crete with a feeling of being at the crossroads of his life. He hated where he worked, and was tired of sitting in the background as the quiet dependable friend, edging towards mid-life obscurity. Tony had vowed to act to change and fate had dealt him a winning card. He now had a confidence that was unshakable.

Kim was waiting for Tony with equal anticipation and with total belief in the future. She had been involved in a holiday fling several years before, but would not stoop so low as to call it a romance. The young good-looking boy from Liverpool had seemed the perfect gentleman at the time, and had easily sweet-talked her into bed with the assistance of many glasses of sangria. Like so many girls before her, Kim wrote long passionate letters to the Scouse dreamboy on her return. No reply ever came and finally Gill was able to shake her into the real world, and the experience of what men were really like.

For years Kim had waited on the serious-looking man, desperate to know more about him. He was always friendly but never seemed to open up and talk in more than a few sentences.

Kim had decided that destiny was not to be kind, and so had made up her mind to abandon the chase. On her return home she was to find a new job and hopefully change her luck. But destiny was not to be thwarted and conceded that the couple would be united after all.

Kim and Tony embraced with a passionate kiss, before walking along the beach as real lovers, armed with the picnic prepared by Kim the night before. The day would soon be lost in endless gazing, gentle cuddles, playful teasing and longing kisses.

Phil reached for the small bin in the corner of the room and promptly threw up.

'Oh great,' Dave jolted up in his bed. 'And good morning to you, too.'

Phil wiped his mouth with the back of his hand. 'Ugh… sorry, mate. I think I must have copped something bad last night. Probably the curry.'

'No, Phil, that would be coming out the other end,' Dave eased out of bed. 'Which incidentally is where mine should be exiting very shortly, if the burning sensation in my arse is anything to go by. I think your problem was the ten pints and then the extra large burger on the way home.'

Phil could taste the very greasy burger from last night and promptly threw up again. Dave moved towards the bathroom, breaking wind loudly several times as he went. Just as he got to the sink there was a knock at the door.

'Dave, Dave, Are you up? It's Gav, Elsie's here, mate.'

Dave bolted to the door with realisation of the strong stench lingering in the air, concocted from puke and gassy farts. 'Is she actually with you, mate?'

'No, she's by the pool. I said I'd come and get you in case you weren't decent,' came Gavin's reply.

'Brilliant,' Dave clenched his fist. 'Listen, Gav, can you go and tell her I'll be ten minutes? Just keep her entertained… and don't fucking tap off with her.'

'Okay,' Gavin gave a little laugh before jovially adding, 'can't make a promise on the last bit though, mate. She's a babe.'

Dave rushed everything from shave to shower to dressing, with added layers of deodorant and aftershave. It was as if Phil and his bucket of sick were not there as he breezed to the door, with a last minute acknowledgment of 'Catch you later.'

Elsie was sitting opposite Gavin by the shade of the poolside bar, and seemed to be enjoying a joke as she laughed loudly. Once more she was a picture of beauty that forced Dave to an almost standstill. Unusually, she was smartly dressed in bright white three quarter length trousers, and a flowery purple blouse. Closer inspection showed that she was wearing a lot of jewellery and even make-up. Her wild tussles of brown hair had been carefully tied into a neat bunch at the back. Was all this effort an attempt to woo Dave?

'Here he is, the ultra cool Dave Holliman,' Elsie sarcastically announced. 'Well, you're too late, I've fallen in love with Gavin and we're eloping this very day.'

Dave mocked a disappointed face. 'Oh well, might as well go back to bed,' he turned to go.

'Come back,' Elsie seemed in a hurry.

'Well, it could have been true,' Dave turned back again and nodded at Gavin. 'If you knew Gav. It's a good job I got here when I did.'

'Listen, the reason I'm here is that a distant cousin of mine is having some kind of socialite party in a villa up the road in Stalis,' Elsie paused. 'My first thought was what a ghastly idea and I'd rather be seen dead and all that. But then I thought of you and that it might actually be a giggle if we both went. Lots of chinless hoorahs and henriettas to make fun of, plus streams of free alcohol and yummy food. What do you say?'

Dave looked over pleadingly at Gavin.

'Don't worry about Phil, mate,' Gavin got up from his chair. 'I'm sticking around all day. You go and have some fun.'

Dave patted Gavin on the shoulder as he passed him. 'Looks like I'm in then.'

Gavin found Phil looking extremely pale as he sat on the edge of his bed, with his chin resting on his hands.

'Wow you look great,' was Gavin's immediate sarcastic response.

'Fuck off and leave me to die, Rogers,' Phil buried his eyes into his palms.

'I love you too, Mockley, but the reality is that it's me and thee today. Dave's done a runner with Elsie, who is very attractive and very posh by the way. And of course Tony is living a young romantic dream,' Gavin sat down on Dave's bed. 'I tell you what, I really fancy that Elsie myself.'

'Yeah, she's a bit of all right,' Phil tried to focus across the room. 'So the band's split again, eh? And anyway, what about your Irish tart?'

'She's not a fucking tart,' Gavin reacted angrily before calming. 'I'll let you know in good time.'

'Great, well what are we going to do together? We never seem to agree on anything,' Phil lay back on his bed 'What a great fucking holiday.'

'Yeah, total opposites really, aren't we? I like beer, you like lager. I like girls with curves and you always go for stick insects.' Gavin paused with a grin. 'I'm good looking and you're an ugly bastard.'

'Oi, wanker,' Phil jolted up and then burst out laughing.

'I don't know about you mate but I could do with a bloody big fry-up,' Gavin added jovially.

'Now we agree. Give me ten minutes,' a revitalised Phil sprung to his feet and headed for the bathroom.

Dave sat in the back of an old battered taxi as Elsie sat alongside him with one hand placed affectionately on his knee, as she used the other to direct the driver around several small back roads. Eventually, as the taxi pulled out of a long tree-sheltered stretch of road, there was a huge villa and gardens that had all the markings of an English country estate, betrayed only by the distinct Greek architecture. The driver pulled up to large wrought iron gates that were attached to a high perimeter wall that seemed to run forever. Beyond the gate the road continued for another half mile up to the villa.

'Here will be fine,' Elsie tapped the driver's shoulder and passed him some drachma. 'We'll stroll the rest.'

Dave gave a slight grimace due to hunger and the thought that he would have to wait even longer for any sustenance.

Elsie walked up and pressed a button by the side of the gate and spoke into the intercom. 'Hi, Jules, It's Elks. Decided to come to your soiree.'

'Aaaaah daaaarling, super,' came the screamed reply, with muffled yelps in the background as if the party was already in full swing. 'Come on up.'

A large buzzer sounded and the gates moved slowly open, allowing Dave and Elsie to enter before closing behind them.

'Elks?' Dave gurned his face. 'It sort of suits you. And I noticed that you put on an even posher voice than normal. Is that because your mixing with your own?'

'Oh do shut up and stop teasing,' Elsie gave Dave a playful slap.

'No, it's true though,' Dave continued. 'I used to go out with this girl from Birmingham who had a pretty non-descript accent. Then she'd go home for the weekend and mix with all her mates, and suddenly she's yamming with the best of 'em.'

'Yamming?' Elsie looked puzzled.

'Never mind,' Dave smirked. 'Anyway, miss love 'em and leave 'em, who never comes back. How come you came back?'

'Fun,' Elsie answered simply. 'My life is about fun and I saw an opportunity to have some.'

'I'm privileged, I think,' Dave concluded as they reached the marble steps leading to the villa entrance.

The front door suddenly flew open and a screaming girl with large buckteeth came running out with her arms in the air. 'Eeelks, how delightful,' she threw herself into an embrace with all the finesse of a Jonny Wilkinson rugby tackle.

Elsie buckled slightly before regaining a steady footing. 'Hi Jules, I'd like you to meet someone. This is my friend Dave.'

Dave sighed at the 'friend' reference before almost being pole axed by another Jules body slammer.

'Come on in and meet the crew. They are dying to see you both, every one of them.' Jules led them indoors and down a very long, concrete hallway, before entering an even bigger lounge.

Inside the lounge was a group of about thirty people. The

women were wearing either expansive floral dresses or polo shirts and jeans, whilst the men wore either cricket whites, complete with large white woolly jumpers tied around their waists, or polo shirts and jeans. Nearly everyone had a pair of sunglasses resting against their foreheads.

'Look all, it's Elks and a man,' Jules announced with a large screech.

Exulted murmurs, gargles, high-pitched sighs and sheep like mumbles came back in reply.

'Shit, it's Brideshead Revisited meets the House of Lords,' was Dave's instant reaction.

'Bucks fizz, you two?' enquired an extremely tall brunette in a garish floral dress.

'Absolutely, and bacon and eggs, please,' replied Dave, rubbing his hands.

'That was bloody fantastic,' Phil wiped his last piece of toast around the large plate to gather up the remnants of beans and tomato sauce. 'I feel great now, cheers, Gav.'

'No problem,' Gavin finished off his own breakfast. 'And I agree, that was superb.'

'So, what really happened with you and the Irish bird? I mean you seemed so loved up.' Phil stopped as he noticed Gavin's expression turning to a serious grimace. 'Sorry, mate, I didn't mean to pry. Just forget I asked.'

Gavin remained silent for a few seconds before holding up a hand. 'No, no problem. Actually, it's about time I told someone. A problem shared and all that. Mind you I know you're going to think I'm a right prat.'

'Well, I think that already, mate, so no worries there.' Phil gave a cheeky grin that was mirrored by Gavin. 'Shall we have another coffee?'

Gavin thought for a moment. 'No, let's go for a beer.'

Phil checked his watch. 'Ten-thirty in the morning! I like your style, my good man.'

'I tell you, it's bloody Brideshead Revisited.' Dave and Elsie had moved out on to the lawns at the back of the villa. Young toffs were sporadically dotted in twos and fours for as far as the eye could see. Most of the men were lying down, some resting their heads on the knees of a sitting, pretty young girl, as she played with his hair. Otherwise the norm was for everyone to sit in circles with perfect boy to girl ratios.

'Eeeellllks,' Jules suddenly screeched out from the midst of the perfect aesthetic scene. 'Come and join us, and bring David.'

'As if I'd dare leave you on your own,' Elsie winked at Dave.

'No chance,' Dave looked genuinely worried. 'And by the way, only my mum calls me David.'

'David, I'd like you to meet Miles, Anton and Melissa.' Jules moved a hand down the line of two exceptionally tall men and a midget of a girl. Miles was incredibly thin, with a big black bushy moustache, hiding most of his lower face. He was wearing tartan golfing trousers and a white tank top. Anton had chiselled good looks and the physique of a top class second row forward. He was dressed tastefully in expensive white chinos and a designer Armani shirt. Melissa, like Jules, had very prominent teeth and a round rosy face. Like many others she wore an oversized figure-hiding floral dress.

'Hi,' Dave offered with a straight raise of the hand.

'So what do you do, David?' Anton ignored the offer of a handshake and sipped a glass of chardonnay.

'Oh, I work in finance,' was Dave's vague reply.

'Aha, in the city are we. Broker? Fund Manager? Or is it sales?' Anton raised both eyebrows with acute exaggeration.

'Uh, oh nothing so glamorous. I just work in the unit trust department for a local assurance company,' Dave accepted a glass of wine from Melissa.

'My God!' Miles spoke with genuine shock. 'How will you keep Elsie in the lifestyle to which she is so accustomed? Or are you to be a kept man and the bit of rough on the side, eh?'

'No.' Dave really wanted to say, 'Fuck off, you sad wankers,' at this stage, and smack the both of them.

'Mind you, I never worked a day in my life so I shouldn't judge, eh?' Miles sat down on the grass.

'Anyway, our Elsie does not care about material things. She's having her wild period before she settles down and marries me,' Anton leaned over to give Elsie a gentle pinch. 'Is that not right girl?'

'Sounds like a fucking fantasy to me,' was Elsie's stark reply.

'Ooh, I love a girl with spunk,' Anton was not deterred.

'Tosser,' was Elsie's only comment, but it finally shook the pompous grin from Anton's face.

'So, David, do you play any sport?' Anton turned his back on Elsie.

'The odd game of footie,' Dave said guardedly.

'Footie! Cor blimey me cockney china,' Anton attempted a cockney accent which was more Dick Van Dyke than Mike Read.

'What about you, Anthony? Is it croquet or crochet?' Dave's voice finally broke with an aggressive edge.

'It's Anton,' said Anton, staring at Dave. 'And most sports are my bag, and I'm bloody good too. Take tennis, I could have got a Wimbledon wild card last year if I'd played a few more matches. Would have had an English ranking to boot.'

'Wow,' Dave mocked amazement. 'You could have got an English tennis ranking. Don't you get that if you can hold the racket at the right end?'

'Now you're boring me, little man,' Anton grabbed a wine bottle and filled his glass.

'Come on, Tony, I think you asked for it,' Elsie could not resist joining in.

'Oh you really have become an oik, haven't you. If you get any worse you will be like one of those untouchable people in India,' Anton began to sulk, 'who, I am sure that you are best friends with. Surprised that you didn't bring them here.'

'Grow up, Anton,' Elsie spoke as if she was addressing a small child.

'Are you going to cry now, mate?' Dave was now enjoying the moment. 'Shall I call for nanny?'

'Oh this really is the limit,' Anton jumped up. 'Get up and take a bunch of fives.'

Dave reacted by laughing. 'Oh, fantastic, or shall we have a duel with pistols at dawn?'

'No,' Miles suddenly shouted out. 'I have a better idea. The clay pigeon shoot. A competition between you both. The winner takes honour.'

Anton stopped and smiled. 'Done deal. If I can't beat an oik I should be shot myself.'

'Um, okay,' Dave shrugged. 'I'm game.'

Elsie moved over to whisper in Dave's ear. 'Don't worry, Anton's a fucking awful shot.'

'There you go, mate, get that down your neck and whatever you like off your chest,' Phil put two beers on the small table placed on a pavement outside the bar.

'Cheers,' Gavin took a gulp of lager. 'Mmm, not too bad actually. I think that this might be a good session.'

'Yeah, an all-dayer,' Phil sat down and grabbed his beer. 'Haven't had one of those since the Munich beer festival a couple of years back.'

'I bet that was fantastic,' Gavin had almost finished his first beer. 'I went to a festival in Belgium, which was good, but I've always wanted to go to Munich.'

'It was pure heaven,' Phil thought back. 'Basically every brewer has its own large tent, and there's loads of 'em. You just go on one big tent crawl and get so nicely pissed that it's like being on a different planet.'

'I vaguely remember you telling us about it at the time. How long did you drink for?' Gavin had switched off during the original recounting of the trip but was now actually interested.

'From breakfast until the early hours of the next day, with the odd stop for food and…' Phil stopped and smiled.

'And?' Gavin asked.

'And for a shag,' Phil was now laughing. 'The group I went with, from my snooker club, were all staying in this old communal hall in sleeping bags. One of the guys was a scout leader and arranged some cheap digs through a contact. Anyway, I tapped off with this German girl who kept insisting on showing me her tattoos. By the time she showed me a rose on her tit, I knew I was in. With all the romance in the world we slipped back to the hall and just started shagging on this pile of sleeping bags.

We really went for it and she screamed the place down. Then as we both lay there exhausted, something moved underneath the sleeping bags. We both jumped up and out pops this geeky guy called Lance, displaced glasses and all. Turned out that he'd drunk too much and had simply passed out.'

Gavin now laughed too. 'And you shagged on top of him. Quality.'

'Yeah, probably the nearest thing to a threesome that I'll ever get.' Phil pushed his empty glass forward. 'Get the beers in, mate.'

Several round later, Phil and Gavin recalled the days that they lodged together and some of the endless drinking sessions.

'Shit, it really was like *Men Behaving Badly*, wasn't it?' Phil commented. 'Without Leslie Ash living upstairs of course.'

'Hey, but there was always Mrs Gummer, landlady extraordinaire,' Gavin pointed out.

'Yeah right, if you like Nora Batty types. Shit, she was about ninety and she was forever giving it the old sexual innuendo,' Phil drew a short breath. 'I remember when she walked in on me in the shower once. I don't know how I got out alive.'

'She did that to me too,' Gavin pointed at Phil with his mouth wide open. 'I never told you before in case you took the piss.'

'To Mrs Gummer, wherever you are,' Phil raised a toast and Gavin obliged by clashing glasses.

'So, anyway, the lovely Annette.' Phil put his glass down and gave Gavin a serious look, 'Ready to tell all?'

'Subtle as ever, Mockley,' Gavin tutted. 'Well as I said, you'll call me a prat and probably rightly so. The scoop is that she's asked me to move out here with her.'

Phil's face turned even more serious. 'And you said no. Then you're not a prat, you're a super prat.'

'I haven't actually said no,' Gavin paused. 'I need to give my answer by tomorrow. That's why I haven't seen Annette for a while.'

'Well, then you must say yes. There is no dilemma.' Phil became animated, gesticulating in disbelief like a native Italian. 'I mean let's weigh it all up, back to nine-to-five and selling televisions, whilst lodging with a refugee from the IRA versus living in the sun with a full-figured Irish girl who goes like a train and runs a bar.'

'The argument does sound a bit weak when you put it like that, but...' Gavin thought hard. 'Well I'm so stuck in my ways and I need a comfort zone. Mr bloody routine as you always say, and I've never been one to gamble.'

Phil sat back. 'Well now's the time to change. This Campaign is going to bring a lot of change for all of us. I think that you want to say yes, but just know that it's safer to say no. Well, I'm not going to pressure you, but say no and you'll regret it for the rest of what will be your boring life.'

'I just knew you'd give me some sound, worldly advice. Another beer is called for.' Gavin headed for the bar.

Another disc flew into the air. Dave pulled his gun up but accidentally fired before it cleared his shoulder. The disc landed harmlessly again. Anton and Miles almost fell over from laughing, and even Elsie gave a slight reserved titter.

'Okay, okay, that was shit. But I've never had a go before,' Dave conceded. 'I half expected someone to drop out of that tree over there, like in that James Bond film. Or maybe I'll just aim for Anton if he calls me fucking oik again.'

'Pull,' Anton called for his own target and a disc flew into the air. He pulled the rifle up in a smooth motion but fired and missed the disc by some distance. Dave's next go was little better than his previous efforts, as he somehow fired in the opposite direction to the target. Anton also failed to register with his next attempt, and so it went on, with Dave shooting at many obscure angles and Anton becoming more and more agitated as he failed to kill the contest off.

'Right oik,' a red-faced and frustrated Anton declared. 'Last go each and if there's no strike then I'm the winner for being the better shot.'

'Bollocks, Anton, it will just be a draw and you know it,' Elsie bellowed out. 'Actually a sort of moral victory for Dave.'

'Okay, Dave,' Elsie lowered her voice to a whisper. 'Give it everything, feel the force or something. Just wipe the smile of the git's face.'

Dave stiffened up and stretched his arms in preparation. 'Mmm, I think the force is strong in this one.'

'Pull,' Anton shouted for Dave.

Taken by surprise, Dave jolted his gun up and fired. To his utter amazement the disc shattered above. There was stunned silence.

'*Yeeees*,' Dave fell down on his knees and held his gun aloft with both hands, feeling like he had scored the cup final winning goal. Elsie jumped on him like an appreciative team-mate.

'You lucky bastard, oik,' Anton shouted in utter annoyance. 'But it ain't over until the fat lady sings. Pull.'

The disc shot into the air and Anton raised his gun and shot, missing the target once more.

Dave and Elsie screamed in delight and started to jump up and down. Anton stormed off, hotly pursued by Miles.

Elsie jumped on top of Dave and knocked him to the ground. 'Well, David, you won and later I shall give you your prize.'

As Dave lay on the lush lawn looking up at Elsie's gorgeous face, with the backdrop of a clear deep blue sky, he could not have felt any more content.

'What's the time, Phil?' Gavin's eyes were a bit blurry and he was starting to feel very tired.

Phil looked at his watch. 'Fuck, it's nearly four. That's fucking five hours good drinking. Superb. Call for another one I think.'

Phil headed for the bar yet again. He and Gavin had only ever moved from their small stools to either buy drinks or go to the toilet. A bar meal had been the only respite from solid drinking.

Two more beers were placed on the table and both Gavin and Phil gave large intoxicated grins. They both took a swig and acted like it was the first pint of the day.

'This has been fucking tops,' said Phil, almost falling off his stool. 'Endless beer drinking while outside on a red-hot day, watching streams of gorgeous women stroll by. Fucking tops.'

'Yeah, and this could be mine all the time if I decide to say yes to Annette,' Gavin declared, giving another pro for the decision to take up Annette's offer.

'Exactly,' said Phil, pointing a knowing finger. 'So you know what to do.'

Gavin nodded unconvincingly.

'Ayup, lads. Starting early are we?' Albert loomed large in his trademark ill-fitting seventies red T-shirt and baggy old khaki hiking shorts.

Phil momentarily closed his eyes. 'Mind you, living here does have some drawbacks.'

'Hello, Albert, how are you?' Gavin was more hospitable.

'Grand lad, really… what the… shite,' Albert suddenly ducked down with fright as a loud bang echoed from the other side of the strip.

'Um, a bit jumpy are we, mate?' Phil gave Gavin a dumbfounded look.

'Not usually, lad, just when I get caught by surprise like that. Sounded just like a gunshot. I'm the same when cars backfire,' Albert's hand was clutched to his chest as if he had suffered a mini heart attack. 'Someone get me a beer and I'll tell you all about it.'

Phil got up and went to the bar, muttering to himself, and returned a few minutes later with a beer and a sour face.

'There you go, mate,' Phil placed the beer down in front of Albert. 'That'll calm you.'

Albert grabbed the pint and consumed half of it in one go. 'Thanks lad, that's smashing. Now, you see the thing is, that in me younger days I did a bit of freelance fighting. A mercenary I was. Always been a good fighter, and a good soldier after doing me national service in the army like.'

Gavin and Phil looked at each other as if to say 'here we go'.

'Anyway,' Albert continued. 'In sixty-seven a bunch of us, me and three other lads, signed up to fight with the Yanks in Nam. The dosh was really good, and the Yanks were well grateful for support. It was the time of the anti-draft movement and Dr Spock's call to resist authority.'

'Eh?' Phil looked totally perplexed.

Gavin shook his head. 'Nothing to do with the planet Vulcan, mate, or Captain Kirk. Just an unfortunate name.'

'Ahh,' Phil looked none the wiser.

'Anyway, we go out there for a laugh. Sound stupid, eh? But we did lots of drugs and the whole thing seemed like a surreal Cub Scout adventure. And then we got embroiled in the real stuff. Heavy jungle fighting outside Saigon. Constant gunfire, dead bodies with throats slit everywhere and then the bloody napalm that the Yanks dumped themselves. Saw each of my mates killed, one by one, and I was suddenly alone. A young lad miles from home and totally shitting himself. By the skin of me teeth I got back to a Yank camp and cut me leg open deep with a knife to feign injury and get a ride home. And when I was on me way I just cried all the way like a bloody baby. Some bloody adventure.'

There was silence for a moment as Albert stared into space.

'Let me guess, you were nineteen. Nnnn nineteen,' Phil was sure this was another tall story.

'No mate, I was twenty-seven,' Albert replied seriously. 'And I tell you it was just like it was yesterday, the memories are that vivid. Look,' Albert pulled out his wallet and produced a small faded black and white photo of four young guys sitting on a tank. 'That's me, the good-looking one on the right, and the rest are me mates who all copped it. They'll always be close to me.'

Albert finished his beer and stood up to go. 'I tell you, lads, I hope we never have another war like that one. And take heed of this, live life because some buggers never get the chance to.'

Albert walked away and Gavin pointed hurriedly at his left leg, where a large scar was clearly visible.

Phil felt a shiver go down his spine. 'God, I almost feel sober. Best get the beers in.'

It was nearing nine in the evening when Dave was taken back to Elsie's digs. Since the clay pigeon shoot-out they had both consumed as much food and drink as possible at the summer party, whilst skilfully not conversing with anyone else. Elsie directed the taxi driver back to her holiday flat, which she rented for a very small fee from a friend.

The flat was a basic box room on the top floor of a small downmarket complex. It simply had a bed, sink and small wardrobe, which just about filled the whole area. It was not long before Dave was on the bed, naked and on top of Elsie, pumping her for all his worth in classic missionary position pose. It was his winning prize and he was savouring every minute of it.

Across town, Phil and Gavin had arrived back at the hotel in a tired drunken stupor, instantly crashing out fully clothed and into a deep sleep on their respective beds.

Over in Malia, Tony too, was fully clothed and asleep, as he lay with Kim, also fully clothed and asleep, on her bed. A day of romance ended with a bottle of wine that brought contented rest as opposed to the lifting of inhibitions and the need for passionate sex. Neither Tony nor Kim really cared.

Week 2: Day 6 – Out with the Old

'Hey, lover boy, better get up,' Elsie pushed Dave to rock him from his slumber. He rubbed his eyes and looked up to see his dream girl already dressed.

'What time is it? Didn't you fancy some morning nookie?' Dave picked up his watch from the small dressing table. It was only eight o'clock. 'What's the rush?'

'I've got to go and say goodbye to some friends. And then it's adeeo Crete,' Elsie said with a very matter of fact air.

'And do I get to say goodbye?' Dave sat up.

'Well, now I suppose because then I'll just be returning at midday to pick-up my stuff and hit the road,' Elsie collected some toiletries and stuffed them into an old worn soap bag. Dave climbed out of bed and quickly dressed himself, leaving an uncombed mop of hair and unshaven jaw to betray his tired disposition. He walked over and gave Elsie a hug, which she reciprocated. As the couple parted they looked at each other before moving back together for a lingering kiss.

'See ya, then,' Dave muttered in an unconvincing nonchalant voice.

'See you,' Elsie sounded more convincing. 'And have a good life, yeah.'

'I'll try,' Dave headed for the door. He looked back before opening it and smiled. A tear nearly fell from his right eye, which was suppressed to allow Dave just enough to escape from view. 'Soppy git. You're getting old mate,' he aggressively wiped his eye and then walked down the steps.

Tony had woken in the early hours and pulled a sheet over Kim, whilst positioning her on the pillow. He had then lay beside her with a beaming smile.

The next day both Tony and Kim giggled like adolescents at the thought of spending the night together, even though no sexual act had taken place. With old-fashioned valour, Tony waited patiently whilst Kim used the bathroom and then took a shower himself. Then they went for breakfast by the beach.

'This is fantastic,' Tony looked out to sea and then back to his smiley doughy-eyed girlfriend. 'I just want this to last forever.'

'So we… we have a real future then? As girlfriend and boyfriend?' Kim went bright red as she made the statement.

'Of course, I'm ready to take on the world with you by my side,' Tony reached out and clenched Kim's small delicate hands.

'Ugggghhhh,' a loud yell came from the next table. 'It's just a line love, he just wants to get in your knickers. I've heard it all before,' a very fat English girl, with two equally fat female friends, then started to cackle like witches.

Tony closed his eyes and swore under his breath. 'Ignore them.'

'No, let's go, Tony,' Kim felt really uncomfortable. 'I don't want to be around them.'

'Leave him here love. We'll let him 'ave what he wants,' another cackle came from the lead fat girl, echoed by her friends.

Tony and Kim stood up, and Tony slipped the waiter some drachma to settle the bill. Kim then walked quickly towards the exit.

'Give her a good one, mate,' one of the fat trio tried to grope Tony. He managed to avoid the lunge, giving a sour grimace as he looked at the three gross examples of young womanhood, wearing flimsy white blouses over butch muscular arms and micro white miniskirts that stretched around tree trunk thighs. 'I'll take it that you left your shot puts outside, just in case I trip over them.'

'Cheeky wanker,' was the predictable un-ladylike response that rang out as Tony followed after Kim.

From the café, Tony and Kim walked to the taxi rank.

'So this is it then?' Kim stood with tear in her eyes.

'Well, until next week, when you get home,' Tony said with warm smile.

Kim stood silently and looking as glum as if it was a final parting.

'Listen, I will be there for you. I promise. Believe me,' Tony held Kim's face gently in his hands, trying to eek out a faint smile.

'I have to go out with my mates tonight, it's the last night… and I think it's going to be the last Campaign. I owe them that.'

'Yeah, I know,' Kim conceded timidly. 'You must go, I'm just frightened I guess.'

'Frightened?' Tony looked quizzical.

'Frightened of letting you go and losing you. Stupid eh?' Kim now smiled.

'Ridiculous. And besides, you know where I drink my coffee,' Tony embraced Kim.

Kim now laughed. 'Very true. Now you go and have a good time. I'll have a girly night with Gill and bore her to death by talking about you all night.'

After a long gentle kiss, Tony clambered into a cab and waved to Kim. He sat back feeling more satisfied and content that at any other time in his life, and a stark contrast to the despairing lonely figure who had arrived in Crete. He was certainly ready to hit the town and celebrate with a really good Campaign beer-up. Kim also walked away with a confident happy spring in her step, already longing for the second week of her holiday to be over so she could fly home for a reunion with her man.

Phil and Gavin sat in the combined aura of a tired hungover stupor. Silently they ate their breakfasts in a dark shaded recess of the hotel pool area. It was nearly eleven and both had only just got up.

'Do you think it'll just be us two again tonight then?' Gavin finally muttered.

'Maybe,' Phil felt his head to alleviate a sharp tense jab of pain. 'But maybe not,' he nodded to the other side of the pool, where Tony was just climbing out of a taxi.

Tony smiled and waved as he instantly spotted his friends in the shadows. He had just started to walk across the poolside when Dave came running into view from behind and jokingly ruffled his hair.

'So, united once more,' Phil commented as the two wanderers returned. 'The three musketeers, who of course were always really four.'

'Of course, last night and all that. A code of honour exists,' Tony said with assertive conviction.

'Wow, even true love ways cannot halt the last night of the Campaign,' Phil confirmed happily. 'Take a seat and welcome back to earth.'

'How are you, Dave? Good night?' Gavin noticed how quiet Dave was, in almost traditional Tony mode.

'Yeah, okay mate,' Dave tried to convince himself. 'I've had a laugh and now it's time to stick in the old memory bank and move on. Just like every other Campaign.'

'I wish my life was as exciting. Wish I could just move on like you and quickly forget the recent past.' Gavin was still struggling with his decision regarding Annette.

'Anyway, what's the plan tonight?' Tony looked around at his quiet friends, with Gavin and Dave now lost in thought and Phil just hung-over. There was no response. 'Lots of beers and mad dancing?' Tony tried to answer his own question with a predictable suggestion.

'Yeah, I guess that's what it'll be then,' Dave finally acknowledged as Gavin and Phil nodded.

It was not long before the foursome had once more moved to the sunbeds, lying back to either mull over private thoughts or alleviate drink induced headaches. Tony sat and read with a constant smile upon his face, looking up now and again to visualise Kim's face and to remind himself that this was absolute reality.

Phil peeped open his eyes, having fallen asleep under the glare of the sun and glanced down at his watch. It was nearly midday. He sat up rubbing his eyes and now felt surprisingly revitalised before noticing Gavin asleep to his left.

'Fuuuuck,' Phil yelled so loud that the whole of the poolside gave a startled stare in his direction, and both Dave and Gavin jumped up from their slumber.

'What the fuck's the matter?' Dave looked around without knowing what he was looking for.

'Gav, it's twelve mate. You're meant to give your decision to Annette right now. So what's it to be? Routine wanker or Mr finally get a life?'

Gavin stared for a second. 'Oh fuck it,' He jumped up and sprinted for the road.

'Right, okay,' Dave started to correctly piece together what was happening based on Phil's comments. 'So it's midday is it. Elsie will be on her way now... 'Dave stopped and eyes widened, before he jumped up and sprinted off in the same direction as Gavin.

Tony sat transfixed with bewilderment.' Now if you run off, Phil, I'm going to seriously start worrying.'

Dave had almost caught Gavin by the time they reached the strip, thanks to the twice-weekly workout at the gym versus Gavin's mandatory pints down the pub. Gavin filtered off down the side road leading to The Harp and stopped to catch his breath in sight of the pub. Breathing heavily and feeling very bilious, he looked up to see Annette walking away.

'*Annette*,' Gavin screamed with what breath he had left and then launched into a jog.

Annette stopped and half smiled as a very red-faced Gavin approached.

'And I'd just been thinking that you'd made your decision by not showing,' Annette spoke with a little emotion and with unfamiliar nervousness.

'No, I was just being a dozing, unpunctual, clueless prat,' Gavin started to recover his breath. 'In fact, are you sure that you want me as a boyfriend?'

'It depends,' Annette said quietly. 'On if you're ready to be my boyfriend?'

Gavin looked very serious for a second. 'Well, one of my mates thinks I'd be a sad wanker if I said no, and we don't agree on many things but... I can't help thinking that he's right. So what's Christmas like in Crete?'

'Oh warm,' Annette's eyes welled with tears of joy. 'Particularly when you snuggle up to me by the tree.'

The couple fell into each others arms, both gripping hard in a release of tension.

'This could be the perfect scene in a romantic movie, like when Hugh Grant and Andie Macdowell hold each other in the rain at the end of *Four Weddings and a Funeral*.'

'Oh yes, except that we're now both soaked in your sweat rather than cooling rain,' Annette announced with a muffled giggle.

Gavin looked down as his T-shirt and shorts, which were soaked in sweat from his physical exertion. 'Bloody hell.'

Dave managed to find the block of flats where Elsie had been staying straight away, despite only going there on the one occasion. He shot up the stairs and then banged vigorously on the door to the top floor digs. Dave gave a relieved smile as the door opened, only to frown as a young Greek guy confronted him.

'What you want?' the Greek said aggressively.

'Um… I was looking for Elsie,' Dave looked over the man's shoulder and saw another girl tidying. 'Is she around?'

'She's gone, now please leave,' the man turned to go. Dave's chin nearly hit his chest as a sheer wave of frustration came over him.

'Are you Dave?' the girl had walked over and spoke with an English accent.

'Uh yeah, do you know Elsie?' Dave suddenly felt hope.

'Oh yes,' the girl gave a friendly smile. 'Never know when I'm going to see her of course, but yes, she's a friend. I always let her stay in this flat, which belongs to my boyfriend.' The man grunted as he tidied the bed. 'Anyway,' the girl said, 'she mentioned that you might turn up. In fact, I even think that she hoped you would. And she said that if you did then I was to give you this,' the girl handed Dave a small letter.

Dear Dave,

If you are reading this then you obviously came back to see me. A bit late were you not. So what now?

Well that is up to you. I am convinced now that there is more to you than my little office boy, so do not waste what you have got.

I am now heading for Northern Europe and here is a real clue/invitation. Come October I will be in Scandinavia, based in Helsinki for the last two weeks. There's a large outdoor skating rink in the city near where I usually stay. Most days I will be on the ice at some point or in one of the bars or cafes nearby. If you are up to it come and find me.

(PTO)

Join the free spirit!

If you did not come back, I truly hope you have a great life anyway. Except that you will not read this and will never know about this challenge.

Love E

'So what are you going to do?' Phil handed the letter on to Gavin, having been the first to read it.

'Bloody obvious, mate,' Dave replied with real determination. 'Quit my shitty job, rent out the flat and head for bloody Helsinki. I just wish it was tomorrow rather than two months away.'

'Good man, I'll drink to that,' Gavin passed the letter on to Tony. 'Impulsive is now my middle name.'

'Fucking hell,' Phil shook his head as he remembered Gavin's recent struggle of conscience.

'Fantastic,' Tony handed the letter back. 'So this really is to be the last night of the Campaigns. Out with the old and ring in the new eh?'

'Looks like it,' Dave muttered quietly as he wondered how Phil was feeling.

'Yeah,' Phil beamed a large grin. 'They were getting boring anyway. Although with you lot, past records of blowing every relationship, we could all be back next year in yet another Med hotspot. Either that or I'll bluff my way in on an 18–30 and be guaranteed some serious shagging.'

'Fuck all chance on all counts,' Dave shoved Phil's shoulder.

It was nine-thirty and the gang of four were sitting in a bar toasting the end of the Campaign and the end of an era.

'I tell you, we haven't half been to some places over the years eh?' Phil had fond nostalgic memories.

'Yeah and got into some right old scrapes at times,' Dave reminded everyone. 'We could write a bloody book.'

'The fantastic four and their wild adventures,' Gavin announced, before adding quizzically. 'Or is that the Marvel lot.'

'Yes, we could make a million with the stories we have to tell,' Tony concluded. 'I mean everyone likes to read about English guys getting pissed, sleeping, dancing badly and attempting horrendous chat-up routines.'

'Sounds like Hollywood script material to me,' Phil commented with sarcasm. 'I can just see Bruce Willis as me.'

'Anyway,' Gavin decided to end the fantasy. 'I think that we should propose some toasts to the future. I'll go first. To Tony and Kim, married within a year.'

'Married within a year,' came the chorus cheers.

'Yeah probably,' Tony conceded. 'Mine goes to Dave, go and find yourself.'

'Go and find yourself,' was the echo.

'…And Elsie, too, hopefully,' Dave muttered. 'Well mine is to Mockley, for god's sake get the shags in.'

'Get the shags in.'

'Fuck off,' Phil said calmly and without malice. 'Mine's to Gav, no longer a creature of habit.'

'No longer a creature of habit.'

'Okay, one more,' Dave held up his glass. 'To the lads, to life and whatever.'

'To life and whatever.'

'Bye.'

The bags were quickly and unceremoniously dispatched to the underbelly of the bus and the departing holidaymakers herded on board. A stuttering ignition and ballast of engine came just as the lads got to their seats and slumped down silently.

Phil sat next to the window with his right cheek glued to it like a child. He immediately spotted Annette cheerily waving and could sense the reciprocal motion from Gavin in the seat behind.

As the bus moved away, Phil looked on as life in Hersonissos continued in its own inimitable carefree and unflustered way. He was now just an observer to be removed from the scene and returned to mundane reality. It had always been the same with every Campaign, as a slightly heavy heart punctuated the end of a temporary idyll. In fact Phil had felt the same since the summer holidays he enjoyed as a child, now simply substituting beer, women and his mates for fizzy pop, lidos and redcoats.

Part of Phil always welcomed the return home with all its traditional comforts. Showing off a tan, recounting elaborated stories and trawling through the photographs were all part of the ritual, and the feel-good buzz usually lasted through to the first fall of leaves in autumn. And through it all were his three best friends, the unmoving constant in his life from Campaign to Campaign. Phil turned to look at them all as he sat back silently, lost in thought. Change was coming to all of them and therefore to Phil. He smiled with a knowing tinge of sadness.

12 October 2001

Dave stood at the train station with a simple rucksack by his side. He had played the scene many times in his head over the last few weeks, expecting to button his coat against the cold and walk along a grey dreary platform as the drab autumn sky dealt an eerie shrill wind. Like David Banner he would walk away from his friends and into the world alone, moving without pattern from town to town. Except that this Dave had no hideous green alter ego.

Instead the sun shone brightly and the temperature was more like June. As Phil drove Dave to the station, people were milling around in summer clothes and relaxing in pub beer gardens, as hoardings tried in vain to declare that Christmas was just around the corner.

It was a surreal scene but then the world had become a surreal place. On September 1st there had been the disbelieving shock and sheer ecstasy as England thrashed Germany by five goals to one to take them nearer to the World Cup. As Dave, Phil, Gavin and Tony jumped up and down in a beered-up huddle around Phil's lounge, nothing in the world could be more important. And then on September 11th it seemed so unimportant as once again the television was viewed with disbelieving shock, but now with hurt and pain. The events of that day were so surreal and so difficult to comprehend. It seemed a million miles from the carefree beach life of Hersonissos or the nationalistic fervour of a football match. Dave's world was about to change and now the world had changed.

Dave thought of staying in the safety of his hometown cocoon. He then thought of Elsie and knew that he really had to go. The passion of another football match was a tonic as Beckham's last minute heroics took England to the World Cup finals. Many questioned whether the finals in Japan would actually take place the following year. Dave knew that it had to, and that he also must stick to his plans. Life had to go on and so he stood waiting for the train to take him to the airport.

As the train finally pulled in, Dave turned and smiled at his friends. Tony shook his hand and Kim gave him a delicate kiss, before the couple once again placed their arms around each other.

Gavin slapped Dave's shoulder and good luck's were exchanged, with Gavin himself due to leave for Crete at the end of the month. Phil gave Dave a playful punch before hugging him.

Dave then turned and boarded the train as the sun shone brightly and sharply to light up the whole platform. Not how Dave had envisaged it at all.

7 June 2002 – Sapporo, Japan

'*Mockleeeey*,' Dave bellowed down the small mobile phone.

'Who's that?' a tired Phil muttered into the handset as he clutched a cup of coffee. 'Is… is that you, Dave?'

'Ahso… greetings from Japan,' Dave mimicked a stereotype Japanese accent.

Phil's eyes were suddenly wide and alert. 'You're not, tell me you're fucking not.'

'I am, mate. Just about to go in. I have my ticket right here,' Dave held it up and gave it a kiss.

'Bastard,' Phil stood open-mouthed. 'Lucky bastard. You'd better get me a programme at least.'

'Absolutely. How is everyone? Is Tony going to watch the game with you?' Dave now had to shout as hordes of English fans began chanting as they walked by.

'Yeah, Tone's fine. He and Kim will be here any minute. Gonna make 'em a World Cup brunch. And then next week I'm flying out to stay with Gav and Annette. Gav's promised to set me up for a shag,' Phil sounded genuinely happy.

'Well give them both a smack in the face from me won't you,' Dave felt a poke to his ribs. 'Look, mate, I'm going to have to go.'

'Yeah, get in there, mate, and cheer for all it's worth. I'll see you in August at Tony's wedding, yeah?'

'Yeah, too right. We'll be there. Elsie sends her love by the way,' Dave held the phone over to Elsie dressed in an England football shirt and jeans. She screamed above the noise of the crowd. 'Hi Phil, love you. Come on Englaaand.'

Dave clicked the phone off and in unison he and Elsie put on their shades and walked into the throng of England supporters heading for the Sapporo stadium.

The stadium clock showed that half time was imminent and it was still Argentina nil England nil. The atmosphere was so tense as both sets of supporters screamed encouragement driven by sheer nervous energy. In Hersonissos, Gavin sat in The Harp surrounded by friendly, but mocking, Irishmen and a handful of focussed Englishmen. In England, Phil sat on the edge of his sofa with Tony perched by his side. Kim sat quietly in a corner chair. Halfway up the east bank of the Sapporo stadium stood Dave and Elsie, unable to look away from the game for a second.

And then Michael Owen moved inside a defender within the area, priming to shoot when he was upended. In a blur the bald headed Italian referee pointed to the spot. Penalty.

The whole of England, every English supporter in the stadium and every Englishman around the globe held their breath. Beckham was to take it. The demons of four year previous could now be dispelled or the icon's resurgence could be destroyed. Beckham breathed so heavily that his diaphragm visibly lifted his chest.

Focussed, he struck the ball low, hard, and true. It hit the net and for a second the world stopped, before it erupted. Gavin jumped from his barstool and into the arms of the elated band of Englishmen. Tony and Phil bounced around the room as Kim yelped in delight.

Dave looked at Elsie and they both screamed out aloud with the rest of the English crowd as Beckham gripped the three lions on his shirt tightly.

'Yeeeeeeeeeeees!'